THE RIVER HOME

Hannah Richell is the internationally bestselling author of *Secrets of the Tides, The Shadow Year* and *The Peacock Summer*. Her books have been published in twenty-two territories and translated into seventeen languages.

Also by Hannah Richell

Secrets of the Tides
The Shadow Year
The Peacock Summer

The
RIVER
HOME

HANNAH RICHELL

ORION

First published in Great Britain in 2020 by Orion Books,
an imprint of The Orion Publishing Group Ltd
Carmelite House, 50 Victoria Embankment
London EC4Y 0DZ

An Hachette UK Company

1 3 5 7 9 10 8 6 4 2

A CIP catalogue record for this book is
available from the British Library.

ISBN (Hardback) 978 1 4091 5225 5
ISBN (Export Trade Paperback) 978 1 4091 5226 2
ISBN (eBook) 978 1 4091 5228 6

Typeset at The Spartan Press Ltd,
Lymington, Hants

Printed and bound in Great Britain by Clays Ltd,
Elcograf S.p.A.

MIX
Paper from
responsible sources
FSC® C104740

www.orionbooks.co.uk

For Will

PROLOGUE

In sleep, the memories rise unbidden. Trees stand as black shadows marking the way through the orchard. The acid sweetness of apples rises from the long grass, while the river below slides silently by.

In the dark, behind fluttering eyelids, she remembers the fermented fizz of cider on her tongue, light bulbs dancing like fireflies over the wooden jetty, laughter carrying across the water. The sensation of paper pressed against her face, the grip of fingers on skin, thick black mud clinging to her scratched and bloody hands, a pain like broken glass cutting skin.

Lost in slumber, all the scents, the sounds, the colours of her past rise up, and all that she has buried – the secrets, the darkness – return to her.

What have you done? What on earth have you done?

It's something she learned years ago – the hard way – and that she knows she will never forget: even the sweetest fruit will fall and rot into the earth, eventually. No matter how deep you bury the pain, the bones of it will rise up to haunt you, like the sickly scent of those apples, like the echoes of a summer's night, like the river flowing relentlessly on its course.

MONDAY

Not sure if you're still on this number, but we
need you at home. Lucy's getting married. This
Saturday! I know. Call me. E x

Sent 18/09/18, 5:58pm ✔✔

Eve says she messaged you. Please come. I need
you. Luce x

Sent 18/09/18, 8:49pm ✔✔

TUESDAY

I

Margot stirs at the sound of the train horn screaming through a tunnel. Her cheek is clammy where it rests against the window and a familiar scent, sweet and heavy, lingers in the air. Opening her eyes, she meets the gaze of a young girl seated across the carriage table. She wears purple headphones with pointed cat ears stuck to the headband and bites into an apple. Empty wrappers escape from a pink packed lunch box lying discarded between them.

Margot looks from the lunch box to the apple, then back to the girl's face. She is around seven or eight, she thinks, with blue eyes and hair the colour of corn hanging in two neat plaits. There is something reminiscent of Lucy in the girl's appearance, though the girl's hair is perfectly parted and the braids are tight and uniform. Her sister's childhood plaits had never been neat, usually wrestled into unruly braids at the breakfast table by Eve or their father. Lucy had always been a wild tangle of a girl – though no longer a girl, of course, but a grown woman, soon to be married.

4

The messages had arrived the previous night, Eve's flashing first on Margot's phone as she'd let herself into the empty flat. She'd scanned it standing in the kitchen as the kettle boiled and had to read it twice before the meaning had sunk in. Lucy was getting married, in less than a week? Their middle sister had always been impetuous – prone to spontaneous gestures or blurting whatever was on her mind, no matter the consequences – but this latest spur-of-the-moment decision surely had disaster written all over it. It was typical Eve too, her elder sister's exasperation and judgement evident even through the economy of her text message. And perhaps, Margot thinks – turning to the window and studying her reflection in the glass, regarding her bloodshot eyes and tasting the stale vodka still caught at the back of her throat – typical of her too.

The girl seated across from her crunches into the apple, brown pips now visible in the hollow chambers of its core. Margot watches, expecting her to discard it at any moment, or perhaps pass it to the woman – obviously her mother – bent over a book beside her, but the girl bites steadily into the shrinking apple until the innards, the pips and finally the thin brown stalk have all disappeared into her mouth. Yes, just like Lucy. She can picture her so clearly: denim cut-offs and long brown limbs, lying on a blanket amid the fallen fruit under the orchard trees, that wide smile and the tangle of her long blonde hair fanning out about her face.

Margot sighs. She thinks of the trolley service that had rattled by half an hour ago, and of the clinking glass miniatures holding so much promise. She wishes she hadn't held her nerve. She wishes she'd bought even one, just to lift the veil of her hangover.

I need you.

The girl opposite licks her fingers then glances across at Margot, her lips twitching into a smile. Margot gives her a solemn nod, before turning away and leaning her head back against the window. Three words. It was all it had taken to undo her resolve. For Margot knows what it is to need. She couldn't ignore Lucy's plea. Against her better judgement, here she is, travelling home to Windfalls. What on earth was she thinking?

2

Eve stands in the lower orchard, one hand pressed to her chest, the other shading her eyes from the sun as the man from the marquee hire company paces between the trees, tutting audibly. She doesn't like his frown, nor the way he keeps bending down and shaking his head, as if to assess the angle of the hill or the quality of the ground. 'It's pretty boggy,' he says, coming to join her. 'And the slope isn't ideal, but I think we can do it. There's enough space between those trees to put up a thirty- by forty-foot tent, which should give you plenty of room for your guests. Around fifty you said?'

'It's a little over sixty now.'

The man sucks air through his teeth and refers to his clipboard. 'We could do it on Thursday morning. That would give you time to decorate.'

'Great. You're sure it'll be OK down here?' The ground feels ominously soft beneath her boots. It's hard to imagine how the pegs to anchor the marquee will hold. As she pictures a vast white tent lifting up and flying off across the valley she tries, simultaneously, to ignore the tightening sensation in her chest. It's as if a cold fist reaches inside her ribcage and squeezes her heart.

'Don't worry,' he says, reading her expression. 'We'll see you right. Lovely spot you've got here,' he adds, genuine appreciation in his voice.

Eve turns to survey the scene. The fruit trees hang heavy with ripe apples. Birds chatter through the lush green boughs while the sun, just past its pinnacle, drenches the hillside in golden, autumnal light. Below the sloping orchard, a strip of river glints like a mirror, visible through the trees as they move in the breeze. Behind her, the honey-coloured stone chimneys of Windfalls jut into a blue sky. Standing there in the soft September light, the old seventeenth-century farmhouse, with its wide, painted sash windows, grey slate roof and tangled wisteria clinging to its facade, has never looked prettier.

But Eve can't focus on the beauty of her childhood home; she is too caught up in thoughts of untethered marquees, and catering, and what to do if it rains between now and Saturday and the orchard turns into a vast, boggy mudslide. Though all these are mere organisational logistics — jobs to cross off a list. When she considers them alongside the more worrying thought of her family coming back together for the first time in eight years, no wonder she feels panicked.

Hay, she thinks, wishing she had brought a pen and paper with her. A few bales from one of the local farms should do it. It could double-up as a rustic decoration . . . seating, even . . . but it would also be useful should the weather turn against them and the ground becomes too muddy. There is also the matter of a power supply to arrange. A generator of some sort, or cables connecting back to the house. They'll need a dance floor and lights.

Lanterns would be nice, but she's not sure if they'd be allowed to light candles inside the marquee. These are all things to run past the man from the tent company.

She glances round for him and sees he has wandered off among the trees with his tape measure, while appearing along the garden path from the house is her mother, grey-streaked hair spilling from a loose bun, a colourful silk kimono flapping behind her, afternoon sun caught in the white cotton of the long nightdress she is still wearing.

As a teenager, Eve used to crawl with embarrassment at her mother's alternative approach to clothes. She used to wonder if it was because Kit spent so long inside her fictional worlds that she was oblivious to fashion codes or clothing conventions. She'd pondered whether she did it to embarrass her daughters, or shock them out of what she might think their more prudish ways. But, after years of mortification, Eve has come to the conclusion that Kit just doesn't care much about appearances. Buried in her books, she would notice what she dressed in each day no more than she would notice that the fridge was empty or the house was filthy. Fashion choices were no more considered than what lay draped over the armchair in her bedroom and came closest to hand. It is simply the way her mother is made. The man from the marquee company does a double-take at the sight of her, but Eve barely blinks.

'I saw the truck in the drive,' Kit says as she draws closer.

'It's all under control.'

'Is Lucy here with you?'

'No,' says Eve. 'I don't know where she's got to.'

'They'll put it here in the orchard, will they?' she asks, watching the man with his tape measure.

'Yes, it's the best place.'

Kit turns her face to the sky and closes her eyes. 'It's lovely out here.'

'I was thinking we could hang bunting and fairy lights to mark the route down from the house. It would look lovely at nightfall. But of course, all of that will take more work and more time,' Eve adds. At this stage, she isn't sure how they're going to achieve even the basics of this organisational nightmare before Saturday.

'Whatever you think, darling. I'm sure it will look wonderful.'

The fist clenches more tightly in her chest. It's all very well Lucy springing this last-minute wedding on them all, saying she wants to keep the celebrations 'low key . . . a private register office ceremony followed by a "bit of a party" at Windfalls . . . everyone back together . . . no big deal', and while a part of Eve admires her sister's desire to avoid the wedding machine and all the para-phernalia and pressure that comes with it, there is no getting around the fact that these kinds of events don't 'just happen'. No matter how spontaneous Lucy might want to be, no matter how laid-back their mother might seem, there's a reason couples plan their nuptials months in advance. Say the word 'wedding', even at the last minute, and guests will arrive with certain expectations. Food. Wine. Music. Dancing. It's the way it is.

She and Andrew had done it properly. They had allowed a respectable twelve months to organise their day. The venue had been meticulously researched. Mono-grammed save-the-date cards had been sent out months in advance. The catering, dress fittings, disco hire, wedding cake, flowers and photographer had all been arranged with Eve's trademark precision, and despite one broken heel on a pair of bridesmaid's shoes, the day had run like clockwork.

Lucy, on the other hand, seems to expect the music, the decorations, the food and drinks to simply 'happen'. Little wedding fairies sweeping in to take care of everything. Eve sighs. It might have been possible to wing it if the guest list was small, but Lucy, in typical Lucy fashion, had announced her bonkers wedding plan a few days ago, then glibly sent out a blanket email invitation to her friends. 'Don't worry,' she'd said, 'it's such short notice only a few of them will be able to make it. Only the important ones.' But what had started out a couple of days ago as *a simple little party* had since snowballed spectacularly. Sixty-five acceptances at the last count. Five vegetarians. Two vegans. One gluten-free. One dairy intolerant. What was wrong with these people? Didn't they have lives, holidays, calendars hanging on their fridges full of scribbled plans and juggled appointments? It's all *so* Lucy, all so ridiculously naïve and chaotic.

It isn't as if Eve doesn't have enough on her plate, with her own household to run and her part-time job managing the office of a small recruitment agency, Andrew working all the hours at his IT consultancy, and the girls with their ballet classes, piano lessons, science projects and invitations to birthday parties. Throw in organising a wedding in a week and her head feels fit to burst.

'Eve, darling . . . what do you think about fireworks? Or maybe a bonfire?' Kit's voice breaks through her train of thought. 'It would be rather fun, don't you think?'

Eve regards her mother with an even stare. Bonfires and fireworks? Add a load of actual pyrotechnics to the explosive emotional landscape they already have to navigate on Saturday? Great idea.

'Perhaps Andrew or your father could take charge?' adds Kit, failing to read Eve's mood.

Eve doesn't answer. She can imagine Andrew's face when she tells him he's been nominated to manage an impromptu firework display on Saturday night.

'Has anyone heard from Margot?'

'Lucy and I have sent messages, but we've heard nothing.'

Her mother's mouth forms a thin line. 'Well, it's sad, but perhaps it's for the best.'

'Lucy will be disappointed. Though if Margot does show up, we're *all* going to have to find a way to smooth things over.' She throws her mother a pointed look. 'It's Lucy's day, after all,' she adds.

Kit frowns and turns away to face the valley.

Thinking of her volatile little sister and what she might be capable of in the pressure-cooker situation of a family wedding, Eve feels another surge of panic. It had been bad enough two years ago when Margot had come home to celebrate their father's sixtieth, though of course on that occasion their mother hadn't received an invite.

Kit throws her hands up. 'I know, I know. I wouldn't stop Margot from coming and being a part of Lucy's day, but until she offers some kind of apology or explanation, I can't forgive her.' She turns back to Eve. 'Could you, in my shoes?'

Eve frowns. She wonders if she's the only one to have noticed how similar Kit and Margot are, both of them hot and unpredictable, like fire. What Margot did was inexplicable and yes, perhaps unforgiveable. 'Probably not, no,' she admits.

Kit nods, seemingly satisfied. 'I doubt she'll come.'

Maybe it would be for the best if Margot stayed away. Perhaps the last thing any of them need is Margot showing up and raising tensions even higher. Eve returns her hand to her chest and feels the thundering of her heart. Take a deep breath, she tells herself. Everything is going to be OK.

3

Margot leaves the train at Bath Spa station and catches a taxi. Leaving the city's grand crescents and elegant stone terraces with their uniform chimney pots aligned against the sky, the car drives into a valley sliding from late summer to autumn. All is green and gold and bronze, while here and there the purple leaves of copper beech trees shift to flaming amber. They cross the river Avon and begin the slow climb through the wooded vale, following signs to the village of Mortford. Margot twists in her seat to catch another glimpse of the green water snaking through the valley, catching the light like glass. The sight of it brings a shiver.

'I've brought a few punters out this way,' says the taxi driver, making small talk. 'Most of them were fans hoping to find that famous writer. Whatsername? The one that wrote *those* books.'

'Kit Weaver,' she offers, gazing out at the honey-coloured stone buildings passing outside. Margot ignores his lingering emphasis on *those* books.

'Yeah, that's her. K. T. Weaver. My wife loves her stuff. She says a night in with one of her books is better than bingo night down our local and a slap-up meal after. You ever met her? Read her stuff?'

'I've read a couple,' she replies, her eyes never leaving the road.

'She's a bit of a recluse now, by all accounts?'

'So they say.'

'Bit strange, to just stop writing like that. Suppose she made so much money she didn't have to bother finishing the series? All right for some, eh?' The man must sense her mood because he doesn't say anything else. Instead, he steers the car up the narrow lane until the slate roof of Windfalls comes into view and they are driving through a wooden gate and parking behind a white truck with the words 'Main Event Marquees' written in tall, red letters across its side. The vehicle's rear doors hang open, revealing a bare interior, nothing but a few blankets and a toolbox. There is no one in sight.

'Someone's planning a party.'

'Yes. A wedding.'

'Ah, who doesn't love a good wedding?'

Who indeed, thinks Margot.

Whenever she has thought of her home in recent years, it has always appeared strangely colourless in her mind. She's imagined walking into a landscape of muffled grey, blank sky merging with muted earth, everything wrapping itself around her like a suffocating blanket. But here the sky is royal blue, the breeze brisk and warm, and the valley is spread before her in a tapestry of early autumn colour, leaves turning from glossy green to amber. The sun is beginning to settle upon the tips of the horse chestnut trees where the frayed rope swing of her childhood drifts idly in the breeze. Behind the tree, the Bath stone farmhouse glows golden in the light, its windowpanes shining like mirrors. Even with her sunglasses on, the world seems too bright, too intense.

Margot pays the driver, picks up her bag and takes the gravel path winding around the side of the house, past overgrown hedgerows and flowerbeds badly in need of a little care, before entering through the back door into the large flagstoned kitchen. She stands for a moment in the quiet of the house, taking in details so ridiculously familiar it seems impossible she had forgotten them all until now. A colourful crocheted tea cosy slumps over a teapot near the kettle. A terracotta bowl filled with fruit sits on the scrubbed oak table, a fly crawling over the browning skin of a pear. She sees a worn wooden chopping board covered in breadcrumbs, half a loaf, going stale in the afternoon sunshine; dirty lunch dishes stacked by the sink. Faded cushions sag on the window seat, above which is pinned a corn dolly she remembers Lucy buying at the village harvest festival many years ago. There is a huge stack of unopened letters – her mother's unanswered fan mail, by the looks of it – heaped by the telephone, and a box of books, reprints from a foreign publisher, ripped open then simply left to prop open the door into the hall. She breathes it all in and closes her eyes, the slight thud of her headache picking up pace.

A clock on the drawing-room hearth ticks to the beat in her head. On the velvet sofa an ancient black cat lies curled in a small square of sunshine. She scratches behind his ears. 'Hello, Pinter.' The cat opens one rheumy eye and rewards her with a purr before sinking back into sleep. She reaches for an old cushion, threadbare and embroidered with painstaking cross-stitch into the image of a rose, and watches the dust motes rise up and circle in a shaft of light. A glass vase catches the sun, revealing its thin layer of grime. Everywhere she looks there are piles of paper teetering on surfaces, dusty corners and cobwebs strung in high places, plants that need watering and books standing in perilous stacks. She can't help admiring her mother for her dogged *there-are-more-important-things-in-the-world-than-cleaning* attitude. Kit has never been one to bend to social convention and it seems not even the imminent arrival of a horde of wedding guests will change that.

A tray of mugs stands abandoned on the coffee table next to a hastily scrawled list written on the back of an envelope. Margot picks up the piece of paper and reads the words written in Eve's careful handwriting:

catering numbers – confirm with R
napkins
glass hire
photographer
extension leads
jam jars
flowers – check with S
batteries
fairy lights
confetti
Margot?

She scans the list before reaching down to swipe the last biscuit from a plate on the tray. It doesn't escape her notice that she is last – well below such frivolities as fairy lights and confetti – and marked with that wary question mark.

The house feels like a stage, awaiting its players, curtains ready to swing open. Rather than break the stillness by calling out, she makes for the staircase.

Upstairs, the sun falls onto the landing through gabled windows, forming slanted squares of light on the floorboards. Margot steps through them like a child playing hopscotch. She passes the door to her mother's bedroom, glimpsing the scarlet-flocked wallpaper, the heavy velvet curtains and the huge bed, rumpled and unmade. Another pile of teetering books stands on the bedside table, a dressing gown lies in a pool of silk on the floor. There is no discernible evidence of the room ever once having been shared with their father. She ignores the curved stairwell leading up to the turret room on the second floor where Kit has now made her office and heads on instead past the door to Eve's old room, then Lucy's, almost certain she can catch the faint scent of joss sticks and CK One still hanging in the air.

The house is so laced with childhood memories – pictures, scents, familiar objects – that by the time Margot reaches the far end of the corridor, she feels a little strange, almost light-headed, as though her feet don't quite connect with the floor beneath them. It is as if she is floating a few centimetres off the ground, as if she has travelled not just the length of the country but somehow stepped back through the fabric of time, crossed an intersection as fine as gauze, returning to a past she's tried hard to forget.

She hesitates. A night of broken sleep followed by the long trip south makes the thought of her old bed an appealing one, but still she lingers, reluctant and perhaps even a little afraid to close the gap between past and present. What does she fear is behind that door? Her old life? An earlier incarnation of herself? The girl who dropped out of school, packed a bag and left home at sixteen?

After the brightness of the landing, it takes Margot's eyes a moment to adjust to the dim light inside the bedroom. The curtains are half-drawn, only a thin triangle of sunlight falling through their opening, but as she focuses, she is alarmed to find that her bed is already occupied. A figure lies on the pillows, arms outstretched, eyes closed. Blonde, not dark. Not the spectre of her old self, but her sister, Lucy, lying strangely formal – almost corpse-like – on top of the bedcovers. Beneath a familiar-looking denim jacket, her sister's floral dress flows out across the bed and seems to blend with the tangle of flowers climbing the wallpaper. Looking at her, Margot is reminded of a painting she once wrote about at school, of a woman floating on the surface of a river. Millais' *Ophelia*. She dredges the painter's name up from the depths of her brain, surprised to remember it.

In the half-light, Lucy is pale, her limbs angular, almost birdlike, her skin a luminous white. Her long, fair hair flows in its usual wild tangle about her. Lucy opens her eyes and stares at Margot, expressionless. For a split second, Margot is reminded of the girl from the train – her wide, curious gaze – and then she is gone, replaced by the adult Lucy lying on the bed. Her sister's face shifts with recognition. 'You,' she says.

Margot nods. 'Me.'

Neither of them say anything else for a long while.

Margot stands by the door, a small smile breaking at the sight of her sister's stunned face.

Lucy seems to gather herself. 'So are you going to stand there staring at me like a weirdo, or are you going to come and give your favourite sister a hug?'

Margot's smile widens. She walks around and perches on the edge of the bed. 'Hello, stranger.'

'Hello, you.' Lucy grins. She wrestles herself into a cross-legged position on the soft mattress so that she can hug Margot, pulling her close. 'Am I the last to greet you?'

'You're the first.'

Lucy shoots a guilty glance towards the garden. 'Eve's going to be in such a strop. She's had that tight-lipped look – you know the one she gets – ever since I told her Tom and I are getting married.'

'And when exactly was that?'

'Sunday.'

'A wedding in a week.' Margot laughs. 'Poor Eve. You sure know how to send her into a tailspin.'

Lucy throws up her hands. 'I didn't *ask* her to take over. I keep telling her it's supposed to be a low-key party, something fun and thrown together, but you know what she's like. Bloody Martha Stewart. According to Eve, it's not a wedding if you don't have mountains of flowers and food, a cheesy DJ and a fancy three-tier cake.'

'So Eve's your official wedding planner?'

'*Self-appointed* wedding planner.'

'And here you are . . . lazing around without a care in the world . . . in *my* bedroom,' she narrows her eyes, 'wearing *my* denim jacket, while everyone else slaves away for your big day!'

Lucy shrugs. 'I'm hiding. And the jacket looked lonely. It was hanging there on the back of the door. I bet you can't even remember the last time you wore it. I mean, look!' She reaches into the jacket pocket and pulls out a packet of Marlborough Lights and a box of matches and throws her an amused look.

'Give me those,' says Margot, taking them from Lucy and moving across to the window seat set into the alcove, pushing the glass pane open.

'They'll be stale,' warns Lucy, but Margot doesn't care. She sparks up and takes a long, slow inhale before blowing smoke though the open window, offering the cigarette to Lucy as she settles beside her. 'No thanks.'

'Sorry, I forget you're wholesome yoga woman, these days.'

'Anyway,' Lucy exclaims, whacking Margot on the thigh, 'what the fuck! You're here!'

Margot nods.

'You didn't think to reply to our messages? Send warning? Smoke signals?'

Margot shrugs. 'I thought it might be best if I just came. You said you needed me.'

Lucy smiles and squeezes her arm. 'I'm so pleased. My evil plan worked.'

'Your evil plan?'

'Yes, it's brilliant, don't you think? Throw a last-minute wedding and force you home for an overdue reunion.'

'Brilliant,' replies Margot drily. 'Though some might

say a little extreme.' She narrows her eyes. 'So what's the big hurry?'

Lucy waves her hands. 'You know me. I've never been much of a planner. Besides, I didn't want to give you too long to think about it, did I? I know what you're like at finding excuses not to come back.'

Margot, noticing how neatly her sister has dodged the question, directs another stream of smoke out of the window and adjusts herself on the seat. 'So, tell me, how did Tom convince you to settle down to a life of wedded bliss?'

Lucy hesitates. 'It was me. I asked him to marry me.'

'Wow. That's brave.'

Lucy shrugs. 'I love him, Margot.'

Margot nods. 'I'm no expert at relationships, admittedly, but that's probably the best reason.' Margot looks out the window, at the trees standing in the orchard. She sees the river glinting below in the valley. She lifts the cigarette and takes another long drag, hoping the shaking of her hand isn't as obvious to Lucy as it is to her. 'I saw the marquee van out on the drive. Looks like it's going to be quite the "do".'

'Mum and Eve might have gone a little overboard.'

'I'd always imagined you more as the eloping type. Perhaps an Elvis chapel in Vegas, to avoid all the fuss?'

'Me too.' Lucy hesitates and Margot waits, sensing there is something else.

'But Windfalls feels like the right place,' she continues, after a moment. 'The only place. The wedding is a good opportunity to get everyone back here, together. When was the last time we saw you? Dad's sixtieth?'

Margot nods. 'Don't remind me.'

'I'm sure everyone's forgotten by now.'

Margot hasn't. She can still remember the sickening sound of shattering glass as she'd fallen through the glass table at the hotel they'd celebrated at. She still has the scar on her leg as evidence of her horrible, drunken fall, when she'd disgraced herself by drinking far too much, toasting their father with an inappropriate speech, then stumbling into the glass coffee table – an expensive antique that their father had picked up the bill for.

'Anyway,' Lucy continues, her face earnest and open, 'I want *all* of us together. It's important to me. And I think it's time you and Mum sorted your rift out, don't you?'

Margot doesn't answer. *Your rift.* Was that how it was being talked about these days? 'Have you invited Sibella?'

Lucy nods. 'Of course.'

The thought of Lucy forcing them all together and expecting Happy Families is almost laughable. 'You're a braver woman than me.' Margot takes another deep drag on the cigarette. 'I've been following your Instagram feed,' she says, changing the subject. 'Headstands and motivational memes. Quite the inspirational cocktail. You'll be giving TED talks next.'

Lucy laughs. 'These days I barely have time to teach. I'm too busy managing the studio. Besides, Instagram – Instasham. Don't trust everything you see on social media. I'm afraid all that stuff comes with the territory. If you're in the health and wellness industry you have to promote the right image – live the dream.'

'So business is good?'

'Booming. I've taken on more teaching staff to keep up with the demand.'

'You have staff?'

Lucy nods. 'And a new studio in Bath, a warehouse space right on the river. I've had to step back a little though . . . to concentrate on the marketing and operations.'

'Operations.' Margot gives Lucy a begrudging look.

She shrugs. 'It's not all green juices, quinoa and active wear, you know.'

'No. I can imagine.' Margot narrows her eyes. 'You look tired. You're working too hard. Or is it pre-wedding nerves?'

'Bit of both,' says Lucy, gazing out at the garden. 'But what about you? You're still in Edinburgh?'

Margot nods.

'As far as you could get from this place?'

'Something like that.'

'Last I heard you were working in books?'

Margot bursts out laughing. 'Is that what you heard?'

'Yeah. Eve made it sound important. We thought you might be following in Mum's footsteps. What? What's so funny?'

'God love Eve. I sit at a desk five days a week and scan books in and out of the local library. I'm an awesome re-shelver.'

'Well, someone has to put the books back in the right place.'

'True.' Margot smiles, but she can't help feeling inadequate next to Lucy's achievements. She's not done too badly, for a sixth-form school dropout who'd left home with no real plan and just a few hundred pounds'

24

savings in the bank. She'd hung around in London for a while, falling in with a bedsit crowd who had let her doss in with them and shown her how to work the benefits system, until eventually, tiring of the constant hustle and the expense of the capital, she'd packed her meagre belongings and headed north. After a few months of hitchhiking, she'd washed up in Edinburgh.

There had been something about the Scottish city that she had fallen for. She had loved the historic architecture, the winding alleys of the Old Town and the sight of the castle presiding high over the city. She'd spent a year or two waitressing in cafes, until one afternoon, sheltering from the rain in the Central Library, she'd noticed a bulletin on the noticeboard advertising for a library assistant. She'd somehow talked her way into the job and had worked there ever since.

After the pace and uncertainty of the previous restless years, it had proved to be something of a refuge for her, with its quietness, its easy escape to other worlds and places. She's a favourite too with the kids at story time, acting out scenes and putting on funny voices to make them laugh. Though it hasn't escaped her notice that barely a day goes by that one of her mother's books isn't loaned or requested on order. Every time she scans a K. T. Weaver volume through the system, she feels a strange stirring of pride and pain. She's come to think of it as a form of personal torture.

'So you're happy up there? Are *you* seeing anyone?' Lucy asks, her curiosity obviously piqued.

Margot shrugs. 'No. Well... no.'

'You don't sound sure.' Lucy waits expectantly, then adds, 'You could have brought them with you.'

'No. It's better like this. Your invitation was perfectly timed.'

Lucy waits, but Margot doesn't want to elaborate. She stubs the cigarette on the outer edge of the peeling window frame before flicking it down into the overgrown flowerbed below.

'It'll be all right, won't it?' Lucy asks suddenly, her fingers worrying the fabric of her dress. 'I'm not completely mad, wanting to do this here, at Windfalls?'

'No.' She says it with more conviction than she feels. 'Not *completely* mad.'

'You see, the thing I want most of all is for everyone to get along. I want us to feel like a normal family,'

Margot can't help her dry laugh. 'A *normal* family?' At the sight of her sister's crestfallen face, she softens. 'Luce, I'm here, and I'll support you in whatever way you need.'

Lucy hesitates. 'Good, because I thought we might mend a few bridges.'

Lucy is gazing at Margot with such an earnest expression that Margot feels the weight of it like bricks on her shoulders. 'If you're thinking about Mum and me, you might need to let that fantasy go.'

'If you two just sat down and talked ... if you tried to explain? We all make mistakes.'

'You always were the most impossible optimist.' Margot sighs. 'I can't promise a heart-warming reunion, but I do promise to stay away from all sharp blades, flammable items and breakable objects. Who knows, Mum might even surprise us for your Big Day and wear *proper* clothes!' Lucy can't help smiling at that. 'I'll be the model sister, I promise.'

26

'Thank you.'

'Though, of course, it does all depend on one thing.'

'What?'

'You'd better show me the bridesmaid's dress you're expecting me to wear. Because I'm warning you, if there's even a hint of pink ... or ruffles ... or God forbid, flouncy bows, then I won't be held responsible for my actions.'

Lucy laughs. 'No bridesmaids. I already told you, it's not going to be *that* kind of a wedding.'

'Well, thank fuck for that. I was beginning to think I didn't know you at all.'

4

Eve is mentally running through guest numbers and menus for Saturday as she steps through the back door into the kitchen and stops in her tracks. Lucy and Margot sit at the long oak table, their heads bent together – long, blonde curls against razor-sharp dark bob.

Margot is back.

For the moment that Eve goes unnoticed, she watches them. Seeing her sisters together for the first time in ages, seated at the table where they once spent so many hours eating meals, plaiting hair, doing homework, squabbling over toys, clothes and household chores, it is almost as if the ghosts of the children they once were hover over them. Lucy, with her energy and her optimism, no one ever knowing what will come next, now a few days away from marrying Tom. And Margot, the youngest, once so flamboyant, so full of dramatic flair, now so hard to read, sitting there with her dark hair skimming her collarbone and a battered leather jacket hanging over her narrow shoulders. They are light and dark, chalk and cheese.

The sight of them together fills Eve with a strong emotion, the same feeling she gets when she tiptoes up to her daughters' rooms and watches them sleeping at the end of the day, small fists curled under chins, their pale faces slack-jawed in sleep. It's an ache – a deep love and affection – and nostalgia too, for all they have shared, and all the days that have already slipped by.

Lucy says something that Eve doesn't catch and Margot's laughter rings out across the room, the sound at once both familiar and alien, like a distant bell that hasn't chimed for a long time. She feels a yearning to be included – to be part of their circle. 'What's so funny?' she asks, announcing her arrival to the room, though the question, as it leaves her lips, sounds harsher than she'd intended, even a little accusatory.

'Eve!' Margot looks up. 'We were just talking about you.'

Eve studies Margot carefully, looking for signs of a joke on her face, but she can't read her brown eyes. She looks older, more angular and there's a hardness too – an air of cool detachment – that she doesn't remember. Standing at the open door in her striped T-shirt, shapeless jeans and wellington boots, Eve feels as she used to around them: dull, sensible, reliable, frumpy. Old before her time. So often she's felt 'other' to them, somehow on the outer. She supposes it comes from being the eldest – three years older than Lucy, seven years older than Margot – always the more responsible one to their younger, more carefree ways.

'Lucy was telling me how great you've been, helping her with everything.'

Eve smiles. 'When did you get back?'

'Half an hour ago. Are the girls with you?' Margot asks, looking to the back door.

'No. It's a school day.'

29

'School. God, I still think of them both as toddlers.'

'Chloe's in year four now. May has just started reception.' Again, that accusatory tone. Eve checks herself. 'You'll see them at the family dinner,' she adds, 'if not before.'

'The family dinner?' Margot narrows her eyes.

'Yes, this Friday night,' says Lucy. 'I wanted to have a pre-wedding get-together.'

'*All* of us?'

If Lucy notices Margot's frown she ignores it. 'Yes, all of us,' she says brightly. 'So how's it going out there?' she asks, turning to Eve, the hint of an apology in her voice.

'Fine. I left Mum finalising the details with the sales guy.'

'Oh, the poor man,' says Lucy.

'Well, when I say finalising details, I mean Mum was drifting around all daydreamy, pulling branches of hawthorn from the hedgerow and he was doing a bad job of trying not to gawp too obviously at her half-dressed state.'

'The see-through kaftan?' asks Margot.

'And a nightdress.'

'It could be worse. Do you remember her naked sunlounger episodes?'

Lucy laughs. 'That's why I never invited friends back from school!'

'Smart decision to hold your wedding in the cooler autumn months.'

They're still laughing as the back door bangs open and Kit sweeps into the kitchen, holding a large, glossy green branch laden with red berries. She stops dead at the sight of the three girls in the kitchen, her gaze moving between them until it comes to rest on Margot. 'You're here.'

'Hello, Mum.'

The hawthorn branch is dumped unceremoniously into the kitchen sink, red berries scattering like marbles across the kitchen floor. Kit dusts off her hands. 'Why didn't you tell us you were coming?' she asks. 'Someone could have fetched you from the station.' The silver bangles on her arm jangle loudly as she seizes Margot, holding her at arm's length to study her.

Eve can't help but notice Margot's discomfort, her sister's shoulders up around her ears and her gaze not quite meeting their mother's. 'I didn't want to be a bother,' she says.

'A bother! You wouldn't have been a bother.' Kit's laugh is high and shrill. They embrace, stiff and perfunctory, two lines barely touching. Eve glances across at Lucy, but Lucy's gaze is averted, her focus fixed on a loose thread hanging off the table runner, which she tugs free.

'Tea?' asks Eve brightly, as Margot extricates herself from their mother's embrace. 'I'll make a pot.'

'Yes,' says Lucy quickly. 'Let's have some tea.'

'Well, isn't this nice,' says Kit, looking around at them all, her voice filled with false cheer. 'All of you here under the same roof like this.'

'Yes,' says Lucy, again.

'You'll be staying here for the wedding?' her mother asks, turning to address Margot again.

'If that's all right?'

Kit nods. 'Of course. *Your* room's still there, exactly as you left it.'

Silence falls over the four women. Eve clears her throat, grasping for something to ease the sudden tension. 'It will be good to have an extra pair of hands to help,' she says, thinking that perhaps now is as good a time as any to work through the outstanding details. 'There's still an awful lot to get done before the reception here on Saturday afternoon. Perhaps we could share out some of the jobs.' She looks around at them all. 'What? What is it?'

'Don't you ever switch off?' Lucy asks.

'I counted the RSVPs this morning. You're up to sixty-five.'

'Actually,' say Lucy, sheepish, 'I think it's more like seventy. Seems some friends got wind of the party on Facebook. I couldn't say no.'

Eve frowns. 'Right. So in four days you'll have seventy plus guests descending on Windfalls to celebrate with you. They'll need food and drinks and they will expect a certain level of entertainment.'

'I don't think they'll expect very much of any—'

'Lucy! Trust me, your guests will expect food. They will want drinks. They will *need* drinks – we all will,' she adds under her breath. 'They will need to use the bathroom – God, I forgot to put toilet paper on the shopping list – write that down somewhere will you, Mum,' she adds, flapping at Kit over by the kitchen sink. 'They will want to dance and celebrate. That's what a wedding is. And that's what we are laying on for you.' Eve places mugs on the kitchen table and heads back to empty the warming pot, shovelling tea leaves from a nearby tin and pouring hot water over them.

Lucy shrugs. 'Honestly, Eve, I appreciate all your help, I do. But I don't think we need to plan for every eventuality. It was a great idea of yours to ask the pub to supply the food and the booze. And the rest... well, a certain amount of... spontaneity is a good thing, right? I envisaged the day unfolding in a more free-form way. Everyone I love, here, having a good time.'

Eve grits her teeth as she carries the teapot to the table. She tries another approach. 'I've seen some sweet dresses online. If we ordered them today they should be delivered in time. Chloe and May would love them. Perhaps they could hold little baskets, ribbons, throw rose petals, you know the sort of thing?'

'Rose petals?'

Eve turns to Margot to enlist her help. 'I've been trying to persuade Luce that flower girls would be a nice touch.'

Lucy sighs. 'I've already told you, the ceremony will just be Tom and me, with our parents as witnesses. No fuss. The girls can wear whatever they like to the party afterwards. They can have flowers in their hair, wear sparkly shoes, hold posies, whatever.'

'But if they're not *doing* anything then they're not really bridesmaids, are they? Besides, they would look so sweet in the photographs. Actually,' says Eve with a frown, 'while we're talking about this, we should come up with a list of the family groupings that you want photographed on the day.' She moves to the cutlery drawer and searches for the teaspoons.

Lucy groans. 'Formal photographs? I don't want to

spend hours posing for pictures. I want everyone to enjoy the day. Besides, we'll all have our phones.'

Eve rolls her eyes. 'A wedding represents the start of your life with Tom. Don't you think your in-laws might like a professional portrait or two of their son marrying his beautiful bride? Something for posterity, something to show your grandkids when you're old and grey?'

Lucy's shoulders sink. She closes her eyes and exhales deeply, a pained look on her face. 'I don't want a cheesy wedding photographer.'

'I think you'll live to regret it.'

'Eve, please—'

'And about the girls?' continues Eve, the bit between her teeth.

Lucy throws up her hands. 'Fine. I don't mind what they wear.'

'I'll tell them they're bridesmaids?'

Lucy casts about the kitchen for support.

Eve sighs. 'So I'll go home and crush the dreams of two excited little girls?'

'I'm sorry, Eve. I never said anything—'

'No,' agrees Eve. 'You never said. You haven't made decisions about *anything*. Believe it or not, I'm trying to help you, Luce.'

Lucy's face flushes red. 'I didn't ask you plan anything. You're *hijacking* everything.'

Eve stares at Lucy, open-mouthed. Hijacking? Out of the corner of her eye, she sees Margot reach for the pot and begin to pour the tea. Their mother is busy at the fridge, suddenly fascinated by the seal on a bottle of milk. It seems she's not going to find support from anyone else in the room.

'Tom and I, we want to do things a bit differently,' continues Lucy, more gently.

Eve shrugs. 'I guess it's more fool me, then.' She lays the teaspoons she has been clutching onto the kitchen table and reaches for her bag. 'I'll leave you to it, if you don't need my help.'

'But what about that cup of tea?' asks Kit, waving the milk bottle.

'Sorry, Mum, I don't have time.' She knows it's childish, but she can't help herself. She sweeps out of the kitchen, the back door catching in the breeze and shutting behind her with a slam.

Inside the car, she winds down the window then rests her arms and forehead on the steering wheel, letting out a long sigh. Why is Lucy so annoyed with her? Can't she see that she's only trying to help?

Up close, the leather of the steering wheel appears crackled and discoloured. She closes her eyes. It's a unique peculiarity, her family's ability to get under her skin. Why can't she sit back for once and allow them their mistakes? Perhaps then *they* would learn? Instead, there she is with her constant need to help, to try to guide them through their messes and to smooth the way when it all goes wrong. She's like one of those 'helicopter parents' she heard being talked about on the radio the other day. Hovering and doting, trying to do everything for their children. Of course, they never learn. They've never had to.

Lifting her head, she checks the time on her watch and sees that she has nearly an hour before she has to collect the girls. The farmhouse looms large in the rear-view mirror. She wishes she could go back in. She thinks of

35

her mother and sisters sitting around the table, drinking tea. She thinks of Margot and Kit and the difficult terrain they face. She thinks of the list of jobs lying on the coffee table in the living room and all the items that still need to be bought for Saturday, and sighs. Her phone buzzes on the seat beside her. She unlocks the screen and reads the text message, warmth spreading across her cheeks. She stares at it for a long time, her eyes scanning the words, her finger hovering, until she comes to her senses and swipes it into the trash bin. With another sigh, she turns on the car engine and pulls out of the driveway. That's the last kind of distraction she needs right now. There is *so much* to sort out.

5

A heavy atmosphere lingers in the kitchen as the slam of the back door fades to silence. Kit turns to her two remaining daughters, Margot, hunched at the table, with her short dark hair and inscrutable eyes, and Lucy, looking pale and exhausted, slumped in the chair with her hands at her temples.

'Well, I royally fucked that up, didn't I?' says Lucy. 'I don't know what's got into her. She's so tense.'

'Eve's just being Eve. She'll calm down,' says Kit, placing the milk on the table. She pulls out a chair and sits beside Lucy.

'Was I wrong? Am I being unfair?'

Margot shrugs. 'It's your day. You should do it your way.'

'I do want her help.' She sighs. 'But she has such rigid ideas about what constitutes a wedding.'

'It'll be fine,' reassures Kit, patting Lucy's hand. 'Let her calm down a little and she'll be back here tomorrow acting as if nothing's happened. I don't know about you,' she says, standing up and retrieving a bottle of white wine from the fridge, 'but I could do with something a little stronger.' She waves the bottle at them in invitation.

'Not for me,' says Lucy. 'I'm driving.' She checks her watch. 'In fact,' she adds, 'I should probably get back.'

Kit, realising that Lucy intends to leave her alone with Margot, feels a small surge of trepidation. 'Stay for supper,' she says quickly. 'You look tired. I'll cook. You two can catch up.'

'I should get back to Tom. We've got a lot to discuss. As I'm sure you do too,' she adds with a meaningful glance in Margot's direction.

Kit sighs. So that's why she won't stay. She glances across at Margot and sees a similar look of apprehension on her youngest daughter's face.

Lucy makes a show of gathering her belongings and hugging them both. 'Enjoy your dinner,' she says. 'I'll call you tomorrow.'

'Don't think I haven't noticed you're still wearing my jacket,' says Margot.

Lucy blows her a kiss from the back door and is gone.

Kit meets Margot's gaze. She smiles lightly. 'Would you like some wine?'

She sees Margot hesitate, then nod. 'OK. A small one.'

Kit pours two glasses. 'Why don't you go and freshen up? Unpack? I can handle dinner.'

'I'm fine.' Margot stretches her legs out and crosses them at the ankle. 'I haven't brought much with me.'

Unable to bear the ensuing silence, Kit switches on the radio, turning it to a low volume before beginning to rummage for pots and utensils. She fills a saucepan with water and retrieves a potted basil plant from the windowsill.

'Want me to chop?' Margot asks, indicating the herbs.

'Why not,' says Kit.

Margot shrugs off her leather jacket, and begins to pull the leaves from the basil plant, their pungent aroma filling the room. Kit takes a bag of pasta from the cupboard. As she turns back to the hob, she startles. The whole of her daughter's left arm from her wrist to the sleeve of her T-shirt is decorated with swirling black ink, curling vines crawling across her skin in looping patterns. Kit stares at the tattoo. The creeping black ink is shocking against the whiteness of Margot's skin. She clears her throat. Margot lifts her head but as their eyes meet, Kit changes her mind. Leave it be, she tells herself.

She turns back to the pan, filling it with water, placing it on the hob. She reaches for the salt and olive oil, stealing surreptitious glances at her daughter as she chops the herbs. The tattoo is oddly beautiful. She wonders if it hurt. She wonders what it means. Margot is like a distant country she once knew, familiar and yet remote, changed. No longer the soft girl of years ago but a slim, angular woman – beautiful, yes – but somehow hard and unreachable. How changed she is. Kit looks at her daughter and feels the ache of loss. She doesn't know this woman.

'You don't have to worry,' says Margot after a long silence. 'I'm not here to cause trouble.'

Kit lets out a laugh that sounds false even to her ears. 'I know that.'

'I'm here for Lucy.'

Kit gives a small nod. 'Yes. I figured as much.'

'What's the forecast for Saturday?' Margot asks after a time, the blade of the knife moving smoothly over the wooden board.

'Mixed,' says Kit, throwing pasta into the pan of boiling water.

'A little rain on your wedding day is supposed to bring good luck, isn't it?'

Kit stares at the pan of steaming water. 'So they say.' They are talking about the weather. She would laugh again, if it wasn't so awfully sad.

'I'm sure the argument between Luce and Eve will blow over,' says Margot, after another long moment. 'Emotions are bound to be running high this close to a wedding.'

'Yes,' agrees Kit. 'I'm not worried,' she adds. 'Those two never bear a grudge for long.'

An awkward silence rises between them. Kit kicks herself for her poorly chosen words. They hover in the air, lassoing the lingering tension, holding it in place.

'It's typical Lucy, though, isn't it?' says Margot, clearly trying to ease the mood. 'Romantic . . . impulsive . . . doing everything at breakneck speed.'

Kit steals another glance at Margot. She does remember. She remembers so much. She remembers how Lucy, aged four, and Eve, aged seven had doted on Margot as a newborn baby. She remembers how they had lain beside Margot's Moses basket in the long grass in the garden, shaking rattles and fetching blankets, enamoured with the new arrival. She remembers how Margot had tottered behind Lucy and Eve, following them about the house and garden, a little shadow. How she would curl up on her father's lap at bedtime, a thumb jammed in her mouth, as Ted read a favourite book. She remembers nights when she would sit on Margot's bed and scratch her daughter's back, Margot purring like a cat as she made up fantastical stories to send her to sleep. She remembers how Margot would demand their presence in the living room, force them all to sit in a neat row on the sofa as she threw back the curtains of the bay window with a theatrical flourish and performed made-up songs and plays. So too does she remember the summer Margot left, just sixteen years old when she had appeared in the kitchen with a bulging rucksack and a resigned look on her face. *I can't live here any more.* Five words, spoken in a flat monotone and Kit had nodded. 'I think that's for the best,' she had agreed, before turning away, not because she didn't care, but because she didn't want Margot to see how much she did. Eight years had passed since then and they have barely spoken since that day.

Remembering, Kit is overcome by a sudden urge to walk across and seize Margot – to pull her into her arms and wrap her in an embrace. But Margot's face is guarded and Kit doesn't think she would welcome her touch. She turns back to the hob, stirring the simmering pan. At least Margot seems to be trying, pretending that they can be normal. She will too. 'It is typical Lucy,' she agrees. 'When she asked if she could hold the reception here, I was surprised, but of course happy to agree.'

Margot nods, the blade in her hand still singing across the chopping board, the basil leaves falling into thin green shreds.

'Besides, it's good to have something to focus on. Something other than my work.'

The sound of the knife moving on the board falls silent behind her. She turns to find Margot staring at her, the steel blade lit like a flame in the light falling from the pendant above the table. 'You're writing again?' Margot asks, her eyes narrowed, a tight note in her voice.

Kit thinks of the screwed-up pieces of paper strewn around the floor of her upstairs office, the near-blank, untitled document sitting on her machine. 'No. I was thinking of writing a prequel to the Rare Elements series but my publishers would rather I finish the Tora Ravenstone story first.'

Out of the corner of her eye she sees Margot lift her wine glass and take a long sip. She gives a tight laugh. 'Judging by the royalties I receive, the readers' appetite for her hasn't waned. I should be grateful. Though some days, it feels as though I'm shackled to a monster.' Kit reaches for her own wine and takes a sip, trying to quench the stirrings of heat tickling her belly. They both know they are on shaky ground. As Kit places her glass back on the worktop, the words burst unchecked from her mouth. 'If I'm honest, I've found it impossible to immerse myself in my work ever since . . . well . . . it was devastating.'

She waits, her heart beating fast, the blood pumping through her veins. This is the closest they have come in years to confronting what happened and she is unsure what Margot's response will be. She wants . . . yes, what she wants is an apology. 'What was lost,' she adds, frustrated by Margot's continuing silence, unable to avoid another pointed dig, desperate to generate some kind of reaction, 'was *irreplaceable*.'

Margot's eyes harden to flint, the tension evident in the set of her jaw. Her brown eyes – so like her father's – hold a visible flicker of anger, the sight of which pushes Kit straight onto the thin ice spread so delicately between them. Well, good. It's about bloody time she provoked some kind of reaction in her. 'Don't you have anything to say to me?'

'Mum,' Margot says, the word a low warning. 'Not tonight. Please let's have one night, shall we, where we let the past lie?'

'Let it lie?' She could laugh. She has let it lie for eight years. 'All I ever wanted from you was an apology,' she says, pleased at her calm, conciliatory tone. She is not being unreasonable.

'An apology? I haven't even been back one night and you want to dredge up—'

'Yes. I want to dredge it up,' she interrupts, the anger flaring again. The urge to pick at past wounds is rising up, a terrible itch that will only be sated by sharp words. She has felt it simmering for so long. Her pain – her frustration – needs release. She needs Margot to take responsibility, or at least to try to explain the inexplicable. 'What you did was so . . . destructive, Margot. I need you to see that. I need you to understand what was lost. Would it be so hard to say sorry, after all this time?'

Margot takes a deep breath. She looks down at the blade in her hand before carefully laying the knife on the board next to the basil. 'You want to talk about what was lost?'

Kit nods but Margot lets out a bitter laugh. 'How about we talk about what I was going through, *Mum*? How about you think about what it was *I* lost?'

Kit stares at Margot, baffled. She opens her mouth to answer but Margot isn't finished. 'But that's not a story you've ever been interested in. You were always so

43

wrapped up in your own life, your work, your bloody *success!* She spits the last word at her like a curse.

Kit rears back. 'My success? You think *that's* what was important to me? It was *never* about the success. It was only ever about the writing. The story. Though of course it was the success,' she adds, speaking the word as if it pains her, 'that paid our bills, that kept you all in school shoes and put a roof over our heads.'

Two red spots flare on Margot's cheeks. 'But you never saw how it affected us. You were so absent . . . you didn't see what any of us needed, what *I* needed.' Margot reaches for her wine and drains the glass, slamming it back onto the table.

Kit winces. 'Absent? Me? Oh, darling,' she says, shaking her head. 'I may not have been the best parent, but it was your father who left.' Her voice has risen in pitch. 'It was your father who ran off with *that* woman.' She knows her words are hitting the mark. She knows she is hurting her, but she needs Margot to see that she is not the bad person in this. Not the only one. '*I* was here. I was always bloody here.' Kit draws up short, breathing hard, aware how loud her voice is, how tightly she clenches the wooden spoon in her fist.

'Why do you think he left?' asks Margot quietly. 'You ignored him, the way you ignored all of us. Of course he ran into the arms of the first woman who showed him a bit of interest. You were more interested in living in your imaginary world with your silly heroine, than with any of us.'

'Is that why you did it?' Kit asks softly. 'As a punishment? You blamed me for your father leaving us?'

Margot's face flushes a deeper red. 'You will never

understand because you never paid attention to anything except your work. We might as well have lived in a different house. You don't remember the forgotten picnics, the missed sports days? The school play?'

Kit stares at Margot in disbelief. 'This is about me missing a sports day? Not coming to see you in a school play?' The sharp laugh bursts out of her throat. She sees Margot lower her head. 'You punished me for a few missed moments on a calendar? Oh, Margot. Grow up. I'm sorry your father and I split up. Believe me, no one is sorrier about that than me. But you are not the only teenager to ever live through their parents' separation.'

'I know that,' says Margot. She sits slumped on her chair, face to the ground. 'It's not that . . . you never . . . when I tried to talk . . . you . . .' She waves her hand in a dismissive gesture, looking thoroughly miserable.

Kit watches in surprise as Margot bites down on her lip. A single tear slides down her daughter's cheek before she buries her face in her hands, as if she cannot bear to let her mother see her emotion. Kit eyes the tattoo curling up her daughter's arm and sees what she hadn't noticed at first glance: a small black heart nestled amid the vines in the crook of her arm. A black heart. How apt.

When I tried to talk . . . Kit frowns. It is hard now to remember a time when Margot *had* ever wanted to talk to her. But she can remember that year, that awful time when Ted had packed his belongings and left Windfalls for good. Yes, she hadn't dealt with it in the best way, throwing herself into her writing, focusing all her energy on the final Tora Ravenstone book that her publishers were pressing for. But Margot wanting to talk, she cannot remember.

That year, it had seemed as if their normal, loving girl – yes, a little more dramatic perhaps than Eve or Lucy, a little more rambunctious and unruly, but always sunny – had transformed overnight into a classic, reclusive teenager. She remembers the curtain of dark hair falling across her face, the way she had slunk about the house like a silent shadow, the headphones permanently jammed over her ears. She remembers knocking at bedtime, hearing Margot's muttered 'goodnight' from behind her locked bedroom door. She was a girl who hadn't wanted to be disturbed – touched – seen. *She* had put the barriers up, not Kit.

The change in Margot had come around the same time Ted had left – the awkwardness of those hormonal teenage years clashing with the disruption of Ted's departure. There could never be a *right* time for a father to desert his family, but perhaps for Margot it had been particularly bad timing. Though whenever Kit had tried to raise their separation with her, Margot had always clammed up. It was unfair of Margot to suggest otherwise. Besides, parents split up all the time. Of course it was hard – hard on all of them – and perhaps, yes, hardest on Margot who had been fifteen and the last of their three daughters still living at home, but it was no excuse. There was no excuse for what Margot had done.

Behind her comes the sound of the pan boiling over on the hob. Kit turns to adjust the gas flame, mopping at the spilled water. 'Well, I'm sorry I was such a terrible mother,' she says after a moment, turning back to Margot. 'I'm sorry I was such a let-down to you. I'm sorry I missed a couple of school events and ruined your entire life.'

Margot stands so quickly her chair screeches on the flagstones. 'You can spin this story any way you like, Mum, but the truth is you were too blinkered to see what was happening right in front of you.'

Kit can't help a sad smile. 'I wasn't blinkered, darling. It's called multi-perspectivity. Same events. Different viewpoints.'

Margot eyes her coldly. 'Save me the fancy literary tropes. It doesn't change anything.'

'No. You're right,' agrees Kit. 'It doesn't change anything. It doesn't bring back what you destroyed.'

Margot stares at her for a long moment. The breath seems to have been knocked out of her, a spectrum of emotion washing over her face – disbelief, anger then sorrow. 'I'm sorry,' Margot says at last. 'OK? I'm sorry about everything.'

Watching Margot, Kit feels something collapse inside of her, a sandcastle destroyed by a wave. She fights the urge to reach for her, unsure if she did how Margot would react. 'Talk to me,' she says, more gently. 'Tell me, Margot. Why did you do it? Help me understand why you wanted to hurt me.'

'I . . . I . . .' Margot wrestles with the words. She closes her eyes. 'I didn't . . . I can't . . .'

Kit feels a physical pain, watching her youngest child's struggle. She wills her to carry on but Margot takes a deep breath and when she opens her eyes, Kit sees that her face has re-formed into a tight mask.

'It's hardly an apology,' she tries, pushing her, 'if you can't explain why you did it.'

Margot shrugs and turns her face to the floor, a defeated, stubborn stance that propels a memory of her daughter's sixteen-year-old self straight back to Kit. *What is it?* she wants to scream. *What happened to make you like this?* But instead, she just sighs. 'Fine. Have it your way. We have to navigate the next few days in the same house. All I ask is that you don't ruin this for your sister.'

Margot nods. 'I already said, I'm here for Lucy. I'll be leaving again and out of your way before you know it.' She looks down at the pile of herbs on the board in front of her. 'I think I'll pass on dinner,' she says quietly. 'I've lost my appetite.'

Kit doesn't try to stop her leaving. She waits until she can hear Margot's footsteps on the upstairs landing before reaching for the bottle of Chardonnay and refilling her glass. At the sound of the bedroom door slamming, she takes a long sip, then stirs the pasta, hooking out a strand of tagliatelle and testing it between her teeth. She drains the pan and stirs in butter and the herbs that Margot has chopped, a few toasted pine nuts and a sprinkling of parmesan, before serving herself a bowl and carrying it to the table.

She sits and stares down at the pasta. Silence settles around her. Her heart begins to slow in her chest. This is exactly what she'd been worried about: Margot returning and bringing her dark moods with her. She'd hoped time might have softened her angry, unfathomable daughter, but Margot has returned in full 'Margot' mode, simmering and resentful. Kit is frustrated to feel so affected. It's still painful to remember the devastation Margot had inflicted. It is maddening to be no closer to understanding what happened. What comfort does an apology bring when it is forced and unexplained?

After a few mouthfuls, Kit finds that she too has lost her appetite. She pushes the dish away before scraping the remains into the rubbish bin and washing up at the sink. One pan. One wooden spoon. One bowl. Her solitary existence marked in the single items passing through her hands. The cat appears in the kitchen, mewing plaintively as he winds himself hopefully around her legs. She throws a handful of biscuits into a bowl and strokes him behind his ragged ears as he crunches slowly.

It hasn't always been this way, of course. She remembers the years at Windfalls when the girls were younger. When she and Ted were still together – days passing in the interminable juggle of family life, distracting and dysfunctional – it somehow always felt as if there were never enough time for her and her thoughts. And those distant days before the girls, of course, when it had been her and Ted playing house, stumbling happily and obliviously through the early days of their relationship, navigating their way around the rambling farmhouse, Ted working on his plays and Kit full of excitement for the future ahead of them.

How strange, she thinks, that it should be her living alone at Windfalls, her struggling with her work at the desk in the turret room, her standing at the kitchen window gazing out upon the apple trees in the dusk-lit orchard where in a few days' time they will celebrate Lucy's wedding.

Lucy. Getting married. She lets this thought expand in her mind, testing how it feels. When Lucy had told her about her sudden plan, Kit had murmured reassurances that of course they could hold the reception at Windfalls and yes, everyone would come – yes, perhaps even Margot. She'd agreed that everything would be fine. Only now does she wonder if she's embraced the reality of it. That sweet, fair-haired baby, that boisterous toddler who would sit in the high chair and bang her spoon on the tray burbling cheery nonsense at them all at the top of her voice, the leggy girl with the tangled hair cartwheeling and handstanding her way around the garden, the laid-back teenager who struggled with her exams and academics but given a netball or a hockey stick could put anyone else to shame, the girl who had become a woman, travelled the world and set up her own business – that girl was now grown up and getting married. The transformation stuns her, as if someone has accidentally pressed a fast-forward button on her life.

So much has changed: all three of their girls now adults, Eve a mother, Lucy getting married and Margot doing God knows what in her self-imposed exile. Standing at the kitchen window, she is struck by another of time's vagaries: how strange, to stand here, a woman in her fifties, the wrong side of the menopause, as her present self merges and intersects with the memory of a younger self, standing right here, in the same spot, gazing out upon the same view as Ted and an impatient estate agent hovered at her shoulder. Her two different selves connect; time concertinas, two points meeting each other like the folded corners of a piece of paper. She closes her eyes. *This is the place,* she'd told him. *I can feel it.*

The memory of the words brings Ted's arms circling

50

her waist, his breath warm on her neck. She focuses on the remembered sensation of Ted, pressed against her back, him holding her, and both of them holding the shared future they dreamed of. How delicate it had been. How fragile. Oh Ted, she thinks, this was supposed to be the place.

She opens her eyes. In the falling dusk, her solitary reflection stares back at her from the darkening window pane. She turns and leaves the kitchen and makes her way up the creaking stairs to her bedroom. A light shines from under the gap of Margot's bedroom door. She hovers for a moment, feeling an ache of regret, wondering whether to knock. There is movement behind the door, footsteps, then the fast unzippering of luggage. Several heavy items – books, perhaps, are dropped onto the floor. More shuffling, then the creaking of bedsprings. Kit thinks of all that remains unsaid between them – all the words that have been lost – and with a sigh she turns and moves down the corridor towards her own room.

As she shrugs off her nightdress she notices the spindly grey cellar spider that has taken up residence in the far corner. Every day this week she has watched her weave her web, stringing silver threads into intricate, spiralling patterns. Eve, ever industrious and always neat, would have swept it away by now, shooed it out the window with a towel or broom, but Kit has found a certain comfort in watching the creature's progress. She likes to see her quiet, controlled work, the circular web growing in size. It gives her a modicum of hope for her own stalled work. The slow but steady process she had once practised of laying words down, one after the other, threading them into their own distinct patterns.

She brushes her teeth over the cracked porcelain sink in the corner of the bedroom, pulls on a clean nightie, then climbs into her unmade bed, drawing the sheets up to her chin, her eyes still trained on the spider as her thoughts meander back and forth, weaving and spiralling inwards from the present to the past before spooling out towards the future, like the web being cast in the furthest corner.

The days to come worry her: the wedding; the connection of the past with the present; the stirring of old wounds. She thinks of Ted across the valley, lying in another woman's arms. With the thought comes a familiar sensation. It is the cold grip of panic, the same awful dread she had felt standing helplessly watching smoke and flames spiral into a night sky.

Kit shifts under the bed sheets. The darkness looms over her, heavy and oppressive. She could lie for hours wrestling with the insomnia that has become her recent bed companion. But rather than remain there sleepless for an entire night, her thoughts circling endlessly until the dawn chorus, she slips out of bed, pulls on a silk robe and treads the spiral staircase to the turret room where her desk with the computer and a chaotic spread of books and papers is laid out. She lifts a page and studies the messy paragraph written there, words scrawled and scratched out, thick black pen criss-crossing the page. Her latest attempt to return to the world of her imagination has stalled once again. She screws up the paper and throws it towards all the other crumpled pages spilling from the overflowing bin. Then, with a sigh, she settles into the familiar curve of the chair at the desk. She thinks of the spider, reeling out her web, strand by strand. She tries to sweep all thoughts of her family from her mind, as she switches on the computer to face the emptiness of the blank screen once more.

THE PAST
1986–1987

6

Before Windfalls – before Eve, and Lucy, and, of course, Margot – there was Ted and Kit, young and in love, sitting in a London flat staring at a small, square advertisement on the back page of a national newspaper. *Somerset: Deceased estate. Characterful six-bed farmhouse with land. Offers invited.*

'What would we need with six bedrooms?' Ted laughed, but something about the tiny black-and-white image of the stone farmhouse had captured Kit's imagination and unabated, she phoned the estate agent the next morning and made an appointment to view the property.

They drove out of London two days later, Ted behind the wheel, quiet and thoughtful, while Kit sat beside him, buoyant and girlish with excitement. En route, they stopped at a small roadside cafe where they drank tea and shared a plate of egg and chips. 'We're not buying it,' he said. 'We're window-shopping.'

'Right,' Kit agreed. 'Of course.'

Back in the car, Kit wrestling with an ordnance survey

map, they drove on through wooded vales, the trees resplendent in autumn livery before entering the village of Mortford, a quaint cluster of stone houses and cottages perched on a hillside above the River Avon. They passed a post office and a pub, following the road over a narrow bridge. The house, when they eventually found it, sat alone at the end of an unmarked lane, on the upper edges of the village.

'This is it,' Kit said. Ted brought the car to a halt, leaning over the steering wheel to take in the full effect of the attractive stone building, a solid L-shape nestled into the hillside with gabled windows and twisted wisteria branches splayed across its facade, the huge sky stretched in a canvas above a sloping garden and a fruit orchard leading down into the valley below where a ribbon of river wound, visible through the trees. The lawn was scruffy and littered with buttercups and puffed dandelion seed heads. The first of the autumn leaves blew in spirals from the surrounding trees. A fraying rope swing dangled listlessly from the gnarled branch of a sweet chestnut tree. It was definitely the place from the newspaper photograph, but seeing it there in front of them, the illusion dropped away. Ted felt his trepidation building. It was one thing to sit in a London flat with Kit and dream up a fantasy future, it was a completely different story to step into that fantasy and make it real. Looking around at the house and grounds, Ted couldn't help but feel that the whole place echoed with a certain melancholy. 'I wonder who used to live here. What did you say it was called?' he asked.

'Windfalls.' They both sat silently for a moment. 'This is the place,' she said.

'The place?'

She nodded. 'I can feel it.'

Looking across, he knew from her look of serene satisfaction that they were in trouble.

The estate agent, a small, harried woman dressed in an ill-fitting suit with huge shoulder pads that dwarfed her slight frame, arrived moments later, gripping their hands with a surprisingly firm handshake before taking them through the house, pointing out damp patches and rotting floorboards. Ted knew she had already written them off as time wasters – a young bohemian couple on a country jaunt from London, playing make-believe – which in turn only seemed to make Kit more determined to tour the house slowly, hesitating at windows to admire the views across the valley, pointing out the honey-coloured hue of the Bath stone walls, the enormous, blackened hearth in the drawing room, the intricately engraved brass door handles. By the time he followed her up the curved staircase leading off the second-floor landing, Kit taking the steps two at a time, to a strange little turret room at the very top of the house, he knew the matter of them moving to the property was a done deal in Kit's head.

'It's perfect, don't you think? You could write up here.'

'It may have escaped your notice, but I've not been writing much at the moment.'

'Why is that? Why aren't you writing?'

He shrugged. 'There's that saying, isn't there, that art requires discomfort... pain, even. Perhaps I'm simply too happy.'

'*Too* happy?'

He nodded and turned to her. 'I blame you.'

'I guess I'd better set about making you deeply unhappy then?'

'Please don't,' he murmured, pressing his lips against hers.

Looking over her head through the small arched window he saw the overgrown garden and the fruit orchard sloping down towards the river. 'All this land? What would we do with it?'

'We can let it go to pasture. Let the children roam like wild things. We'll give them a proper childhood, outdoors in the fresh air, swimming in the river.'

'Children, plural?'

'Yes. Didn't I say? We're having a big family. Monstrous. Kids everywhere, climbing the walls and swinging from the rafters.'

'I'm not sure we've discussed it.' He placed a hand on the gentle curve of her belly. 'Rather like we didn't discuss this one.'

Kit beamed at him. 'I'm a great believer that sometimes you have to just dive into life. You wouldn't want him to be an only child, would you? You've always told me how much you hated being an only.'

'Him?' he asked with a raised eyebrow.

'Or her.'

Ted glanced down at the property particulars again. 'It would take almost my entire inheritance from my parents, and a good chunk of my royalties. There wouldn't be much left over.'

'But our living costs will be lower out here than in London. You'll have the peace and quiet you need to write. There will be new plays. Surely that's the joy of creative genius?' He rolled his eyes but Kit continued, unabated. 'The house is called Windfalls. It's a sign of good things to come.'

'And what would you do out here in the wilds of Somerset? Won't you miss London?'

She waved her hands airily. 'Oh, you know me. I'm easily distracted. Besides, I'll be busy making the babies.'

'Not on your own you won't.' He kissed her again, feeling that familiar stirring, marvelling at the pull she had on him. He found it hard to deny her most things.

The agent waited for them out on the doorstep before locking up the house and driving away in a spray of gravel. Ted was already halfway to the car when he heard Kit calling. 'Come on,' she said, leading him down into the tiered garden, through the orchard where the trees stood bowed with apples. She stopped near a rickety wooden gate and Ted came and stood behind her, drawing her towards him, his hands resting on her waist. She leaned her head back against his chest and he breathed in her scent – a fresh, lemon fragrance mingling with the first breath of autumn hanging in the air and the sweet aroma of the earliest windfall apples lying at their feet.

'Aren't you tired of the city?' she asked. 'Don't you feel hemmed in? Rushed all the time? We can leave behind the parties and the people, all those distractions crowding our days. Here we can think, and breathe, and you can write. Besides,' she added, 'look around you. If it all goes wrong, we'll make scrumpy and live off apples.' She turned and smiled her most winning smile and Ted knew it was a lost cause. From the moment he'd first clapped eyes on her, there was something about Kit that got under his skin.

She had been standing almost completely naked on

a stage in front of an audience of several hundred, the very first time he'd seen her. He had been attending the opening night of a new play – a pretentious, experimental piece written by an old college friend. Kit had been one of four female nudes, dressed in nothing but flimsy G-strings and white body paint, hired to stand motionless on plinths dotted about the stage, part of the 'art gallery' set design. Between each scene, as the lights faded to black, the naked actors would assume a new statue position on their plinths, then stand rigid as another scene played out. Halfway through the final act, as the two leads had laboured through a painful scene, Ted had heard the man seated a row in front state in an unfortunately loud whisper, 'I think those statues might be the least wooden thing up there.'

His companion had agreed. 'Though second from the left has a rather impressive rack,' he'd added, making several people nearby giggle,

Ted had been trying hard not to gaze at 'second from the left' for most of the play. How on earth she managed to maintain stillness under such scrutiny, knowing at least a couple of hundred pairs of eyes were roving over her naked body, he had no idea. Wasn't she cold? Bored? Her Zen-like trance was something to behold. She's a serious artist performing in a theatre, he told himself sternly. Not just a naked body to drool over like a teenage boy.

Afterwards, standing at the cramped theatre bar, awaiting his turn to order an overpriced drink and wrestling with what he might say to his playwright friend Timothy that wouldn't sound disingenuous, he had felt someone squeeze into a non-existent gap beside him. Turning, he had found 'second from the left' pressed up against him. He almost hadn't recognised her, clothed now in a dress splashed with bright flowers, her dark hair loose about her shoulders, though the traces of white make-up still visible in her hairline convinced him it was her. 'Congratulations,' he'd said, unable to turn his body but acknowledging her with a tilt of his head. She'd given him a small nod, but hadn't taken her eyes off the bartender. 'I thought you made an excellent statue,' he'd added.

'Are you taking the piss?' she'd asked, not even bothering to meet his gaze.

'No!' Ted had blushed, mortified that he might have offended her. 'No . . . I . . . I thought . . . you were very . . . well . . . very still.'

'*Still*?' A small space had opened up at the bar and she'd taken the opportunity to shuffle in before turning to regard him.

Meeting her gaze, feeling her eyes sweep his tall, no doubt horribly dishevelled appearance, Ted had blushed. 'Yes. Very. Is it difficult . . . being that . . .' Looking into her hazel eyes, his words faltered.

'Still?' she had finished for him, one eyebrow raised.

Ted had experienced a strange lurching sensation, a little like stepping out and finding a void beneath his feet. He'd nodded, still lost for words.

'I've had some practice.'

'You practise being a statue?'

'No.' She'd looked at him, bemused. 'I work as a life model at a local art college,' she explained.

'Right. Yes. Of course. Good. That's good.'

The barman had appeared in front of them and Ted had offered to buy her a drink.

'I tell myself stories.'

'Excuse me?'

'You asked how I stay so still. I make up stories in my head, to pass the time and to distract myself from those annoying itches and cramps that creep up on you.'

'What kind of stories?' he'd asked, genuinely interested.

'Oh, anything. At the moment, it's mainly revenge fantasies. I'm taking great pleasure in imagining awful endings for the man who wrote this play.' She'd leaned in. 'He's insufferable. He insisted on casting all the nudes personally, at his *home* address. He made me parade naked around his living room then thought I'd be so grateful for a part I'd shag him there and then on his nasty velour couch.'

Ted winced, horrified though not altogether surprised to hear of Timothy's appalling behaviour. 'I'm sorry.'

'Oh, don't worry. I slapped him and told him I'd report him to Equity for sexual harassment if he didn't give me the part. So it all worked out in the end.'

Ted gave her an impressed look. 'Good for you.'

She'd glanced around and Ted had wondered if she were searching for someone to rescue her, but then she had turned back to him. 'What is it that you do?' she'd asked him.

'I write.'

'A playwright?' She'd pulled back a little to appraise him. 'Like Tim?'

'Yes, though not exactly like him, I hope.'

The volume around them had risen to such a pitch that

she had to stand on tiptoe to shout in his ear. 'Would I know your work?'

At the sensation of her breath on his skin, Ted had felt a stirring. What was wrong with him, he'd wondered. He *was* no better than bloody Tim, no better than those old men seated in the row in front of him. He'd tugged at his shirt collar and taken another quick sip from his pint. 'I suppose that depends on whether you've any interest in tragic works about dysfunctional father–son relationships.'

She'd narrowed her eyes. 'What was it called, this play of yours?'

'*Lost Words.*'

At that she'd smiled, a dazzling, showstopper of a smile revealing her even, white teeth. 'I've seen it. Twice.' She'd given him a begrudging look. 'I was offered a couple of tickets by one of the lecturers at college, in lieu of payment. I loved it so much I queued for returns and saw it again the following week. It's a beautiful play. Heartbreaking, yet somehow uplifting.'

'Thank you.'

'Ted Sorrell,' she said, pulling his name from her memory.

He'd nodded and she'd held out her hand. 'Kit Weaver.' Her skin was warm but when he looked down at her hand resting in his, he'd seen more traces of the white body paint on the back of her hand, as if she were somehow fashioned from fine porcelain.

'I read the piece in the *Evening Standard* about you,' she continued. 'They said you were one of London's brightest young talents. They said your follow-up to *Lost*

Words would be one of the most anticipated theatrical productions of the decade.'

He'd scuffed the floor with his shoe. 'Yes. Nothing like unexpected success to cripple one under the weight of expectation and self-doubt.'

'You're struggling?'

He couldn't help his dry laugh. 'You could say that.' The conversation had faltered. 'I like your dress,' he'd blurted out. 'It's very . . . unusual.'

'Thanks. I made it myself. From a pair of old curtains, would you believe?'

'Yes. I'm sure my mother had the same ones hanging in her drawing room.'

She'd laughed at that, then knocked back her drink in one impressive swig, the ice sliding and clinking in her glass. 'Shall we get out of here, Ted Sorrell? There's a halfway decent pub round the corner and I wouldn't mind going someplace else, you know, where the *entire* room hasn't seen me naked.'

They'd stayed in the pub until last orders and afterwards, she had been the one to take him by the hand and lead him back to her flatshare. She had been the one who had pulled him onto her bed and whispered in his ear that if he didn't make love to her that very minute she might die. She had been the one who, when they couldn't bear to leave each other's side the next morning, had invited him to Camden Market where he had sat beside her on the stall she ran with a friend, selling crystals and homemade dreamcatchers.

'Aren't they just overpriced lumps of rock?' he'd asked, lifting a pale-pink egg-shaped stone from the table, feeling the weight of it in his hand.

'That's a piece of rose quartz. It's a heart stone, filled with feminine energy. It will stimulate connection, self-knowledge and inspiration. It's good for creative types,' she'd added, with a nudge of her elbow. 'You should buy it. I'll give you a discount.'

He'd laughed. 'That's an impressive sales pitch. Did you make that up on the spot?'

'No! It's true.'

'How do you know this stuff?'

'Picked it up, I suppose. I've always had an interest in myths and legend, ever since I was a little girl. Ancient history, Celtic tales . . . I started a degree in ancient and medieval history a while back. Didn't last too long though,' she'd added with another shrug. 'All those lectures and essays . . .' She'd trailed off. 'I'm not good with timetables and deadlines. I'm too much of a dreamer. I was the eternal frustration to my parents. They washed their hands of me a couple of years ago when I dropped out of college.'

'So what is it that you want to do?' Ted had asked. 'I'm assuming life modelling isn't the anticipated pinnacle of your career.'

'Is that judgement in your voice, Ted? Do you mind that I take my clothes off for money?' she'd only half-teased.

Ted had shrugged. If he were honest, he didn't like the thought of others ogling her body. 'Maybe a little,' he admitted. 'What would happen if you didn't go back to the theatre?'

'Tonight?'

'Yes.'

She had narrowed her eyes. 'I'm not someone that needs rescuing, Ted.'

'I don't think that,' he'd added quickly. 'It's your choice. I support your right to express yourself however you wish. Creative freedom is important.' He knew he'd never try to stop her from doing what she wanted. He wouldn't dare. 'I simply meant I'm enjoying your company. I don't want today to end. And that play was . . . awful. You have to admit that.'

'You're not going to get all possessive and weird on me?'

'No. I don't believe in holding anyone too tightly.'

She'd regarded him for a moment before throwing her arms around him and pulling him closer. 'Yes. Let's hold each other, but not too tightly.'

'So come on,' he'd said after a while, pulling away from her, 'you didn't answer my question. What would you *like* to do with your life?'

'I'm still figuring that out.'

'Well, you're young. You've got plenty of time.'

'You talk as if you're an old man. You're only a few years older than me.'

'Nine years.' Ted had reached into his pocket for his wallet. 'I'm buying this crystal, for you. If I'm right, I'm giving you an expensive piece of rock. If you're right, I'm giving you self-knowledge and inspiration. We'll see, shall we?'

'Thank you,' she'd said, accepting his gift with a kiss. 'We shall see.'

They were already a long way from those incarnations of themselves two years ago. Ted couldn't help musing on the changes in them both, nowhere more evident than when he glanced at Kit walking beside him down the hillside towards the river and saw the transformation of her body, blooming in early pregnancy. They were going to be parents. The thought was wonderful and terrifying and utterly mind-boggling to him. 'What?' she asked him, catching his eye.

'Nothing,' he said, smiling.

Through the trees, a building emerged, a small, round stone structure with a low, thatched roof, set a short distance from the water, a wooden jetty nearby with an old rowboat tied to a stump. 'A boatshed?' Kit asked.

'No. It's an apple store. The estate agent told me there was one down here. The farm used to transport the orchard fruit to market along the river.'

Kit moved closer to the sweet little building and peered through a grimy window. She was surprised to see a cleanly swept room, empty of clutter bar an old table and a few empty wooden crates stacked in a corner. 'It looks dry.'

'It would make a lovely summer house,' Ted said with a smile.

'Lazy days messing about on the river, picnics and boats?'

'Yes, exactly.'

'A camp for the band of river pirates we'll raise, wild bandits ambushing innocent ramblers, adventuring away on the high seas, returning with stolen treasure to keep their slovenly parents in the manner to which they've become accustomed.'

Ted gave her an appraising look. 'Do you know, I think there might be a writer in there, trying to get out.'

She laughed and kissed him. 'I think one writer is enough for any family.'

Turning to look again at the scene spread before them, he noticed the willows on the far bank bowing to the river, trailing their shimmering leaves in the water. The towpath came past the bottom of the orchard and disappeared around a bend in the river. Across the valley, the hills rose up to meet the sky in a spectacular patchwork of countryside. There was no denying it was beautiful, though he also couldn't deny that the picture Kit painted of their possible future here made him nervous. The rural location, the isolation . . . it felt a million miles away from the life they lived in London.

Yet they would have each other – and the baby, of course. A new kind of life would open up for them here. Kit seemed so utterly convinced, and so convincing, that standing there beneath the swaying trees and thinking it all through, he knew he couldn't deny Kit this future. Perhaps this was exactly what he needed to relaunch his writing again. He wanted to believe her, so much: good things were coming their way. 'Yes,' he said, drawing her closer and kissing the top of her head. 'This is the place.'

They moved to Windfalls in late November and woke on their first morning to a fretwork of frost creeping across the inside of the draughty sash windows and an ailing hot-water system that had given up the ghost. The house had been sold to them with many of the previous owners' belongings left in place, a strange array of furniture: a vast oak desk wedged into one corner of the dining room, floor-to-ceiling bookshelves in the sitting room, a long oak table in the kitchen, a moth-eaten rocking horse with one missing eye in one of the smaller bedrooms and a huge mahogany bedframe, as big as a boat, that took up most of the master bedroom. While the furnishings were not exactly to their taste, they were grateful for the legacy. Their own scant belongings – a mishmash of the few items Kit owned jumbled up with all that Ted had inherited from his deceased parents – barely grazed the sides of the rambling house, the building swallowing them up like fish disappearing inside the dank, cavernous interior of a whale.

But it didn't matter. It didn't matter that Kit spent her mornings wrestling with a temperamental range, burning toast and sometimes herself; her afternoons stoppering draughts with screwed-up newspaper; the evenings shivering under piles of blankets in front of a smoking fire. It didn't matter because they were dizzy with happiness and high on the novelty of their new home. When Ted woke her with tea in their huge boat-bed and left her to doze and dream as he wandered off to write for the day, Kit lay under the covers and stroked the growing curve of her belly. She watched how the winter light caught in the web of the dreamcatcher she had hung over their bed – a favourite she couldn't bear to part with when she had left the market stall. She ran her fingers over the rose quartz Ted had given her that she now slept with under her pillow. She told herself that this was enough. Love. Intimacy. They had it in spades. It was enough to move about the house and hear the tapping of the keys on Ted's typewriter and to know that they were where they were supposed to be.

There were adjustments to make, of course. Gone were

the parties and pubs, the Saturdays spent rummaging for fashion in flea markets, the nights spent drinking with friends in basement bars and mornings spent sipping tea and smoking in greasy cafes. Gone too were the cold mornings working at the market, watching shoppers browse her stall before wandering away, and those painfully slow hours modelling naked at the art college, where, lulled by the sound of charcoal moving over paper or brushes caressing canvas, she had killed time by disappearing inside her own head, letting her imagination run wild as she made up fantastical worlds and stories. She sometimes pondered Ted's question to her: *what is that you want to do?* But she truly didn't know the answer. Next to Ted's obvious talent she felt lacking. *He* was the real deal. *He* was the writer. She felt the itch of something unfulfilled building in her, and assumed it was the pull of motherhood calling to her, the need to feather their nest and focus on the new life forming inside of her. She was determined with the move and pregnancy to channel her energies into a new job: she would be a mother, of the very best kind.

In their new home, she distracted herself with the workings of a temperamental sewing machine left behind in an upstairs cupboard, running up wonky curtains for their bedroom and attempting baby clothes and maternity wear from tracing paper patterns. She borrowed a recipe book from the local library and spent afternoons in the kitchen perfecting soups and boiling jams until the kitchen windows were permanently clouded with steam. She sanded down an old oak table she'd found abandoned outside a barn, polishing its surface until it shone.

69

Ted, desperate to finish another play, moved his typewriter first from the second-storey turret room, then again from one of smaller bedrooms on the floor below, until he finally settled at the huge oak desk left behind in the formal dining room. 'It's warmer down here,' he said. 'Besides, I like to hear you moving about the house. It makes me feel less lonely.'

She knew Ted worried, sometimes, about the life they were leading in such an isolated place, but the sound of Ted's fingers bashing against typewriter keys helped to reassure her, in rare moments of doubt, that they had made the right decision. Ted needed to finish a play. Kit knew it. Ted knew it. Ted's agent, Max Slater, knew it. It had been three years since his last. Without the distractions or pressures of the London literary scene, he would be free to create again, and he had to deliver something new, if only to prove to himself that he could do it again.

She left him in peace until late afternoon when, as the sun began to dip in the sky, they would take a twilight walk together, foraging for firewood, Ted stopping once in a while to pull Kit to him, nuzzling her neck or strok-ing her growing belly. In the evenings, they huddled together under a blanket, her feet in Ted's lap while scratched LPs played on the old record player, books splayed all around them.

'I suppose I should make an honest woman of you?' Ted asked her one late spring night, peering at her from over reading glasses that made him look so much older than his thirty-one years, sheets of writing paper scat-tered all about him across the floor.

'Do I still strike you as the type to need a piece of

paper for you to prove your love?' she asked, patting her huge belly. 'Besides, how could we afford a wedding? All our money has gone into this place.'

He nodded. 'I'm glad. I don't need a ring to know that I am yours, and you are mine.'

That's exactly it, she thought, smiling back at him. That's exactly how it was supposed to be. They may not have had much in the way of financial security, but they were happy. Soon, they would be a family of three. The future felt laden with possibility and promise, like the boughs of the trees down in the orchard bearing white blossom.

The baby arrived on a warm May evening, all flailing limbs and piercing wails. They had planned and pre-pared as best they could, decorating one of the smaller bedrooms a buttercup yellow, sanding and painting an old cot they had found tucked in a dusty corner of the attic and folding cloth nappies into a snowy white tower of promise, but what neither Kit nor Ted could have foreseen was how the arrival of Eve – named for the soft, dusky light that had bathed the valley as Ted had held his daughter in his arms that first time – would disrupt their lives. She was a sweet torture neither of them could have anticipated.

Kit had imagined a strong maternal instinct would rise up in her – natural and protective – the moment she held her baby in her arms, but as an only child herself and inexperienced around babies, she'd found herself flailing in the earliest weeks of motherhood. People had been having babies since time immemorial, and yet Kit could not fathom how anyone survived it. Gone were their serene days at Windfalls, her and Ted in their bubble and the world kept at bay. Gone were those long walks and cosy nights by the fire. Instead, there was a third among them, a third who ran to her own punishing schedule and punctuated their hours with the rudest of interruptions. Night after night, it seemed Eve's shrieks and cries could not be abated. There were endless thunderous, stinking nappies that had to be soaked and scrubbed in a vile plastic bucket, bottles and laundry and streams of milky puke and always the crying, the tears flowing freely from both mother and daughter.

'It's exhaustion,' Ted said, finding Kit in the kitchen weeping quietly into the squawking bundle pressed against her shoulder. 'You need to rest. Let me take her.'

'No, you can't.' Eve shook her head. 'This is *my* job. You're supposed to be writing. Besides, you can't feed her. Only I can do that,' she said, looking down in misery at the damp circle leaking through her straining bra onto her shirt. 'It's the only thing I *can* do right now.' Not even her body and its responses felt like her own any more. She had always regarded herself as strong and in control. She had taken a certain pride in her physicality – and yes, she had enjoyed how others had appreciated her form. But all was changed. She was soft, blurred, a picture half rubbed out. She didn't recognise herself in the mirror.

It was relentless. The cycle of waking, crying, feeding, changing. The sleepless nights sitting in the creaking rocking chair, the baby at her breast and her poor, tired brain capable only of the most muddled lullabies and nursery rhymes pulled from the dustiest corners of her brain. Twinkle twinkle. Polly put the kettle

72

on. Rock-a-bye baby. She sang odd fragments of long-forgotten songs like a demented soul – a woman going slowly mad as the keys of Ted's typewriter clicked a quiet accompaniment.

Eventually, Ted came up with a plan. Two secretive but industrious afternoons out in the garden and he was standing in front of her in the kitchen, cobwebs in his hair and a look of boyish excitement written on his face. 'I've been thinking,' he told her, 'you need something of your own. Something more.'

'More? I can barely cope with what I've got right now.'

'What you need is a little head space away from me and Eve. You know how you need to dream. Come on,' he said, pulling her up from the chair. 'Follow me.'

He led her down towards the river and right to the entrance of the old apple store. 'Go on, take a look.'

Kit threw him a puzzled look before pushing open the wooden door and entering the space. Inside, the room was transformed. The table had been pushed beneath the window and covered with an old curtain from the house. An armchair was nestled in the corner, a crocheted blanket draped across the arm. There was an old apple crate, turned on its side and stacked with a few favourite books, a jug of sweet peas and a pot of paintbrushes. Standing on the windowsill was the piece of rose quartz he had given her, while in the middle of the table was a large sketch pad and an old Olivetti typewriter, a spare of Ted's.

'What is this?' she asked, turning to look at him, still unsure.

'It's yours. A room of your own. You can come here whenever you need a little space. To read. To write. To

73

paint. To make your dreamcatchers. To do whatever you like.'

She reached out and pressed a key on the typewriter, hearing the satisfying click of the letter striking the ribbon.

'Whatever I like?' She looked at him, confused. 'What about Eve?'

'Bring her down here with you, or leave her with me. I don't mind having her from time to time. Besides,' he added carefully, 'I thought you might feel inspired. I thought you might like to try a short story or two. I've heard you spinning your stories for Eve at bedtime. You didn't know I was listening but you're a good storyteller. I think you might surprise yourself. A little hobby might make you feel more like yourself.'

Kit stared at Ted, surprised and touched by his thoughtfulness, and a little bit fearful.

'Don't dismiss the idea yet,' said Ted, seeing her scepticism. 'Give it a try. Nothing ventured . . . an hour away from the baby, sitting down here reading, sleeping, whatever you need . . . it will be good for you.'

Kit, pushing aside her doubts, gave him a long hug. 'You are so kind. Thank you.'

More from exhaustion and defeat than any real sense of enthusiasm, she began to experiment with his idea. For a couple of afternoons a week, Ted would whisk Eve away and usher Kit gently down to her new 'studio'. To Kit's surprise and yes, annoyance, Eve seemed to settle more easily away from her. Only Kit hadn't. She had wandered the studio room feeling listless and lost, a dull ache in the back of her throat and the constant sting of tears in her eyes. She flicked aimlessly through the books on the makeshift shelves and spent an age sitting on the wooden jetty, her legs dangling over the river, staring at the reeds drifting beneath the water like the hair of a drowning girl. She pulled branches of willow from the trees and attempted a small, rustic basket, but something didn't feel right.

She felt that she was wasting time. Rather than help, Ted's plan had only seemed to emphasise how useless she was in her current state. Who even was she? She should be supporting Ted, enabling him. Was this another way for him to procrastinate, spending hours with his daughter to avoid the unfinished play sitting on his desk? Was this an even faster route to plunging them further into debt?

After a few days, drifting aimlessly about the apple store, she gave up completely. She wandered back to the house, drawn by Eve's hungry cries. 'Let me take her,' she said, lifting the baby out of Ted's arms. 'It was a lovely idea, but I don't think it's going to work.' She put the baby to her breast and promptly burst into tears. 'None of this is working, Ted. I'm a useless mother. Your play will never be finished.'

'I'll finish it, love. I promise.'

She lifted her head and threw him a despondent look. 'I've seen it, Ted. I've seen the draft sitting there on your desk. You haven't touched it in weeks.' She sighed. 'I thought this would be the place. But it's not. It's stifling us.'

Ted, seemingly lost for words, filled the kettle and made tea. He placed a mug in front of her then rubbed her shoulder. His tentative touch made her want to scream. 'Maybe I should call the doctor?' he asked gently.

She shook her head.

'I'm trying, Kitty. Honestly, I'm trying.'

Eve began to cry. Kit unbuttoned her blouse and put the baby to her breast. She turned away. Kit tried again but still Eve fussed and jerked. 'For heaven's sake,' she cried. 'What do you want?'

'Maybe a little fresh air would help?' he tried. 'Take a walk?'

Kit eyed Ted. He wanted her out of the house. Of course he did. How could he possibly work with them hanging about as distraction? Without saying another word, she swaddled a mewling Eve in a fabric sling, tucked a blanket around her and left the house.

She took off through the garden, weaving her way down the orchard, past the apple store standing as another symbol of her failings, until she reached the river. For a moment she stood and watched the water slide silently by. Two elegant white swans appeared from around the river bend, gliding among the reeds. A little behind, a line of scruffy grey cygnets paddled in formation. You make it look so easy, she thought, staring at the proud parents drifting by. She turned away from the water and continued along the towpath, Eve still grizzling in the sling.

Kit trudged on, following the river, the shadows lengthening around her as her mind began to empty. When she turned, she saw the sun dipping lower over the hills. She should probably head back, though the thought left her heavy and defeated. At the slowing of her movement, Eve's protests escalated.

Kit looked around and saw a flat ledge jutting from the riverbank. Untying the sling, she perched on the rock and unbuttoned her shirt, offering her breast to the baby again. This time, Eve latched hungrily, the tears drying on her cheeks as she fed. Kit looked down at the little creature suckling and felt her own tears begin to fall again.

She had heard of postnatal depression, but truly had no idea that having a baby would compress her life and steal her breath and make her feel so utterly claustrophobic that most days she felt like a drowning woman. She looked down at the face of her daughter. It is too much, she thought. The weight of this is too much.

All around, the shadows seemed to creep closer, as if drawn by her darkest thoughts. What had she sacrificed for this baby? She didn't recognise herself, or her relationship with Ted, now so different. The way he touched her, no longer the desire of a passionate lover but more careful and cautious. She looked down at the baby in her arms and narrowed her eyes. 'It's all your fault, you little beggar.'

Wrapping the baby, now sated and quiet, tightly in the blanket, she lay Eve down on the flat rock and, with her heart thumping in her chest, took a step back. She tried to see the baby as a stranger might, one small fist breaking free of the knitted blanket, flailing in the air. Her small, round face stretched with a yawn. She let out a cry.

Kit took another step backwards, then another, putting several metres between her and the baby. The invisible thread between them stretched gossamer thin. An ache rose up in her chest. Could she do it? Could she leave her daughter here on this slab of stone? Could she offer her up to something else? A different life, or perhaps even death? Would it be for the best? Kit closed her eyes, listening to the pounding of the blood pumping through her veins.

On the walk back to Windfalls, she fixed on the tread of her footsteps on the towpath, though something began to niggle at her, like a small stone in her shoe. So used to the fog of her brain and the cotton-wool numbness she had existed in all these postnatal weeks, she pushed it away. But there it was, returning, pressing insistently. Kit allowed her mind a moment to focus and felt something unfurl.

The baby.

The rock.

A sacrifice.

Walking beside the river, she allowed her mind to follow its meandering trail and by the time she had arrived at the turning from the river path to the house, she was walking a little faster, a little more purposefully. She hesitated at the entrance to the apple store. The trees beyond, heavy now with summer fruit, showed her the way back to the house but turning away from them, she opened the door and closed it behind her with a gentle click.

Holding her breath, she unwrapped a now sleeping Eve from the sling and carefully lowered her onto a nest of blankets on the floor. Please, please, please, she willed. Eve gave a small cry. Kit froze, then let out a long breath as the baby fell quiet. 'Sleep on, little one,' she breathed.

She lit the old oil lamp Ted had hung on a nail for her, then moved to the table where the typewriter and that blank piece of paper lay waiting. She glanced back once at Eve and then, with her hands resting lightly on the keys and the faintest thrill of anticipation caught in her throat, she began to type.

WEDNESDAY

7

Lucy wakes to the sound of rain. Her body is drenched in sweat and her mind filled with a terrible sense of foreboding. She lies still, blinking in the dark, racing to catch up to the truth her body already seems to know. After a second or two it comes to her: the last-minute wedding, Margot back at Windfalls, all the high emotion of the next few days to navigate. A wave of nausea hits. She sighs and reaches out for Tom, who murmurs in his sleep and rolls towards her, one arm pulling her closer, not yet ready to wake.

She doesn't want to disturb him, but nor does she want to lie there fighting the panic and discomfort. She reaches for her phone and starts to mindlessly scroll through her social-media feeds, cycling through glossy photos and upbeat posts from friends and strangers, all living their shiny, happy lives. She knows it's unhealthy to torture herself with the false images of others' imperfect realities, but she cannot look away.

Her gaze fixes on a striking image. One of her instructors at the yoga studio has posted a photo of herself in an impressive standing splits pose with the words 'Live your truth' scrawled in cartoonish neon letters along the perfectly straight line of her leg. The instructor is a new hire but her dynamic classes are already proving popular with their clients. Lucy reposts the image onto the studio's Instagram feed and moments later her phone starts to buzz with notifications.

Tom stirs. 'All right?' he murmurs, turning to her. 'You're awake early.'

'Yes.' She nestles into him, resting her head on his warm chest. His heart thumps a slow, steady beat beneath her ear. Lucy listens for a while, trying to match her breathing to his.

'Sorry I got in so late. Just a little more overtime though, and I can be off with you all next week. How was it at your mum's?'

'Margot's back,' she says, a small smile on her lips. 'Told you I'd get her home.'

Tom squeezes her shoulder. 'I'm glad. How was your mum?'

'Tense. I left them to it. Hopefully they talked it out.'

'You do know it's not your responsibility to single-handedly fix your family, don't you.'

'I know.'

'You can't change other people. You'll only waste your energy trying. I don't want you putting that pressure on yourself.' He nuzzles into the crook of her neck. 'You have enough on your plate.'

'I know. But I think the next few days could be good for them – good for all of us.'

A lone motorbike screams down the street outside the flat, the sound of tyres splashing over wet tarmac and the engine noise fading away. 'How are you feeling this morning?'

'Fine.'

'Fine?' He leans away and eyes her with suspicion.

'Tired,' she admits. 'A little nauseous.'

'You need to take extra care of yourself this week. Don't go taking on everyone else's problems and exhausting yourself. Promise me.'

'I've got all next week to put my feet up.'

Tom sighs. 'I'm going to make sure you do nothing next week except look after yourself.'

'You're such a mother hen.'

'Isn't that why you love me? For my formidable fussing?'

'Yes.' She reaches up and strokes one of Tom's earlobes. 'Because you are a wonderful fusser, and because you have the most perfectly shaped ears.'

'I do?'

'Has no one ever told you that?'

'Funnily enough, no.' Tom pulls her close, his breath warm on her skin. He kisses her where her shoulder meets her neck. 'Are you sure you want to tell them at the dinner? Why not wait until after the wedding?'

She sighs. 'I'm sure.' She stares into the darkness. 'I want to tell them all together.'

Tom squeezes her gently. 'OK.'

'Go back to sleep. It's early.'

Lucy knows she won't sleep again, but she rolls away from him to lie on her side, one hand resting lightly on her stomach. The yellow light of the street lamp outside the first-floor terrace flat falls in a triangle onto the duvet. Three days until the wedding. Three days until she marries the wonderful, uncomplicated man lying gently snoring beside her. Grounded. That was how her dad had described Tom after their first meeting. It was a good word for him. He was grounded – solid, and down to earth. They'd met in a rave tent at Glastonbury two years ago and she'd known from Eve's eye-rolling and her mother's muted response when she had first told them about her new boyfriend that they were all expecting yet another flaky stoner Trustafarian. But Tom, with his warm smile, his steady, optimistic outlook and his good nature had won them all over. Even Margot, back for their father's sixtieth, had found a moment to whisper in her ear, 'He's a good one, Lucy.'

Lying in the darkness, her thoughts loop back to the previous night. She hopes her mother and Margot managed to get through their dinner unscathed. Perhaps they even found a little common ground to stand upon. She knows she needs to reach out to Eve too, after their disagreement. She'll get up soon and head to the studio. There are new memberships to process and next month's timetable needs updating. She is hoping to contact a local artist about painting a mandala on the studio wall and there is a delayed order of new yoga mats to chase up. All jobs to get done before Saturday and their time together next week.

Life is moving so fast. It's as if a fat clock hangs over her head ticking relentlessly, everything rushing forward in a way that makes her heart leap. She wants to slow everything down, put the world on pause. Not yet . . . not yet.

Live your truth. The garish neon words come back to her, as if scratched across her eyelids, and she feels a pang of guilt. She knows she is right to tell them all together. One hit, face to face.

She sweeps thoughts of the weekend ahead from her mind and tries to focus instead on the rise and fall of her breath, concentrating on the techniques she has used in her many yoga classes, teaching stressed-out professionals and too-busy parents how to relax, how to breathe. Funny, she thinks, how something so natural – so instinctive – should sometimes feel so hard to do. If she were to let it, she knows fear could steal in through the open bedroom window and wrap itself around her. But she won't let that happen. Not with Tom lying there beside her. She won't think about the wedding, nor the fractures in her family still to be healed, nor the news she has to share. Not now. Right now, all she has to do is breathe.

8

Margot is lying in bed, tearing strips of paper from the wall beside her. Something about the sight of the sun-faded flowers from her childhood – poppies and tangled roses – makes her skin itch. How many mornings has she woken in this bed, her eyes opening to the sight of this wallpaper? There is something so achingly familiar about the sag of the mattress beneath her and the sight of these flowers that for one strange moment, Margot no longer feels like a grown woman. She is a teenager again. That strange, hollow girl.

Her fingers trace a petal and her nail snags of the seam where two sheets of paper meet. She lifts it, then tugs harder, watching as another triangular strip comes away from the wall in a single, satisfying shred. It curls in her fingers like apple peel. She studies its twisting form before dropping it down the side of the bed to join the other pieces she has already discarded. When she leans back, she is amazed to see a blank patch of wall, a scar about the size of her face staring back at her.

What is it about a homecoming that can strip a person of all that they have become? What is it about the return that propels someone instantaneously back to the shades of who they once were? As if the act of walking through the door of her childhood home is an act of regression? She tests herself. Yes, it's still there, buried deep, hidden beneath the layers of herself, but still present, simmering at the nub of herself. Pain. Shame. An unpleasant ache that throbs through her being. It is infuriating to be so undone by a place.

Unable to lie there a moment longer, she slides from the bed and dresses quickly. As she pulls a T-shirt from her bag, she catches sight of the bottle of vodka lying among her clothes. She rewraps it tightly in a sweater before sliding the whole bag under her bed. She's promised herself she won't touch it. Emergencies only. Glancing back at the wall, she arranges a couple of pillows to cover the ugly scar over the bed, then leaves the room.

The house is quiet. In the kitchen, she feeds Pinter, the old cat coiling himself hopefully around her legs, then makes coffee and sits drinking it on the back doorstep. She had heard Kit's creaking footsteps on the stairs leading up to the turret room late last night. She knows from experience that her mother won't stir for a while yet. Kit has always seemed to keep different hours to the rest of them. When she'd been writing one of her novels, Margot had thought it like living with a family member in a perpetually different time zone. She used to resent the fact her mother was so absent. This morning she is grateful for the solitude.

The garden outside is damp and expectant. The early morning rain has stopped and an extraordinary sea of spiders' webs lie strung across the grass as far as she can see, silver nets catching the dew, suspended over the green. A little further away, in the orchard beyond, she hears the dull thud of an apple release from its branch and fall to the ground. She wonders how long it will take for the rot to claim it. A familiar scent drifts towards her, the damp river rising up from the valley and with it an image surfaces unbidden: green water, dark mud, ragged fingernails. Margot swallows and lowers her face to her cup, replacing the fragrance and the image with the bitter scent of coffee.

Last night was the first time she had been alone with her mother in several years. Lucy's clumsy ploy had worked. Certainly, Margot had been prepared to try. She had wanted it to feel normal – had wanted sitting at the table, helping her mother prepare supper, to feel like something that could happen on any other night. Wine. Dinner. Conversation. A mother and daughter catching up after a period of absence. What could be more ordinary?

Would it have been so hard for her mother to draw a line under everything that had gone before, if not for her, then for Lucy? She was here, after all. That said something, surely? No, it had been Kit who had raised the spectre of the past. Not raised it but hurled it, flaming and explosive, right at her. All her past wrongs wrapped up in a neat Molotov cocktail of words, emotion and underlying recrimination, and Margot, sitting at the kitchen table, the blood pumping in her veins, had wondered, for a moment, if she had heard her right. Yes. She was doing it. Her mother was going there. *Talk to me*, Kit had said. *What made you do it?*

It had been a close-run thing. Part of her had wanted to tell the truth, to draw her mother close after all these years. But still there was that burning shame. And there was Lucy too, with her impending Big Day and the memory of her sister's plea that they be a *normal family*. Perhaps that, more than anything, had stoppered her words and driven her from the room.

It's obvious Lucy is hoping they will play happy families. Her sister seems to believe that by drawing them all back to Windfalls she can smooth over the past, that their parents will become friends again, that Kit and Margot will gloss over the events of a few years back, that everything will magically resolve itself. But Lucy has always been full of naïve optimism, because Lucy doesn't understand the full story. How could she? Kit and Margot are two women standing on different sides of a river, with the past, a vast, unfathomable flow churning between them. Four days to get through. Four days to navigate and hold herself in check – to be the sister Lucy needs her to be, to do the right thing – before she can leave.

Thinking of Lucy and the wedding and remembering the tension with Eve the night before, she reaches for her phone and taps out a quick message to her sisters: *Give me some jobs. I want to help. M x* Almost as soon as she presses 'send', the screen shifts and a shrill ringing noise makes her leap on the step. 'Jonas' flashes on the screen. She hesitates, then silences the phone and places it beside her, waiting for the screen to clear. A wood pigeon coos its morning song. Her moment of stillness has gone. She needs to move.

There is a softness in the garden. Leaves drip with the residue of early morning rain and the ground gives beneath her feet as she follows the silver-green slope of the garden down the hillside. In the orchard, she passes a familiar tree, a twisted Bramley apple leaning over the stream meandering down the hillside, its trunk bearing the scars of five initials carved into its bark like black brands: K. T. E. L. M.

Margot stares at the letters, remembering the blade of the penknife flashing silver in Lucy's hand as she leaned against the trunk and sliced into the bark. She reaches out to trace the letters. Another time; another Margot. The memory hooks around another, of that same penknife, years later, in her own hand, meeting its mark, scratching deep. A woman's shout. The knife clattering to the ground. Margot's feet slamming hard on tarmac. She swallows the bile rising in her throat.

The steep sides of the valley create a natural echo chamber, birdsong bouncing off the hills, and amplifying the drone of a distant tractor. At the far end of the orchard, she can see the iron gate leading to the towpath and the river. She stands, her hand resting on the tree trunk, wondering whether she is brave enough. She hasn't passed that way in years.

She closes her eyes. She can feel it building in her, that same destructive itch that saw her tugging wallpaper from her bedroom wall. It's a compulsion – like the irresistible need to pick at a scab – to make herself bleed. Opening her eyes, she continues down the hillside, moving on to where the river flows.

Through the gate, she joins the towpath running beside the river, a smooth expanse of green water moving silently before her, the hull of the old rowboat slumped and rotting on the bank. She takes a steadying breath, keeping her face turned to the water. Another breath. Then another.

A trio of ducks takes flight, disturbed by her arrival. She leaps at the sudden sound, then feels her heart settle as the birds flap away along the river, shadows skimming the water, their disgruntled quacking fading with their departure. She ignores the tangle of ivy and timber standing in the shadows to one side of the towpath and instead makes for the jetty stretching out into the water. The planks of wood creak beneath her feet. She sits on the damp platform, her feet dangling over the edge, and gazes out at the eddying currents playing on the surface, the flies and midges hovering above and the reeds streaming like mermaids' hair beneath.

After a time, a dragonfly lands beside her. She watches it, marvelling at its luminescent wings, metallic greens and blues shimmering as it flexes gently in the breeze. It looks end-of-summer weary. I know the feeling, she thinks. Keeping her eyes on the insect, she takes up her phone again and plays back the voicemail message waiting for her.

Margot. It's me. I think we should talk. Call me. Please.

The sound of Jonas's voice – the particular cadence of his Scandinavian accent, the skipping delivery of his words – makes her close her eyes. She can see his scruffy blonde hair, his unkempt beard, his sky-blue eyes. Jonas. Another perfect example of what happens when she lowers her defences and lets people too close. Confusion. That dark, creeping shame. She's an idiot – an idiot with another mess to clean up. With a sigh, she hits the redial button and waits.

'Hey,' says Jonas, answering almost immediately, his voice soft and low.

'It's me.'

'Hey you.' He hesitates. 'I'm glad you called. I thought you might be avoiding me.'

'No.'

A silence falls over the line. 'You left so suddenly.'

'I wrote you a note.'

'Right. "Family stuff". Course. Made complete sense.'

'My sister's getting married,' she says, as further explanation.

'Oh.'

'Yeah . . . She sprang it on us all, last minute.'

'I see.' There is a long pause. 'And you didn't need a "plus one"? . . . A helpful photographer friend to come with you?'

'Thanks, but aren't you working this weekend? Besides, I doubt Luce could afford a hot-shot photographer like you.'

'I wouldn't have expected to be paid. I'd have done it as your friend.'

The silence expands between them. Margot is back in Jonas's bedroom, lying naked on his bed. She sighs and blinks away the image. A complete fuck-up.

'Should we talk about the other night?' he asks.

'Yes,' she agrees, wanting to do anything but that.

'I don't think we can ignore what happened.' He hesitates. 'I don't want to.'

She doesn't know what to say, so Jonas continues, filling the silence. 'I know when you answered the ad for my spare room it was supposed to be a practical arrangement. But since I've grown to know you a little . . . well . . . you've become important to me, Margot. A good friend.'

'Yes,' she says, seizing upon his words. 'We're friends.'

'Yes. Only the other night . . . what happened . . . it took me by surprise but it made me realise that I . . .'

Margot closes her eyes. Don't do this, she thinks.

'. . . I have . . . feelings for you.'

Margot holds her breath.

'So I was . . . uh . . . I was wondering if you—'

'Don't stress, Jonas,' she says, interrupting him again. 'It's all good. We were both drunk. It didn't mean anything.'

He waits a beat. 'It didn't?' The silence between them expands. 'It's . . . I thought . . . I felt maybe there was something—'

'We're mates, Jonas. OK? Flatmates. Let's not over-complicate it.'

Jonas is silent for a moment. 'Yes. Of course.'

Margot gazes out across the river. She hates the hurt she can hear in his voice and feels an unpleasant ache, a swelling in her ribcage that requires her to place her hand over her chest and hold her thudding heart. 'So, we're good then?' she asks, her voice tight and falsely bright.

'Yes.' Jonas hesitates. 'And *you're* OK? You'd tell me if you weren't? If you needed anything? As a friend?'

'Yes,' she lies. 'I would.' Her gaze catches on something on the far side of the river. Something white trapped in a tangle of overhanging branches.

'Good.' Muffled voices drift down the phone line. 'Yes, the light reflector, and the spare battery.' Jonas is talking, his mouth a little way from the phone. 'Sorry,' he says, his voice returning to full volume, 'I'm on a shoot. Boy band.' He adds under his breath, 'All complete divas.

You've never seen so much hair product in your life. I should go. You'll be home next week?'

Home, Margot thinks. Is that what she calls it? 'Yeah, back next week,' she says. She blinks and refocuses her gaze on the object caught in the tree branches. A cluster of white sticks in a neat, curved pattern, arced like the spine of a boat's hull. 'I'll see you then.'

'Fine, Margot. See you.' The line goes dead.

Margot holds the handset to her ear for a long time, listening to the silence echoing back at her as she stares across the river. While they have been talking, a thought has come to her, horrifying to her for its possible truth. Perhaps walking through the door of Windfalls is not so much an act of regression, but more acknowledgement that for all her running – for all those years she has spent away from this place – she is still the same person, unchanged. She cannot run from who she was – who she is.

Gazing out at the far side of the river, she swallows. The shape of the strange bundle of white sticks grows clearer. There is a recognisable pattern to their curved shape. Not sticks, she realises with a creeping dread. Bones.

She stares across the river for a long moment, wondering if her eyes are deceiving her, until she stands and moves to the furthest point of the jetty. Definitely bones. The blood is rushing in her head. She can hear her heartbeat in her ears, feel her breath catching at the back of her throat. She wonders what to do. She dips a hand into the water and shivers. If she were Lucy, she would peel off her clothes and dive into the water, but she is not Lucy.

Glancing around, she notices the old rowing boat lying on the riverbank. She eyes it for a moment. Moving closer, she can see it is in a sorry state, but from what she can tell, it looks watertight, no obvious holes or damage. A lone paddle lies across the seat bench. She kicks the timber hull, reassured to hear the solid thunk as her shoe hits the wood. With another quick glance around, she unties the frayed rope securing it to the jetty and begins to push the boat to the river's edge.

9

Eve stands in the shower, warm water falling onto her skin. She can hear the far-off sound of her daughters laughing as she scrapes a blunt razor over the curve of her armpit. May's high-pitched giggles are followed by the slightly deeper laughter of her older sister. 'Stop, Chloe. Stop!' screams May, in the maniacal strains of a six-year-old who doesn't want her big sister to stop at all. Eve sighs. They are supposed to be getting dressed and packing their school bags. Andrew is downstairs. He can deal with it.

She closes her eyes and rubs shampoo into her hair. Washing the foam away, she imagines she is somewhere else . . . in a dark bar, seated at a stool, cocktail glasses and a candle flickering on the polished wood in front of her. She conjures a man on the stool beside her. He leans forward, his arms reaching out to draw her into his embrace, the hot press of skin—

'Muuuum!'

Eve opens her eyes then quickly squeezes them shut again, too late, as shampoo runs into her eyes. 'Fuck,' she says, groping for a washcloth.

'You said a bad word.'

'Yes. Yes I did.'

She puts her head under the full force of the water, rinsing the last of the shampoo away and when she opens her eyes again, she sees May standing on the other side of the shower screen, the top half of her body dressed in school uniform, the bottom half still in pink unicorn pyjamas, her hands and mouth smeared with Marmite and her face screwed into a tearful scowl. 'Mummy, Chloe's trying to kill me.'

'No she's not, darling.'

'She is. She's sitting on me and making me smell Daddy's shoes.'

Eve rolls her eyes. 'And why such torture?'

'Because she wants to watch *Scooby Doo* and I want *Paw Patrol*.'

'I thought I'd said no television before school.'

May pouts. 'Daddy said we could.'

'Did he now?' Eve sighs. 'I'll be down in a minute. I'll talk to Chloe . . . *and* Daddy. OK?'

May takes this as a win and lunges at the screen. 'I love you, Mummy,' she says, kissing the glass then stepping back, leaving an imprint of sticky, brown Marmite hands and lips smeared across the glass.

Eve eyes the mess, telling herself it doesn't matter, trying to relish the moment of affection. She bends down and presses her own lips against May's imprint. 'I love you too. Now please get dressed, and stay away from your sister.'

May saunters out of the bathroom, leaving Eve to dry and pull on clothes. She checks her watch. Twenty minutes before they have to be in the car.

Downstairs, she finds Chloe, still in pyjamas, hair

unbrushed, sitting on the back of the sofa lazily tossing dry Cheerios into her mouth. Sofa cushions are scattered across the floor, a vase of flowers lies tipped on its side, water spilling onto the carpet. The shoe basket from the front door has been dragged into the lounge and upended. The TV blares an annoying theme tune. 'Chloe! What on earth?'

Chloe drags her glazed gaze from the screen.

'Why aren't you dressed? What's all this mess? Where's your father?'

Chloe shrugs, the nonchalant, carefree shrug of a nine-year-old with no apparent timetable. 'Dad's in the kitchen.'

May sidles into the room, still only half-dressed, though now with the unfathomable addition of rabbit ears perched on her head.

'Why are all the shoes in here?' Eve asks, her exasperation growing.

'May threw them at me.'

'She called me a baby.'

'She *is* a baby. She's scared of *Scooby Doo*.' Chloe's gaze slides back to the television.

It is the last straw. Eve reaches for the remote control and snaps the TV off, ignoring Chloe's shout of protest. 'Tidy this mess up. Both of you.'

'But it's not fair,' wails May. 'I didn't make the mess.'

Eve picks up the vase of flowers, watching as the last of the water cascades onto the carpet. 'Now,' she roars. 'I don't want to hear another word.'

Chloe stomps across the room, rights the shoe basket and drops one of Andrew's trainers into it with a dramatic sigh.

97

'You're such a meanie,' says May, forgetting that she has drawn her battle lines against her sister, both of them now united in their resentment for their mother.

She finds Andrew in the kitchen, hunched over his laptop, surrounded by dirty cereal bowls, plates of crusts and cups. Music blares from the radio on the window-sill. A congealed porridge saucepan waits in the sink. A puddle of coffee grounds sits on the kitchen counter. The half-full milk bottle stands next to the fridge, warming nicely. She stands in the doorway, watching her husband, the frown on his face pinching the skin between his brows into deep furrows. 'All right?' he asks, glancing up.

'No. I'm not all right.' She stalks across and snaps the radio off.

'I was trying to drown them out,' he admits, smiling up at her. 'Everything OK?'

'Other than the girls trashing the lounge and neither of them being ready for school?'

'Sorry. I got a little distracted with this spreadsheet. It sounded like they were having a great time.'

Eve raises an eyebrow.

'What?'

'World War Three was about to break out and you were completely oblivious. You said you'd help out a little more in the mornings.'

'I'm here, aren't I?'

'Not exactly. Not *here* here. Your head's still in your work.'

'They're not babies, Eve. They don't need watching every second. Besides, something urgent came up.' He smiles at her. 'No harm done. All present and accounted for.'

Eve sighs. It's hardly the point. She looks around at the mess in the kitchen then thinks of the imminent battles to be had with hairbrushes and shoes, the inevitable race to the school gates, the forgotten musical instruments and PE kits. She thinks of her own looming day of admin at the recruitment agency – perhaps not nearly as important as Andrew's – but still a commitment, still a job that needs to be done properly. She thinks of the coming weekend and the ever-growing list of tasks to get done before Lucy's wedding on Saturday and the simmering tension between Kit and Margot, then adds the image of Sibella seated at the same table as them all on Friday night and wonders how on earth they are to navigate such turbulent ground with emotions running so high. She thinks of it all and feels defeated.

Has it always been this way, she wonders? Has she always borne the strain of holding everything together? When she thinks back to the packed lunches she would make for her sisters whenever their mother forgot or wasn't awake to make them after yet another late night working, or the school uniform she would pull out of the dirty laundry and scrub clean with a damp cloth, or the plaits she'd tie and the school notes she'd nag Kit to sign, it feels as though she has lived most of her life with responsibility resting on her shoulders. It is, in part, why she is so determined to be a different kind of parent to her own children, present and reliable. Only it's hard to be present when you have so many balls in the air. Increasingly, she feels as though she's about to drop them all.

Andrew stands and flicks the kettle on. 'Let me make you a cup of tea.' He reaches for her, drawing her to him. 'Don't be cross with me. I'm sorry. I'll try harder.'

Eve nods and bites her lip, leaning her body against the reassuring solidity of his, just as her phone buzzes. She pulls away to check the screen and sees a message from Margot. Well, that's something, she thinks. A little help would definitely be welcome. She types a quick reply, presses send, then punches out another to her father.

Andrew sighs and turns back to the kettle. 'How is Operation Last-Minute Wedding going?' he asks, pouring water into a mug for her.

'Fine,' she says, laying down her phone. 'Though I'm afraid it looks like you and Dad might be on bonfire duty now. Mum was talking about fireworks but I think I may have dissuaded her.'

'Bonfire? Fireworks? I thought it was supposed to be a low-key thing?'

'If you call seventy guests and rising low key.'

Andrew gapes at her, then laughs. 'Your family.'

Eve feels a rush of irritation. She turns away and begins to rinse the cereal bowls before dumping them in the dishwasher. 'I've got a school governors' meeting tonight. You'll be here for the girls?'

'Tonight?'

'Yes. Seven o'clock.'

'God, Eve, sorry, I have a work dinner. I thought you knew?' He slides the mug of tea across the counter towards her.

Eve studies him evenly. 'It's not on the calendar.'

'Isn't it?' He unplugs his laptop and slips it into his

bag. 'Sorry, love. My mistake. I didn't realise you needed me to babysit.'

She feels the blood rush to her cheeks. 'How many times do I have to tell you, it's not babysitting when they're your own kids?' She sighs. 'So what am I supposed to do?'

'It's just the PTA. Can't they go ahead without you?'

She slams another bowl into the dishwasher. 'That's not the point. I made a commitment.'

'Well, book a babysitter.' Andrew glances up. 'Sorry, but I can't miss the dinner. They're an important client.' He softens slightly. 'I know it's your way, but you're working yourself up into a state over school meetings and your sister's wedding. You do too much.'

Eve throws a handful of cutlery into the holder, a knife missing and clattering to the floor. 'Right. I do too much.' She bites back a retort about others not doing enough and waits at the sink, hoping for Andrew to notice how upset she is, but he continues to pack his belongings before moving to kiss her on the cheek and throw her a cheerful 'goodbye'. She stands there for a moment longer, trying to control the rising emotion. She counts to ten, squashes it down, then leaves the kitchen, yelling at the girls in a voice she can't bear, 'If you two don't hurry up and get dressed, you'll be explaining to your headmistress why you've arrived at school in your pyjamas! Don't think I don't mean it.'

'Wow,' she hears Chloe mutter from the lounge, 'worst mum ever.'

10

'Do you think it's going to be all right?' Ted is leaning in the doorway to Sibella's studio, a cup of coffee warming his hands. The mug he brought for Sibella sits on the bench beside her while her hands shape a lump of white clay on the wheel spinning in front of her.

He marvels at her skill, the way he has marvelled ever since he first witnessed her at work. The rise and fall of the clay, the ripples of the material moving through her hands, her foot urging the wheel on. Her green eyes are fixed in concentration and there's a streak of white on her left cheek. Behind her stand tall shelves, row upon row of ghostly white pots drying on boards.

She dips her fingers in a bowl of water and places them in the centre of the clay to hollow the vessel. It sinks a little then rises again, thinner, taller. She pinches a rim before curving it over into a neat lip. In his work, he pulls words out of the air and strings them together to make fictions. He moves characters upon a stage to tell a story. But Sibella has a *real* craft. There is nothing fictional about what she does. Plates. Jugs. Bowls. Pots. Her work is physical, practical and real. Some days he can't help but feel envious of the solidity of her craft.

She doesn't look up as she answers. 'You mean the wedding?'

'Yes.'

Sibella considers his question. 'I'm sure everyone will be on their best behaviour.' She glances up from the wheel. 'You're frowning.'

'I like Tom, I do, but I don't understand the need for them to rush like this.' He takes a sip of tea. 'She must be pregnant.'

'Perhaps. Though you're hardly the sort of father to march a young man up the aisle to make an honest woman of his daughter. You wouldn't have a leg to stand on!'

'True,' says Ted with a dry laugh. 'Kit and I certainly have form on illegitimate children.' He looks down at the thin gold band on his hand. He remembers the moment Sibella slid it onto his finger. Why it should have felt so important for him to marry this woman, when he had spent all those years with Kit, proudly unmarried, he still isn't entirely sure, but he knows it was a good decision.

'Perhaps it's simple: she loves him. It's the right time for them both.'

Ted smiles. 'I guess I can understand that. I suppose for all her impetuous ways, Lucy also has a strong streak of romance in her. Though she's certainly a conundrum. All my girls are.'

'That's women for you,' says Sibella, dipping her fingers in water again before smoothing the edges of the vessel. 'I'm surprised you haven't figured that out by now, surrounded as you are.'

'Another baby in the family . . . wouldn't that be

something? A real blessing. Perhaps they are saving an announcement for the reception?'

Sibella smiles. She slows the wheel then leans back to appraise the pot in front of her.

'You're continuing with the porcelain?' Ted asks.

She nods. 'There's something about it . . . a fragility. It requires such lightness of touch. It's not easy on the wheel but I'm enjoying learning.'

Ted notices how the light streams through the studio window, glancing off the delicate, white pieces drying on the shelves behind her. She's right, he thinks. There is a wonderful purity to them.

'You were up early,' she says. 'Working?'

He nods. 'I wanted to revise the final scene before I send the new draft to Max.'

'You're feeling good about it?'

Ted considers Sibella's question. He has spent the last few months buried in a new play, delving into the complex, often unfathomable terrain of father–daughter relationships. 'I am. I don't want to get ahead of myself, but I think it could be good. Perhaps even my best. Though you know how it goes,' he adds. 'One day it flows. The next . . . well, it's the equivalent of me trying to craft something at your wheel here. A misshapen disaster.'

She laughs. 'We all have those days.'

'I booked a table at The Bridge for Friday evening,' he says, changing subject. 'You are coming still, aren't you?'

Sibella frowns. 'Do you really think it's a good idea?'

'Lucy asked specifically that you be there.'

'I just think . . . with Kit . . . it might be easier if I—'

'This isn't about Kit. This is about Lucy and Tom. I

know they'd both like you there. Besides, the dinner the night before might pave the way for a more ... *harmonious* day on Saturday?'

Sibella bites her lip. 'Anything that brings me closer to your girls ... you and I both know it drives Kit crazy.'

'That's her problem,' Ted says, firmly. 'Lucy wants you there.'

Sibella sighs and leans back on her stool, her gaze meeting Ted's. 'Then I shall be there,' she says.

He steps forward, kissing the top of her head, her red hair soft and warm as it brushes against his lips. Ted is still inwardly counting his blessings for the beautiful, creative woman sitting before him when his mobile phone gives a shrill beep in his pocket.

'Who is it?' asks Sibella, glancing across, seeing his frown.

'Eve. She's asked me to add one more to the dinner reservation on Friday.' He looks across at Sibella. 'Margot's back.'

Sibella raises an eyebrow. 'That's good, I suppose?'

Ted lets out a low laugh. 'Have you forgotten my sixtieth?'

'You've missed her. I know you have.' Sibella smiles gently. 'It might be ... healing ... for everyone.'

He hesitates. 'Yes, it might.'

'Maybe coming back will force her to face up to what she did? She can't run from it for ever.'

'No,' says Ted with a frown. He looks out across the valley and sees the sun slide behind a grey cloud. The effect is like a curtain being drawn over the surrounding hills. His youngest daughter, Margot: what *is* she running from?

Sibella reaches for her cup of coffee and takes a sip. 'I suppose, if we're looking for a silver-lining, at least I won't be the *only* persona non grata at the table on Friday.'

Ted nods and tries to conjure a smile, though his eyes remain fixed on the dark shadow hanging over the valley.

II

Halfway across the river, Margot realises the folly of her plan. Navigating the channel with one paddle is proving harder than she'd imagined. Even worse, far from being watertight, the old rowing boat seems to be leaking at an alarming rate. Looking down into the hull, she can see a pool of muddy water gathering around her feet. She fixes her gaze on the far bank, where she has seen the white bones, and does her best with the paddle.

A little further on, the current begins to tug her off course. She feels its pull and imagines letting it take her, the boat bobbing down the river until eventually she is spat out into the great churn of a cold, unforgiving ocean. But remembering the bones caught in the tree on the other side of the river, she adjusts her course and paddles with fresh resolve.

It is impossible to get close. The tangled branches jut awkwardly into the river and prove hard to draw near. After a couple of attempts, one near miss losing the paddle and several painful scratches, she manages to grasp one of the larger branches, and pulls herself, hand over hand, until she is almost eye-level with the bundle caught in its watery nest.

Up close, she sees straight away that she was right. The ribcage – the arced section she had noticed from the jetty – is still in perfect formation and attached to a curved spine, on top of which sits a skull. Stripped clean by scavenging birds and fish, they are the stark white bones not of a human, as she had feared, but of a deer. She stares into the hollow eye sockets and regards the smooth muzzle with fascination and relief. She wants to laugh at the sheer ridiculousness of finding herself in a slowly sinking boat in the river, staring at the skeleton of a dead animal.

Feeling the water seeping into her shoes and creeping up the hems of her jeans, she awkwardly adjusts the prow and paddles back across the river towards the jetty. Halfway across, she takes a rest, the muscles in her arms burning with the effort of using the paddle. She catches her breath, staring down into the dark water, hearing the quiet sound of it lapping at the wooden hull. She is reminded of a summer's afternoon from years ago, when she had jumped into the river and let herself sink below the surface. Gazing into the dark water, she can almost imagine she sees herself there below the surface, gazing up towards the light, isolated momentarily in a submerged world of silence and shadows. The thought makes her shudder.

With a deep breath, she picks up the paddle and resumes her efforts. The boat is filling more quickly now, proving heavier and harder to steer. It is a relief to eventually feel the bump of the solid jetty against the hull, her wet shoes squelching as she jumps out and drags the boat up onto the riverbank. She secures it to its post then strips off her jumper, warm after her exertion.

Catching her breath, she studies the sleeve of tattoos, tracing the heart near her elbow. She trails her fingertip across the vines looping in their spiralled patterns on her skin. It had been the small black heart she'd had inked first into the crook of her arm, returning to the tattoo artist again and again to add to the design, needing to feel that sharp buzz of the needle against her skin – the heady electric thrill of it breaking through her numb state. She *could* feel. She could feel pain. The sight of the ink marking her skin was the proof she had needed.

Her phone vibrates in her back pocket. She reads the message from Eve – a reply to her text from earlier – asking her to visit Sibella and check that all is on track with the flowers for Saturday.

Good, she thinks, a job that will keep her out of the house and out of Kit's way for a little while longer. Her trainers are wet but it isn't too far to go across the valley. She wanders back onto the towpath, before turning left, away from Windfalls, away from the collapsed pile of charred wooden timbers, barely visible beneath a tangle of brambles and ivy, lying slumped in the shadows that she has so carefully avoided this whole time, heading instead for the path that will take her across the bridge and on to the far side of the valley.

Lucy walks down Milsom Street, her trainers making a satisfying slap against the cobbles beneath her feet. A thin shard of sun breaks through the cloud overhead, transforming everything grey to dazzling silver, the Bath stone warming to honey in the light. Lucy isn't thinking about the spreadsheets she has left behind in the studio office, or the multitude of appointments ahead, or any of the organisation still required for the coming weekend. She thinks only of the miracle of her feet hitting the ancient pavement, the damp air on her face, the light breeze catching the tassels of the silk scarf hanging at her neck as she turns down a narrow lane, making for a shop at the far end of the street. She is one of many, part of a steady flow of humanity treading these cobblestones — those who have gone before and those still to come. She takes comfort in her insignificance.

On the pavement a little further ahead, a mother races to catch up with two young children, pigtailed girls aged about three or four, dashing in front. 'I am running. I am running,' sings one girl, looking down to watch her feet as they move. 'Here I am. Here I am.' It is such a simple refrain that her sister cannot resist joining the chant as she runs giggling behind. 'Here I am. Here I am.' They are both so obviously delighted with the moment, with their movement, with themselves.

Lucy, following behind, smiles. She remembers being with her sisters at Windfalls, chasing each other around the garden, throwing themselves down the hillside in a crazy tumble of roly-polies. The joy of movement. *First to the old apple tree!* Eve and Margot had given it a good shot, but she had always won those races. She will smooth things over with Eve later. Bringing them together for the weekend is going to be good for them all. She knows it. Here I am, she thinks, breathing the fresh autumn air, filling her lungs.

The bell over the shop door jangles as she enters. Dorothea, the owner, looks up from her sewing machine, and waves a greeting, mumbling something that sounds like 'Hello dear' through her mouthful of pins.

Lucy smiles and waits. 'You're early,' says Dot with a smile, as soon as she has finished her seam and removed the pins clamped between her lips.

'Yes. I'm excited.'

'Of course you are. It's hanging back there,' she says, nodding towards the curtained-off cubicle at the rear of the shop. 'Go through. Shout out if you need a hand.'

Five minutes later, Lucy pulls back the changing room curtain and twirls in front of the long mirror. 'How does it look?'

'Beautiful,' exclaims Dot, rushing to adjust the hem. 'It fits perfectly.'

The dress is long and made of vibrant scarlet-coloured silk. It is a flamboyant stop-sign of a dress. Lucy runs her hands over the fabric, pleased to see that it does fit her well. She'd spotted it hanging in the window of a vintage clothes shop in Bristol, and had known immediately that she had to have it. An unconventional dress for an unconventional day. She knows it is, by far, the most beautiful item of clothing she will ever wear. 'You've done wonders. It looks like it was made for me.'

'Perhaps it was,' says the other woman, smiling. 'You're going to stun them all this weekend.'

Yes, thinks Lucy, studying her reflection in the mirror, a small frown falling over her face. Yes I am.

Dot wraps the dress in tissue paper, placing the parcel carefully into a large cardboard bag. At the door she kisses Lucy effusively on the cheek three times. 'I wish you both a lifetime of love and happiness.'

Lucy squeezes Dot tightly, overcome by a sudden wave of emotion, holding the seamstress close enough so that she cannot see the tears welling up in her eyes.

The cardboard bag is so light, the silk dress inside not much heavier than the tissue paper wrapping around it, as it swings in the breeze, occasionally bumping Lucy's thighs as she walks. She is still swinging it in her hands, passing the tall stone obelisk in Queen Square when the wave of nausea comes over her. Taking deep breaths, she reaches for the iron railings surrounding the square and steadies herself. She spots an empty bench and makes her way to it, then sits hunched, waiting for the worst of the sickening sensation to pass.

The wind moves through the cherry trees, leaves whispering overhead. Hurry, hurry, they seem to say. But she can't move. Not yet. She takes several deep breaths, and tries to concentrate on the people passing by. An upright man in a dark pinstripe suit, swinging a briefcase. Two grey-haired ladies in headscarves discussing the weather. A young man wearing huge headphones nodding his head to a beat. A woman pushing a stroller, the toddler strapped into it slumped in sleep. As they pass, a small blue teddy bear falls from the pushchair and lands at Lucy's feet. 'Excuse me,' she calls, reaching for the toy. 'You dropped this.'

'Thank you,' says the mother, returning to the bench. 'That would have been a disaster.' The young woman tucks the bear safely beside the sleeping child before carefully adjusting the blanket. Without any warning, Lucy bursts into tears.

'Oh,' says the mother, seeing her distress. 'Are you all right?'

Lucy can't reply.

'Can I ... do you ... is there someone I can call for you?'

'I'm sorry,' says Lucy eventually, finding her voice.

The woman looks around helplessly before manoeuvring the stroller next to the bench and perching beside her. 'How about I sit with you for a minute?'

Lucy nods. She wipes her eyes and then, before she can stop herself, she blurts, 'I'm getting married on Saturday.'

The woman's eyes widen. It's obvious this is not what she has expected Lucy to say. 'Oh. That's wonderful ... isn't it?' she adds carefully.

Lucy nods.

The woman rummages in her handbag. 'I'm sorry, it's all I have,' she says, handing Lucy a crumpled tissue. 'You must be feeling ... overwhelmed?'

Lucy gazes out at the square, at the leaves trembling

113

on the trees, at all the life moving past the bench. 'I feel like I'm on a bloody seesaw. It seemed like such a good idea to rush into the wedding. But now . . . now I'm not so sure.'

'You're having second thoughts?'

She blows her nose and wonders how to tell this stranger her truth. 'Tom's such a good person. So generous and kind. He's always driven to do the right thing.'

'Call me crazy but they sound like good reasons to marry him.' The woman looks down at the thin gold band on her ring finger. 'I remember the days leading up to my own wedding. They were a terrible blur of emotion and exhaustion, not to mention all the family squabbles and politics. I don't know why we put ourselves through it.'

Lucy nods wearily. 'Yes, exactly that.'

'It's easy for me to say – I don't know you at all – but if you love him, and if you think he loves you, try not to worry about the rest. Your family will rally together and what you will remember, when it's all said and done, is the fact you were together, with the people you love. There isn't much more important than that.'

Lucy turns to the woman and smiles. 'Thank you.'

The woman pats her hand. 'After this one was born,' she nods her head in the direction of the stroller, 'I spent the first six months crying . . . tears of joy, tears of sorrow. Life's big moments can do that to us.'

Lucy smiles. 'I'm so sorry to ambush you with my emotion.' She studies the sleeping child. 'Is it nice,' she asks, 'being a mum?'

The woman's smile lights up her face. 'It's wonderful. The best job in the world.'

Lucy sees the toddler's long lashes flicker against his perfect, smooth skin. She lays her hands comfortingly over her own belly.

'You know what I'd do?' says the woman, gathering her bag. 'Hit the shops. Treat yourself to a little something. That'll make you feel better.'

'Thank you for being so kind.'

'It's the least I could do after you saved us from a bedtime drama without Bear.' The woman stands and reaches for the stroller. 'Good luck on Saturday. I hope you have a wonderful day.'

Lucy sits in the square for a while longer, letting the last waves of nausea settle and her tears dry. Eventually, she gathers up her cardboard bag and walks the cobbled lanes of the city. The woman is right. Retail therapy might help. She could buy gifts. Something to appease Eve and to say 'thank you' for all her help. Something for Tom, too. He will need cufflinks for Saturday. It's not the sort of thing he will have thought of, spending every day dressed in his casual clothes at the Woodland Trust, with mud under his fingernails and sunglasses propped on his head. Out in the wilds of Somerset, working on his conservation projects, clearing out contaminated sites and preserving reserves and wildlife habitats, there isn't much call for shirt sleeves or cufflinks. Yes, she'll buy him a pair, a gift for their wedding day.

She enters the department store and browses the jewellery counters on the ground floor, trying not to get side-tracked by elegant drop-earrings and pretty Art Deco hair combs that would look so lovely with her dress. After a short time, she spots two simple gold bangles, ivy leaves twisted into a delicate circle, that she feels certain Eve and Margot would like. She asks the assistant to wrap them for her, before spotting the cufflinks in a cabinet a little further away. 'Would you like to look at any?' asks the eager assistant, sniffing another sale.

Lucy studies the rows of brightly enamelled studs. Dominos. Mini Coopers. Stop signs. Champagne bottles. They're all far too 'city boy' for her down-to-earth Tom. 'I'm looking for something simple,' she says. 'Something less . . . showy.'

'What about these?' the shop assistant suggests, unlocking the cabinet and pulling out a small black velvet tray on which a collection of simple, silver cufflinks lie.

Lucy scans the selection and spots two in the shape of acorns. She holds them up to the light and smiles. 'Acorns from the oak tree.' Natural. Strong. Everything Tom is.

As the assistant wraps her purchases in tissue paper, the sound of a familiar laugh catches her attention. She glances across the shop floor and sees a man standing several counters away, tall and broad-shouldered, dressed in a suit, his dark hair slightly receding. He holds a glittering earring up to his companion – a petite lady with dark curly hair and full, red lips. The smile on Lucy's lips falters.

The woman beams up at Lucy's brother-in-law, her face a picture of adoration, the diamond earring glinting at her lobe. Andrew leans in closer to the woman and narrows his eyes. 'They suit you,' he says, Lucy just able to lip read his words. Lucy frowns. The woman looks young – several years younger than Eve.

Andrew hands the earring to the assistant behind their counter and pulls out his wallet. The young woman at his side grabs his arm and squeezes it tightly. Lucy, watching, feels a cold shard of dread slide into her guts like a knife. Andrew is buying jewellery for this woman? This woman who is clutching his arm and smiling beatifically up at him, like she has won some kind of prize?

Reeling with shock, Lucy can't decide whether to march over and punch them both, or duck down behind the counter before she is spotted and an embarrassing confrontation ensues. Before she can decide, the shop assistant is handing her purchases over. 'Thank you for shopping with us today.'

With a small nod, Lucy snatches up the cardboard bag and leaves the store. Andrew? Having an affair? She can't believe it. Poor, poor Eve.

Eve leaves the cash-and-carry at a virtual run and throws the shopping bags of tea lights, paper plates and napkins into the boot of her car. She checks the time on her phone and sighs. It's going to be tight to make it for school pick-up.

She was only supposed to work a half-day in the office, but as usual, her boss had appeared at her desk at a quarter to twelve with a pile of signed letters that just *had* to go out immediately. She had been playing catch-up ever since. The queues at the cash-and-carry checkout had been so frustratingly long she almost hadn't bothered, except she'd known this was one of the last opportunities she had before Saturday to get what was needed for Lucy's big day.

Scrolling quickly through her messages, she sees one from Margot sent earlier confirming that she will head to Sibella's, and another from Lucy saying that Tom has tracked down a friend to DJ at the reception and – even better – that he'll be bringing his own decks and speakers. Maybe her strong words the previous night had got through. It wasn't exactly an apology, but perhaps Lucy had begun to grasp what was going to be required and was finally pulling her finger out. The last message on her phone is from Ryan at the pub, a reminder that he needs the final numbers for the food and wine for Saturday. His message ends with a string of emojis: champagne bottles, a cocktail glass, a dancing girl and a winking face. She starts the engine and pulls out of the car park.

The route to school is unusually clear and as she draws near, a car pulls out of one of the few coveted parking spaces. Hardly daring to believe her luck, she darts into the spot, leaps out of the car and rushes through the school gates. By some miracle, she is only a couple of minutes late.

May sees her first, rushing at her, an oversize rucksack banging on her back, a large, brightly coloured painting of unidentifiable splodges clutched in her hand. 'Mummy!'

'Sorry, darling. Busy day. How are you?' She hugs May and throws a smile of greeting at the teacher over her daughter's head. 'What do you have there?' she asks.

'It's pop art.'

'It's lovely.'

'I fell over at lunch,' May says, lifting the hem of her school skirt and pointing to a bandage on her knee. 'Mrs Greenaway gave me a plaster.'

'She was very brave,' calls the teacher.

'Thank you,' says Eve, ruffling May's hair and giving the teacher another smile. 'That's my girl.'

Chloe appears at her other side. 'Do I have to go to my piano lesson tonight?' she asks, scuffing at the ground with the toe of her shoe.

'Don't do that Chlo. They're new shoes.'

'I hate piano.'

'We agreed you'd see it through to the end of term. If you aren't enjoying it then, we'll talk about dropping it.'

Chloe huffs. 'Fine.'

She throws the bags into the boot, checks the straps on May's booster seat. 'I need to make a quick stop at the pub on the way,' she says. 'I have to sort out the last details for Auntie Lucy's wedding on Saturday,' she adds, to head off any grumbling.

Chloe eyes her in the rear-view mirror. 'Can we have a Coke?' she asks.

'Nice try,' laughs Eve. 'But no, we don't have time. You girls will have to wait in the car.'

The pub car park is empty when they arrive. The lunchtime session has finished and it's way before evening opening hours. 'I won't be long,' she tells them, parking out the front before walking around to knock at the rear entrance. She hears footsteps thundering down a staircase and a key turning in a lock before Ryan appears at the door, barefoot, dressed in jeans and a polo shirt. 'Just the woman I needed to see,' he says, beaming at her. 'Though I wasn't expecting you till later. Come in.'

'I can't. I've only got a couple of minutes. The girls are in the car.'

He nods. 'Better make it quick then.' He holds the door open, allowing her to step into the entrance hall. 'So,' he says, 'business first. You've got the numbers for Saturday?'

She nods. 'Trying to get a straight answer from Lucy on anything is virtually impossible, but I think we'll be safe if we assume eighty people.'

'You're happy with the menu? The platters and the vegetarian options?'

'Yes.'

'Great. And the grog . . . red, white, champagne and some kegs of the local beer?'

'Grog?' she laughs. 'You're *so* Australian.'

He shrugs. 'You say that like it's a bad thing.'

'Yes to the grog,' she says. 'It all sounds perfect.'

'No problem. I'll give you a refund on anything you return unopened.' He smiles and takes a step towards her. 'So now we've got the boring stuff out of the way . . .'

'The girls,' she says, weakly. She's told herself the whole way from the school that she wasn't going to let this happen. 'The car's round the front.'

'Come here,' he says, either oblivious to her reticence or ignoring it. 'I've been thinking about you all day.' And then he pulls her closer, leans down and kisses her on the mouth.

She knows it is wrong. She knows she shouldn't respond. She knows she should tell him that she can't – she's married – and what they're doing is wrong. But it's as if a switch has been thrown. Feeling a rush of desire, she wraps her arms around his waist and presses herself up against him until they are leaning against the open doorway. He feels so different – so other to Andrew – with his hard, muscular body and his strong arms that it shocks her. She pulls away with a groan. 'I have to go.'

'I know.' Ryan gives her a solemn look. 'But we're still good for tonight?'

'I'm sorry. Andrew has to work.'

Ryan frowns. 'Is this about the other night?'

'No! God, no. Of course not.'

He nods. 'So it's OK between us? I've been wondering, you know, after what happened.'

'Yes.'

'Good, because I want to see you again. It will be . . . better . . . next time. I promise. Tell me when.'

Eve frowns. Alongside the lingering desire, she feels something else – something unexpected. There, loitering among her want is a tremor of irritation, exasperation that there is someone else needing something from her. 'I don't know,' she says. 'This weekend I'll be flat out with family stuff. I won't be free until next week, at the earliest.'

And even then, she thinks, realisation creeping over her, does she really want this? After their last encounter, she has wondered more and more what she is playing at. Ryan is not the type of man she has ever been attracted to in the past. He is loud, bombastic, physically strong and full of masculine energy. She's seen him propping up the bar late at night with his guests, his ruddy cheeks evidence of his tendency to overindulge. Unlike her husband, there is something so raw and physical about him – immature, yes; unreliable, probably; a drink problem, quite possibly – and yet . . . and yet, here she is, standing weak-kneed in his arms.

Ryan shrugs. 'No worries. Next week. You know where I am.'

Eve's stomach plunges at another realisation. 'But you'll see me on Friday night,' she says. 'We're all coming to the pub for a family dinner.'

Ryan raises an eyebrow. 'Well, *that* will be interesting.'

Eve groans. 'I'm sorry. Not my idea, obviously.'

'Obviously.' Ryan grins and folds his arms across his broad chest. 'Don't worry. It'll be fine. I'll be on my best behaviour.'

Something in his words brings Margot to Eve's mind. God, she thinks, so many people on their 'best behaviour'. What a minefield the next few days are going to be. She imagines, momentarily, an evening when they are all together and on their 'worst' behaviour and a hysterical laugh threatens to escape her. But then she is forgetting all about Margot and the looming dinner because Ryan is leaning in again and kissing her hard on the mouth and she is only thinking about the fire building in her belly and the pulse of desire between her legs. She is remembering the spark of attraction that she had first felt for him – a risky, reckless abandon, a feeling of being desired and desirable, a sense of falling away from all the responsibility and convention holding her in check.

They are still kissing as a car pulls into the car park and pulls up near the back entrance. 'Shit.' Eve jerks backwards, pulling herself from Ryan's grip, her eyes on the blue car. 'Who is it?' She rubs her lips. 'Did they see us?'

'No.' Ryan peers at the car. 'It's only Stacey. Coming to prep the bar for later. She wears specs like Coke bottles. She won't have seen a thing.'

Eve slaps Ryan's arm lightly. 'Don't be rude.'

'What?' He mock protests. 'It's true. I'm not sure she sees much of anything.' He smiles broadly. 'Not judging by the state she leaves the bar each night.'

'You shouldn't be mean about her.'

'I'm not. Stace is all right.' He winks. 'I think she might have a little crush on me.'

'What if she saw us?'

'Calm down, we're fine.' He reaches out and rubs her arm. 'God, I want to kiss you again. You're such a MILF.'

This time she does hit him. 'I told you, don't call me that.'

Stacey's footsteps crunch across the gravel towards them. 'Hiya,' she calls, flashing Ryan a smile.

'Hi, Stace. So I'll drop your order round to the house about midday on Saturday?' he asks Eve pointedly, his tone laughably businesslike.

'Thank you.'

'And we'll sort a date for that meeting next week, to go over the figures,' he adds with a wink.

On the way to Chloe's piano lesson, the radio playing a little too loudly and the girls babbling away in the back, Eve allows her mind to wander back to Ryan.

It had started innocuously enough at the school summer fete. She had arrived for her rostered shift on the BBQ stall to find the new manager of the Bridge Inn standing in front of the smoking BBQ wielding tongs. She had held out her hand. 'I'm Eve. Nice to meet you. You don't have kids here, do you?'

'No. No kids. No wife – at least not any more. She left me,' he'd added. 'I'm Ryan.' He'd squeezed her hand firmly.

'Oh. Sorry.' She hadn't known what to say. 'So how did you get roped into this?'

He'd waved his branded Bridge Inn apron at her. 'The pub is sponsoring the BBQ today.'

Eve had leaned back, impressed. 'That's very generous.'

'Thought you Poms might need a proper Aussie to show you how it's done.' He'd grinned at her. 'Besides,

124

it builds good will with the local community. I tend to think you get back what you put in at these sorts of events.'

'Well, you'd better budge up,' she'd said, pulling her own apron over her head. 'I'm your helper for the last hour.'

The air was hot, sticky and grease-scented. Eve's hair had turned limp. Sweat had trickled down her back. But Ryan had maintained a cheerful demeanour and soon they had devised a simple but clear delineation of responsibilities. Ryan had flipped the burgers and sausages while Eve had stood beside him taking orders, buttering rolls and pouring squash for thirsty kids. She'd found herself enjoying the simple task of serving the crowds and Ryan had made it fun. 'We make a good team,' he'd said, watching her slap cheese slices onto the burgers sitting on the grill.

'We do,' she'd agreed, grinning back at him.

'Nice buns,' he'd added suggestively, nodding over at her towering pile of pre-prepared rolls awaiting sausages.

She'd laughed and cringed simultaneously.

Once or twice their hands had met as she had passed napkins or bottles of sauce. And afterwards, when the last sausage had been sold and the gas bottle turned off, he had pulled two beers out of an icebox and clinked his bottle against hers. 'We've earned these,' he'd said, and then, before she'd known what he was doing, he'd reached out and stroked the side of her cheek with his forefinger. 'Mustard,' he'd said, smiling, putting his finger to his tongue.

'Oh.' Eve had blushed, looking down at her grease-stained apron. 'I'm such a state.'

'No,' he'd said. 'You're gorgeous.'

One touch. One compliment. It was all it had taken. A sudden rush of heat had risen within her – a surge of desire so strong she'd had to turn away and busy herself with tying off a huge black bin bag of rubbish and wiping down the sticky tables. Men like this – full of energy and confidence, the life and soul of the party – were to be avoided. He was a flirt. She knew it didn't mean anything.

Only later that night, at home, she had studied her reflection in the bathroom mirror. Her nose was sunburnt. There were shadows under her eyes and crow's feet when she squinted. She'd sucked in her cheeks, then turned sideways and pulled in her stomach. *You're gorgeous*. The way he'd said it, so openly, in that broad Australian drawl. What *had* he seen in her? She couldn't fathom it. Was it some inappropriate fetish for haggard women with bad roots and shapeless mum jeans? She was a wife and mother. She wore those badges plainly, for the world to see, in the gold ring on her finger and the extra pounds she had carried since childbirth. She wasn't special. She wasn't gorgeous.

She had returned to the living room where she'd slumped into her usual position on the sofa, Andrew lifting his feet then dropping them again unceremoniously into her lap. She'd only half-watched the tense medical drama he'd had playing on the TV. She'd been too distracted by thoughts of Ryan.

With the arrival of the summer holidays, Eve's days had been filled with the mind-bending juggle of children and work. There had been a strained week away as a family of four on a stark, volcanic island where an unseasonably cold spell had arrived, a brisk wind blowing for the full seven days, bringing storms and rain. Andrew had grumbled about how his week out of the office was a washout and Eve had reminded him that it was supposed to be a holiday for all of them and that surely the fact of their being together should bring him some joy. Frankly, it had been a relief when the girls had gone back to school and the familiar routines could be picked up again.

She hadn't thought of Ryan at all until she had walked into the Bridge Inn for the first PTA meeting of the new school year, relocated to the pub thanks to a clash with a school choir rehearsal. Ryan stood polishing glasses behind the bar, and had given her a cheeky wink as she ordered a red wine. Joining the other parents and teachers grouped around a table, she'd wondered if she was imagining the weight of his gaze.

The first meeting after the holidays was always a long one and the session had run late as the committee had debated the placement of a climbing frame and the logistics for a new, online payment portal. As the debate had droned on, Eve had found herself glancing back to the bar. Her eyes had met Ryan's. The second time it happened, as the school treasurer had stood self-importantly, hiking his trousers up over his belly and clearing his throat, Ryan had rolled his eyes at her and Eve had feigned a cough to cover up her laughter.

At the meeting's close, there had been a sudden rush for the exit, but Eve had lingered, gathering a few empty glasses and carrying them to the bar. 'We owe you a big thank you,' she'd told Ryan. 'We raised over two thousand pounds for the school last summer.'

'It was my pleasure. Always happy to help. One for the road?' he'd offered, waving a half-open bottle of red at her.

'I shouldn't. I'm driving.'

'Shame. I was going to ask for your help with some cocktail tasting. I need a new recipe for our autumn menu.'

She'd smiled. 'Sounds fun. Another time.'

'You're the last to leave,' he'd said, looking around. 'Let me walk you to your car. Just to be safe.'

'There's no need.' But he had followed her out and as she'd turned at her car door to wish him goodnight, she'd found him standing a little closer than strictly necessary. 'I . . . um . . . I should get going.'

He'd nodded. 'Look, I know I shouldn't say this, Eve, but I think you're really hot.'

Eve had stood frozen, her heart thumping in her chest as Ryan reached out and took her face in his warm hands. She was reminded of the moment he had touched her cheek at the fete and the response it had generated in her. Before she could stop herself, she had leaned in and kissed him.

At the unfamiliar sensation of his lips and the taste of beer on his breath, Eve had felt a flutter of panic. What on earth was she doing? But there hadn't been time for any other thought, because Ryan had been kissing her back and the sensation had been so intense, she had let out an audible moan and parted her lips. His hands had been under her shirt, moving over her skin, hers found their way to his belt buckle. Moments later, they were having sex in the shadows of the car park, leaning against her Volvo.

Afterwards, they'd stood there, gasping and laughing at the sheer unexpected frenzy. Eve had pulled up her jeans and tucked in her shirt. 'I don't ... I'm not ...'

'It's OK,' he'd said, taking her hand, raising it to his mouth. 'I'm not going to get weird on you. Just a little no-strings fun, right?'

'Right.' She'd nodded. She'd been going to say that she had never done that before – that she was happily married and didn't know what had come over her. But perhaps it didn't need to be said. She certainly didn't want him to get weird on her. So that was good, at least.

She had skulked home that night, relieved to find Andrew fast asleep in bed. After a shower, and a long moment spent gazing at her reflection in the bathroom mirror, searching for traces of her betrayal, she had slipped silently between the sheets beside her snoring husband and lain for hours, unable to sleep, unable to believe what she had done. Her – Eve – shagging a virtual stranger in a car park? It was unfathomable.

The following morning she'd barely been able to look at Andrew – or the girls – not that any of them had noticed. The morning had passed in the usual manic routines of packed lunches, lost homework books and missing school shoes, and before she'd known it, they were all out the door and heading off to their standard days of work and school, as if nothing seismic had occurred at all. Thinking about it on her drive to work, she'd let the full weight of what she had done sink in. She had broken her marriage vows. She hadn't even been drunk. She didn't even have that excuse at her disposal. The memory of what she had done made her breath catch in the back of her throat and her heart beat a little faster, yet laced with the shame and regret was something else – something unexpected – the intoxicating thrill of having done something so wrong, so utterly un-Eve-like.

She was the girl who had studied Business Studies at university, choosing something practical and as far removed as possible from the unpredictable artistic chaos of her parents' jobs. She was the woman who had settled down with the first man she had seriously dated, married him, borne two perfect children and moved into their carefully renovated semi-detached Victorian home. She was the woman who now shopped for plants at garden centres, followed a familiar weekly cycle of recipes, and managed a multi-columned family calendar filled with strictly kept appointments and events. She had worked so hard to construct a balanced life of order and harmony. This new development in her life was baffling.

'What's for tea?' May asks from the back of the car, breaking through her reverie. 'I'm hungry.'

'It's shepherd's pie tonight.'

The girls groan in unison. 'I hate shepherd's pie,' says Chloe.

'Since when?'

'Since always.'

'That's news to me. You ate it last time I made it.'

'It's disgusting.'

'Well, you can have beans on toast then.'

There are further grumblings from the back seat, before the girls fall blessedly quiet again.

Ryan may have promised not to get weird, but he had begun to pursue her with fervour and every time she had tried to apply logic or common sense to the situation, every time she had tried to distance herself from his attentions, she found her body responding in a different way. He sent increasingly explicit texts. He wanted to fuck her. He wanted to taste her. He told her in intimate detail all the things he'd like to do to her and she would read his messages, a complex mix of desire and shame rushing through her, then delete them quickly before the incriminating evidence could be discovered. Her sex life with Andrew had always been good – until those baby years, of course – but Andrew had never said anything like that to her in their ten years of marriage. She couldn't decide if she was excited or horrified. To be so desired was enlivening. Abandoning her responsibilities and principles was liberating. It was, she knew, as if she were hell-bent on wilful self-destruction.

It was a week later that she'd called in sick at work and driven to a small chain hotel off the M4, a location far enough away to feel safe from prying eyes and bland enough for neither of them to worry about the pressure of romantic expectation. Eve had arrived in the dreary restaurant attached to the hotel, wearing her sexiest underwear beneath her boring work clothes. She'd felt sick with nerves, and the most horribly alive she had in months. Even the sensation of the silk on her skin, knowing that she was wearing lacy black knickers and her best push-up bra for a man who thought she was *gorgeous* had been enough to leave her a little breathless. She'd barely eaten a morsel of the lunch they had ordered and when Ryan had suggested they take their drinks to the room down the corridor, she'd nodded in relief.

Perhaps the appeal was in submitting to him. To not being the woman she was expected to be every other moment of her life – controlled, respectable, tightly held. Perhaps it was a desperate attempt to feel youthful again. Or perhaps it was a desire to not feel like 'this' was it, for the rest of her life. Whatever it was, she wasn't entirely sure, but Ryan's interest had unlocked something inside of her. Lust. Desire. It was as if a sleeping part of her had woken with a roar.

Ryan had fallen on her as soon as they'd entered the room. Thrillingly, he'd taken charge, pushing her up against the wall as the door had closed behind them, tearing at her clothes, his mouth on her neck, his hands on her breasts. She'd been desperate to be touched, happy to submit to his physical desire. It was everything she'd been fantasising about, which had only made it all the more disappointing when, moments later, they'd found themselves lying side by side on the bed, contemplating Ryan's inability to achieve an erection. 'Don't worry,' she'd said. 'It happens.'

Ryan had covered his eyes with his hands. 'I . . . it . . . it's not the first time. After the other night, I thought . . .'

Eve had reached for his hand. 'It's OK,' she'd reassured him and he had curled in to her and rested his head on her chest in a strangely childlike way.

'My ex-wife wasn't as understanding. She ran off with my best mate. Took the dog. Said she needed more.'

As she'd listened to Ryan's faltering apology, Eve had felt something give. It was not the fantasy she had imagined. Instead of the passionate sex she had been picturing, there she was lying in a bland roadside motel room comforting him, stroking his hair as he lay like a giant man-child on her chest. Oh God, perhaps that was it? Perhaps it was an older woman thing? A mummy complex? The thought had made her shudder.

She was starting to realise that the 'fantasy Ryan' she had been communicating with in her head was a step apart from the real, living, breathing man. Baggage. They all had it. She just wasn't sure she wanted to deal with someone else's, not when all she thought she had signed up for was a quick, no-strings fling. An affair with a man like Ryan had nowhere to go and she, of course, had everything to lose. But what she didn't know how to do now, was let him down without hurting his feelings. It was a minefield. Next week, she tells herself. As soon as the wedding is out the way, she will tell Ryan they are done.

Still wandering the complex maze of her thoughts, Eve pulls out onto a roundabout. From her right comes the violent screech of wheels, closely followed by the loud blast of a horn. Eve hits the brakes, her handbag flying from the passenger seat beside her, pens and mobile phone and purse spewing over the footwell as the girls in the back are thrown against the front seats. May lets out a high shriek. When Eve looks, she sees a white van has shuddered to a stop inches from their bumper, only narrowly missing them. A surly driver leans out of his window and gesticulates. 'Stupid fucking cow!' he shouts. 'Look where you're going. You could've killed someone.'

Eve stares at him, horrified. Her heart jackhammers in her chest, her lungs seized. She can't seem to draw a breath. In her mind, she has fast-forwarded to a different scene: the two vehicles colliding, her daughters in the back seat taking the full impact of the white van as it smashes into the side of the car.

Several pedestrians have stopped to stare. The van driver shakes his head and gesticulates again before pulling away from the roundabout with loud spin of his wheels.

'Mummy!' says Chloe from the back seat. 'Mummy?'

'Yes,' says Eve, returning to the present. 'Sorry, girls, are you OK?'

'Yes. Are you?'

Eve nods, not trusting herself to speak.

'That man said a rude word,' says May primly.

'Yes,' says Eve again. 'He was angry. I wasn't looking where I was going.'

Another horn sounds behind them.

Eve takes a deep breath and puts the car into gear. She drives to a side street where she parks behind a silver Volvo and leans her head against the steering wheel. 'Mummy?' says Chloe again, more uncertainly. 'Are you sure you're OK?'

'I just need a moment.'

The girls don't say anything else, but she can feel their worried glances as she sits at the wheel and weeps silently, a cascade of warm tears sliding down her face and falling in her lap. After a little while May's voice comes from the back seat. 'What about Chloe's piano lesson?'

Eve sighs. 'Yes,' she says. She lifts her head and wipes her eyes before turning the key in the ignition. 'Sorry, girls.' She checks her mirror and indicates before carefully rejoining the traffic. What is wrong with her? She needs to get a grip. That man was right. She is a stupid fucking cow, sitting there daydreaming about a sordid little affair. She could have killed someone. She could have killed them all.

14

Margot traverses the small stone bridge over the river, avoiding the shadows falling beneath its arches, before taking the path leading up the far side of the valley. She walks beside stubbled fields of shorn wheat and corn, dodging deep, muddy troughs where roaming cattle have churned the path. Here and there, rags of sheep's wool flutter on the barbed-wire fences.

Making for the small stone cottage, Margot sees its stable-style door standing half open. She leans over the lower gate and spots Sibella seated at the kitchen table, its wooden surface barely visible beneath a mass of dried lavender and stalks of golden wheat. 'Hello,' she calls.

Sibella twists in her chair. 'Hello,' she says, seeming not in the least surprised to find Ted's daughter standing at her door after all this time. 'Come in,' she beckons. 'Would you like a cup of tea?'

Margot leans over and unlatches the lower half of the door. 'Yes please.'

Sibella stands and places a copper kettle on the range. 'There's a packet of ginger snaps in that jar over there. Your dad's out in the garden somewhere, digging up vegetables.'

'Problems writing a scene?' Margot retrieves the biscuits and sits at the table.

Sibella smiles. 'How did you guess? I'm sure he won't be too long.'

'It's OK. I'm here to see you too. Eve sent me.'

'You can report back that I'm hard at work. No shirking here.'

It's Margot's turn to smile. 'I'm not a spy. I'm here to help.'

'Did you fall in?' asks Sibella, noticing Margot's squelching trainers.

'Something like that.' It seems ridiculous now, her escapade to the other side of the riverbank.

'You can borrow some slippers if you like?' She indicates a pair of embroidered shoes near the open hearth.

'Thank you.' Margot removes her wet shoes and socks before sliding her feet into the soft slippers.

Sibella fills a pot with tea leaves and boiled water, before returning to the table. Margot watches as Sibella's long, pale fingers carefully sort through the cuttings. The light from the window falls onto her red hair, making it shine like copper. Margot is reminded how pretty she is – high cheekbones and smooth, pale skin that makes it hard to place her age, though Margot knows she is in her late forties. 'What can I do?'

Sibella pushes a pile of lavender towards her. 'We had a good crop this summer. Eve had the good idea of using some for Saturday's flower arrangements. Tied up with some of this wheat, it will look lovely. There are roses too, but I won't cut those until Friday. I'm stripping any damaged stems for the buds.' She indicates the large earthenware bowl already a third filled with the grey-blue flowers. 'I thought I'd make lavender sachets with the remainder.'

Margot nods and reaches for a handful of stems, beginning to sort the lavender into two piles, mirroring Sibella's. As she works, her gaze occasionally drifts to take in surreptitious details of her surroundings. Dried herbs. Copper pots. A stack of well-thumbed recipe books teetering on a dresser. What looks like an old bird's nest perched on the old, wrought-iron hearth. Earthenware dishes. A porcelain vase standing in the window – so fine it is almost translucent in the sunshine falling through the glass behind. Her father has lived here for the best part of nine years, and while his presence is detectable in the worn slippers by the back door and the folded newspaper on the arm of a chair, it still feels very much Sibella's place.

'It's been a while since you were home,' says Sibella carefully. 'How does it feel?'

'Fine.' Margot doesn't want to get drawn into anything heavy.

'Lucy and Eve must be pleased?'

'Yes.'

'And your mum?'

Margot shrugs again. 'I guess.'

Sibella waits a beat. 'Is it still . . . tricky?'

Margot nods.

Sibella takes up another frond of lavender. 'None of my business, I know.'

'It's not that.' Margot thinks for a moment. 'It's strange. You go away and when you come back, nothing's changed. Nothing in the slightest. We're stuck in stalemate.'

'Perhaps if you tried talking to her?'

Margot thinks back to their angry confrontation the night before. 'What's the point? It's all water under the bridge.'

Sibella lifts her gaze to meet Margot's. 'Is it?'

Water under the bridge. Margot glances at her damp trainers standing by the back door and feels the blood rise to her face. She takes a deep breath, inhaling the heavy scent of lavender, and tries to scour the unwanted memories from her mind.

'The past can have a funny way of haunting us if we don't face it head on . . .' says Sibella, gently. 'Ghosts can linger.'

'There's nothing to face.' Margot's voice is flat and final. She reaches out and runs her hand through the bowl of lavender, the buds moving like grains of sand through her fingers.

Sibella pours two mugs of tea, pushing one towards Margot. 'I've come to realise,' she says after a while, 'that the events that cause us the most difficulty can often, if we let them, become the experiences that make us stronger.' The lavender rustles in her hands as she takes up another stem. 'I suppose what I'm trying to say is that pain can alter us, and its in the facing of it – in the surviving of it – that we find ourselves changed . . . perhaps a little wiser, sometimes a little braver? Does that make sense?'

Margot nods, though she's not sure she agrees. What if life weakens you? What if events *do* transform you – not for the better, but for the worse?

'We all make mistakes, Margot.'

Margot swallows.

'We're all just doing our best.' Sibella fixes her with a kind look. 'Including, I'm sure, your mum.'

At the mention of her mother, Margot bristles. Talking this openly with her father's girlfriend – no, his *wife* – feels like treading a tightrope. How many times has she longed for a conversation like this with her own mother? Would it have made any difference if she had talked to someone – her mum; Sibella, even – all those years ago?

Could she tell this woman what she has never told anyone before? As she picks at a loose thread on her jeans, she wonders what Sibella's reaction would be. For one wild moment, she imagines speaking out loud the words she has held so tightly and feels an instant, creeping shame. The thought of sharing the worst thing she has ever done makes her feel sick. Far better to bury it, to hide it somewhere deep.

She reaches for her tea and takes a sip, before returning the mug to the table with a sigh. There is no denying there is something soothing about sitting here at this kitchen table. Perhaps, she thinks, it's the heavy scent of lavender hanging in the air, seducing her with its pungent aroma. She breathes it in again, then lets out a long exhalation and feels her shoulders sink a little.

'Like I said,' she says finally, yanking the thread loose from her jeans and rolling it into a tiny ball between her fingers, 'it's water under the bridge.'

There is a loud stamping of boots outside the back door. Ted enters the kitchen, pulling off muddy gardening gloves. He stops near the doorway, startled at the sight of Margot at the table. 'Margot, darling, I didn't know you were here.'

'Surprise!' she says with a half-hearted shrug, standing

to greet him. He hugs her close and though still tall and solid, weathered from time spent out in the garden, she can't help noticing how much greyer he is now, his face a little more lined.

'There's tea in the pot,' says Sibella.

'Thank you.' He turns back to Margot. 'We're growing gigantic vegetables, positively gargantuan. Look at these.' He goes to the door and retrieves a wooden trug filled with huge, soil-covered onions and parsnips. 'I was coming in to get a bowl for the blackberries. The bushes are teeming with them. Put some boots on and you can give me a hand.'

The garden is a wild tangle of plants and brambles, a scruffy lawn crowded by overhanging trees and hedgerows. The blackberries hang like plump jewels from the thickets surrounding the vegetable patch where Ted has been digging. A robin, perched on the handle of his spade, takes flight as they approach.

'I think Lucy has chosen rather a good weekend to celebrate her wedding,' says Ted, dropping several plump blackberries into his bowl.

'Why's that?'

'It's the autumn equinox on Sunday, the point when our hemisphere begins to lean away from the sun, bringing shorter days and longer nights. Rather apt, don't you think, to celebrate the last long day of the season, the last moment we lean towards the light, rather than away?'

Margot nods. 'How very Lucy. I wonder if she knows.' She moves along the hedgerow, drawn by a cluster of fat berries hanging on a nearby stem.

'I can remember blackberrying with you when you

were little,' says Ted, after a moment of companionable silence. 'I'd hoist you onto my shoulders so you could reach the juiciest berries,' he adds, eyeing the prize fruit way out of reach on the brambles high above their heads.

'I remember,' smiles Margot, picking a berry and popping it into her mouth. She looks across at her father, at his stooped frame and grey hair and marvels at the thought of being small enough to sit on those shoulders, steering him by his ears like a biddable pony. It makes her chest ache to remember. 'Eve always gathered the most. She was the most patient. Lucy would get bored too quickly, and you and I, we always ate more than we put in the bowl.' She hesitates. 'It was good, wasn't it . . . back then?'

Ted nods. 'It was good.'

'We were lucky we got to spend so much time with you. Not like lots of dads. It was hard . . . when you left.'

'I know you don't understand, but Sibella is good for me. I love her. I hope you can see that?'

'Weren't you worried about Mum?'

He clears his throat. 'Yes. Of course. But our relationship had broken down by then. Truth be told, I wasn't sure your mother would be that affected by my departure. She was so wrapped up in her writing. I'm sure you remember? We had become two adults sharing living space. It wasn't enough for me.'

Margot nods and feels that stirring in her chest again, that ache of longing – the feeling Margot is starting to associate with her return home – a nostalgic yearning for an unreachable past: her sisters a constant, effervescent presence; her father still living at home; and her mother . . . well, her mother still the same complicated, distracted woman, but all before . . . before. She swallows, the taste of blackberries souring on her tongue.

'It was an act of self-preservation,' Ted continues. 'You girls were mostly grown. Kit and I weren't making each other happy – hadn't been for a long while – and I felt stifled, creatively. I don't think it's a coincidence that I've only felt able to write again since I moved here to be with Sibella. That's not to blame your mother. That's on me. My issues. I'm not proud of that.' He clears his throat again, as if awkward at how much he has revealed. 'What about you, love?' he asks, changing the subject. 'Is there anyone special in your life? A boyfriend?' He coughs. 'Girlfriend?'

Margot smiles. 'There was someone . . . he's just a friend though.'

'Oh yes?' Ted waits but Margot doesn't know what to tell him. She's certainly not going to share the details of her last confused encounter with Jonas. She turns away and busies herself with a blackberry bush, working her way down the hedgerow. How to make sense of that last night in Edinburgh?

It was the vodka, of course – always the drink – too much consumed on the same night Eve's message had arrived on her phone. She'd read the text revealing Lucy's last-minute wedding plan and flicked off the kettle, instead pouring herself a large drink – three fingers of vodka mixed with the last of the orange juice from the fridge. Then she'd taken her glass and the bottle to the living room where she had weighed up her options. Damn you, Lucy, she'd thought.

There was no doubt in her mind that it would be

easier not to go. Not that Lucy or Eve would see it that way. She knew they would never forgive her for missing the Big Day. She'd been all but ready to send a carefully worded reply when Lucy's message had come through, as if she had somehow, all those miles away, heard Margot mentally constructing her excuses. *Please come. I need you.*

Beyond the top-floor living-room window of Jonas's flat, the Edinburgh skyline had glowered against a dusky sky, her gaze settling on the familiar brick outline of the old townhouses across the street, the spires of St Giles's Cathedral jutting in the distance. Ever since that first afternoon when she had stepped from the train with just one rucksack on her back and no real clue of what she was doing or where she was going other than trying to put as much distance between herself and Windfalls as possible, the city had been a refuge for her. The beautiful, built-up cityscape couldn't have been more different to the landscape of home, with its soft greenery, its swaying trees, the rushing river and birdsong. Could she step back into that place and hold the pieces of herself together? Was she ready? Could she navigate her way through a few days with her family and leave unscathed?

Finding it impossible to ignore Lucy's request, she had downed her drink and opened her laptop to research the train times and connections from Edinburgh to Bath. By the time Jonas had returned home a couple of hours later, staggering in under bags of camera equipment, she had already booked a return ticket and made a serious dent in the bottle of vodka.

'You're back,' she'd said, struggling to sit upright

on the sofa, aware how drunk she was. 'How was it? Switzerland, wasn't it?'

'Great. Terrible flight home though. Turbulence. I could do with one of those.' He'd nodded at the vodka bottle.

'Be my guest.'

Jonas had retrieved a glass from the kitchen and slumped next to her on the sofa. Margot had studied him with a sideways look. He'd caught the sun while away and the blonde stubble on his jawline glinted gold in the lamp light. He'd downed a shot, neat, then reached into his battered leather jacket. 'I brought you a gift.' He'd pulled something small, wrapped in a brown paper bag, out of the pocket.

Inside, she'd found a key ring, a plastic cuckoo clock dangling from its chain. 'Wow, that's . . .' She'd struggled to find the words. 'Really . . .'

'Kitsch?' He'd grinned at her. 'Pull the chain. Go on.'

She had and the tiny ornament had *cuckooed* at her, surprisingly loudly. She'd laughed. 'I love it. Thank you.' Leaning back as he'd topped up their glasses, she had studied him more closely.

There was no denying that their relationship had changed over the past year, from that polite first meeting when she had answered the 'room to let' sign on the library noticeboard. On the phone, he had told her that he was looking for someone 'quiet and easy-going' to share the rent and bills on his home. She had gone round that evening to inspect.

'What do you do?' he'd asked her, as she'd stood in the doorway to his spare room, staring around at the sparse furnishings.

'I work in the library.'

'You're a librarian?'

'Kind of. In training. I'm general dogsbody ... though I run the kids' story times,' she'd added, trying to find something she could share with him that would make her sound a little less flaky, a little more responsible and reliable as a potential flatmate.

She'd noticed he spoke with an accent, the words leaving his mouth in an offbeat rhythm, his vowels containing an unusual, almost musical lilt. Scandinavian, she'd decided, with his dishevelled blonde hair, olive skin and blue eyes. He was tall too, with the sort of strong hands that wouldn't have looked out of place swinging an axe in a forest. In the kitchen, she'd eyed a photo tacked to the fridge of a striking blonde woman sitting beside a lake, a flare of sunshine caught in her hair. The family resemblance was obvious. 'Your mum?'

'Yes.'

'She's lovely.'

'Thank you.'

'Did you take it?' she'd asked, having already clocked the bags of camera equipment lined up in the hall.

'Yes.' He'd hesitated. 'She died five years ago.'

'I'm sorry.'

'You don't look like a kind-of-in-training librarian,' he'd said, eyeing the ink on her arm and clearly trying to change the subject.

She'd shrugged. 'Well I am.' She'd felt momentarily disconcerted – self-conscious about what he might see standing opposite him: a slim, dark woman in torn black jeans with a severe bob and furrowed brow.

146

But whatever he'd seen obviously hadn't caused him too much concern. 'When can you move in?'

She had hesitated. He seemed friendly enough and looking around at the flat's neat interior and at the Edinburgh rooftops glistening beyond the window, she knew it was a damn sight better than the hostel she had been camping out in. More comfortable – more private – and, best of all, almost affordable now that she had regular work at the library. 'Next week?'

At first she'd kept out of his way, hiding in her room, avoiding the lounge whenever he was home, scuttling to and fro between the small bathroom and kitchen. Truth be told, she'd been a little suspicious of his good looks and glamorous-sounding job. 'A photographer,' he'd told her, confirming her guess. 'Editorial portraits and the like, for magazines and media agencies. I'm often away on shoots. You'll hardly see me.' But after a couple of months, he'd knocked on her bedroom door. 'Listen, Margot, I know I said I wanted a quiet flatmate, but I didn't mean invisible.' He'd waved a bottle of red wine at her. 'I don't like to drink on my own. Would you like a glass?'

Their friendship had grown, slowly, carefully, with the odd glass of wine and the occasional shared meal perched on the sofa, or a box-set binge on one of his rare weekends off. She liked him. She liked how he always asked her about her day, how he hadn't seemed at all fazed when he'd found out who her mother was, and how he hadn't been afraid of the silences that fell in their conversation. He didn't race to fill the space, but let the conversation settle, with their thoughts. She liked how he sometimes showed her his work, scrolling through images on his computer screen, asking her which ones she liked best, as if her opinion mattered to him. 'You have a good eye,' he'd told her. 'There's a creative side in you wanting to break free.'

'I once thought I'd like to be an actress,' she'd said, surprised to hear the words leaving her mouth.

'What changed?'

She'd shrugged. 'I suppose life gave me a reality check.'

'It's not an easy industry to crack,' he'd agreed, and she hadn't said any more on the matter.

Placing the cuckoo-clock key ring onto the coffee table between them, she had smiled at Jonas. 'Thank you.'

'Want to hear something strange?' he'd asked, taking a big glug of his vodka, stretching his arm along the back of the sofa.

'Always. I like strange.'

'I missed you.'

She'd laughed. 'That wasn't what I was expecting you to say.'

'I know.' He'd held her eye and Margot had been the first to look away. His eyes were so blue and his mouth seemed so . . . so close.

'Margot?'

'Yes.'

'Is it just me?'

'Is what just you?'

He'd raised an eyebrow. 'Are you going to make me spell it out?'

She'd hesitated, and then, as if driven by some magnetic pull, she had leaned in and kissed him.

'Are you sure?' he'd asked, pulling back to search her

face and Margot had nodded and kissed him harder, proving to herself as much as to Jonas that yes, she was sure.

They had undressed quickly in his bedroom, a tangle of clothes and limbs and for a while, they had lost themselves in the sensation of each other. He was so known to her now, and yet so physically unknown. A surge of longing rose up in her, something she hadn't allowed herself to feel for a long time. She felt it building: a need to be close, to be touched, to be seen. She didn't think about their friendship or the complications of them sharing a flat. She gave in to the moment.

Only with the rising desire had come the sting of something else. She'd opened her eyes and tried to focus on Jonas – her friend – kissing her. But the sting was unfurling into something dark and miserable, wrapped in the rank scent of rotting apples and fetid earth. Something dark was seeping out of her and stealing the moment and she couldn't stand it. Margot had thrown her head back and moved Jonas's hands to her throat. She'd clamped them around her neck and squeezed tightly. Jonas had held her for a moment before pulling his hands away. She'd guided them back. 'Do it,' she'd said. 'I want you to.'

Jonas had frowned. 'Margot,' he'd said, her name soft and low, a warning.

'Please,' she'd said. 'Do it.'

'Margot. I'm not going to hurt you.'

She'd studied him, her gaze meeting his in the darkness, the fleeting pressure of his fingers on her throat still prickling against her skin. She'd looked away. 'Well, that's killed the mood, hey?' she'd said, sitting up and reaching for her T-shirt.

'Come here,' he'd said, pulling her back to him. 'It's OK. Let's lie here for a bit.'

And so they had, the two of them lying on his bed, his fingers tracing the ink on her arm. 'What does it mean?' he'd asked.

She'd stared down at the tattoo. 'Nothing.'

He had stayed quiet for so long that she'd thought he'd fallen asleep, until he'd spoken again. 'What was that about, Margot?'

'It was nothing.'

'Nothing. Like the tattoo.'

No, she thought. Nothing, like me.

'There's something about you, Margot. You act so dark and angry. You hide so much of yourself. Yet I see something else in you — a light — that's trying to escape.'

'I don't think you should trust what you're seeing.'

'But I do, Margot. I have to. It's my job. Seeing. Revealing. Exposing. The best photographers always find the light.'

In the darkness of his room, she had lain with her head on his chest. His breathing had reminded her of an ocean tide, rising and falling. A car had driven past on the street outside. There had been the sound of a bottle smashing. A high-pitched laugh. For some reason her mind had returned to the image of Jonas's mother tacked to the fridge in the kitchen. The thought of that blonde, glamorous woman made her feel deeply uncomfortable — so opposite, so golden, so wholesome-looking. A man like Jonas couldn't be with someone like her.

She'd closed her eyes and tried to match his breathing

– tried to fall sleep beside him – but his arm had lain heavy across her, the hot press of his skin on hers, the weight of it growing uncomfortable. Eventually, she'd given up, slipping out from between his sheets and retrieving her scattered clothes. She'd packed a bag, scribbled a brief note and left at dawn, taking the first train from Edinburgh, the first beats of her hangover rising with the sun.

Standing in Sibella's overgrown vegetable garden, with the hedgerows rustling and the distant sound of cattle lowing echoing across the valley, that city – the flat, Jonas – all seem a world away. Margot sighs. She likes Jonas – a lot – and his home and his friendship have been something of a haven to her over the past year. Only she'd gone and messed that up now with their clumsy encounter. The Queen of Self-Sabotage. The only way she could see to salvage the good thing it had once been was to steer them back onto familiar territory. Landlord and tenant. She had to hold him at arm's length, the way she held everyone else.

Pushing thoughts of Jonas away, she looks down at her bowl and sees that it is almost spilling over with blackberries. Her fingers are stained a deep red with the juice. A little further away, Ted has also filled his bowl. 'Not sure I can pick any more,' she calls. 'Leave the rest for another day?'

Ted nods and they turn back for the cottage, but before they get to the stable door, she feels her father's hand on her arm. 'Margot, hold up,' he says, his voice serious.

'What?' She turns, startled.

He seems to steel himself. 'There's something I need to know.'

'What?' she asks again.

'Why did you do it?'

Margot freezes, the blackberries held before her.

'Why did you burn it? All that work, years of it spent on that last blasted book, gone up in smoke. Do you know what that did to her? Personally. Professionally.'

Margot holds her father's gaze for a moment before looking away.

Ted sighs. 'I don't understand. I know you're not a bad person, but it seems so . . . so malicious.'

Margot swallows. Not a bad person. Of course he wants to believe that.

'If you were upset at my leaving you both, why punish *her*? You could have come here, set fire to my work. God knows,' he says with a grim laugh, 'at that point in my career, you'd have been doing me a favour. Whichever way I look at it, it doesn't make any sense.'

'No,' she says. 'I don't suppose it does.'

'Tell me. Help me understand.'

She lifts her head. She can see the confusion in his eyes, the sadness and something else . . . is it fear? Fear, perhaps, of who she is – of what she is capable of? Fear that she isn't the daughter he thought she was? Fear that he might not know her at all? At the sight of it, she feels something shift inside of her. She cannot tell him. She cannot tell any of them. She turns away.

Perhaps sensing that the moment is lost, that she has withdrawn, Ted sighs. 'Come on, we'd best get back to Sibella.'

She nods, grateful that he isn't going to press her further.

As they walk back to the house, a question comes to her. 'Are you happy for Lucy?' she asks, curious as to what their father's opinion might be of her sudden race down the aisle. 'Do you think she's making a good decision?'

'I am . . . and I do,' he says, turning to her. 'Though between us,' he adds, with the hint of a smile, 'I suspect there might be a little more to their decision to marry than they've let on.'

Margot nods. 'I know. We'll have to try and act surprised.'

'So I'm not the only one to think so?'

Margot shakes her head.

'Well, I hope so. I'd be delighted for them both.' He reaches out and steals one of the plumpest berries off the top of Margot's pile. 'Will you stay for dinner or would you like me to drop you back at Windfalls?'

Margot hesitates. 'I was wondering whether I could stay the night? I'll sleep on the sofa,' she adds quickly, at the sight of Ted's frown. 'I won't be any trouble, I promise.'

'Won't your mother mind?'

'She won't care.'

'I think she might,' Ted says carefully.

Margot ignores the comment. 'I'll text her and let her know – that is, if it's OK with you both?'

Though he still wears his worried frown, he nods. Margot punches out a brief text on her phone and presses 'send' before he can change his mind.

As she slides the phone back into her pocket, her

gaze catches once more on the berry-red stains marking her hands. She stares at them for a long moment before turning to follow her father back to the cottage.

THE PAST

2005

15

'Go on, Margot. Jump.'

Margot stood on the rock ledge, her arms crossed and her toes curled over the edge, watching Lucy swim in circles beneath her. The river flowed deep and green, sun refracting on the surface, the reflection of the clouds distorted by her sister's splashing. Lucy called to her again, then, losing patience, she gave an exasperated sigh and dived below the surface of the river, a pale blur moving through the water. Eventually, slick and seal-like, her long blonde hair plastered dark against her scalp, she popped back up to check on Margot's progress.

Margot peered down into the water, thinking about the fish lurking in the depths and the clinging weed that might tangle round her legs. She eyed her sister. How come Lucy found the jump so easy? How come she never tired, never felt the cold? Margot was starting to regret her decision to follow her up onto the ledge.

'Come on, scaredy cat,' called Lucy. 'What are you waiting for?'

It was late in the summer. A 'watershed moment'. At least that's what their father was calling it, before Eve left for her Business Studies degree at Birmingham University, Lucy faced a dreaded year of GCSEs and Margot moved up to the local secondary school. The three girls had spent the summer revelling in their freedom, lounging in the garden, walking the woods, shopping with friends in Bath and – Lucy's particular favourite – wild swimming. If Lucy had had her way, they would have spent every day in the river, rain or shine, though that morning it had been Ted's suggestion to have the picnic down on the riverbank, at the tucked-away spot near the weir where locals in-the-know gathered to take the plunge. He'd raised it at breakfast. 'Who knows when we'll all be together next,' he'd only half-joked, his hands on Kit's shoulders, kneading the knots in her neck as she'd stood waiting for the kettle to boil.

'What was that?' she'd asked blankly, seeming to surface from a reverie.

'I said, let's all picnic today by the river.'

'What a lovely idea. Though I won't be able to join you until later. I have a headful of ideas to get down.'

Ted had frowned. 'But I thought we'd all walk there together, make a morning of it.'

'I don't want to lose the thread of my story, Ted. I can't stop the creative flow just because the sun is shining. Why don't I make us all sandwiches a bit later and I'll bring the picnic with me, so it doesn't get too hot in the sun while you swim.'

Ted had been about to argue, when Eve had jumped in. 'It's fine,' she'd said quickly, sensing the rising tension. 'We don't mind. Do we?'

'No,' Margot and Lucy had chimed in obedient unison.

Margot unfolded her arms and held them outstretched for balance as she gazed down at the water. It hadn't looked particularly high when they had spotted the raised ledge jutting out from the opposite bank, where the land rose more steeply from the water's edge. Both Margot and Lucy had agreed that it would be easy to swim across and scramble up. Lucy had gone first. She had scaled the bank and stepped out onto the rock, leaping without hesitation into the river — a narrow dart disappearing into the water. Margot had watched, impressed, before clambering up to take her own turn. It was only as she had walked out onto the ledge that her fear had kicked in, the perilous nature of the crumbling rock and the dark water below making her uneasy.

A little further up the riverbank, just a short distance from the towpath, she could see Eve sitting in an old rowboat still moored to the bank, a towel draped over her bare legs, her nose buried in a book, far too sensible to be drawn into their daredevil antics. Ted sat beneath a nearby willow tree, wrestling with the pages of a newspaper. He folded them into a manageable rectangle then threw an irritated glance back in the direction of Windfalls. They had left Kit working in her riverside studio with promises to join them in a couple of hours, though predictably, she was running late. When Ted looked back in Margot's direction she gave a tentative wave from her perch. Ted lifted his hand in a mock salute.

For such a glorious day, the river was surprisingly quiet. There was no one in sight bar a single figure climbing over a stile in the far distance. It was now or never. She turned back to the river.

Sensing her wavering resolve, Lucy began the count-down. 'Three... two... one!'

Margot took a deep breath and stepped out from the rock, plunging down into the water below. She let the force of the fall take her as deep as she could go, right into the black depths of the river. Submerged, she opened her eyes and allowed the burning sensation to build in her lungs. All was muffled. An eerie silence surrounded her. It felt as if she had dropped into an alternate world, one cutting her off from everything and everyone above. Disorientated, caught by a sudden tremor of panic, she looked up and saw faint shards of sunshine rippling down through the gloom. With an effort, she kicked toward the light, until she broke the surface, elated and relieved.

Practising their underwater handstands nearer the riverbank, she plucked up the courage to ask Lucy one of the questions that had been troubling her all summer. 'Luce, what's a "bonkbuster"?'

Lucy burst out laughing. 'Are you serious? Let me guess. You overheard someone talking about Mum's books?'

Margot nodded. 'Brian Hansen said his mum said our mum wrote "bonkbusters". He said she said her books are "smut that weren't fit to be in the public library".' She blushed, knowing that whatever Mrs Hansen thought of their mother's writing, it wasn't good.

'That's hilarious. Ignore them, Margot. Brian Hansen is an acne-ridden twerp and his mum... well, she's a sanctimonious old prig.'

Margot didn't know what sanctimonious meant any

more than she knew what bonkbuster meant, but she nodded in agreement.

'It means sex, Margot,' Lucy said, seeing her puzzled expression. 'Mum's books have lots and lots of sex in them.'

Margot grimaced. 'Gross.'

'Yep.' Lucy dived down beneath the water, her feet and ankles emerging moments later, toes perfectly pointed.

Margot waited until she had reappeared, gasping at the surface. 'Why does she write that sort of stuff, Luce? Why can't she write *normal* books.'

'Why does she have to wear nighties in the day? Why does she have to sunbathe naked and wander round barefoot? Why does she forget our packed lunches and send us to school in odd socks and too-small shoes? It may have escaped your notice, Margot, but our mother is not like other mothers. I mean, look around, where is she? She was supposed to be here ages ago with the picnic. I'm starving!'

It was true. Margot supposed she had always known her mother was different. While other mums baked cakes and served fish fingers and could grapple long hair into elaborate French braids, Kit *was* different. A woman of two halves. There was the quiet writer entombed in her studio, typing words onto paper on that clackety old black typewriter, the words flowing magically from virtual stillness. That woman was a mystery to her. Inscrutable. A closed book. She was the famous author – K. T. Weaver – creator of fat, historical novels with flashy, gold-embossed covers. She was the woman who people queued to meet at bookshops and festivals, the woman people sought autographs from, the woman who took 'important' phone calls from her publishers and conducted interviews with journalists from all around the world behind shut doors. She was the woman who would tut if you knocked and opened the door, her hand beckoning you with an irritated flick of the wrist. 'Yes, yes?' she would ask. 'What is it?'

That woman was her mother, but a shadow of the woman who came after, the one who surfaced from the riverside studio after a long day of writing, blinking and stretching like one of the cats stirring on the sofa. She would appear from the garden rolling her stiff shoulders, her tangled bun slightly askew on her head, her clothes rumpled. She would make a cup of strong, black tea and sit at the table, slowly acclimatising to the atmosphere of the house around her.

Only then was it that their mother would attempt to make up for her hours of seclusion, shaking off her intro-spection with a sudden manic intensity. 'Come here, my darlings. Come and tell me about your days.' It was then that the record player would go on and music would blare as eggs boiled on the stove top and toast popped in the toaster. And Kit, as if wildly compensating for the hours of quiet stillness she had spent lost inside her own head, would return to them all.

There were moments of intimacy. Margot could re-member them still. Bedtimes, when Margot, limbs still jumping with adrenalin from the day or anxious about what lay ahead tomorrow, would lie in bed and Kit would come to her, sit at her bedside and smooth her hair and stroke her bare arms, run her fingers round the palm of her hand, over and over, until Margot felt an easier peace begin to descend. Though, as the years passed, those moments grew shorter, less frequent, her mother's attention so obviously elsewhere as her fingers drifted across her skin. Then often, with a gentle tap at the door, Ted would interrupt to say that someone important from the States was on the phone and could Kit please come?

Margot found it confusing, this gradual retreat. The blowing hot and cold as Kit did; one moment warm and maternal, the next distant and aloof. Margot sometimes felt like one of her fans queuing for her attention, hoping for a moment in her spotlight. As she became more aware of her mother's success, it was hard not to get drawn into the myth of her, to place her on that unreachable pedestal.

Lucy was under the water again. Margot waited for her to reappear before she asked her next question. 'Who *is* that with Dad?' She pointed to the riverbank.

Lucy followed her sister's finger. The figure Margot had seen earlier, clambering over the stile, had now reached the copse of shimmering willows and stood talking with their father in the shade of the trees. She was a tall, slender woman, dressed in green trousers, a loose white shirt with a light yellow scarf wrapped around her neck. Her long red hair caught in the breeze, streaming like ribbons around her. She seemed to be holding a handful of brown fronds – pheasant feathers, from the looks of it.

The woman said something to their father. Margot couldn't hear her words, but the loud laugh that followed from Ted echoed across the water.

'I think that's the woman who bought the cottage

across the valley,' Lucy told Margot. 'The *widow*. Mrs Ash.' She spoke the word 'widow' in a dramatic whisper.

Margot stole another look at the woman. It was hard to tell admittedly, but from that distance she didn't look more than about thirty years old. 'She doesn't look like a widow.'

Lucy swam closer to Margot, her chin below the surface, her blue eyes gleaming in the light bouncing off the water. 'A freak accident, I heard. Squashed by a tractor. Can you imagine? Apparently she was the one who found him, but it was too late.'

Margot shuddered and dived down beneath the water to try and banish the horrible picture that had formed in her mind. Inspired by Lucy, she reached out, groping for the riverbed, hoping to find purchase against the silty floor to kick up into a handstand, though finding herself woefully off balance, she collapsed and launched herself back to the surface for a breath. 'Try again,' said Lucy. 'Keep your legs together.'

Determined not to be outdone by Lucy, she dived back down. This time as her hands met the riverbed, any sense of triumph disappeared as a razor-sharp pain sliced into her palm. With a yelp, she launched back to the surface, clutching her hand as she choked on swallowed water.

Raising her arm, she saw the blood oozing over her hand, dripping like ink into the green water. 'Lucy,' she whimpered, staring at the gore. 'Lucy, I've cut myself.'

'Oh my God.' Lucy took one look at Margot's hand and shrieked. 'Dad!' she yelled, calling out across the water. 'Dad, quick! Margot's hurt herself.'

Lucy was still helping Margot to clamber up the stony

bank as Ted, Eve and the woman who had been chatting to their father arrived at the water's edge. Seeing Margot's distress, Ted waded out into the reeds and grabbed Margot, hauling her up onto the bank. She held her fist squeezed shut, warm blood running in rivulets down her wrist and arm. Dizzy with shock, she whimpered at the sight of it.

'You must have cut it on something pretty nasty,' said Ted, blanching.

The woman beside him reached out and took Margot's hand in hers. 'May I look?' she asked Margot, who nodded and tried to unclench her hand.

The woman peered at her palm then curled Margot's hand back in on itself before reaching up and removing the pretty yellow scarf hanging around her neck. 'If you can open your hand again, I'll wrap this around the cut to stop the blood. Can you be brave for me?'

Margot nodded, mute with pain. She uncurled her hand and let her gently bind it with the scarf, the pale fabric turning pink almost instantly where it met the wound. The woman turned back to their father. 'You should take her to the hospital. She might need stitches, probably a tetanus shot too.'

Ted nodded and Margot noticed for the first time that he too was looking a little green around the gills. 'Eve,' he said, 'pack up our things. We'll head back to the house right away. Damn it! Where is your mother when we need her?'

The woman squeezed Margot's shoulder. 'You're a brave girl. You're going to be fine.' Seeing that both she and Lucy were shivering, she wrapped each of them in their towels then helped Eve throw the last of their belongings into the big wicker basket. As they turned to leave the river, the sun disappeared behind a cloud, turning the water black. 'Thank you,' called Ted to the woman. 'Thank you very much. I'm sorry about your scarf!'

'Don't mention it,' called the woman. 'I hope she's all right.'

'Did Mum forget?' Lucy asked, hopping along beside Ted as he marched them back down the towpath.

Their father didn't answer, but as they reached the section of river leading to the old apple store and the jetty, he ushered them through the garden gate and urged them on. 'Go up to the house,' he said, his mouth fixed in a grim line. 'I'll tell your mother what's happened. Eve, can you help Margot change into dry clothes so I can drive her to hospital?' They all knew from the way he let the little wooden gate slam shut behind them that he was livid.

As they began to wend their way up through the orchard they could hear his loud knocking on the studio door, followed by the sound of raised voices. 'For God's sake, Kit. One damn thing! You couldn't spare us one precious hour from your desk?' His words echoed among the trees.

They found the picnic basket sitting half-packed on the kitchen table, exactly where they'd left it. Eve sighed and swept it off the counter. 'Best not let Dad see that,' she said, hiding it in the larder.

Margot was still sporting the sturdy white bandage on her hand two days later when the journalist came to the house to interview Kit. Eve had already spent an hour tidying downstairs when she arrived in the kitchen to find thick black smoke wafting through the air and her youngest sister, still in pyjamas, perched precariously on the kitchen counter, her bandaged hand clumsily grappling with a knife jammed deep into the toaster. 'What are you doing?' Eve cried. 'You'll kill yourself!'

Flying across the kitchen, she switched the appliance off at the wall and grabbed the knife from Margot's hand. Carefully, she prised the burnt toast from the machine with her fingers and threw it into the bin. It was only then she saw the feathers scattered across the floor, as if a pillow had exploded mid-fight. 'Those bloody cats!'

Margot nodded and threw another two slices of bread into the toaster. 'I think it was a pigeon. Look, there's a special present over there.'

Eve glanced to where her sister pointed and saw a pile of coiled entrails glistening on the back doormat, deposited by one of their thoughtful new family members. Ted had brought the three kittens home a few months ago, rescued from a local farmer who had been talking about drowning the poor things, so overrun were his barns by the feral creatures. Since then, Pinter, Miller and Mamet had taken up residence at Windfalls and had shown daily appreciation for their rescue by bestowing various ghoulish hunting trophies on the family. 'I'd just tidied the kitchen,' groaned Eve.

'It's not like the journalist is going to come in here. I don't know why you're so worried. It's only another stupid interview.'

Eve sighed. Why *was* she so worried? Why had she spent the early hours of the morning tidying the house, vacuuming and dusting the lounge and trying to coax her mother into wearing something a little less... informal... a little more... appropriate? She knew why. It was bad enough that their mother was renowned for writing the sort of books that her friends passed dog-eared copies around, sniggering and laughing at the 'rude bits'. It was bad enough that they were known locally as *that* family: parents unmarried, father out of work, girls always dressed in each other's cast-offs. They didn't have to publicise their family dysfunction and slovenliness to the entire world, did they? Muttering to herself, she reached under the sink for the dustpan and brush and began to sweep up the feathers. She had no idea how they were going to cope when she packed up and left for university at the beginning of next week, but even though she felt guilty for wanting her freedom, Eve, for one, couldn't wait to be free of them.

Smoke cleared, feathers swept, entrails removed, order restored, the journalist arrived promptly an hour later. She had been sent by a leading women's magazine to write an exclusive 'at home' pre-publication feature on Kit before her book – the highly anticipated fifth volume in the Rare Elements series – was released that autumn.

The girls had been asked to stay out of the way, to entertain themselves in the garden or stay up in their rooms, but Eve couldn't resist. She sat halfway up the stairs chewing her nails, her head pressed against the wooden balustrade, her gaze fixed on the view through the open door into the living room below, where her parents perched side-by-side on the green velvet sofa.

Her mother was straight-backed, her knees pressed together and, thankfully, she had taken Eve's heavy hints and had both brushed her hair and changed into a dress

– a proper one with buttons down the front and a belt at the waist, the fabric pulled taut over her thighs as the sunshine fell through the window onto her lap. Her father, in contrast, was one broad shoulder, a cord-clad leg, a brown shoe and a tanned hand resting lightly on her mother's knee. The one brogue Eve could see tapped out an unheard rhythm on the worn rug. He sat beside her mother, half a man.

The visitor had her back to the door. All Eve could see of her was the stiff sweep of her grey, feathered hair and the dramatic puffed sleeves of her silk shirt, the pussy bow tied at the side of her neck quivering like school blancmange whenever she bent to consult the notebook on her lap. A recording device sat whirring on the coffee table between them.

'Well, this is lovely,' said the journalist, looking around the living room. 'It's exactly how I imagined a writer's home would be: intimate, cosy, inviting.'

Eve smiled and congratulated herself for her foresight in dusting off the coffee table and arranging the freshly picked garden flowers in an earthenware jug.

'I'm sure our readers would love to know how it felt,' the woman continued, her voice high and nasal. 'It must have been life-changing, receiving that phone call from your agent?' Her head was angled towards her mother.

Eve imagined the journalist's 'readers' as an orderly army of quiet librarian types poring over issues of the magazine, the satisfying *swish* of pages flicking in unison.

Kit smiled. 'Do you remember, Ted? You sent the first rough draft to Max as a favour, thinking he might have a contact or two who would take a look at it for me. The last thing either of us expected was his phone call two weeks later. When he told me the news, I screamed and dropped the telephone.'

Eve had heard this story before, but she always enjoyed reliving her mother's excitement.

Kit turned back to the journalist. 'It was Ted who continued the call. I couldn't take it in. A bidding war!' Kit's face wore the same look she had when standing by the Aga mindlessly stirring a pot, or when she sat at her desk, chewing aimlessly on a pencil. She might have been present in body, but in her head at that moment she was somewhere else.

'We had nothing in the house to celebrate did we?' Kit continued after a moment, turning back to Ted. 'Certainly nothing as extravagant as champagne. We couldn't afford the good stuff back then, could we?' She nudged Ted with her leg and smiled again. 'But you insisted.'

Eve heard her father's murmured assent.

'Ted dashed to the local pub,' Kit continued. 'He forced them to open up and sell him a bottle of champagne!'

The journalist was nodding enthusiastically. 'A true Cinderella story, rags to riches, our readers love that sort of thing.'

Her father let out a strange, strangled noise, but neither of the women appeared to notice. 'I wouldn't say *rags*,' said Ted.

'And I wouldn't say riches,' smiled her mother. 'At least, not back then. The offer was beyond my wildest dreams, of course, but I don't think any of us could have anticipated how popular the series would become. The first book, *Eye of the Stone*, was a slow build. It took several months before it appeared on the bestseller list.

Then everything seemed to . . . snowball. Other countries came on board and I was commissioned to write the rest of the series. It was the readers, you see. They were the ones who took the story of Tora Ravenstone into their hearts and began to spread the word.'

'And spread the word they did! You've written four international bestsellers and the fifth novel, *The Quartz Heart*, is scheduled this autumn?'

Kit nodded. 'There are to be seven in total. I know some critics have dismissed my books as racy potboilers, and readers probably wonder why I can't churn them out more quickly, but you can't rush inspiration. It takes as long as it takes. You have to follow the thread of your ideas, let it guide you. You have to bow to the Muse.'

'Right,' said the journalist, sounding a little baffled. 'And presumably there is a fair amount of research for each book?'

'Yes. I like to get the historical detail right, to make the characters and the world they inhabit feel as authentic as possible. We're so lucky, living around here, close to fascinating historical sites like Stonehenge and Glaston-bury. The landscape feels imbued with a certain kind of mysticism and magic. Can you feel it? It is inspiring.'

The journalist tilted her head, then cleared her throat. 'Um . . . yes . . . I think so. I've been researching what your fans particularly seem to respond to in your writing. It's not only the historical detail, but also the way you write about the female condition, the experience of being a woman in a male-dominated world.' She hesitated. 'Is it true that you conceived the idea for the whole series while out walking with your baby daughter? You mentioned in one interview you had been wrestling with postnatal depression. Writing became a form of release for you? A way of saving yourself?'

'Yes. I found early motherhood challenging. It involves such sacrifice, such a loss of self. The opening sequence in the first novel is something that came to me in a moment of extreme emotion and tiredness: what would compel someone to sacrifice a newborn child to a higher power? To leave a baby on a riverbank and walk away?'

The journalist murmured. 'Indeed.'

'It was through the writing that I began to feel like myself again. It was a surprise as I had never written anything before I started the first novel.'

'You've written all of your books here, at Windfalls?'

'Yes.'

'Do you have a particular method? I know Stephen King, for example, always writes in the morning and won't stop until he has written at least six pages every single day.'

Kit nodded again. 'It's a silly superstition, I know, but I write each book the exact same way as I wrote that first one. There's a potency of energy down by the river. It feeds my creativity. I write in my studio – an old apple store at the bottom of the garden. It's nothing fancy, but it is comfortable and quiet. I write on an old Olivetti typewriter Ted gave me.' She patted Ted's knee. 'It brings me comfort to follow the same method for each book.'

'A typewriter!' Eve saw the woman lean back in surprise. 'How – how . . .' She seemed to struggle for the right word.

'Antiquated?' Kit suggested and laughed. 'Yes. Ted's constantly haranguing me to update my methods. He's trying to drag me to the dark side with endless talk of Apple Macs and USG sticks.'

'USB,' Ted muttered.

'But I can't be bothered with all that modern technology. I don't trust it. I like to work on one typed hardcopy. It's how I've always done it. Far simpler and easier for me to keep track of the story that way.'

'Fascinating.' There was a short silence as the journalist flicked through her notes. 'It's certainly a picturesque spot. Have you always lived round here?'

'Since the late 1980s,' said Ted.

'It's a lovely house, but like most old places, it's in need of constant upkeep,' continued Kit. 'Truthfully, Windfalls would have fallen down around our ears by now if my readers hadn't proved such loyal followers.' Kit smiled. 'I'm grateful to them.'

Eve noticed Ted's foot fall still. There was a sudden shift in atmosphere, a sort of tightening, as if a door had been closed somewhere in the house, altering the air pressure or temperature with it. Eve leaned a little closer, the balustrade pressed hard against her cheek.

'And how have your friends and family taken to your success? Is everyone thrilled for you? Have you encountered any . . .' the journalist gave a light laugh, 'personal or professional jealousy?'

'Oh no. No jealousy. It helps that my partner is a writer. You understand what it takes, don't you, darling?'

Ted gave a grunt, which sounded like agreement, though Eve wasn't entirely sure.

'Readers have followed your flame-haired heroine, Tora Ravenstone, from her earliest, tragic beginnings where her family are brutally murdered and she herself narrowly escapes sacrifice by her tribe to the pagan gods, through to her rise as a skilled healer and warrior. Many reviewers have credited you for the strong feminist angle of your novels. You've been praised for empowering your heroine, giving her true agency. No doubt you have even bigger plans for Tora in the coming books?'

Kit gave a light laugh. 'I can't give away my secrets, but I think it's safe to say that readers have only seen the tip of the iceberg as to what Tora is capable of and what her future holds. Not even Tora understands, yet, her full power.'

The journalist nodded. 'I feel I should ask . . . some critics have taken . . . issue, shall we say, with the numerous and rather graphic sex scenes. One broadsheet reviewer called your books "gratuitous and titillating . . . well-thumbed bonkbusters for bored housewives." Do you read your reviews? Do you mind such comments?'

'I try not to read them. I find them distracting. My job is to write for my readers. Not the reviewers.'

'Would you mind if your daughters read your books?' The journalist had leaned forward in her seat. Eve too found herself craning forward a little, interested in her mother's reply

Kit shrugged. 'Why not? It's only sex. We humans have such a strange, uncomfortable relationship with our bodies and our desires. Shame is such a destructive emotion. I'm happy for my girls to read whatever they please, though I suppose Margot, our youngest, might want to wait a couple more years before she tackles Tora's story.' She laughed. 'Truly, I'd be surprised if they had any interest whatsoever in my career. To them, my job seems terribly dull.'

No, thought Eve. No interest whatsoever. She'd got halfway through the first book a few years back before throwing it across the room. As a blossoming teenager, it had been far too horrifying to read sex scenes that had been dreamed up in her mother's head. It was bad enough to know all her friends were reading them.

'Your daughters aren't impressed by your career?' the journalist pressed.

'Oh no. My daughters think my job is awfully boring. I sit alone in my studio every day. I spend too much time in my own head. It's hardly glamorous. Margot told me the other day she'd much prefer it if I were a vet, or a shopkeeper, like her friends' parents. Puppies and free sweets are far more exciting than bestseller listings, when you're eleven.'

The journalist laughed then turned her head, casting her attention for the first time in Ted's direction. 'And you, Ted, how about you?' she asked. Eve could hear the woman's smile, rather than see it. 'Do you mind the *erotic* nature of your wife's work?'

Eve heard her father clear his throat. 'It's not for me to say. Kit must write whatever she pleases. That's the way creativity works.'

'Yes, of course, I suppose you would understand that better than most, being a writer yourself? You enjoyed a little success yourself, back in the day?'

Eve noticed her father's hand close over her mother's knee, the knuckles whitening to bone. 'A little, yes,' he said tightly. 'Though these days you'll find me caring for the girls and running the house. I'm Kit's chief enabler.'

Kit took his hand in hers, lifting it and giving it a gentle squeeze. 'He's being modest. Ted is the *real* writer,' she said. 'He's a brilliant playwright. I'm sure you remember *Lost Words*?'

Kit paused but the journalist remained silent so she continued, 'It ran for several seasons in the West End and then toured around the country. There was even talk of taking it to Broadway but, well . . .' She trailed off. 'This was a few years back. You're writing again, aren't you, darling. Another play.' Ted remained silent so Kit turned back to the journalist with a forced smile. 'He's being secretive, but I know that it's going to be brilliant.'

The journalist nodded. 'Terrific,' she said, but Margot wondered if she was the only one to notice that the scratchy sound of the pencil moving across her notepad had fallen silent. 'Do your daughters show signs of following in your footsteps? Any young writers blossoming here under your roof?'

Kit looked thoughtful. Eve leaned closer to the banister. 'Eve, our eldest, is far too practical. She has her head screwed on. She mothers us all.' Eve couldn't help feeling a little disappointed. Kit made her sound so . . . so dull. 'And I doubt Lucy, our middle child, would manage it. She can't sit still for more than a few minutes. She's a free spirit, far too physical for the discipline writing requires. And then there's Margot. I'm not sure about her. She has the imagination, I think, but she's showing quite the dramatic flare. I think she might like to be an actress. It's fun, isn't it,' she added, smiling at the journalist, 'imagining where life might take them. Though, of course, those are stories they will create for themselves, in time.'

'They're wonderful girls,' said Ted, speaking up. 'We're proud of them all.'

The journalist closed her notebook and uncrossed her legs, leaning forward to switch off the cassette player. 'Terrific. I think I've got what I need. It's going to be a lovely feature. It will run in our September issue. I'll make sure your publicist gets copies.'

Eve, caught out by the conclusion of the interview, shuffled a few steps backwards up the staircase, careful to duck out of view as Kit ushered the journalist from the room and said goodbye at the front door. She heard Ted's loud exhalation of air and the creaking springs of the old sofa before Kit returned to him in the living room.

'Thank God that's over. I'm telling you, Kit, that's the last time I'm doing one of these interviews. *"You enjoyed a little success yourself, back in the day?"*' he mimicked in a high voice.

'I think you're being oversensitive, Ted. She was interested.'

'Interested?' He let out a harsh laugh. 'Do you have any idea how it feels to sit there like a ruddy fifth wheel while journalists gush over your work? I may as well have been invisible. I may as well have been banished to the garden with the girls.'

'That's why I told her about the play, and about your new writing.'

'Throwing me a bone, were you? Spare me your hand-outs, Kit.'

'Don't be like that.'

'Like what?'

'A petulant child.'

Ted let out a groan. 'And all that rot about the house falling down around our ears.'

'I was spinning a story for her, Ted. That's what writers do.'

Eve, still hidden on the stairs, held her breath as Kit continued, her voice more conciliatory. 'It's publicity, silly hoops I have to jump through. We should be grateful for it. The more books I sell, the less financial pressure on us as a family. I'm envious of you. I'm tied into this blasted contract. Tora bloody Ravenstone is going to be with me for years yet. You are free to write whatever you like, or not.'

Ted didn't answer.

Kit sighed. 'Perhaps it's time to think about the life you want to lead, Ted. Perhaps it's time for a little honesty.'

'What's that supposed to mean?'

'It's been *years*, Ted, years that you've been putting yourself under this pressure to write. Haven't you ever wondered if you might be happier if you found something else to do? Perhaps if you diverted yourself into something unrelated the words would come again.'

'Write a few shoddy bestsellers and you are the font of all wisdom on the creative process? Is that it? I can't bash out any old nonsense. I want my work to *mean* something.'

A long pause followed. 'And what would have happened to us, to this family, if I hadn't written my "shoddy bestsellers"? Tell me that?'

'Christ, Kit, can you hear yourself?'

'You can blame me. You can blame everyone else. Haven't you noticed Ted, the one person you can never seem to blame is yourself – the only person who can

176

change this situation. You're the only one who can write your plays.'

Kit swept out of the living room and Eve waited a minute, checking the coast was clear, before skulking back down the stairs and slipping out into the garden.

The picnic blanket lay empty on the lawn in front of the house, a chess set abandoned mid-game. Listening, Eve could hear her sisters' laughter coming from the orchard. She followed the sound to the little clearing by the stream where it pooled beneath a twisted apple tree before flowing away down the hillside towards the river. With the sun behind them, her sisters were silhouettes, midges darting in the air around them like flecks of gold. She couldn't see what they were doing until she drew closer and saw the penknife flashing in Lucy's hand. 'Ta-dah!' she said, stepping back to show Eve their handiwork.

'What are you doing?' asked Eve, narrowing her eyes. Across the tree trunk were now scored five white letters, hacked into the bark with Lucy's knife. K. T. E. L. M.

'For posterity.'

Eve frowned. 'Why?'

Lucy smiled. 'Because you're leaving, and because no matter where you go, or when you're next home, this tree will be evidence that you belong here. We all belong here.'

'You're such a dork.'

Lucy shrugged. 'Yep.'

Margot, noticing the apples hanging in the branches of the old tree, reached up and wrestled three from their stems, awkward with her bandaged hand.

'It's too soon,' said Eve. 'They won't be ripe yet.'

'Who cares?' laughed Margot.

Eve took her apple and bit into it. She was right. It was sour – too acidic. She spat out the flesh and threw the whole apple into the hedgerow, the bitter taste lingering on her tongue. Her eyes drifted back to those five letters carved on the tree trunk. *You belong here.* Perhaps Lucy was right, but Eve couldn't wait to find out what else awaited her, away from the confines of Windfalls.

Ted stomped down the gravel path and out onto the lane. He didn't know where he was going, but he knew he couldn't bear another minute in the house. He couldn't bear another moment of being undermined by Kit.

When they had first got together she had listened to him. Oh, how she had listened. He knew it was poor form to admit it, but her adoration had made him feel good – it had made him feel manly – to feel so supported, so revered by a spirited woman like Kit.

Only somehow, over the past few years, the respect and admiration she had felt for him seemed to have crumbled. There had been a clear but seismic shift in the balance of their relationship.

It's been years, Ted, years that you've been putting yourself under this pressure to write. Haven't you ever wondered if you might be happier if you found something else to do?

Her words had cut like a blade, all the more painful as they'd only echoed his own private fears. It *had* been years. So many years since he had enjoyed that first sweet taste of success, when he had been heralded as one of the country's finest young playwrights. Look at him now: a washed-up, middle-aged, unemployed man living off his wife's royalties. He was an embarrassment. A nobody. And she ... she was the world famous K. T. Weaver.

Chief enabler. He'd meant what he'd said. He had put his ambition on hold to run Windfalls as best he could, and to parent their three daughters. It wasn't a conversation they'd ever explicitly had about how they might share the division of duties, but as Kit's writing career had escalated and the pressure to hit her deadlines had increased, Ted had fallen into the primary parenting role. Small hands clasped in his on the walk to the village primary school. Plasters on grazed knees. Pushing swings and helping little legs to scramble up tree trunks. Swimming lessons in the river and reading books at bedtime. He'd been there for all the cherished moments of his daughters' childhoods. He'd felt lucky, in many ways, to be surrounded by such spirited souls, to be his daughters' guide and their protector. But he was traditional too. He had values and expectations embedded in him from his own more formal upbringing. He couldn't help feeling that he was lacking, as a man. That he was failing them in his duty to be not just their protector, but also their provider.

'You're not like a normal dad, are you?' Lucy had commented one day on a walk home from school.

'What do you mean, Luce?'

'Well, you don't work. You don't wear a suit or tie. You don't drive one of those big, fancy cars.'

'No. I don't.' He'd looked down at her heart-shaped face. 'Do you mind?'

Lucy had shaken her head. 'No. I like you just the way you are.'

Ted had smiled and squeezed her hand. 'And I like you, Lucy. Just the way you are.'

Such simple acceptance. Yet Ted knew he'd be lying if he hadn't admitted a degree of resentment. How swiftly, how easily Kit had assumed that Ted would take the brunt of it. When the school phoned to say one of the girls was sick, it went without saying that Ted would be the one to collect them, bring them home and tuck them into bed. When the holidays rolled around, it was Ted who planned their days and managed their care. Increasingly, he had slid into a space once shared between them. He could never regret the closeness he had built with his daughters, but such closeness only seemed to increase the growing rift between him and Kit. He couldn't help but feel resentful at the many assumptions she had made. Without any debate, their roles had been set and defined.

Even Max, his agent, had relegated him to the list of has-beens. 'Ted, old boy,' he'd greeted him on the phone last week. 'Great to hear your voice.' Somewhere from down the phone line Ted had heard the distant siren of an emergency vehicle moving through the streets of London. The sound had conjured such a yearning in him, to be back walking those gritty pavements, surrounded by a throng of humanity. To be back as the man he once was.

'If you're calling about the script . . .' he had started, about to launch into a pleading defence, when Max had interrupted.

'No, Ted. It's Kit I want. I need a quick word with her about the Japanese contracts. A small sticking point. Nothing to worry about.'

'Of course,' Ted had replied through gritted teeth. 'I'll fetch her for you.' And off he had trundled, the obedient lackey.

It wasn't that he didn't rate Kit's work. He had read her first two novels with his heart in his mouth. He had been transported – gripped. She wrote a rattling page-turner and he had felt both surprised and proud of her – perhaps even a little in awe too. God knows, he knew better than most what it took to sit down at that desk every day and face the blank page. No, it wasn't that he didn't rate her work. Ted's problem was that he no longer rated himself.

He had written *Lost Words*, his first play, in a storm of grief. It had felt like an urgent process, a necessary act of survival to pen the script, to make sense of the years he had spent as a teenager watching his elderly father suffer dementia, caring for a man who was essentially slipping away, watching the slow erasure of a parent he had loved the only way a boy could love a certain type of kind but emotionally distant man from the silent generation. Without the buffer of his mother between them, the two of them had been all at sea. After his father's death, the words had poured from him, sprung from his grief. The work had meant something – everything – to him.

Perhaps that was the difference between them. Kit's work involved daydreaming and fantasy, a wild flight of fancy into a make-believe world. Ted, on the other hand, seemed to need his work to be grounded in reality. He wanted to use his words to interpret the baffling realities of the life he lived. He wanted to say something real, something meaningful. Yet the problem he faced, day after day seated at his desk, was that he seemed to have nothing to say.

He'd spent years now, distracted by the girls, feeling stalled and frustrated, unable to finish a single damn play, that haunting voice of self-doubt perched on one shoulder, the fear of failure on the other. He'd been paralysed, and the greater a success Kit became, the smaller he shrank by comparison. He was supposed to be a man of words, and yet he had no words. He was a voiceless man, silenced by the success of his partner, quietly unravelled by jealousy. That was the ugliness inside of him – the ugliness he couldn't tell her. *It's been years, Ted*. She could never know how her words stung. He felt like Samson, living with his very own Delilah. It was as if she had taken up scissors and shorn him of his strength. *Lost Words*. The irony of the title of his first play had not escaped him.

He walked for a while, head down, his gaze fixed on the tarmac as his shoes stamped heavily down the lane, past the church, taking the bridge over the river. Midway across he stopped and gazed down at the churn of water moving below him. The river level was higher than usual after a night of heavy rain. Reeds billowed under the surface, and he could see the rocks and pebbles shifting visibly under the sheer force of the flow. He thought of those river stones, bouncing along, knocking against each other, being worn smooth by the movement of the water. It seemed somehow apt, those particles of rock being slowly removed, the edges rounded and worn away. Evidence of another slow process of erasure, like his relationship with Kit, like his career, like his sense of self. Attrition, that was the word for it. He was atrophying here at Windfalls. What was it Kit had thrown at him? *Perhaps it's time to think about the life you want to lead?* Was there truth in that?

Halfway up the far hillside, he lifted his head and looked around. He had left the river and was surrounded now by farmland and fields. A short distance away, if he were to carry on over the crest of the hill and through the wooded copse beyond, he knew he would come to a small, stone cottage nestled at the edge of a cornfield. He sucked in a breath and lifted his head a little higher then turned his face to the sun and kept walking.

It was only as he arrived at the cottage that he wondered what he was doing. He almost turned back, but as he stood deliberating, one hand hovering at the gate latch, the woman had emerged from one of the nearby outbuildings wiping her hands on a cloth as she squinted at him in the sunlight. 'Hello,' she said. She was wearing a green dress, the colour of moss, and her long red hair was pulled off her face with a comb, loose strands falling about her face, glinting copper in the sunlight. 'Have you come to buy one of my pots?'

'Er . . . I didn't . . .' He patted his pockets, realising he hadn't thought to bring his wallet, and it was only when he saw the smile creeping across her face that he realised she was teasing him.

'How is your daughter?' she asked.

'She's fine. You were right. A few stitches and an injection but they sent us home within the hour. She was lucky. Any deeper and they said she would have damaged the tendons.'

She winced. 'Well, that is fortunate.' She threw the cloth back in through the open door behind her. 'I was about to put the kettle on. Fancy a cup of tea? I have biscuits,' she added, in that teasing voice again. 'Chocolate ones.'

Ted considered the return walk to Windfalls, the dry taste in his mouth and the frosty atmosphere waiting for him back at the house. 'Why not?' he said, relenting. 'Thank you.'

In the kitchen, she washed her hands at the sink then fetched mugs and a glass jar of tea leaves while the kettle boiled. 'Sit,' she urged, seeing him hovering awkwardly at the table, so he pulled up a chair and watched her for a moment. He noticed how she moved with an easy grace, performing the tea-making ritual with a lack of self-consciousness that belied the fact she had a perfect stranger sitting at her kitchen table watching her every move. He saw traces of dry clay in her hair, a red powdery smudge up one arm. The sight of it somehow brought the memory of Margot's accident spinning back. He recalled the way she had unwrapped her own scarf and swathed Margot's hand so tenderly, and caught there in the memory was the sight of her slender fingers and the whiteness of her wrist in the bright sunlight.

With the tea brewing in the pot, she settled into the chair in front of him, exhaled a long breath and turned her attention to him. He felt a certain kind of stillness settle over him as his eyes met hers. It was a calm, open sense of being studied, observed. No judgement. She smiled and he noticed the fine lines creasing at the corners of her eyes. The small heart-shaped mole on her left cheek. She poured two mugs and pushed one towards him. He took a sip of his tea, scalding his mouth, swallowing it too quickly and feeling it burn the back of his throat.

'It's hot,' she warned, still with that slight teasing tone in her voice.

He wasn't sure what had come over him. Perhaps it was the walk in the sunshine. Or perhaps it was the stillness of the day, the intimate air in the kitchen. He glanced about again, suddenly unable to meet her eye. Pots and pans, hanging over the hearth, caught the light from the lead-pane window. A wooden armchair with a patchwork cushion on the seat stood nearby. He saw a bowl of pine cones on a dresser. It all looked surprisingly inviting. He turned back to find her still watching him. They smiled, a flicker of recognition at the strangeness of the shared moment, and Ted relaxed. He was being ridiculous. He stretched out his hand. 'I'm Ted. It's nice to meet you, properly.'

'Sibella.' As she took his hand in her warm one, he felt a small pulse of electricity travel up his arm.

'I owe you a thank you,' he said. 'For your help, for being so calm and kind, and ... well ... for sacrificing your lovely scarf.'

Sibella smiled. 'It was nothing. The main thing is that your daughter is OK.'

The sound of a clock ticking somewhere in the kitchen filled the silence. Sibella eyed him over her mug. 'Are *you* OK? You looked a little shaken by the accident. These things can be a bit of a shock, a reminder of our fallibility. I imagine it is hard to see your child in pain.'

Ted was surprised to be asked how he felt and even more surprised to feel a lump forming at the back of his throat. 'Yes. I'm OK. Of course.'

He took another sip of his tea. Her skin was the colour of milk, he decided. Her eyes the same moss green of her dress. She'd be in her late thirties, he supposed. 'You're a potter?'

'Yes.'

Too young to be stuck out there on her own with nothing but her clay pots and her kiln for company. He wondered how she bore it. 'I heard you lost your husband,' he blurted out, unsure why he felt the need to mention it, but feeling somehow as if it were the right thing to do. 'I'm sorry.'

When she looked up, he found himself falling into her green-eyed gaze. 'Thank you,' she said.

He fought the urge to reach out and touch her arm, to try and comfort or reassure.

'It'll be seven years this month since my husband died,' she said quietly.

'What was his name?'

'Patrick.'

'Do you mind if I ask how he died?'

'No. We ran a dairy farm in Staffordshire. He was out in the fields on the tractor and hopped off to shut a gate. A safety switch on the vehicle failed. The machine rolled back onto him. It was a terrible, freak accident. That's what the coroner called it.'

Ted looked down into his tea. 'I'm so sorry. How long had you been married?'

'Two years.'

Ted didn't interrupt, sensing she had more to say.

'I was nine weeks pregnant at the time. I lost the baby two days after his funeral. I had to sell most of our land to pay off the debts we'd accrued after a couple of poor years on the farm. Overnight, the life I knew – the future I had imagined – vanished. It was loss heaped upon loss. In the end, I decided it was best to move away from the place of so much pain. Though, of course,' she admitted with a sad smile, 'you can't outrun it. You carry it with you.'

'I'm so sorry.' Ted reached across the table and took her hand, squeezing her warm fingers in his own. Sitting there, Ted thought for a moment how strange life was, to find himself holding a virtual stranger's hand, and for it to feel like the most natural thing in the world. How odd it should be, the feeling he had to comfort her, the feeling that he didn't want to let go.

It was Sibella who pulled away first, reaching up to brush a tear that had trickled down her cheek. 'I'm sorry. Seven years later and it can still rush up on me.'

'It's not fair, that you should lose him like that. And the baby.' He shook his head.

Sibella shrugged. 'No. It's not.'

'It's not the same, but I lost my parents a few years back. My mother when I was young, then my father, to dementia, when I was a teenager. I was his carer in the final years. We weren't close but I still found the loss hard to bear. I can't imagine how you have coped. Grief is confounding, wild and unpredictable.'

She nodded. 'It is.'

'You never remarried?'

'No.'

'Don't you get lonely out here all by yourself?'

She shrugged again. 'Sometimes. But it's peaceful.' She let out a sigh and threw him a small smile. 'I'm sorry. I don't know why I told you all this. I don't usually bombard strangers with my tragic past over a cup of tea. It's hardly the sort of small talk exchanged between new friends, is it?'

'No. But at least it's real.' Ted thought it might be the most real conversation he'd had in months. They held each other's eye and Ted felt it again, a strange energy passing between them. Understanding. Connection. He wasn't sure what it was, but he felt rattled by it. He looked down at his teacup and noticed it was empty. 'I should get going.'

She nodded. 'Yes. Of course.'

As he stepped out into her courtyard, he saw a shard of light breaking through the clouds, falling like a spotlight onto the valley below. High above, a buzzard wheeled in tight spirals across the sky, its cry echoing over the valley. The scene was breathtakingly beautiful. He turned to her and smiled. 'Thank you, for the tea, and the conversation.'

'You're welcome.'

For some inexplicable reason, he found it took all his willpower to turn and walk away. At the gate he stopped and looked back. She was still there, watching him.

'I'll come back next week,' he shouted. 'With my wallet. I'll buy one of your pots!'

She raised her hand in acknowledgement and he felt her smile lift him like nothing else had in a long time.

THURSDAY

16

Kit wakes early, pulled from sleep by a disturbing dream in which she has stood by, watching helplessly as Windfalls and everyone she loves is razed to the ground in a terrible inferno. It's a nightmare she hasn't had for a while, but last night it revisited her in full Technicolor. Pushing herself wearily from the bed, it's almost as if she can still smell the acrid smoke, can still hear the echo of her cries: *What have you done? What on earth have you done?*

The lingering fragments of the dream are enough to drive her from her bedroom and send her up to the turret room. She settles into the chair, presses the power button on the computer and listens to the whirr of the machine starting up.

There is a stillness to the house, an emptiness that seems to expand with every moment that she sits there in Ted's worn leather chair, the one she had commandeered from his study the day after he left, the one she had refused to give up to the men who came with the van to claim his possessions. The seat still carries the memory of him, worn into the cushion from all those hours he occupied it while labouring over his writing. It offers comfort. The physicality of him is still present in this one small way, even though most days she is the only inhabitant of this draughty old house, bar Pinter, the sole survivor from Ted's kitten rescue all those years ago.

She stares at the blank screen in front of her. Just write, she tells herself. Write something. Anything. She reaches out to the keyboard, fingers hovering, diverted suddenly by the sight of her hands. It's the back of them that stuns her. When did those lines form, the creases gathering around her knuckles and wrists, the shadows of those first age spots? She is not a young woman any more. She knows this intellectually, of course. She is neither mad nor delusional, thank goodness. Yet, sitting there, staring at her hands, at her blunt fingernails and her lined skin, and yes, the lack of jewels or adornment – the lack of wedding ring – she feels every one of her fifty-three years. With the ache of loneliness expanding in her chest, Kit lowers her head to her arms and weeps.

She cries until the sleeve of her silk dressing gown is soaked through, then lifts her head and rubs her face. She lets out a loud groan. She hates herself for this self-pity. If only she could do what she once did and disappear inside an imaginary world – fictional characters feeling fictional emotions – but she can't seem to conjure herself away from her current pitiful state. Single. Spinsterly. Alone.

Last week, before Lucy had announced her madcap wedding plan, two plumbers had arrived at Windfalls to replace an old enamel bath and fix a broken cistern.

Their cheerful presence in the house, the sound of their radio and the banter they had shared, had lifted her lonely spirits in such a way that, as she had waved them goodbye, she had found herself silently willing their van to return back down the drive. 'Don't go,' she'd wanted to cry. 'Don't leave me here, to this.'

The reality of her life rises up and hovers before her eyes. This isn't how she'd imagined it would be. This wasn't what she'd dreamed of all those years ago, when she and Ted had started their family and dared to envisage what a life together might hold.

'I'm embarrassed to show you,' she'd said, when Ted, curious as to what had kept her in the riverside studio for so many weeks, had asked if he could read her work.

'Don't be embarrassed. We all have to start somewhere, Kitty.'

Reluctantly, she had handed him the first hundred pages of the manuscript she'd begun after her fateful walk with Eve, then left him to it, strolling the towpath, back and forth, unable to bear the thought of Ted – her wonderfully clever Ted – reading her clumsy words.

He'd been waiting in the kitchen on her return, tapping the table impatiently, the pages strewn before him. 'Where's the rest?' he'd asked, a gleam in his eyes. 'Show me the rest.'

'What? All of it?'

'Yes,' he'd nodded, urgently. 'All of it.'

It had been Ted's idea to send it to Max, his literary agent in London.

'I don't know, Ted.' She'd worried it was too unpolished, too rough for professional eyes.

'What have you got to lose?'

That question. It was laughable, now. 'Nothing,' she'd answered. How wrong she had been. It was, perhaps, the greatest irony that it had been Ted who had encouraged and indulged her, urging her to nurture her creativity in those earliest days, the way you might encourage an ailing patient to take a necessary and restorative turn around a garden. Though of course neither of them could have predicted the success of her first foray into fiction or the rift it would eventually drive between them.

She sighs and leans back in Ted's chair. The familiar creak of its seatback and the noise of the castors shifting on the wooden floorboards are the only sounds to be heard in the entire house. Margot hasn't yet returned from her night at Ted and Sibella's. She glances out to the valley beyond the window and tortures herself with thoughts of Ted, surrounded by love and laughter.

A memory rises and pricks on the surface of her mind. Margot, aged about six or seven, struggling with a sudden bout of bedtime anxiety. It had seemed to rise from nowhere, their once confident little girl suddenly afraid of shadows, disturbed by the dark space beneath her bed, lying awake, sleepless and worried. She remembers how Margot had called for her, and Kit, abandoning her work, would go to her and sit on the edge of her bed. She remembers the fairy tales she would make up for her, revisions of classics where the princesses would wield the swords and slay the monsters. She remembers Margot, lying tucked beneath the covers, wide-eyed and rapt, the sleeve of her pyjama top rolled up to reveal a skinny bare arm, an invitation for Kit to trail her fingers over her daughter's skin, soothing away her worries, until at last she would let sleep take her and Kit would tiptoe from the room. That sweet little girl. Those shared moments had felt so precious. They had been an anchor, a reminder of her place in the family. Until one night, it had been Ted Margot had called out for, not her, and Kit, though stung, had brushed off her daughter's rejection. It was fine, she told herself. More time to write.

It was a tug she found hard to bear. A constant push–pull sensation between work and family. It wasn't so long ago that she'd craved silence and solitude. The eternal family noise, the constant interruptions had meant she'd felt sure she would be happier and more productive if she could shut them all out. Yet as soon as the house became hers – the proverbial empty nest – the silence became unbearable and her words somehow stifled by the quietness. It's hard to write from an empty place. It was a painful lesson to learn, but the fertile ground of the family, the solid foundation of it underpinning her existence, was the soil she needed to nurture her work, her sense of self. Without it – without them – she is lost.

Of course she'd known what was going on with Sibella, and not just because Ted had done a terrible job of hiding his infatuation. Yes, even someone like her, distanced by her work and closeted away from them all, had intuition enough to know that the man she loved was slipping from her grasp. She could sense it in his distracted gaze, his long sighs and the curve of his back, turned away from her in bed each night. She'd decided to turn a blind eye. What was that saying? If you love someone, set them free.

She remembered their first promise to each other, to hold each other lightly, and had felt worldly and wise, allowing him his fling, knowing how gracious she was being, how generous. She knew that ultimately, she and Ted belonged to each other. What was it he had once said to her: *I don't need a ring to know that I am yours, and you are mine.* Who said relationships had to be monogamous? Infatuation with another didn't have to mean the destruction of their partnership. Their connection was stronger and deeper than that.

But that didn't mean she wasn't curious. Who was the woman who had caught Ted's eye? It hadn't been hard to piece things together. It was a vase Ted had brought home one afternoon, an elegant cream vessel which he had placed in the living-room window and sat gazing at all evening, as if preoccupied by its form. 'I saw it in a shop,' was all he offered when she asked. 'I thought it would look nice here. Don't you like it?' In all the time they had lived at Windfalls, Kit couldn't once remember Ted showing any interest in home furnishings. As soon as Ted had gone to bed, Kit had turned the vase over and read the artist's looping signature scratched into the dried clay. Sibella Ash.

She had tracked her down to an artisan market in Bath. Slipping out of the house one Sunday morning, Kit had arrived at the crowded market square and wandered among the stalls, buying a pot of local honey and a pretty woven bag for Lucy's birthday, before finally spying what she had come for: a stall laid out with an impressive array of ceramic pots, plates and jugs, behind which stood an attractive red-headed woman, dressed in a navy-blue pinafore dress. Certain of her anonymity, Kit had approached casually, and while the woman served another customer, she had allowed herself to inspect the woman's craft more closely.

They were nice pieces, she supposed, *if* you liked that sort of thing. Rustic, homely, though showcasing a certain amount of skill. She'd glanced again at the woman, noting her slender waist, her almond-shaped eyes. She was younger than Kit by a few years. Was that what Ted was drawn to, she wondered? Her youth?

'Can I help you with anything?' the woman had asked, startling Kit so that she had almost dropped the bowl in her hands. Kit had placed the item back on the table and looked at the woman, and it was then, as the woman's green eyes had widened with recognition and her face had reddened, that Kit had realised her mistake. 'It's Kit, isn't it?' the woman had asked in a low voice.

Kit had nodded, surprised that the other woman should recognise her. Though perhaps, she realised, she shouldn't have been. Her photograph had appeared on enough book covers and magazine articles in recent years. Or perhaps Sibella had simply taken the trouble to research her competition. 'Yes. I'm Ted's . . .' She'd hesitated. Not his wife. What should she say? 'I'm his partner,' she'd settled on. 'You're Sibella?'

The woman had nodded.

Kit, realising that she was taking a small amount of satisfaction from the other woman's obvious discomfort, had eyed her evenly. 'You do realise that he has a happy home with me, and three daughters who he dotes upon?'

Sibella had had the good grace to drop her gaze. 'Ted said that you . . . that he . . .' She'd petered out, awkwardly. 'It wasn't my intention to come between you.'

Kit had straightened her shoulders. 'I'm sure what Ted *said* . . . what he *wants* . . .' She'd given a hollow laugh.

'Well, we all know what men *want*, don't we?' She'd fixed her in her sights. 'Do *you* have children, Sibella?'

The woman had shaken her head, seemingly unable to meet Kit's gaze again.

'No. I didn't think so. If you did, I'm sure you would tread a little more carefully, treat people with a little more respect.'

'I'm not proud—'

'No,' Kit had interrupted, coldly. 'I don't suppose you are. Oh, don't worry,' she'd added quickly. 'I won't tell Ted that I was here. He need never know that we've met. And you may have your sordid little affair with *my* Ted. I'll grant him that. But please don't be so foolish, Sibella, as to think you could ever take him from us. He'll never leave. You are a flight of fancy, a momentary diversion. Nothing more.'

Before Sibella could reply, Kit had turned and marched away through the crowds, her legs shaking but her sense of triumph to have said her piece rising like a cresting wave. Later that afternoon, as she had knocked the cream vase to the floor, she had felt nothing but the same sweet triumph to see it shatter into pieces. 'Oh, how clumsy,' she'd said, unable to meet Ted's gaze as she'd swept the shards into a dustpan. 'Unfortunately, darling, I don't think it's worth saving.'

She had tried so hard to give him everything. She had tried to turn a blind eye to his indiscretion. What was it was she so guilty of? Working hard? Achieving success? Giving him his freedom? And for what? Ted's paralysis had seemed to deepen with her own escalating career. His detachment from her, and his desire to be with Sibella, had only seemed to grow the more books she had sold, until the day he had confronted her with his decision to leave.

That she had been devastated was an understatement. Kit didn't know who she was without Ted. She didn't know *why* she was at Windfalls. The dream they had shared dissolved with his departure, and of course their girls growing up and spreading their wings. A 'momentary diversion', she had told Sibella. She wasn't ever supposed to be his *future*.

To hide from the pain, she had disappeared into her work. She had submitted to the pull of her creation, absorbing herself even more deeply in her writing. Kit took to spending long hours in the studio, working on the manuscript, moving her characters like chess pieces playing out a complex game, all the while avoiding the pain of her own failed relationship. The seventh book was going to be her best yet. She felt it in her bones. Kit's own life might be falling apart, but her heroine, Tora, was reaching the pinnacle of her story. Her character had seen off countless threats and foes. She had become a mother in the sixth volume and the transformation – the maternal power – had added a compelling new dimension to the character and the writing. Kit had felt inspired in a way she remembered from those earliest days in the studio. After a day of escape into Tora's world, she would lift her head, amazed at the speed in which the day had passed, and leave her riverside writing studio, drained but content, eyeing the growing stack of typed pages with a sense of satisfaction, certain it was her best work yet and thrilled to know that her vision was nearing completion.

Only she had neglected one important piece of her

own real-life puzzle. Margot. She had failed to notice Margot's loneliness and despair at Ted's departure.

It still caused Kit physical pain to remember the spring night she had looked out of the kitchen window and seen the flames rising up through the trees in the orchard. Lost in her own thoughts, she had seen the flickering orange fire dancing down in the valley and had stood for a moment, entranced. How beautiful, she had thought. But as the flames grew in strength and the black smoke began to billow from the trees, Kit had snapped out of her trance. Realisation dawned. A fire, down by the riverside. Gripped by a terrible dread, she had run through the orchard to the studio and found the entire building engulfed in flames and Margot crouched on the jetty, looking dark and deranged. If she could have entered the building and grabbed even one page of that novel she had poured her broken heart into she would have, but the old apple store was an inferno and it was clear nothing would survive the force of such wilful destruction. Her only draft – her best work yet – had gone up in smoke and Margot didn't seem to have any explanation for what she had done. 'He's gone,' was all she'd said, as Kit had stood over her, shaking with rage. 'He's gone.'

'I know he's gone,' Kit had screamed at her. 'He left me too, you foolish, foolish girl.' She'd stared about, aghast as the flames had risen and the sparks of her work had spiralled away into the sky. 'As if this could have brought him back!' Kit didn't think she could ever forgive Margot for such a cruel betrayal.

All this before the final kick in the guts when, just a few months later, Ted made his triumphant return to the West End. Though she nursed her own deep wounds and maintained a hurt and frosty silence with him, she'd had the good grace to find an iota of joy for Ted's achievement. She knew what it would mean for him, after all these years, to have finished a play. It was only when the first reviews of *Attrition* had started to appear, and she had understood what exactly his new work was about, when the phone had started to ring with sly requests from journalists asking for comment and opinion on the themes of her ex-husband's play ('not my ex-husband – we were never married') that she had begun to understand what he had done. For *Attrition,* it transpired, was a contemporary spin on the biblical story of Samson and Delilah. It was an exploration into the descent of a man, eroded slowly by a more powerful, more successful lover. A well-known Hollywood actor had been cast as the West End lead and the play was being hailed by critics as a gruelling examination of the collapse of a once loving relationship, a dissection of the power struggle between a man and woman and a topical analysis of modern-day gender roles and politics. The broadsheets were calling it a revelatory modern master-piece. The tabloids were calling it 'sensational' and pored over it as if it were a free for all on the machinations of Ted and Kit's failed relationship.

When, a few weeks later, Margot had appeared in the kitchen, just shy of her seventeenth birthday, and announced that she too was leaving home, there hadn't seemed any point arguing with her. Kit could barely stand to look at her still. But with Margot's departure, it was as though the final door had slammed shut on Kit. Was it any wonder, after the last few years, that she had constructed walls around herself? She had built her defences high, and retreated behind them, certain that she would not risk such personal or professional pain again. In the new reclusive world she inhabited, her only battlegrounds were loneliness and middle age.

This weekend, in front of Lucy's wedding guests, will be the most public she has been in years. She hopes she is ready. It will be hard to face them all: Ted, Sibella, Margot. But she will cope. She will do it for Lucy. This weekend is not about her. Perhaps the greatest gift she can give Lucy is to put aside her own pain. She can keep it hidden and buried – as she has become so adept at – and maintain her uneasy truce with Margot. She will do her best to welcome Sibella to Windfalls, without fuss or histrionics. As much as it hurts, she will do it for Lucy. She will prove to them, as much as to herself, that she can be the mother she knows none of them believe her to be.

Blinking in the morning light, she turns away from the window and rests her gaze on the blank computer screen in front of her. The MacBook she now works on sits waiting. A hard drive hums beneath the desk, next to the printer she uses to spit out backup hard copies of her day's work. Somewhere, an invisible 'Cloud' waits to gather up her words and store them safely. Eve and Andrew had come one day and set it all up for her. It feels like an alien way of working, a world away from the satisfying thunk of typewriter keys hitting ribbon, but at least, should she find herself ever putting words down, they will be kept safely.

Perhaps someday, she will find a way to return to the Rare Elements story. Perhaps somehow, she will find it in her to battle the terrible block she has faced these eight long years. Perhaps, at some point, the words will start to flow again. Oh Ted, she thinks, I understand now. I understand so much.

Far below, she hears the sound of the back door opening then closing. Margot has returned. Minutes later, there comes the high beeping of a truck reversing up the driveway. Voices drift up through her open window, her daughter's mingling with the deeper, rougher voices of the men from the marquee company. Footsteps crunch on the gravel path. There is the sound of truck doors sliding open. Kit wonders if she should go and help supervise but something holds her in place. She sits there, listening to the industry below, hiding behind her wall for just a little longer.

17

The men are fast and efficient. They drag the poles and white canvas down to the orchard and start to erect the tent frame between the trees. Margot watches them work, feeling helpless. She sends Eve and Lucy a photo from her phone as the bones of the marquee begin to take shape. 'Too late to back out now!' she jokes.

She hears the sound of another vehicle on the driveway and moments later Tom appears in the orchard, wandering down through the trees in his work gear and muddy boots, aviator sunglasses masking his eyes. 'I was checking on a conservation project nearby and thought I'd pop by to see if you lot needed a hand with anything.'

'I think the guys have got it under control,' says Margot. 'But thanks.' She casts about for something to say. 'What's the project?'

'A bumblebee corridor.'

'A what?'

Tom smiles. 'We're working with farmers and land owners to create nectar-rich sites that help bees travel and pollinate. It's important for their survival, and agriculture. A win for everyone.'

Margot smiles. 'I like that. A bee super-highway.'

'Exactly.'

They stand side by side watching as the workmen raise wooden posts and drive huge metal pegs into the earth with mallets.

'It's exciting,' says Margot.

'It is,' says Tom, though something in his voice makes her turn.

'Everything all right?' she asks.

'Yeah,' he says, rearranging his face into a smile. 'Everything's great.'

One of the men, wrestling with a corner of the white canvas, loses his grip. The fabric catches in the breeze and cracks like a whip, the sound echoing out across the valley. Tom heads across and helps to pull the fabric in place, before returning to Margot's side. 'Lucy's dead chuffed that you came back for the wedding,' he says.

'Of course I came back,' says Margot.

'I realise you and I don't know each other well, but I hope you trust I'll always do my best to look after your sister.'

Margot laughs. 'To be honest, Lucy has never struck me as the kind of person who needs "looking after".'

'Well then, just know that I'll always have her back.'

Margot turns and studies Tom's tanned face. She sees the earnest expression in his blue eyes. 'I hope so.'

'I'm looking forward to getting to know you a bit better over the next couple of days. You are coming to the dinner tomorrow?'

Margot nods. Truthfully, she had been wondering whether she could make up an excuse and avoid the whole excruciating pre-wedding family line-up. With the buffer of more guests, she knows it will be far easier to avoid confrontation and conflict at the wedding. The intimacy of the family meal scares her.

'Good,' continues Tom, 'because it means a lot to Lucy to have you there, and my folks are looking forward to meeting all of you.'

'I hope you've warned them we're a little—'

Tom grins. 'All the best families are, Margot.'

She smiles at that.

He clears his throat. 'Lucy has pinned a lot on your return, Margot.' Margot turns to him with a raised eyebrow. He holds up his hands. 'I know she can sometimes be wildly unrealistic, but I want her to enjoy this weekend. I don't want her distracted by family politics and fighting. I guess I'm just saying, if you could find a way to, well, keep things calm...' He trails off, seeing the flare of indignation on her face.

'She's the one that called us all back together,' Margot says, bristling at his suggestion. 'I'm perfectly happy to let the past remain in the past, but I don't suppose you've had this little chat with our mother?'

He at least has the good grace to look guilty. 'I shouldn't have said anything.'

Margot eyes him warily. 'I don't know what Lucy has told you, but trust me, you don't know the full story.'

Tom nods. 'Sorry. Forget I said anything. Luce said to tell you that she will be over to help with the decorations. I'd best get back to work.'

Margot watches Tom walk up towards the house, upset and more than a little irritated at his interference. When she turns back to the orchard, she sees that the men have performed a miracle. Where once there was only grass and trees, now stands a huge white tent. It rises and falls, the fabric breathing like a giant lung in the morning air. She studies it for a moment, watching its undulating movement. Yes, she thinks. Just breathe.

18

Lucy drops her bombshell as they are balancing on chairs in the marquee, a string of fairy lights between them. 'I think Andrew's having an affair.'

'What?' Margot nearly drops the lights, only just catching them in time. 'You're kidding?'

'I wish I was.'

'How do you know?'

'I saw him with another woman. He was buying her jewellery. It didn't look exactly . . . innocent.'

'Did he see you?'

She shakes her head.

'Fuck.'

Lucy eyes Margot. Her sister has gone a furious red, the wire string of the lights wound tightly in her hands. 'What's wrong with him? What about Eve, the girls?'

'I know,' says Lucy. 'I don't know what to do. I don't know if I should tell her.'

'Of course you should.'

'She'll be devastated. You know what she's like, how in control of everything she has to be.'

Margot sighs. 'What a bastard.'

'I should have confronted him when I saw them

together. I was tempted. I could have wiped the smug smiles off their faces.' Lucy imagines the conversation she has played out in her head a hundred times since her shopping trip. She could have pulled Andrew up there and then and reminded him of his responsibilities to his wife and kids.

'I always thought those two were rock solid.' Margot thinks for a moment. 'She's seemed pretty odd these past couple of days – so tense and cagey. Maybe she already knows?'

'She would have said something, surely?'

'Unless she didn't want to burden you before your big day?'

Lucy frowns.

'Well, whether she knows or not, he's still a complete bastard for cheating. Honestly, what is it with men? Why are they such untrustworthy, philandering bastards?'

'Not *all* of them are like that.'

Margot throws her a sour look. 'Dad left Mum, didn't he? Now Andrew's fooling around behind Eve's back. Men are weak, Luce. They just can't keep it in their trousers.'

'Er . . . you do realise that I'm marrying the love of my life on Saturday?'

'I hope Tom's different. I really do,' says Margot quietly.

'Well, thanks for the vote of confidence. Of course he's different.'

Margot doesn't say anything and Lucy feels her indignation rise. 'Are you OK? You seem a little . . . rattled.'

'I'm fine.'

Lucy leans up to attach the wire over the entrance to

the tent, stretching to pin it to the corner. Her chair tilts slightly in the soft ground, making her wobble. 'Shit,' she says, reaching down to steady herself.

'Here,' says Margot, reaching across for the lights. 'You get down. I'll take it from here. Can't have you injuring yourself before your big day, not in your—'

'What?' Lucy gives her a look.

'Nope. I insist,' says Margot, wrestling the lights from her hands. 'Why don't you fetch the bunting from the house? We'll hang that next.'

Lucy sighs but does as she is told. When she returns, she finds Eve has arrived and is helping Margot, the two of them untangling another string of lights between them. She eyes her elder sister, trying to read her face for signs that something might be off. Eve looks more tired than usual, perhaps a little less 'put-together' than she'd expect, with her brown hair scraped back in a messy bun and her shirt creased and untucked.

'Thanks for coming to help,' says Lucy carefully. She glances at Margot. 'We weren't expecting you.'

'I wanted to check on the marquee and thought you might need an extra pair of hands.'

Margot clears her throat. 'Everything all right at home?' she asks.

Lucy throws her a frown but Eve is oblivious to Margot's clumsy question. 'Of course.' She glances up from the lights. 'This is a rare moment of quiet, with the girls at school and Andrew in the office.'

'Great,' says Margot, nodding. 'That's great.'

Eve gives her a suspicious look. 'Everything OK with *you*?'

'Uh-huh. Everything's wonderful. Isn't it, Lucy?'

Lucy shoots her another warning look. 'Yes. Fine.'

Margot shakes the tangled wires. 'Ugh. This is a disaster. Why don't we forget the lights and put candles everywhere. It would look lovely.'

'We can't,' says Eve. 'The hire company said it would be a fire risk. Can you even imagine? This whole place would go up in flames.'

Margot's hands, still fiddling with the string of lights, fall still. The three sisters look at each other, the same image hovering before their eyes at the same time. Lucy swallows. This is ridiculous. They have to talk about what happened. It's the only way. 'Don't you think it's time you gave Mum an apology, Margot?'

Margot shoots her a steely look. 'If you really want to know, I apologised the other night.'

'Well, that's good,' says Eve brightly.

'Not much good it seemed to do. She's hell-bent on holding a grudge.'

Lucy sighs. 'You destroyed years of her work. A six-hundred page manuscript, up in smoke, like that.' She clicks her fingers.

Margot winces. 'I know.'

'Have you even tried to imagine what it must have felt like for her? Is it any wonder she hasn't been able to finish the series, that final book?' Lucy sees Margot scuff the grass underfoot, her face turned to the ground and feels a wave of anger. 'You did that, Margot. You're the one that paralysed her.'

'Lucy,' warns Eve. 'I don't think—'

'Yes. I know that,' says Margot quietly. 'Of course I know that.'

'Have you considered counselling,' she continues. 'Tried talking to someone?'

'What good would that do?'

'How do you know if you don't try?'

Margot looks utterly dejected, her face still fixed on the ground. 'It's just words, isn't it? It doesn't change anything.'

'Yes, Margot. Just words. Words that you need to stop bottling up and start sharing. This silence you shroud yourself in, it's not healthy. You owe Mum. Not only a proper apology, but an explanation as to why you would do something so . . . hurtful.'

Margot raises her head and rolls her eyes. 'Would you listen to yourself? You act like we lived this idyllic childhood. As if Mum and Dad never put a foot wrong. The truth is that *none* of you know the *real* truth. Or perhaps it's simply that none of you wanted to see it. Far easier to believe in a fantasy than accept the shitty reality, right?'

Lucy throws Eve a confused glance. 'What *are* you talking about?'

'Forget it.'

'No. Tell us.'

'What's the point? There's no coming back from this. I'm sorry but the fantasy of "happy reconciliation" that you hold is rubbish.'

'You don't know that. It's obvious from how hurt and angry you and Mum are that you both care. There is still love between you, and where there is love, there is hope.'

Margot shakes her head.

'You won't even try?'

Margot still won't look at her. 'I get it, Lucy.'

Lucy lets out a groan of frustration. 'No. You don't.'

'What?' Margot raises her head, a look of anger flashing across her face. 'You think being the blushing bride this weekend gives you the right to do whatever you want? You think that having the perfect life, a great job, the ideal relationship, means you get to say whatever you want? You get to make your demands and trample over the rest of us?'

'It's not perfect, Margot. Nothing is. And no. I don't think that. The only person who trampled over anything is you, Margot. I'm the only one in this family prepared to tell you how it is. What you did to Mum was awful. We all think so. There isn't a teenage temper tantrum in the world that could justify it.'

Eve puts a hand on Lucy's arm. 'Lucy, I know you're all for straight-talking, but I don't think now is the time—'

'If not now, then when?' She turns to Eve in frustration. 'Now *is* the time, don't you see? Now is all we have. We've spent far too long tiptoeing around each other. I think Margot needs to know—'

'She knows, Lucy.' Eve gestures to where Margot stands. 'Look, she knows.'

Lucy turns back to Margot and sees her standing crumpled in on herself. She is bent over with her face in her hands, her shoulders shaking.

'Margot?'

She doesn't answer.

'Margot? Are you—?'

But before she can say anything else, Margot has spun on her heel and fled the marquee.

Eve throws Lucy a worried look. 'Well done, Luce.'

Lucy sighs and throws her hands up. 'Somebody had

to say it.' She stares after Margot, at the light falling through the opening of the tent, wishing she could shine a light on the secrets her sister seems hell-bent on keeping. 'What do you think she meant?' she asks, turning back to Eve. 'The *real truth*? What was she talking about? What didn't we see?'

Eve stares at Lucy for a long moment. 'I have no idea.'

THE PAST

2009

19

The day Ted moved out of Windfalls happened to be the same day Margot auditioned for a part in the school production of *Romeo and Juliet*. There had been more student interest than usual in the casting of the play, thanks to the arrival of Mr Hudson, an enthusiastic new drama teacher who had joined the faculty and was proving popular with the pupils.

The line for auditions had snaked through the school corridor but Margot, just shy of sixteen, thought she would try out. She was taking Drama GCSE and hoped she might continue on to theatre college, if her results proved good enough. Her audition, Juliet's balcony monologue, was delivered to Mr Hudson and two self-important sixth-formers who had sat blank-faced at a table and, rather frustratingly, given nothing away. Margot was still replaying the speech in her head, trying to gauge how she might have been received, as she returned home to find Ted dragging two suitcases out to his car. 'What's going on?'

Kit appeared at the back door, her arms folded across her chest. 'Your father's leaving.'

Margot looked from Kit's tight frown to Ted's resigned face. Her father gave a small nod and Margot felt something heavy drop in the pit of her stomach.

'I'm sorry, Margot. It's better this way,' Ted said. 'I'm not going far. I'll still see you all the time.'

It was happening. That woman – the one they had all pretended he wasn't carrying on with – was taking him away.

'Your mother and I—'

Kit didn't allow him to finish his sentence. 'Your father, at long last, has tired of sponging off me and my "shoddy bestsellers". Now that you girls are grown up and his star is on the rise again, he doesn't need us any more. He's shacking up with *that tart*, across the valley.'

'I'm sorry,' Ted said, ignoring Kit's barb and turning back to Margot. 'I thought we might be able to live like this but it's damaging all of us. I've found someone who makes me happy.'

'We don't make you happy?' Margot frowned at him.

Ted shook his head. 'It's not like that, darling. Of course you make me happy. I'm your father. I'll always love you.'

'But you're choosing *her*?'

'Yes,' spat Kit. 'He's choosing her.'

'Kit!' said Ted, sharply. 'That's not fair.'

'Not fair? Not fair?' her mother screeched. 'Do you want to know what's not fair? It's not fair to live with a man who has spent the last four years carrying on with another woman, turning a blind eye in the hope that he would one day realise what was waiting for him at home. I never placed any demands on you. I never asked for a ring. I never asked for *anything*. I gave you your freedom. And it still wasn't enough.'

'Spin it any way you like, Kit, but we both know this is no way to live. Our relationship died years ago. Sibella *sees* me. She supports me, emotionally, in a way you long ago stopped doing. I should have left years ago.'

'What about the "support" I gave you, all those years when you weren't working? When I was having babies and writing books and doing everything I possibly could to allow you to reach your "creative potential"?'

Ted's face flushed an indignant red. 'Artistic impulse isn't something that can be turned on and off, Kit. I could have chosen an easier route, but I'm striving for more than commercial gain, something more than obvious cliché.'

'Cliché?' Kit reached down and seized the nearest object to hand. He ducked, just in time, as the muddy wellington boot flew past him and landed on the bonnet of his car.

'Kit, stop,' said Ted. 'I want to be with Sibella. I love her. I'm going to marry her.'

Kit grabbed another boot and hurled it at Ted. 'Marriage? You fucking bastard. After all these years—'

Margot couldn't bear to witness any more. She left them, blocking out the shouts and thumps as more shoes followed in quick succession. She headed into the house, dragging her school satchel up to her room and flopped onto her bed where she turned her face to the wall.

Now you girls are grown up. Her mother's words echoed in her ears. *Was* she grown-up? She'd been having periods for a couple of inconvenient years, and her breasts, though disappointingly small, had definitely grown. They'd had the sex talk at school and she'd heard the whispers and giggles from some of the girls about Tanya and Darren going *all the way* at a house party last month. But Margot hadn't even kissed anyone. She'd tried to imagine what it might feel like. She'd watched from the shadows at a summer disco as a group of her friends had played spin the bottle, girls strutting confidently across the circle to plant long, open-mouthed kisses on some of the boys from their year. But to Margot it was all a little unappealing – frightening, even – and somehow tied to that sense of discomfort and shame she had felt when she'd first realised her mother's books were judged by some as little more than 'smut'.

She had read one last year. She'd stolen a paperback edition of *The Dreamcatcher*, the third of the Tora Ravenstone books, from the shelves now lining the walls of her mother's riverside studio and had raced through it in three late-night clandestine readings over Christmas; no mean feat given the hefty size of the book. She had found it extraordinary: a whole, fantastical world peopled with imaginary characters that had sprung from *her* mother's head. She had loved the heroine – her courage, her spirit, her drive to do the right thing in a world ruled by outlaws and violence – and had been drawn into the quest. And then the dashing, misunderstood warrior Aeron had arrived on the scene, Tora's great love, and Margot had understood why her friends would smirk whenever her mother came up in conversation, and why copies of the book were stowed away in school backpacks and passed furtively from pupil to pupil.

What those characters *did* to each other! It was an education in itself. Margot couldn't stop reading, turning the pages with increasing speed, feeling an uncomfortable mix of shock and interest and strange twinges of warmth spreading through her as she read on and on late into the night.

The morning after she'd finished the novel, she'd sat studying her mother over breakfast. The reading experience – the sheer excitement of the story and the appeal of Tora – still remained, but were now mingled with a new and complicated understanding. Her mother had written those scenes. They had come from her mind.

'What is it?' Kit had asked her, looking up from her coffee. 'Why are you staring at me like that?'

Margot had considered her words carefully. It would have been easier not to say anything, but she'd suddenly found herself blurting out, 'I read one of your books.'

'Oh yes?' Kit had smiled. 'Which one? Did you enjoy it?'

'The third.' She'd hesitated. 'The one with Aeron.' She'd blushed as one of the more heated scenes between Tora and her lover returned unbidden in her mind.

Kit had nodded, her smile widening. 'What did you think?'

'It was, well . . .' she struggled to find the words, '. . . kind of *rude*.'

Kit's laughter had erupted like Coke fizzing from a shaken can. 'Yes, my darling,' she'd said, as soon as she'd composed herself. 'I suppose it must have seemed a little *colourful*.' She'd eyed Margot keenly. 'You know, it's natural to feel curious about these things at your age, and to feel a little self-conscious too. Your body is changing. Hormones are raging. It can be a confusing time.'

Margot shook her head. 'No,' she'd said firmly. 'I'm not confused. I just think it's . . . gross.'

'Well, I doubt you'll feel that way for long. You're growing up fast. It's normal to be interested in the opposite sex, to be curious about your body, about masturbation and—'

'Mum!'

'Margot, it's only natural. Your body is something I hope you will learn to feel proud of, to enjoy. Sex can be a beautiful, transformative thing. All I ask is that you respect yourself, and take precautions. But fancying boys – or girls –desiring sex . . . it's nothing to be ashamed of. It's part of your biology.'

Margot hadn't been able to meet her mum's gaze. Her cheeks had flushed bright red. 'This is too embarrassing. Stop, please.'

Kit had thrown up her hands with another laugh. 'Fine! But I bet one day you'll look back at this conversation and realise I was right. At least, I very much hope you do. Sex between two people who love each other is a gift to cherish.'

Margot had shaken her head and pushed her chair back from the table. 'I think I can hear Lucy calling.' She hadn't been able to leave the kitchen fast enough.

Margot sighed. Outside, she could hear low thrum of her father's car engine starting, audible over the sound of her mother's shouts. Why was he doing this? He had said that Sibella *saw* him. She didn't like to think of her dad with Sibella, but his words had hit home. What she wanted to do was stomp back outside and ask her parents 'who sees me?' For at that moment, she had never felt more invisible in her life and lying there on her bed, she felt a very long way from what she'd ever imagined 'grown-up' would be like.

It was a quiet and hellishly slow weekend. A removals van arrived the following morning and two men, supervised by a grim-faced Ted, came and whisked clothes, books and Ted's large oak desk from the house. Spaces opened up at Windfalls – gaps both physical and emotional – that her father and his belongings had previously occupied. The voids hurt. Margot tried to avoid them, spending the weekend tactfully revolving around a quietly distraught Kit.

It was a relief to escape back to school on the Monday morning and her mood improved greatly when Mr Hudson announced the cast list as the bell rang to end the day. 'Well done,' he said, handing Margot a script. 'There's a lot of work ahead, but I'm excited to see what you can do ... Juliet.'

Margot couldn't believe it. She walked home from the school bus stop glowing with pride, the emptiness awaiting her at home forgotten for a short while, until she entered the back door and saw all over again the absence of coats on the once over-burdened pegs. And by the back door now, just her own muddy boots and a moth-eaten pair of her mother's velvet slippers. She placed her school shoes next to the slippers before going to the fridge and pouring herself a glass of milk. Cheers, she toasted herself. Her mother would be writing in the studio, lost in her private world. No point attempting to share her good news. Instead, Margot pulled the script from her school satchel and found a patch of sunshine to curl up in the drawing room as she began to mark her lines on the script with a yellow highlighter.

Lucy congratulated her on the phone that night. 'I knew you'd get a good part. You're a natural. How's things at home?'

'Quiet.'

'I'm sorry. Is it strange without Dad?'

'Yes, but in some ways it's better than the constant rowing. Mum's in denial, burying herself away down in the studio.'

'She's still deep in the final book?'

'Yes, working all hours.'

'I'm sorry. It must feel lonely. Why don't we meet in Bath after school tomorrow?' Lucy suggested. 'I'm almost finished packing. I should have a relatively clear day before I fly out. We could go shopping. I'll buy you a hot chocolate, shout you a cake at that cafe you like.'

'I can't. First rehearsal's tomorrow.'

'Well, that's good,' she said encouragingly. 'That will keep you busy. How's Romeo? Is he hot?'

Margot laughed. 'No. Jamie Kingston is three inches shorter than me and has terrible acne. The new drama teacher seems nice, though. He's not like the other teachers,' she added, by way of explanation. 'He seems to like the students, for starters.' It helped, Margot thought, that he was at least fifteen years younger than the rest of the faculty. His classes were fun and full of energy and he always seemed interested in his students' opinions.

His more modern reimagining of the Shakespeare play had got the whole cast fired up.

'Great,' said Lucy. 'A good teacher can make all the difference. Who knows, I might have passed my exams if I'd had some good ones. Look, Margot, I know it's tough for you stuck there with Mum, and her so busy with the book, but keep your head down, work hard, throw yourself into the play and I'll be back from Kerala before you know it. The yoga course is only three months. And you've still got Eve, right?'

'Mmmm,' said Margot. They both knew that Eve had disappeared into a vacuum, setting up home with Andrew and looking after their new baby daughter.

'It will be OK. I promise.'

Margot hadn't answered, afraid that if she spoke, the only words that would leave her mouth would be a plaintive, 'Don't go. Don't leave me.'

In the coming weeks, Margot immersed herself to some extent in her schoolwork and, more wholeheartedly, in the play. She found it easier to ignore the gaping holes at home – the crushing loneliness, the boredom – when she was learning her lines and rehearsing scenes. She filled the void with the camaraderie of the cast and the kindness of Mr Hudson.

'Think about the words, Margot,' Mr Hudson coached her at one of their after-school rehearsals. 'Think about their meaning. Try to feel what Juliet is feeling. She's young and in love for the first time. There's an innocence to her, yes, but also an exuberance. I want you to try to convince us, the audience, of her love, her longing.' Mr

Hudson spoke with such passion, his green eyes sparkling as he enthused over the script.

Margot looked over at her Romeo – Jamie Kingston busy stamping on an empty juice carton with his friends, kicking it into an imaginary goal. She wanted to please Mr Hudson, but convincing a room full of people of her love for Jamie was going to be a stretch. He was annoyingly unfocused in rehearsals and hadn't bothered to learn any of his lines yet.

'I know it's not easy when some of the other cast members aren't taking the play as seriously,' the teacher had added, following her gaze, 'but I see something special in you. You have talent, Margot. You deserve this part.'

Margot nodded and wished her cheeks wouldn't blush quite so furiously.

Midway through the term, Ted issued a tentative invitation for Margot to join them for tea at Sibella's house after school. Margot wasn't keen, but her father had pleaded with her to give Sibella a chance, and of course, if she went, she could ask him face-to-face to come to her play.

It was an awkward encounter. She felt traitorous walking up the lane to the house and realised as soon as she stepped into the kitchen that she didn't want to know about her father's new life. It was easier to block it from her mind than picture him with a new woman in this strange, cluttered cottage perched on the far side of the village. Margot didn't want to sit at Sibella's table, eat her food and play happy families with them both when she knew that across the valley, her mother sat alone at her desk, the rooms of Windfalls echoing with absence.

'I'm vegetarian,' she said, eyeing the plate of shepherd's pie and vegetables Sibella had placed in front of her.

'Oh,' Sibella said, her cheeks flushing red. 'I'm sorry. I didn't know.'

'Since when?' asked Ted, looking at her in surprise.

'Since you left.' She held his gaze, daring him to be the first to look away.

Ted nodded, understanding dawning. 'Fine. I'll make you some toast.'

'Oh, we can do better than toast,' Sibella said quickly. 'I'll rustle up something else.'

'No. Toast is fine,' said Ted, sharply.

Margot shrugged, smarting a little at her father's obvious anger. Why was he taking *her* side? How could he know she was lying? For all either of them knew about her these days, she *could* have turned vegetarian.

The stilted conversation continued as Margot told her father about the play. 'Tickets go on sale next week. Will you come?'

'I'm sorry, darling. If I'd known sooner I might have been able to make arrangements, but I'll be up in London that week for castings. Nigel wants me at the auditions. It's all gathering pace at a rather exciting rate.'

Margot sank down in her chair. Of course her father's new play was more important than a silly school production, but it still felt like another rejection.

Sibella cleared her throat. 'I could come?' she suggested. 'I mean, I could . . . if you'd like me to?'

Margot shook her head. 'No. It's OK. Mum will be there. I think it's best you don't.'

223

'Oh. Of course,' said Sibella, and Margot took a small amount of satisfaction to see her cheeks flush bright red.

They were all relieved when Margot pushed her chair back from the table and made her excuses to leave.

Two weeks before the production on an overcast Saturday afternoon, Mr Hudson invited the whole cast to his house to watch the Baz Luhrmann adaptation of *Romeo and Juliet*. He let them into his modern townhouse in one of the new cul-de-sacs on the edge of town, a tidy sandstone house with a black front door and a red Ford Focus parked in the drive. Mrs Hudson, his pretty wife, her belly huge with the late stages of pregnancy, buzzed around in the background offering biscuits, squash and cups of tea as they all squeezed into the lounge, perching on sofas and sprawling on cushions on the floor. It had been a fun afternoon, until the scene where Claire Danes and Leonardo DiCaprio kissed in the lift at the Capulet's masked ball. Margot had felt her face flush as the whole cast laughed and jeered. She glanced across at Jamie, who wore an equally pained expression. Would they be expected to kiss like that?

After the movie, as the rest of the cast trooped down the drive, Mr Hudson called her back. 'I saw your face earlier. You needn't worry or feel embarrassed. There's plenty of time to go over the balcony scene. Have you and Jamie found a moment yet?'

She shook her head. 'He's been busy with football practice and . . . er . . . homework.' She blushed. 'Or maybe he doesn't want to kiss me,' she added, trying to make a joke out of it.

'Rubbish. You're a pretty girl. What teenage boy wouldn't want to kiss you?'

Margot blushed and buried her hands deep into her pockets.

Mr Hudson leaned closer, smiling kindly. 'Have you kissed anyone before?' he asked, his voice low.

It was as if he could read her mind. She shook her head, embarrassed.

'You're worried?'

A nervous giggle escaped her lips. 'Of course. I have to kiss Jamie onstage in front of the school. In front of my *family*.'

'You don't like Jamie?'

'I like him, I'm just not sure I want to *kiss* him.'

'What you need to remember is that it's not Margot kissing Jamie, is it? It's Juliet, kissing Romeo.'

'Yeah. I know.' She knew what he was trying to say, but she also knew that it was her – Margot's – lips touching Jamie Kingston's . . . in front of the whole school. It didn't matter what Mr Hudson said. Everyone knew that.

Mr Hudson smiled again. 'Put yourself into the character of Juliet. She's a girl blossoming into a young woman, feeling all the powerful emotion of first love. Or perhaps you just need a little practice. Take the pressure off. Disassociate.'

She let out that high laugh again. 'My friend, Amy, says you can practise on your hand. She told me to make a fist and kiss the curled-up thumb and forefinger.' As soon as she said it out loud she felt embarrassed.

But Mr Hudson didn't laugh. Instead he made a fist with his hand. 'Like this?'

She nodded. 'Stupid, right?'

Mr Hudson shrugged. 'Then move not, while my

prayer's effect I take,' he quoted. Before she understood what he was doing, Mr Hudson pressed his curled hand to her mouth. Her lips brushed against his warm skin. She froze, then turned her face away and blushed an even deeper red.

He laughed. 'Oh Margot, you're a sweet kid.'

'I'm not a kid,' she said quickly, mortified.

'No, of course you're not.' He squeezed her arm. 'Sorry. Sweet sixteen.'

'Almost sixteen,' she corrected.

'Do you know how old Shakespeare's Juliet is?'

Margot shook her head.

'Thirteen.'

'Oh.' Margot's eyes widened. 'Wow.' She didn't know whether to be shocked or embarrassed. If Juliet, at thirteen, could fall in love and marry Romeo, she must be a real prude to not want to kiss Jamie Kingston.

'Yes.' Mr Hudson nodded. 'Society today would consider her a child still, but Shakespeare understood. He saw a girl on the cusp of womanhood.'

She didn't know what to say. This was all new terrain for her, talking about love and kissing with a teacher. She was so inexperienced. She worried Mr Hudson would regret casting her as Juliet. Margot glanced away down the drive. Everyone had left. She'd be walking home on her own.

'It's all about trust. As a cast and crew, we have to build it between each other. We have to work to make each other feel comfortable, to break down our barriers. A few more rehearsals with Jamie and I'm sure you won't be feeling so nervous.' He hesitated. 'You want my advice?' he asked, after a moment.

226

She nodded, hoping he was about to tell her that there was no reason for her to kiss Jamie Kingston, not if she didn't want to.

'If Jamie isn't your idea of Romeo, close your eyes and think about kissing someone you do like.' He smiled. 'Is there someone?'

Margot shook her head. 'I... er... no. I don't think so. I'll have to think.'

He smiled again. 'You're lovely. Don't worry, Margot. You're going to make a wonderful Juliet.'

She thought of all the other students in the play who would have been better for the role. 'Perhaps someone else—'

'No,' he said firmly. 'We'll have none of that self-doubt. You're perfect for the role. We need to work on building up your confidence.'

Margot walked away down the cul-de-sac moments later feeling a little lighter. *A wonderful Juliet.*

She held his words close all evening and replayed them in her head in bed later that night. *You're perfect.* Mr Hudson thought she was perfect for the role. She pressed her closed fist to her lips and tried to imagine kissing someone. In the dark, Jamie Kingston's face dissolved and was replaced with another. A man with green eyes and a head of dark curly hair. She smiled. Of course, he meant her acting, but still... no one had ever called her lovely before.

Two weeks later, standing offstage, hidden in the wings, Margot peered out at the gathering audience. She scanned the rows of faces and found Eve on the aisle of the third row from the back, bouncing baby Chloe on her lap. There was an empty seat next to her, but no sign of their mother. Yet.

'Two minutes till curtain up,' called Mr Hudson. Margot took a deep breath and shared a nervous smile with Jamie. The teacher stood beside them both. 'Now remember, the most important thing is . . .'

'. . . to enjoy ourselves,' they chanted in unison.

He laughed. 'I've taught you well.' He reached over and adjusted the strap of Margot's white gauze dress. 'Your bra strap is peeking out,' he whispered, and gave her shoulder a squeeze. Margot felt a shiver pass through her, her skin tingling where his fingers had brushed her shoulder. An image of his warm fist pressed against her lips rose in her mind. She had thought of that moment, alone in her bedroom, perhaps more times than a pupil should strictly think of a teacher, imagining once or twice her lips meeting not his hand, but his lips.

'Break a leg, Margot,' Jamie said, smiling at her.

'You too.' She peered out once more at the audience but the lights had dimmed and all she could see were dark figures, waiting expectantly for the curtain to rise.

Halfway through the second act, as Friar Laurence laboured through a painful monologue, the unmistakeable sound of a baby's piercing wail erupted from the audience. Margot peered round the stage curtain. She could just make out Eve standing and whispering her apologies as she snuck out of the fire exit, the sound of Chloe's cries disappearing behind the heavy thump of the closing door. Margot tried not to mind too much. Perhaps she'd make it back in time to catch the next act.

Perhaps her mother had crept in at the last minute and was sitting there too, hidden somewhere in the darkness.

At the final curtain call, Margot quickly scanned the faces in the audience. Eve's seat was still empty and there was no sign of her mother, not in any of the rows. Margot bit her lip and tried to smile as she took a final bow. All that hard work and not one member of her family had seen her performance. As soon as the curtain had been drawn across the stage, Margot fled. 'What's up with her?' she heard someone ask as she pushed past the cast and crew.

It was Jamie who found her in the makeshift dressing room, removing her make-up with a blend of Vaseline and tears. 'Are you OK?'

She nodded. 'I don't want to talk about it.'

He sat down beside her. 'You were good, you know. By far the best of all of us.'

'Thanks.'

'I hope you're coming to the after-party?'

'I don't know.' She stared at her reflection in the mirror, the eyeliner smudged down her cheeks. 'I don't feel like it.'

'You have to come,' said Jamie. 'It wouldn't be the same without you. Besides,' he added, lowering his voice, 'Riley's nicked a keg of cider from his dad's shed. Mr Hudson's so cool, he's pretending he doesn't know anything about it. Come on, it'll be fun.'

Margot stared again at her face in the mirror. She could either stay for the party, or go home, and she knew what waited for her there. Absolutely nothing.

Back in the school hall, the kids had cleared away the rows of chairs and set up a trestle table with drinks and bowls of snacks. Someone passed Margot a plastic cup. Beyoncé blared from a nearby speaker. She took a sip and tasted a strong kick of alcohol lacing the tropical fruit punch. Jamie winked at her. 'Strong, right?'

Margot downed the drink in one go and reached for another. Soon, she had forgotten her disappointment. She sipped the cups of punch that were passed to her and let Jamie drag her up onto the makeshift dance floor with the rest of the cast until the school caretaker appeared at ten o'clock, threatening to lock them all in if they didn't leave.

'Where next?' asked a tall boy from the lower sixth.

Some of the sixth formers wanted to decamp to the pub, but the sensible ones among them knew a large group of underage school kids would never get served.

'You can all come back to mine,' said Margot.

'Won't your parents mind?'

Margot shrugged. 'It's just my mum, and I doubt it. She's probably working.'

'You come too, Mr Hudson,' cried a couple of students. 'Come on!'

'Yes,' said Margot, gripped by a sudden desperation for the night to continue a little longer, for the emptiness of the days ahead – the vacuum that finishing the play would create – to remain at bay for a little longer. She turned and gave him her brightest smile. 'Come on, Mr Hudson. Everyone back to mine.'

Mr Hudson threw up his hands up and smiled. 'You lot are too persuasive. OK,' he said. 'For a little while. Someone needs to chaperone you lot.'

They ended up as a crowd of about twelve or so, a motley crew of those with an extended curfew, and those still standing after the spiked punch. Margot squashed into a sixth-former's car and directed them to Windfalls. They parked at the top of the drive then followed Margot down on foot towards the house.

As they rounded the corner and saw the house ahead, Margot's heart sank. Contrary to what she'd assumed, Kit wasn't working late in the studio. There were lights on in the house, the shadow of her mother moving behind the drawn blind of the kitchen window.

'It doesn't matter,' she said quickly. 'We'll go down to the river.'

'Are you sure, Margot?' Mr Hudson frowned. 'Maybe we should call it a night. I don't want to upset your parents.'

'No!' she said urgently. 'It's fine. Mum won't care. It's perfect. Down there we can be as loud as we want.'

She led the way, weaving through the orchard, stumbling a little on the uneven ground. Trees loomed out of the darkness, their edges strangely blurred, the stars overhead fizzing in the sky. Jamie, sloping down the hillside beside her, caught her arm as she tripped on an unseen tree root, steadying her. 'OK?' he asked, taking her hand and squeezing her fingers.

When Jamie didn't let go, she pulled her hand gently from his. 'I'm fine,' she said, not entirely sure why she felt self-conscious in front of the others, but knowing that she didn't want anyone getting the wrong idea, least of all Jamie.

Sensing rejection, Jamie hunched his shoulders and slunk ahead into the dark.

Someone else tripped and cursed. There was a loud burst of laughter, followed by hurried shushing. Up ahead, she could make out the dark glint of the river. Margot felt a sudden tremor of panic. It had been her idea to bring them all here, but outside, in the darkness, her head swimming and with only the moonlight to guide them, the night seemed to have taken on a new momentum, a furtive sort of atmosphere, as though the normal rules no longer existed. So what, she told herself. There was no one to care what she got up to. Besides, Mr Hudson was with them. He would make sure things didn't get too out of hand.

She turned to check and saw him a few steps behind, talking easily with a couple of the sixth formers, laughing at something one of the girls said. A twinge of jealousy caught in her belly. She wanted to be the one walking next to him. She wanted to be the one to make him laugh. She wanted to feel the glow of his admiration for just a little longer. Raising his head, he caught her looking and smiled. 'All right, Juliet?' he asked.

She nodded and smiled, turning her face back to the river.

As the rest of the cast made for the jetty, Margot groped her way to her mother's studio where she flicked an outside switch on the old apple store wall, illuminating a string of bulbs hanging from trees along the riverbank and across the jetty. The lights were met with enthusiastic cheers, though the sight of them swaying in the dark made her feel even more unsteady, as though she were standing on a rolling ship. A large grey moth ghosted out of the darkness, batting against one of the bulbs. There was the sound of cans of beer fizzing open, the clunk of glass bottles rolling on the wooden jetty.

Laughter and a few cheers. Something fell into the water with a splash.

'So this is where the magic happens?' The voice made her leap. She spun round to find Mr Hudson leaning against the studio wall, his white teeth shining in the light from the bulbs. 'Where your mother writes,' he added. 'What a great spot.'

Margot smiled, feeling a small thrill at his approval. 'Yes, this is her studio.'

'Will you show me?'

'I think it's locked,' she said but when she tried the door handle, it turned easily, the door opening into darkness.

'A peek?' He grinned. 'I'd love to see where the famous K. T. Weaver comes up with her ideas.'

Margot shrugged. It was her mum's boring office, but it was Mr Hudson and she didn't want to disappoint him.

It was darker inside, the light from the moon and the swaying bulbs not quite reaching the studio interior. It took Margot a moment for her eyes to adjust. Scents of incense, paper and her mother's familiar floral perfume hung like an afterthought in the air. She reached to switch on the desk lamp.

'Don't,' said Mr Hudson. 'They'll all come. You don't want that rabble in here, messing up your mum's special place.'

He was right. She didn't want anyone else to come. There was something exhilarating about having Mr Hudson all to herself. In his company, she felt as if a warm spotlight had fallen upon her. She didn't want to share it with anyone else.

'So this is it,' she said, indicating the desk with a stack of typed white paper fanned across the surface, a rose-coloured crystal paperweight, the mug of pens, the framed photo, too dark to see though Margot knew it held an image taken years ago of her, Eve and Lucy balanced as a precarious, smiling trio on the garden swing. The office wasn't that special. She hoped he wouldn't find it too disappointing.

Mr Hudson moved towards the desk and lifted one of the typed pages, peering at the words. 'The last novel?'

Margot nodded. Her words appeared to be stuck in her throat. She was alone with Mr Hudson in a dark room and with the quietness and the close proximity of him, all that came to mind were those moments she had imagined in the stillness of her bedroom. Thank goodness he couldn't read her thoughts.

He studied a couple of lines of text, before turning to her with a wink. 'Pretty racy stuff, hey?'

Margot wanted to sink into the floor.

He placed the paper back on the desk. 'Do you like your mum's books?'

Margot shrugged. 'I don't know. They're all right.'

'I bet you've learned a lot from them.'

Margot shook her head. She couldn't feel more embarrassed than the thought of Mr Hudson reading her mum's racy sex scenes. 'Not my thing.'

She licked her lips, her mouth suddenly dry. She had imagined being alone with him before now, but somehow in her fantasies it never felt like this. It had been a different Mr Hudson, an imagined man, a cardboard cut-out character she had always been in control of, not this unpredictable living, breathing person standing in front of her.

'You did well tonight,' he said. He was so close she could feel his arm brush against her own.

'Thank you.'

'Especially the balcony scene. I know you were nervous about it, but you couldn't tell. It was very moving.'

'Thanks,' she said again. She took a step backwards, feeling the desk pressing into her legs.

He picked up the crystal and turned it over in his hands. 'So did you like kissing Jamie?' he asked, not quite meeting her eye.

Margot let out a small, embarrassed laugh. 'No.'

'Did you take my advice? Did you think about someone else?'

Margot nodded, her breath caught in her throat.

He returned the paperweight to the desk. 'Who did you think about, Margot?'

Margot wasn't sure if it was the darkness or the punch or the unfamiliarity of being alone with him that had her swaying slightly. Should she tell him? He would think her so silly. 'I thought about . . .' She knew she shouldn't say it, but the burning anger earlier at her mother's no-show and the cider fizzing through her bloodstream made her feel bold, somehow devil-may-care. The room felt cast in a strangely intimate air and the thrill of his closeness felt mixed with fear, that racing feeling of everything moving too fast, too much beyond her control. He loomed in front of her. She was afraid that he might kiss her; she was afraid that he might not. She looked down at the desk, at the stack of typed pages fanned neatly across its surface, and remembered her mother's heroine. Memories of the book she had read last Christmas returned. She should be more like Tora, she thought. She should be a little bolder, a little more courageous, a little more grown-up. *It's nothing to be ashamed of. It's part of our biology.* Her mother's words echoed back at her. Margot opened her mouth. 'I thought about . . . you.'

The final word escaped in a whisper, so quiet she wasn't even sure he'd heard her. She blushed, grateful for the cover of darkness, and looked down, unable to meet his gaze, surprised to feel his hand reaching for hers.

'Oh, Margot.' He squeezed her fingers and Margot, looking up to meet his gaze and seeing his smile, realised he wasn't laughing at her. 'From my lips, by thine, my sin is purged,' he said, quoting Romeo's line.

Before she even knew what was happening, he leaned down and kissed her. Margot, with her lips pressed against his, froze, her eyes wide, staring up at him. Was this happening? Was she kissing Mr Hudson? The moment she had thought about so many times – that confusing, stomach-churning fantasy she had entertained in the privacy of her bedroom and written about secretly in her diary – was actually happening?

It didn't feel at all how she had imagined. His mouth felt firmer than Jamie's, his skin rougher, his kiss less soft, less tentative. She could feel the stubble on his chin rasping against her cheek in a way that wasn't altogether pleasant and she could taste the sickly sweet punch on his tongue. It felt exciting . . . and somehow all wrong.

She leaned away, trying to catch her breath and focus

on his face, smiling with embarrassment. 'Sorry,' she said. 'I shouldn't have said that.'

'Don't be embarrassed.' He pulled her into a hug. Her face was squashed against the buttons on his shirt, beneath which she could feel the beat of his heart. 'Uh . . . should we go back?' she asked, glancing at the door.

He didn't answer. Instead, he drew her more tightly into him. She let him hold her, though it felt awkward, her face pressed against his chest and the weight of his head pressing down on hers. There was the faintest scent of sweat rising off his shirt. 'Oh Margot. You're like a flower, ready to bloom.'

She wanted to laugh but he was reaching and tilting her chin, moving her face so that he could kiss her again, his lips pressing hard against her own, his tongue moving between her lips.

Kiss him, she told herself. Don't be a baby. Don't make a fuss. But as his fingers crept up to her breasts, his thumbs rubbing her nipples through her T-shirt, Margot jerked away. She covered herself, horribly embarrassed. 'I don't think we should.'

'Don't hide yourself. You're beautiful. Do you remember what I said? It's about trust, isn't it? Breaking down barriers. You trust me, don't you?'

She nodded. From outside, the sound of laughter burst up from the riverbank. 'I think we should go back,' she said again.

He frowned, his eyes glinting in the darkness. 'But I thought you liked me? I thought you *wanted* to kiss me?'

She nodded and tried to smile. 'I do. I did.' She was going to add that she did like him, but she knew that kissing him was wrong and could get them both in a lot of trouble, but before she could speak, his mouth was pressed over hers again, his tongue pushing insistently into her mouth and then he was taking her hand and rubbing it across the front of his trousers where a hardness rose up against her palm. 'See how much I like you, Margot? See what you do to me?' And then his own hand was between her legs and he was touching her – too hard – making her squirm. 'You like that?'

'Don't,' she said, pushing his hand away. 'I don't want to do that.' There was a lump building at the back of her throat. Don't cry, she told herself. It was Mr Hudson. Her teacher. Her friend.

'How can you know what you want if you've never done it before? I thought you trusted me? If you're going to be a good actress, you're going to have to learn how to let yourself go, Margot.'

'I know. It's just...' She didn't know what to say to ease this strange atmosphere that had arisen between them.

'Good. Because I'd hate to think you were a tease. You know, one of those little girls who gets a man all worked up and then sends him away. No one likes those girls, Margot. I thought you were more mature than that.'

'No!' She laughed, a strange, high-pitched sound. 'I'm not like that.' She tried to push him away again, playfully, as if it were all a big joke. Because surely that's what it was? A joke. But Mr Hudson stood firm, holding her trapped between his legs, with her back jammed against her mother's desk and as the moonlight shifted from behind a cloud, she saw his face again, staring intently at her and shivered. It was Mr Hudson, she reminded herself. There was nothing to be frightened of. It was a misunderstanding. She had wanted... wanted... what had she wanted? His attention? To be alone with him? To be praised and called beautiful again? Yes, maybe even to be kissed?

Only now that they were there together, in the dark, she wasn't sure. Mr Hudson – her teacher and friend – didn't feel like Mr Hudson any more. He was like a stranger. His mouth so insistent and his hands grabbing at her in a way that made her feel afraid, his leg nudging between hers. She had drunk too much and her head was spinning. She couldn't think straight. She could try to push past him, but she didn't want to be rude.

'Tell me what you want, Margot,' he said, his hands on her waist, sneaking up under her T-shirt. 'Tell me what you think about. I've read your mother's books. You must know the expression: the apple doesn't fall far from the tree? Tell me what you think about, when you're alone.'

It was almost as if he could read her thoughts, those silly moments when she had imagined kissing him. She didn't want to share that with him. 'I want to go back to the others,' she said. She didn't want to offend him, not when he had been so kind to her – but all she wanted was to be back outside, laughing and joking around by the river.

'We will,' he said. 'But not yet.' He leaned in again, pushing her hard against the desk, grinding against her. The cider on his breath reminded her of the apples falling to waste in the long grass of Windfalls' orchard, rotting and fermenting on the hillside. In her growing panic, the scent seemed to seep up off the floor and ooze from the walls of the old apple store, sickly and cloying. It made her want to gag.

'The others will wonder where we are,' she said, turning her head, her hands on his chest, pushing him, willing him to step away and release her.

'I *said* not yet.' He wasn't smiling, teasing Mr Hudson any more, but a dark, looming figure pulling her ponytail, a little too hard, so that her scalp sang and her head tilted back, exposing her neck to his mouth. She moaned – not in pleasure but in fear – her body arching away from his.

'You like that, do you?' He was breathing hard now, his hands on her belt buckle.

'No. Please—' she said, but the word 'stop' was lost as his mouth covered hers again. He tugged roughly at her jeans and then spun her around, one hand at his own belt, the other pressing her face down onto the desk.

'Don't,' she said, her voice high and scared, but he didn't listen; instead, he forced her legs apart with a knee, spreading her across the desk like the white pages of paper her face was now pressed against. His hand gripped her shoulder, his thumb pressing into the soft curve of her neck.

Margot choked back a scream. Searing pain ripped into her like grinding broken glass. She could hear the others on the jetty still, their chatter and laughter but the thought of any of them stumbling in and seeing this – seeing Mr Hudson doing what he was doing to her – was too much. She clamped her mouth shut, willing it to be over. She wanted to stop this thing she had started with her silly smiles and her thoughts of kissing. But Mr Hudson wasn't stopping. 'Why are you doing this?' she sobbed through the tears that had begun to fall.

He'd leaned over her, his mouth beside her ear. 'Because I know you want me to.'

As the paper crumpled under her and the desk juddered, Margot lay pinned beneath his weight. She closed her eyes and tried to block the pain – tried to take herself away from the horror of the moment – as the sickly scent of apples rose up to fill her lungs and outside, the silent river flowed relentlessly on its course.

20

Standing in the living room, Margot can see the marquee through the window, the white fabric billowing ghost-like among the trees. This time tomorrow, Lucy will be married and the house will be filled with the commotion and revelry of family and strangers. For now it is silent, just her, the ticking clock, the cat stretching on the sofa, and her mother hidden somewhere in the house.

Over on the bookshelves, she spots a copy of *The Quartz Heart*, her mother's fifth book in the Rare Elements series. She reaches for it, opening to the first page where a dedication is typed upon the white page.

```
For my girls - the most precious elements
   of all.
Love wildly. Live boldly.
```

As Margot studies the words, emotion rises in her, a sickening, see-sawing tug of love and pride and anguish. *Most precious.* Is she precious? She doesn't feel it. She knows what they all think of her. She knows how they judge her.

And the rest of it: *love wildly, live boldly.* If only it were that simple. She sees the way Lucy throws herself at everything, optimistically, with her heart open and full of hope, but Margot cannot live like that. She tried, and the result was pain and violence. Imprisoned by her experience, she cannot seem to escape the confines of her trauma.

Try as she might, she can't help but feel her wound is somehow linked to her mother's absence, to her mother's words, and to her wafty, liberal attitudes about sex and relationships. Is it any wonder Margot struggles to let people close now? Is it really that strange that any feelings of desire and intimacy she has are laced with a need for punishment? She glances down at the dedication, then shuts the book, returning it to the shelf.

Upstairs, she tries hard to ignore it, but the call of the vodka lying hidden in the bag beneath her bed is impossible to resist. Those unsettling thoughts about her mother and her growing unease about the family dinner ahead, compounded by the fact she hasn't spoken to Lucy since their confrontation in the marquee, have stirred a need in her. Just a little, she tells herself, to calm her frayed nerves and blunt the sharp edges of her anxiety.

She drags the holdall out from beneath the bed and unwraps the bottle from her clothes. The first swig scours the back of her throat, but by the third she is all heat and blissful numbness. She takes another couple of swigs before returning the lid to the bottle and lying back on her bed. That's it. Just enough to take the edge off. She doesn't need any more.

After Lucy's sharp words in the marquee, she had been tempted to get a train straight back to Edinburgh. She'd gone so far as to look up the return train timetables. Screw Lucy and screw her stupid wedding. Screw them all. She had come all this way to be with them. Why couldn't that be enough? Why was Lucy pushing so hard? She doesn't know what she is asking of her.

Margot turns her face and sees the ripped patch of wallpaper beside the bed. It's tempting to work a little more off the wall, but the sound of her phone beeping startles her from her reverie. She unlocks the screen and finds a message from Jonas. A single jpeg attachment. No words.

Confused, she clicks on the thumbnail and watches as the screen fills with a black-and-white photo. She frowns. A face stares back at her. Her own.

She recognises the location. The Edinburgh skyline is visible as a black silhouette behind her. The shot was taken in Jonas's flat. She thinks back, and it comes to her, a day a few months ago when he'd returned home from work with a flashy new camera lens. 'A few portrait shots,' he'd begged. 'So I can test it out. I'll delete them right away, I promise.'

'Fine, but I'm not posing.'

'I don't want you to pose,' he'd said, lifting the camera and taking a photo.

'Wait, I wasn't ready.'

'It's fine. I want you like this. Natural. Candid. Perfectly yourself.'

She'd sat there, feeling self-conscious and stiff, until the repetitive sound of the camera's shutter opening and closing had sent her into an almost meditative state.

'That's it,' he'd said a few minutes later, scrolling back through the frames. 'You were great.'

She hadn't asked to see the images. She had assumed, incorrectly, that he had stuck to his word and erased them from the camera. As she peers at her phone screen, studying the image a little more closely, a second message appears.

'See,' he has written. 'Beautiful.'

She stares again at the photo. She doesn't agree that she looks beautiful, but there is certainly something rather startling about the portrait, if only for the light captured in her eyes and the softness in her face, the way she gazes into the middle distance, her lips slightly parted. It's not how she usually sees herself.

'You said you'd delete them,' she texts back.

'I did. All but one. This one was too lovely to lose.'

Too lovely to lose? She's not sure about that, but the image certainly carries the hallmarks of Jonas's work. There is a candour to the photo, a clarity he has become well known for, that has seen his demand as a photographer rise steadily in recent months. For some reason, she finds herself thinking of the photograph tacked to the fridge in the flat – the shot he took all those years ago of his mother beside a lake in his hometown in Sweden.

'Where are you?' she types, wanting to imagine him, wherever he might be.

'Somewhere near York. En route to my next job.'

'Hope it's a good one,' she replies, confused by the sudden sense of longing she feels to be near him. She throws the phone back onto the bed and, before she can stop herself, reaches again for the bottle standing beside the bed.

Eve is wrestling May into a dress when Andrew calls from the office. 'I'm leaving now,' he says. 'Can we talk when I get home?'

She tucks the phone between her ear and shoulder and pulls the fabric over May's head. May squawks in protest. 'I can't breathe,' she complains from beneath the dress. 'It's too tight.'

'You'll be fine if you stop wriggling.'

'Eve? Are you there?'

'Yes, I'm here. Sorry, getting the girls changed. You haven't forgotten about tonight's dinner, have you?'

'No. That's why I'm leaving early.'

'Good.'

'So, can we talk? When I get back?'

'Yes. Of course.' Eve hesitates. 'Is everything all right? It sounds important.'

'It is. Look, I'll talk to you when I get there, OK?'

'Right.' Eve feels a flutter of anxiety.

'Have the girls ready and I'll be there as soon as I can.'

'OK.'

Andrew rings off and Eve sits for a moment on the

floor in May's bedroom, while her daughter grumbles and tugs at the dress.

It's not like Andrew to sound so . . . intense. What could he possibly want to talk to her about? His job? Their relationship? She sighs. She's been dreading the family meal. It was bad enough that Lucy had stirred tensions with Margot yesterday. Combined with the thought of navigating a dinner with Andrew at her side and Ryan in residence at the pub, she's been feeling nauseous all day. And now Andrew is acting strangely. Could he know? Or could it be something else?

She picks up the second dress by her side. 'Chloe,' she calls. 'Come and get changed, will you?'

'In a minute, Mum,' comes a small voice from downstairs.

'Not in a minute. Now!'

Chloe huffs up the stairs. 'Sheesh, Mum.' Her daughter's eyes fall on the dress in her hands. '*Not* the frilly one.'

'Come on. Do it for me. You look so lovely in this.'

Chloe groans. 'Oh Mum, you're the worst.'

Eve eyes her daughter. 'Yes, Chloe. I am. Now come here.'

Forty-five minutes later and with Andrew still not home, Eve checks the clock in the kitchen. They will need to leave in ten minutes if they are to get to the pub on time. She finds a stick of scarlet lipstick in her handbag and applies it in the hall mirror. She is just wondering if it looks a little *too* red – a little too 'scarlet woman' – when her phone rings again. 'Sorry, love, the traffic's been terrible. I'm five minutes away.'

'Girls, get your shoes on. We need to be ready to leave as soon as Daddy gets here.'

Moments later, Andrew rushes through the door. He pecks her on the cheek. 'I'm sorry. There was an accident on the London Road. I'll change and we'll be off.'

She nods. 'What about that chat? Shall we do it in the car on the way?'

Andrew eyes the girls. 'No. Later.'

Eve watches her husband rush up the stairs, two at a time, and feels a terrible sense of unease. Why does it feel as if everything is about to unravel?

22

'Have you been drinking?' Kit reaches for her arm as they draw close to the pub, her grip surprisingly firm.

Margot stops and turns back. 'What if I have?'

'Oh, Margot.'

'*Oh, Margot* what? What do you think I'm going to do? What are you so terrified of, Mum?' Margot can hear the slight slurring of her words and tries hard to annunciate more clearly. 'I'm here, aren't I?'

'Yes,' sighs Kit. 'You're here. Behave yourself, OK?'

'You don't need to worry,' mutters Margot. 'None of you need to worry.'

The table has been set for an unlucky thirteen. Margot spots Ted and Sibella as she enters the pub. They are already in their seats at the far end of the table next to Tom's family. Tom's father, a grey-haired man in a crumpled suit with a walking cane propped next to his seat was, Margot remembers Lucy telling her, a respected professor of physics at some university somewhere until taking early retirement due to a Parkinson's diagnosis. The trembling of the man's hands is obvious as he leans across to chat with Ted and Sibella. Tom's mum, a small, birdlike woman with Tom's beaming smile, sits beside her husband, deep in conversation with Tom's younger sister, Sarah, a primary-school teacher. At least, if she's not a primary-school teacher, thinks Margot, taking in her rosy cheeks, floral dress and tied-back hair, she should be. She looks exactly how a primary-school teacher should look, clean and wholesome. The sight of her makes Margot feel the exact opposite.

Lucy sits on her own at the centre of the table, looking lovely in a pale green shirt-dress. She is fiddling with the bangles on her arm, drumming her fingers on the table. Spotting Margot and Kit, she waves then gestures at Tom, who is up at the bar, ordering drinks. 'Just in time,' he says, kissing first Kit then Margot on the cheek. 'What can I get you?'

Kit orders a glass of wine. 'Vodka tonic, please,' says Margot. 'A double,' she adds, ignoring the angry glance from Kit.

'You must be Margot,' says Ryan, pouring half her tonic into a glass. 'I've heard about you,' he adds, as she shrugs off her leather jacket, revealing the full extent of the tattooed sleeve creeping up her bare arm.

'All bad, I assume.'

He laughs and slides her drink across the bar.

'You're the new manager here?'

'For my sins.' He holds out his hand. 'Ryan.'

The door to the pub swings open and Chloe and May burst through, wearing matching blue dresses, closely followed by Eve. 'Auntie Margot,' they cry, leaping all over her. Andrew follows behind, laden with an assortment of iPads, pens and colouring books.

'Oh my goodness,' says Margot, hugging the girls tightly in turn, feeling a little of her tension release at

their effusive greeting. 'Who stole my nieces and replaced them with these giants?'

Eve lets out a long exhalation and looks around, nodding at Ryan, before glancing at the table laid out at the
far end of the pub. 'Are you OK?' she asks Margot, her
voice low.

'Couldn't be better,' replies Margot, her voice a little
too loud. Eve flinches. 'Are *you* OK?' Like Lucy, Eve looks
weirdly tense. And she thought she was the only one
who'd been dreading tonight?

'Yes. I'm fine,' says Eve, though she looks anything
but.

She glances across at her brother-in-law who is
trying to shake Tom's hand and simultaneously wrestle
Chloe out of a pink, furry coat. 'Had an argument with
Andrew?'

'No.'

'Evening, Margot,' says Andrew, coming to kiss her
on the cheek.

She turns away slightly and offers him her coldest
'hello' in return.

Ryan pushes a glass of red across the bar towards
Eve. 'And for the good gentleman?' he asks, turning to
Andrew.

'Well, cheers,' says Margot, clinking her glass against
Eve's. 'Here's to an uneventful evening,' she adds, so that
only Eve can hear.

'Yes, quite,' Eve agrees, taking a sip of her wine.

Kit heads to the table. 'Ted ... Sibella,' she says coolly,
before offering a warmer greeting to Tom's parents.
Margot watches the awkward interlude, noting how her
mother chooses a seat a tactful distance from Sibella and

Ted, at the far end of the table. Eve and her family crowd in around Kit, leaving the only empty seat beside Lucy. Margot slides into it and carefully stands her drink on the coaster in front of her place setting. They haven't spoken since she fled the marquee the previous afternoon, but Margot has already decided to pretend the altercation never happened.

'Well, isn't this nice,' says Kit, raising her glass at them all from the head of the table, though Margot can see from the tight line of her mother's jaw that her jolly tone is forced. Her gaze comes to rest on Margot's tattoos and she winces visibly. Margot raises her own glass at her in response.

Ted, seated at the other end, picks up on Kit's cue. 'We should toast the happy couple,' he says. 'Let's wish them the best of luck for their big day tomorrow.'

'Yes,' agrees Kit. 'Best of luck, Tom and Lucy. May you have a long and happy life *together*.'

'Thanks,' says Tom, squeezing Lucy's arm. Lucy nods at her parents but looks oddly grim-faced. Margot catches Eve's eye and smirks. So this is how it's going to be: false bonhomie and snide digs.

'I like your tattoos,' says May, gawping at the inked patterns winding up Margot's arm. She reaches out and traces a spiralling vine with the tip of her finger until she comes to the small heart near the crook of her arm. 'When I grow up, I'm going to get one just like it. We can match.'

'Yes,' says Margot with a wink, 'I thought I might do the other arm too,' she adds, holding out her bare right arm.

'Yeah!' says May. 'Me too.'

'Thanks for that,' murmurs Eve.

Gradually, the chatter turns to discussions of the menu. Margot leans in towards Lucy. 'Shall we try and forget yesterday?' she suggests. A peace offering. 'Focus on tonight.'

Lucy turns to look at her. 'Yes, all right,' she says.

Margot nods, though she doesn't feel particularly re-assured. Lucy looks pale and distracted, not herself.

'Are you OK?' she asks quietly. 'You look a little ... peaky.' She knows she shouldn't stir, but it does seem ridiculous that her and Tom are making such a meal of it. The way they're acting, such cloak and daggers, it's as if Lucy is the first woman on earth to ever conceive a child.

'I'm fine,' she replies, reaching for the untouched glass of Prosecco in front of her. Tom throws his arm around her. 'Feeling OK?' he asks, kissing her cheek.

Lucy nods.

'I just asked her that,' says Margot. She narrows her eyes. 'Do you think she should?' she asks in a low voice, gesturing at the wine.

'What do you mean?' Lucy looks at the glass in her hand and then flushes red.

'You know, in *your* condition?' Margot nudges her. 'Come on, Luce,' she carries on. 'You might as well tell us all now.'

Tom leans across, and speaks so that only the two sisters can hear, 'Back off, Margot. Let her tell you in her own—'

'Tom,' warns Lucy.

Margot throws up her hands, annoyed at Tom's inter-ference. His overprotectiveness is misplaced. He doesn't need to shield Lucy from *her*. 'Sorry, I didn't realise a

253

prerequisite for marriage was the removal of a woman's backbone.'

'Will you two stop it,' says Lucy, more loudly perhaps than she'd intended because the whole table falls silent and turns to look at the three of them.

Mercifully, Ryan chooses that exact moment to arrive at the table. He starts taking orders at Eve's end, beaming round at them all, seemingly oblivious to the rising tension. As he gathers the menus, Margot waves for his attention and orders another vodka tonic, ignoring the look of daggers from her mother. Turning back to Lucy, she finds Tom talking to her sister in a low, soothing voice. Margot sighs. When did she become so passive and simpering?

With the easy distraction of the menus removed, an awkward silence falls over the table. Ted clears his throat, as if to speak, only to fall silent again. Margot sees Sibella lay a hand over her father's. The gesture only infuriates Margot further. What is wrong with everyone? Ted ditched their mother for Sibella. Andrew is having an affair right under Eve's nose. Tom is smothering Lucy like some overbearing minder. Why should she be the only one to be judged – to feel shame? 'You know,' she says, turning to address the table, 'you all act like I'm the only person in the world to ever do anything bad, but maybe some of you should take a look at yourselves.' She lifts her near-empty glass in a toast to the rest of the table and finishes it with a swig.

'Margot,' says Lucy, pleadingly. 'You said you wouldn't do this.'

'Do what? What?' Margot looks around at everyone. She sees her father's crestfallen face, her mother's

254

tight-lipped fury and Eve's weary resignation. Tom's sister is gazing intently down at her lap. His parents wear baffled expressions. 'What's wrong with you all? This is supposed to be a party, isn't it?'

'Yes,' says Andrew, speaking up from beside Eve. 'You're right. I could do with another drink.' He pushes his chair back from the table. 'What can I get everyone?'

Margot watches him go, imagining she has touched a nerve. She nudges Lucy, wondering if she has noticed too, but Lucy won't look at her; she is, instead, doing everything in her power, it seems, to ignore her.

Margot frowns. Has she gone too far? She picks up the nearest bar mat and starts to rip it into small pieces. She can't seem to stop herself. There is a pressure building, a strange buzzing. Images and memories she doesn't want to think about threaten to rise up. She reaches for her drink again, but this time Eve stretches across and places her hand over the top of her glass. 'I think that's enough, Margot, don't you? How about a little fresh air?'

Margot feels the blood rush to her cheeks. 'Yes, of course. God forbid I should do anything to *embarrass* the family.'

Kit shakes her head. 'I don't understand where all this anger comes from, Margot.'

'Of course you don't.'

'Margot.' Eve says her name, a low warning.

Kit eyes her coldly. 'Why don't you go and cool off, before you say something you'll regret.'

'Oh, don't worry. I'm going. I'll be a good girl and go and "cool off", as *Mummy* suggests.'

As she pushes her chair back, swaying a little at the sudden movement, caught off balance, Margot hears

May's giggles followed by a loud whisper, 'She called Granny *Mummy!*'

Chloe, perhaps from the look on Eve's face, seems to know not to laugh and nudges her little sister in the ribs. Both girls drop their heads to their colouring sheets.

'Would you like me to come with you?' Sibella asks from the far end of the table.

'Oh for God's sake,' mutters Kit, shaking her head.

Margot doesn't bother to reply. Instead, she follows the corridor to the ladies bathroom where she stands for a moment leaning against the sinks, pressing her forehead against the cool glass of the gilt-framed mirror. She studies her eyes – red-rimmed and bloodshot – and sees the flicker of a younger girl in a grey, shapeless hoodie standing in the same spot, looking into the same mirror. No, she thinks. She is not that girl. Not any more.

She bursts out into the back car park, gasping for air, sucking it into her lungs in deep breaths. Outside, in the night sky, the stars seem to fizz and blur. She is definitely more drunk than she'd intended. Squinting across the car park she sees someone sitting on a step near the kitchen. A teenager, wearing a striped apron, smoking a cigarette. He is clearly on a break from kitchen duties. She heads straight for him and hits him with what she hopes is her most winning smile. 'I don't suppose I could bum a cigarette off you?'

'Sure.' He pats his pockets and then holds out a box of cigarettes. His lighter follows. Margot cups her hands around his and leans in, the cigarette hanging from her lips as he lights it for her.

'Thank you,' she says, taking a deep drag before

exhaling smoke up into the dark sky. She wraps her arms around herself, her bare arms tingling in the cold air.

'No worries.'

'Australian?'

'Yeah.'

'Backpacking?'

He nods. 'I'm on my gap year. I was hoping for a little adventure before uni.'

'And you washed up here in the buzzing metropolis of Mortford? Lucky you.'

He laughs. 'Ryan's my uncle. He offered me the job. What brings you here?' he asks, eyeing her tattoos. 'You don't look like the usual type we get in here.'

'Family.'

The boy nods again and throws his cigarette butt to the ground, scuffing it beneath his trainer through the gravel. 'Can't live with them. Can't live without them,' he says.

'Isn't that the truth.'

'I'd best get back to it,' he says, indicating the kitchen with a tilt of his head.

'Sure. I don't want to get you on the wrong side of your uncle. Thanks for the cigarette.'

'No worries,' the boy throws the words over his shoulder at her as he ducks back inside the kitchen.

She stays outside a minute longer, gazing up at the stars. Now she is alone, it doesn't feel so rebellious to be sitting there puffing away on the cigarette. It's cold too, without her jacket. She rubs her arms and thinks about the smoke circulating in her lungs. She thinks about the grotesque health warning she'd glimpsed on the packet as the boy had handed them to her. She is old enough to know better.

She throws the cigarette to the floor and stubs it out, just as a movement in the shadows across the car park catches her eye. She peers more closely through the darkness, and sees what looks like a man and a woman standing together in the shadows, near a car. Something about the stance of the couple makes Margot's blood run cold. She blinks, trying to clear the vodka haze that has set in. Something in the closeness of their bodies, the fierce gesticulations, the looming height of the man makes her feel afraid. She knows she should shout – try to help the woman – but she is paralysed and her words are caught in the sour bile rising up her throat. The man reaches out and pulls at the woman's arm. Margot's heart thumps in her chest.

A cat runs across the car park gravel and triggers a security light. As the yellow glow sweeps across the couple's faces, Margot sees another truth. The man is no stranger. It is Andrew, and he looks ashen-faced, as the woman he is with – the barmaid from the pub – gesticulates angrily. She turns slightly away from him and folds her arms.

Andrew, glancing around, notices Margot standing by the back steps of the kitchen, still caught in the glow of the security light. She gives him a long, cold stare then turns on her heel and re-enters the pub. Fucking Andrew. Lucy was right.

Back inside, Lucy and Tom are standing at the bar conducting an urgent-looking conversation. As she stalks past she hears Lucy say, 'Not now. Not with all this tension.'

'When then? You said you'd tell them tonight.'

'It's all wrong, the wrong atmosphere. Margot has ruined it.' Lucy catches sight of Margot and looks away guiltily.

'No,' says Margot, plastering a smile on her face. 'Tom's right. You should tell us all now,' she says. 'Put us out of our misery,' she adds, a slight taunting tone in her voice. 'I mean, it's not like most of us haven't guessed already. It's so obvious.'

Lucy stares at her. Margot rolls her eyes. All this carrying on like nobody knows, as if they have this huge, precious secret to divulge. They are so wrapped up in their own lives – the drama of it. So what. Lucy and Tom are having a baby. The way they are carrying on is ridiculous. 'The pitter patter of tiny feet?' She glances down meaningfully at Lucy's stomach then raises an eyebrow. 'Come off it, we're not idiots.'

Lucy stares at her, the colour draining from her face.

Margot shrugs. 'Oh, I get it. You want to revel in your big moment. I won't spoil it for you.' She snatches up the nearest glass from the bar and raises it, drops of wine spilling onto her hand as she does. 'But between us, let's toast . . . to babies. The next generation of little fuck-ups.'

Tom's arm tightens around Lucy's shoulders. Margot sees it and feels a surge of anger. He doesn't need to protect Lucy from her. Surely he knows that? She loves Lucy – always has, always will. She'd never do anything to hurt her.

She spins on her heel, heading back to the table, but it's no better back there. Andrew approaches, pale-faced, his hands jammed in his pockets. He glances in Margot's direction as he slides back onto the bench beside Eve, then wraps his arm around his wife and pulls her in for a kiss. Eve throws him a surprised look. 'Everything OK?'

'Couldn't be better,' he says loudly, eyeballing Margot

Yeah, right, she thinks. You don't fool me. She glares at Andrew and he drops his gaze.

Over the course of the meal, the conversation is false and stilted. Margot has lost her appetite and only picks at her food, settling instead for another glass of wine. Lucy barely touches her food too and Eve sits quietly, distracted and tense. Only the two little girls at the end of the table seem oblivious to the family tensions around them. 'We've finished. Can we go and play on the pool table?' Chloe asks.

'Yes,' says Andrew, with barely disguised relief. 'I'll take you into the games room.'

The plates are cleared and no one seems to want to order dessert. After a tactful amount of time, Margot sees Ted whisper something to Sibella. She nods and Ted clears his throat. 'Well, thank you for a lovely dinner, Lucy . . . Tom. We know you two have a big day to-morrow. I suppose an earlyish night might be in order. We don't want to keep the bride and groom from their beauty sleep.'

'Yes,' agrees Tom's mum brightly. 'We'll all need a good rest.' She pats her husband's hand, smiles pointedly at Margot, then reaches for the handbag on the back of her chair.

Eve, reading the mood of the table, starts to gather up the girls' felt tip pens and sketch pads. Margot, slumped in her chair, her chin propped on her hand, turns and sees Tom give Lucy a little nudge. 'Go on,' he whispers.

'Yes, go on,' says Margot.

Lucy shoots her a look, but then, to Margot's surprise, she stands. 'Would you all stop and listen for a moment. Please. There's something I need to tell you, before you leave, and perhaps it's best that I do it while Andrew is off with the girls.'

Well here we go, thinks Margot with a small smile, leaning back in her chair. At last. The *big* revelation. 'Hit us with it, Luce,' she says. 'Dazzle us with your wonderful news. We're all ears.'

23

Lucy stands, her heart thudding in her chest. She takes some comfort from Tom's solid presence at her side. 'Go on,' he says again. 'I'm right here.'

'What is it?' asks Kit, looking baffled. 'What's going on?'

Lucy takes a deep breath. 'So it's no secret that Tom and I have rather rushed this wedding. It was just over a week ago, in fact, that we decided to get married, which didn't give anyone much time to plan or prepare. For that we're sorry.' She pauses. 'But we are incredibly grateful that you are all here with us this weekend.'

She looks around the table and sees the bewildered expressions.

'The reason we wanted to get you all together tonight, before the big party tomorrow, is because I have something important I need to share with you all.' Margot is still grinning up at her with such a look of 'knowing' on her face. Lucy can't bear it.

She takes another deep breath. She has rehearsed this moment in her head over and over, but somehow, now that it has arrived, she doesn't feel ready. 'I'm not pregnant,' she says, turning to Margot. She sees the smile begin to falter on her sister's face, her quick glance in their father's direction. 'I'm afraid it's not such happy news. You see, I'm sick.'

'Sick?' asks Kit, with a frown.

'Yes,' says Lucy, turning first to her mother, and then to Ted. 'I have cancer.'

A stillness falls over the room.

Ted coughs.

She sees Margot's expression shift from confusion to disbelief.

Her mother is staring at her, open-mouthed.

Margot breaks the silence with a laugh. 'Luce. That's not funny.'

When she doesn't answer, she sees Margot look uncertainly at Tom, searching his face for reassurances, and slowly the smile on Margot's face fades. 'But you're pregnant,' insists Margot. 'It's been the worst-kept secret ever.'

Eve squeezes Margot's arm. 'Shut up, will you?'

'Sorry. No,' Lucy says. 'I'm not pregnant.' Her hands hang uselessly at her sides, fists squeezed tight. 'I'm sorry for the secrecy. But I wanted to tell you all together. In one go. I thought it would be easier this way. I'm being admitted to hospital on Monday for a procedure. An operation.' She can't help her hands moving to her stomach, covering her sick, traitorous womb. 'Turns out there's a rather large tumour having a party on my ovaries. They'll remove it . . . and . . . anything else that needs to come out.' Lucy takes a deep breath. 'And then it will be down to chemo to slow the disease.'

'Slow it?' asks Eve.

Lucy nods. She feels Tom's hand, warm and reassuring on her arm.

'But they can get rid of it,' says Eve.

Lucy holds Eve's eye. 'The scans I had last week show that the tumour has, most likely, already metastasised. We'll know more next week when they operate, but the consultant has warned that it looks aggressive. Most likely stage four.'

Somewhere beyond the table, Lucy can hear her nieces calling to each other, the crack of snooker balls hitting together, a peal of laughter.

'Metastasised? What the fuck does that mean?' Margot is blinking angrily.

Lucy sees her family, seated around the table, looking bewildered and upset and realises for the first time that perhaps Tom was right: breaking the news to them all in one go like this may not have been the best way after all.

'It means the original tumour has spread. The scans indicate there are probably secondary tumours in my abdomen and lungs. The appointments next week will clarify things.'

'But you're on honeymoon next week,' says Eve.

Margot nods vehemently. 'You're all packed.'

'The only honeymoon I'll be taking, for now, is a stay at the RUH in Bath. The case I've packed is for a hospital visit, not a honeymoon. Not yet, anyway.'

'Oh Lucy,' says Ted, quietly. 'My darling girl.'

'But ... but ...' Margot still seems to be struggling to calibrate, 'you can't have cancer. You're twenty-eight. You're getting married tomorrow.'

Lucy nods and manages a small smile. 'Yes, I'm getting married tomorrow.' She reaches for Tom's hand. 'This is why we decided to speed the wedding up, to go for it. Finding out I have cancer . . .' she sees her mother flinch, 'well, it made me realise what is most important to me. Tom. All of you. Being together.' She feels Tom's squeeze of reassurance. She shrugs and gives another weak smile. 'I wanted to tell you and for it to not feel like such an awful thing – you know – what do they say? Sandwich bad news between good news?'

Margot snorts. 'Hey everyone. I'm getting married. Oh, I have cancer. But let's party.'

Lucy winces. 'Yeah, I suppose it doesn't sound so good when you put it like that.' She shrugs. 'I'm sorry if it feels selfish and as if I've dragged you all here under false pretences, but we *are* getting married and we want it to be fun.' She smiles. 'We insist it is fun. I'm pretty certain the next few months aren't going to be, so let's make tomorrow count.'

Margot still looks furious. 'Why didn't they catch it sooner? How can you go from being completely fine to *this*? It doesn't make sense.'

'I've been struggling with some symptoms for a while. Tiredness. Bloating. Abdominal pain.' She rests her hands on her stomach. 'They thought it was IBS for a time. Apparently it's easy to misdiagnose.'

Ted is shaking his head. 'There are some incredible doctors in London. We'll get you up to Harley Street for a meeting with the best specialist we can find.'

Lucy smiles sadly. 'Dad, it's OK. The medical team at the hospital are amazing. I'm in good hands.'

'But you're not going to die,' says Margot, firmly.

'Margot, we're all going to die, sometime.'

'Stop it. You know what I mean.'

'Dad's right,' says Eve. 'There are all kinds of treatments these days. Amazing drugs and special centres you can visit trying pioneering techniques, not to mention alternative therapies. They'd be right up your street, acupuncture and reflexology, and . . .' She trails off.

Lucy looks at Eve, then Margot and finally Kit, 'I don't know what's going to happen in the coming weeks and months, but frankly, I didn't want the next time you all get together to be my funeral.' She tries to smile. 'I didn't want you having that party without me.'

At the word 'funeral' Kit lets out a choked sob.

Lucy gives her a nod. 'Tomorrow is a celebration of love and life. It's not about death.'

'Why are you talking about funerals?' asks Margot.

'Surely they can fix you?' says Eve, a pleading look on her face.

'If they confirm next week that it's stage four, well . . . they can help me, but there is no "fix". My treatment would be palliative. But I'm not giving up. I'm young and I'm strong.' She squeezes Tom's hand, then turns to fix her gaze on Margot. 'I firmly believe that where there is love, there is hope.' Margot drops her head. Lucy turns to look at Kit, who sits a little apart from them all, her face stricken. 'Mum? Are you OK?'

Kit stares at Lucy. 'I . . . I . . . I don't . . . I'm sorry.' She stands, pushing back her chair with a horrible scrape, then runs from the room, leaving a stunned silence.

'It's OK,' says Lucy, brightly. 'It's a shock, for everyone. I've had a little time to begin to process the news, but it's going to take longer. For all of us.' She tries to smile at them, but all she sees staring back at her is a sea of horrified faces. Eve has a fist pressed to her mouth. Her father looks like he is about to cry, Sibella squeezing his hand tightly. Tom's mum is quietly weeping.

'I think you've been very brave tonight, Lucy,' says Sibella, from the far end of the table. 'Perhaps everyone needs a little time tonight to think over what you've told us?'

Lucy nods, grateful for Sibella's calm presence. 'Yes.'

'Sorry,' says Margot, throwing Sibella a look, 'but I can't sit here pretending that everything is wonderful. You want us to celebrate tomorrow like it's a *normal* wedding?' Margot glances up at Lucy, shaking her head in disbelief.

Lucy nods. 'That's exactly what I want, Margot.'

Everyone is still staring at Lucy as a blast of cooler air rushes into the room. They all turn as a tall, blonde man in a black leather jacket enters the pub. He glances around searchingly, until his gaze comes to settle on Margot seated at the table. Lucy looks down at her sister and sees she is staring back at the man, her mouth open and her eyes wide.

Lucy turns back to the door and watches as the man's face splits into a wide grin at the sight of Margot, a smile that creases his handsome face and makes his piercing blue eyes crinkle. Lucy can't stop staring at him. He looks like a rock star.

'Hello, Margot,' he says.

Margot doesn't say anything, so the man turns to the rest of the table and offers a smile. 'Hello,' he says. 'I'm Jonas.' He speaks with a slight accent, a softening of the 'J' of his name. 'I'm a friend of Margot's.'

Lucy looks from Jonas to Margot again and sees that her sister is blushing furiously. 'I don't mean to intrude,' he continues, 'but I heard there was a wedding tomorrow and I thought you might need a photographer?' He raises an eyebrow at Margot.

Margot opens her mouth to speak, but no words come out.

Lucy turns back to Jonas and nods. 'Yes,' she says, smiling at the man. 'Yes, there is a wedding tomorrow. Welcome, Jonas.'

24

They had intended to spend the night before their wedding apart, but after the way the evening has unfolded, Lucy asks Tom to come back with her. 'It's supposed to be unlucky, isn't it?' he says on the drive to Windfalls.

Lucy can't help her hollow laugh. 'Luck? I'm not sure we need to worry about that right now, do you? I want to make the most of every moment. I want you with me.'

He nods and squeezes her knee. 'Me too.'

They curl up together in her bed, Tom's arms wrapped tightly around her.

In the dark, she can make out the long column of her wedding dress hanging on the back of the door. 'I guess that could have gone better,' she says after a while.

'It was never going to be easy.'

'No.'

'You were brave, telling them all together like that. I'm proud of you. What was Margot's problem, though?'

Lucy stares up into the darkness. 'We've been asking ourselves that for a while now.'

Lucy thinks about Margot's drunken antics in the pub, her rage at the possibility of Andrew's infidelity, and the unexpected tears when she'd confronted her just yesterday about the loss of their mother's work. 'It's so hard to read her. She's so . . . erratic. I don't think any of us know what she's going to do next. I must say, that man turning up out of the blue was something though. He was rather gorgeous, wasn't he?'

'Can't say that I noticed,' says Tom, drily.

'You're not jealous, are you?'

'Me? Jealous of a six-foot-four Scandinavian hunk?'

Lucy laughs. 'You're all the man I need,' she says, snuggling into his arms.

They fall silent. 'Are you thinking about tomorrow?' he asks. 'Nervous?'

'Yes,' she admits.

'It will be fine. You've got me.' Tom strokes her hair before returning his arm to circle her waist. She feels his breath against her neck and pushes her back against him, enjoying his warmth, his strength. Curled in his arms, she feels small and fragile, like an egg sheltered in a nest. After a while their breathing slows and syncs. She is losing him to sleep. She can feel it.

She thinks about the day that lies ahead and of all the people from her life who will converge on Windfalls to celebrate with them. She meant what she'd told her family. She wants the day to feel like a celebration. Not a sad day.

Tom's breathing deepens. Gradually, his grip on her loosens as he succumbs to sleep.

Letting go. It's something she needs to learn too. An image rises up out of the depths of her subconscious, a dandelion head, its seeds drifting away on the breeze, and with it comes a memory of standing on the lawn at Windfalls, blowing dandelion clocks with her father.

'That's it, Lucy,' he'd said, bending low beside her. 'However many puffs it takes to blow the seeds from the stem will tell you the time.'

She had looked at him with suspicion.

'Go on. Try it.'

She had. It had taken five. 'Five o'clock?' she'd asked.

He'd made a great show of checking his wristwatch. 'Exactly right,' he'd said with a wide smile.

She'd frowned. 'But we've just had breakfast.'

'Well, silly us! We must have slept in!' He'd swept her up into his arms and tickled her until she had howled with laughter as the seeds had drifted far away on the wind. 'Watch them go, Lucy,' he'd said, when she had eventually stopped laughing. 'Watch them fly away.'

The memory brings an ache – nostalgia for the past, when everything felt so simple and uncomplicated, for a time when they didn't have to let go of anything more weighty than dandelion seeds. She thinks of the news she has shared. Of Margot's tight, hurt face. All the emotion simmering beneath her skin. What is it, she wonders? What is it that makes Margot, Margot? Why won't she let any of them in? Why won't she let her walls down?

'Tom,' she whispers into the darkness.

The only reply is Tom's slow, steady breath.

'Tom,' she tries again, but she knows he is lost in slumber and the words she wants to share with him, the questions she wants to ask, remain heavy inside of her, turning over and over, keeping her from sleep.

THE PAST

2009

25

The gift arrived a couple of days after the *Romeo and Juliet* wrap party, a box covered in gold paper and tied with a red ribbon, dropped on the front doorstep of Windfalls. Margot felt her blood chill as she read the message inside the attached card. 'Bravo, Juliet! You were superb. With best wishes, Mr Hudson.'

She studied the words for a long time before unwrapping his gift to reveal a large box of chocolates, the kind you'd see on special at the tills in the supermarket at Christmas. She sat looking at them for a long time.

'How lovely,' Kit said, wandering past. 'Something to put a smile back on your face.'

Margot didn't say anything.

'Still feeling poorly? I can't tempt you to eat a little something?'

She shook her head.

'You're not dieting, I hope?'

Margot pushed the box of chocolates across the table at her. 'You have them.'

Kit frowned. 'But they're yours.'

'I don't want them.'

Kit shrugged. 'Thank you, darling.' She selected a triangular-shaped chocolate from the box and popped it in her mouth. 'Maybe you'll fancy them when you're feeling a bit better.'

Margot looked down at the card. *You were superb.* A vile loathing surged from the pit of her stomach. She took a deep breath. 'Mum.'

'Mmmmm.' Kit was still chewing.

She swallowed. 'You know the night of my play?'

'Yes. I do. And I've already apologised profusely for forgetting.'

'It's not that.' She shook her head. 'Something happened.' Margot didn't know how she was going to tell her mum. To speak the words out loud felt impossible. But her mother was right there, standing in front of her, a rare moment of attention and she felt a trace of courage rising up. If she could explain how it happened, how she had wanted . . . wanted something . . . to be seen . . . to be kissed . . . but not *that*. *Never* that. Maybe her mother would understand. 'Something bad,' she added.

'But I thought it had all gone so well?' Kit was studying the card inside the selection box, trying to decide on another flavour. 'A triumph, Jamie Kingston's mother told me.'

'I don't mean the play. I mean, afterwards. At the party.'

'Oh.' At last, Kit turned her attention from the chocolates and fixed her with a searching gaze. 'Yes. I was going to talk to you about that.'

Margot stared at her mother. 'You were?'

Kit placed the selection box menu on the table between them. 'Yes. I know all about it.'

'You do?' Margot's felt her cheeks flushing bright red,
though a sensation a little like relief began to creep over
her too. Perhaps she wasn't going to have to explain the
bad thing in quite such horrendous detail after all.

'Yes. I wasn't going to bring it up, not when you had
done so well in the play and, well, I'd messed up myself.'
Kit gave a light laugh. 'But as you've raised it...'

Margot held her breath.

'Clearly you tried hard to cover your tracks, but there
were several beer cans left on the jetty and I could tell
from the way my desk had been left that you and your
friends had been inside the studio.'

Margot frowned.

'Now, I don't mind you having a few friends over
once in a while,' she continued, fixing Margot with a
stern look, 'but can I please ask that you stay out of my
studio. It's so important that everything remains as I left
it. Imagine if anything had happened to the draft of my
novel.' Kit shuddered. 'It would be devastating.'

Margot, realisation dawning, felt a new sort of anguish
take hold of her. She lowered her head and nodded.
Devastating. 'Yes. Course. Sorry.'

'I think it's best if we say the studio is out of bounds
to you and your friends, don't you?'

Margot nodded again. On this, she could agree. She
hadn't stepped foot in there since the night of the play.
She couldn't imagine ever doing so again. 'Perhaps you
should back-up your work,' she offered quietly, after a
long moment.

Kit laughed and popped another chocolate in her

mouth. 'Oh, you know me and technology. I struggled enough with that damn DVD player your father brought home all those years ago. The old ways are the best ways. Besides, if you stay out of the studio, I won't have to, will I? Problem solved.' She stood and squeezed Margot's shoulder. 'Thank you for understanding, darling. I promise I'll make it up to you, as soon as this book is written. Besides, no harm done on this occasion. Let's forget it, shall we?'

Margot listened to her mother leave, the soft click of the back door closing, the sound of Kit's fading footsteps as she wandered down through the garden.

She missed the final days of the summer term, crying off sick and instead took to her bed where she lay for hours, a cat curled at her feet and her face turned to the wall, studying the flowered wallpaper in minute detail. It was her fault. Those nights when she had lain in bed imagining what it would feel like to kiss him, her own curved fist pressed to her lips. She wanted to scour herself clean. She wanted to scrub those traitorous lips and cut off that stupid hand.

See what you do to me.

She had made it happen. The shame that ate away at her was a sign: she must never tell anyone what she'd made happen. How she had wanted Mr Hudson to notice her, to kiss her. It was a mess of her making. She locked the incident in a private place, hid those horrible moments somewhere deep inside.

Who did you think about, Margot?
Tell me what you want, Margot.
You like that, do you?

When the fragments escaped from that locked place and rose up in her mind, she tried to transform it into something more palatable, something softer, more romantic, something other than what it was. He couldn't help himself. Maybe he loved her? But always, there was the sensation of his hands grabbing at her hair, the pain of the desk pushing into her thighs, the sickening taste of his tongue probing her mouth.

In late August, a letter arrived with her GCSE results: nine passed at grade A or higher. She had aced her drama exam. She should have been delighted, but none of it seemed to matter any more. 'Aren't you going to go out and celebrate with your friends?' Kit asked.

'I don't feel like it.'

Kit frowned. She walked to the fridge and produced a bottle of champagne. 'My French publishers sent me this last week. Let's have a glass, shall we, to celebrate?' she offered. 'You deserve it. I'm proud of you. We all are.'

Margot didn't want it, but she forced the champagne down. The sweet wine coated her tongue, reminding her of the sickly taste of punch and cider. Warmth began to spread through her belly, a gentle buzz dulling the sharp edges in her mind. When Kit returned to her studio, Margot retrieved the open bottle from the fridge and poured another glass. She drank fast, until the bottle was almost empty.

Upstairs, the muffled silence of the house felt frightening. She stood for a long time staring at her reflection in the bathroom mirror. *You're like a flower, ready to bloom.* She stared at her face for a long time, fighting the urge to scratch her skin, to rake her cheeks with her fingernails.

In Eve's room, she lay on the neat wrought-iron bed

and hugged one of her sister's cushions to her chest. She let the tears come, wishing Eve was there with her calm, practical advice. Eve would know what to say and do. Instead, there was only the quietness – the aching loneliness.

In the bottom drawer of a chest she found a pile of Eve's old clothes, faded T-shirts, a pair of tracksuit bottoms and a grey hoodie she could remember Eve wearing on those 'fat days', when she would walk around the house scowling, a hot water bottle clutched to her stomach. Margot raised the sweatshirt to her face and breathed, inhaling the forgotten scent of her sister. Feeling a little comforted, she pulled the hoodie on. She liked the way it felt – too big, swamping her frame, hiding her from view.

In Lucy's room, the void seemed even greater, the constant energy and momentum of her sister all the more obvious for its absence. The room stood like a messy time capsule, littered with a tangle of teenage memorabilia. She studied old posters of boy bands and photos tacked to the wall, of Lucy lifting school hockey trophies and posing with triumphant netball teams. There was another photo of the three of them from a long time ago – the sisters seated on the jetty down by the river, all of them gazing into the water. She couldn't remember the photo being taken, but presumed it had been their father who had shot it. She couldn't have been more than about six or seven. She looked at the girls they once were, then turned away.

Lucy had left so many of her belongings. On the desk Margot saw a messy spread of pens and books, old bottles of nail varnish and a stack of well-thumbed paperbacks piled haphazardly. There were old cinema tickets and lipsticks, a beaded necklace lying tangled with a pair of headphones. Beside a dusty lamp, she saw her sister's penknife lying discarded next to a half-empty bottle of patchouli oil. She reached out and tested its weight in her palm before releasing the blade and turning it to catch the light. She remembered a moment by the stream in the garden, Lucy using it to carve into a tree. The knife felt cool and solid in her grip. She slipped it into the front pocket of the hoodie and left the room.

Outside, the day was cool and grey. There was no sign of Kit. She knew her mother would be down in the studio, working on her precious words. Pulling the hood up over her head, she turned and walked down the drive, away from the house, away from the river.

Whether it was the champagne she had drunk, or the sensation of Eve's hood pulled up around her face, or the strange numbness that seemed to have taken hold of her body, Margot wasn't sure, but all felt muffled. Her footsteps landing on the road, the sound of cars passing, the laughter of little kids playing on a swing set, it was as though she existed in a separate state. Not part of the world but oddly other.

She didn't know where she was going. She walked with her head down, her feet treading their monotonous beat, her hand curled around the handle of the penknife in her pocket, now warm in her grip.

It was only as she reached the entrance to the cul-de-sac that she realised she had known all along where she was headed. The black front door stood as she remembered, the red car parked on the driveway. A few short weeks ago, she had been standing there with the rest of the cast, waiting to watch the film with their beloved Mr Hudson. She could feel the blood pumping through her veins. She felt the breath catching in her throat. Squeezing the handle of Lucy's penknife a little tighter, she stepped forward and pressed the doorbell.

At the sound of the chime, a piercing wail rose from within the house, the cry of a baby. It was followed by other sounds, the murmurings of a woman's voice, the silencing of a television. 'Just a minute,' someone called from behind the door.

It was his wife's voice that pulled her from her muffled state – or perhaps the sharp cries of the baby. Either way, seeing the light shifting behind the glass panel of the door, knowing that at any moment it would be thrown open, Margot spun quickly on her heel.

She walked fast, back down the front step and onto the driveway. It was only as she reached the car that she lifted the knife from her pocket, stretching out her hand to allow the blade to meet the vehicle, dragging it in one long, screaming streak along the painted metal.

'Hey!' she heard the woman's cry behind her but Margot didn't turn around. She didn't run. She dropped the knife to the pavement with a clatter and kept walking – fast – her shoulders hunched over and her face buried in the hood of the sweatshirt as she turned the corner and carried on, no longer numb and muffled but alive and pumping with blood and a fierce, hot anger.

She hid for the rest of the summer, turning down party invitations and afternoons swimming in the river. She avoided trips into town, afraid she would bump into friends from the play – or worse – Mr Hudson himself. It was easier to stay at home than face anyone.

By the time she returned to school at the start of the autumn term, Margot had constructed a careful wall around herself and the experience with Mr Hudson she had locked somewhere deep inside. She was braced for her return, steeled to see Mr Hudson walking the corridors, smiling at her in class. It was done. She would never let him close again.

What she hadn't expected was the head teacher to stand up in their first morning assembly and announce Mr Hudson's sudden departure from the faculty. The head relayed the information to them in the briefest statement, with no explanation as to why he should have abandoned his post. 'I know you will all join me in welcoming Mrs Ashcroft as our Head of Drama and I ask you please to make her feel at home.' Margot sat, numb and silent, as the rest of the assembly politely applauded the new teacher.

It didn't take long. By lunchtime, the whispers were all around her, a flurry of hushed rumours passing from student to student like the flashing messages on their contraband mobile phones.

'Dirty perv.'

'It's so gross.'

'I always knew he was dodgy.'

Margot slowed as she walked by a group of fifth years, craning to hear.

'Apparently he kept her back after class one day and put his hand up her shirt.'

'Ugh. You could tell something wasn't right. He was such a try-hard, acting like he was everyone's friend.'

'Do the police know?'

'Sasha's parents said they'd forget the whole thing if the school got rid of him.'

'Yeah, I heard they wanted to avoid the police, didn't want her name getting in the newspapers, not when she's applying to universities.'

'It's his wife I feel sorry for. Apparently, she's just had a baby.'

Margot listened to the rumour mill with a growing sense of panic. Mr Hudson had tried it on with Sasha Hart and Sasha, unlike Margot, had been smart enough to know what Margot had not, she had seen the teacher for what he was, had been able to do what she had not and fight him off. Mr Hudson was a *dirty pervert*, a fact it seemed everyone else had grasped except her. She felt sick to her stomach listening to the other students churning through the details of his spectacular fall from grace.

The gossip only confirmed what Margot had known all along: it *was* her fault this had happened to her, and now that she had held the shameful secret so long, now that *everyone* knew what he was, it was even more crucial that she keep it from the rest of the world. A whole summer had passed. If she spoke out now, wouldn't they wonder why she hadn't told anyone? Unlike Sasha, it wasn't just his hand up her shirt . . . he had . . . he had . . . and then they would know that she had *asked* for it.

See what you do to me?

Everyone would know. Her family. Her friends. The school. The police. The newspapers. Dread grew like a huge black mass inside of her as she remembered the

281

whispers of the other students. They would all know. She couldn't bear the thought of it. She could never, ever utter a word about what happened that night, down by the river.

SATURDAY

26

Margot wakes from a nightmare with a dry mouth and her head pounding almost as hard as her heart. She kicks off the duvet and casts about, trying to ground herself in the present. As her vision adjusts to the grey dawn light, she sees the curled shape of a man lying on a mattress on the floor across the room. Jonas.

Slowly, through the fog of her hangover, fragments of the night before come back to her. The meal at the pub. The drinks. The tension around the table. Andrew's white face illuminated in the car park security lights. Lucy's announcement. Jonas's surprise arrival.

As she cycles through her memory, an icy horror trickles down the back of her throat. Lucy's announcement. Margot stiffens.

Lucy isn't pregnant. She is sick.

The word that has been lurking in her subconscious rises: cancer.

Margot rolls onto her back and stares up at the ceiling, replaying what she can remember. She sees Lucy, standing there beside Tom, with that tight, brave smile on her face.

Lucy has cancer. It hits her like a punch to the stomach. Words float in her mind: ovaries . . . stage 4 . . . metastasised. Unable to stop herself, Margot slides quietly from the bed and retrieves the laptop from her luggage. She sits on the edge of the bed and boots up the machine, typing quickly into the search engine. What she reads doesn't help. Lucy has clearly tried her best to shield them from the worst, but there is nothing reassuring to be gained from Dr Google. She scans a brief summary of symptoms and treatment options on a cancer charity website and clicks through to a chat room where a whole stream of people have joined threads discussing symptoms, treatments and prognosis. She shuts the laptop and closes her eyes. Oh Lucy.

Why had she kept this from them? These past days she'd been hiding this most awful secret, protecting them from it. She thinks back to the plaintive text message she had received at the beginning of the week: *I need you*. What had at first seemed so selfish – drawing them all back for a last-minute wedding – now seems nothing short of heroic.

Margot releases a long breath. She knows what it is like to hold a painful secret. But this? Margot feels something crack inside of her.

She lies back on the bed and a wave of emotion rises up. She tries to fight it but it's like a huge, crushing weight pressing down on her and it's all she can do to let the tears fall as she tries to draw her next breath.

After a while, she becomes aware of the sensation of

someone moving onto the mattress beside her, a warm hand coming to rest on her arm. 'Margot?'

She can't speak. She can't look at him. The pain is too much. She holds herself apart from him, using every ounce of her energy to keep the pieces of herself together. If she lets go now, she will surely fly apart into a thousand brittle shards.

'Margot,' Jonas says softly. 'I'm here.'

At those two words, she turns and buries herself into him. She lets him hold her as she sobs into his shoulder, releasing her burden of pent-up pain and sadness.

'I *should* be annoyed with you,' she says, a little later, lying beside him on the bed, both of them staring at the ceiling overhead. 'Barrelling in here like that.'

Jonas nods. 'I know.'

'How did you find me?'

'It's not hard to track down the name of the village where the famous K. T. Weaver lives. Your mum's Wikipedia page is full of useful information. I came into the pub to sweet talk the locals into giving me directions to your place and there you were, sitting at that table as I walked through the door. A sweet serendipity.'

'Why did you come?'

He shrugs. 'I don't know. I felt . . . I felt as if you might need a friend and when I realised that the worst that could happen would be that you would tell me to fuck off, I knew that I should try.'

'And would you have? Fucked off?'

'Of course. I'll fuck off any time you ask me to.'

She can't help her smile. 'I think that might be the nicest thing anyone's ever said to me.'

'So you're not annoyed?' he asks, still gazing at the ceiling.

Margot thinks for a moment. 'No. Do you want to know what I felt when I saw you walk through that door last night?'

Jonas tilts his head to give her a sideways look. 'I'm not sure. Do I?'

'I felt relieved. Life is so messed up,' she says, after a long moment. 'Lucy has cancer.'

'I know. You told me last night.'

'I did?' Margot puts a hand to her temple, and realises that she has no memory of leaving the pub, or of being put to bed. She sighs. 'It's not fair.'

'It's not fair,' agrees Jonas. 'Life isn't fair.'

Margot remembers the photograph of the beautiful, blonde woman seated beside the alpine lake pinned to Jonas's fridge. She squeezes his hand. 'I'm sorry.'

'And I'm sorry for you. For Lucy. For your family.'

Margot sighs and turns away, rolling into a small ball. What she doesn't say – what she can't bear to admit to Jonas, to anyone – is how horribly wrong this is. How guilty she feels. How the most unfair thing about it all is that Lucy – who has always lived with such joy and optimism – should have to deal with this. Surely fate has dealt this hand to the wrong sister, because if anyone in their family deserved this kind of sentence, then why not her? She has lived for so long with such shame, such emptiness. It should have been her.

'Talk to me,' says Jonas, sensing her turmoil.

'I don't know why you're here. I don't know how to live a good life. I've got nothing to give you. I'm hollow.'

Jonas is quiet for a long while. 'You say you're hollow,

Margot, but that's bullshit. I see the emotion in you. It's there. You hold it all so tightly inside. A nut that won't crack. You may not love me – and I may find that hard to take – but don't ever think you don't have the capacity to love. You love. I see it in you. The way you came straight back here for Lucy, even though it's the place that gives you nightmares. You're not empty. You're afraid. Let yourself feel. Let yourself feel it all. What's the worst that could happen?'

'I'm afraid I will crack.'

'If you crack, perhaps you might start to heal?'

'What if I don't? What if I break?'

'Then I will be here to hold the pieces.'

27

Kit stands outside Sibella's cottage for a long while before she knocks at the door. She doesn't know why she has come. All she knows is that she woke with a desperate need to escape Windfalls. She couldn't bear the thought of all that lay ahead of them: the forced joviality, the laughter, the toasting of a future now so bleak and uncertain. The marquee, standing empty in the orchard, perhaps the ultimate symbol of the pointlessness of it all – the flimsiest, most impermanent space – here today, gone tomorrow. She couldn't bear to look at it, knowing, in part, why it was there and the reason behind Lucy's rush down the aisle.

She had walked for a while along the river, beneath the bowed trees, watching their reflections shifting on the slow-moving water. A single grey heron had stood on a rock in the reeds on the opposite bank, contemplating the shallows. It had lifted its head as she passed by, but remained in place, still amongst the rushes. On a normal day, they'd be cheering the fact that the weather was mild and dry. They would be ironing wedding outfits and popping champagne. But this was anything but a normal day. She wasn't even sure there would be such a thing as a normal day now.

Her daughter had cancer. Terminal cancer. With those two words, the future she had taken for granted had been ripped from her grasp.

She hadn't known where she was headed, but at some point she had found her feet treading the steps of the stone bridge leading across the river and following the path rising up the far side of the valley, towards Sibella's house.

Sibella opens the door with a small nod of greeting. 'Come in,' she says, taking a step back to allow Kit into the kitchen.

She enters and glances about in bewilderment at the cluttered, homely space. This cottage where Ted now resides is a mere mile across the river from Windfalls, yet she's never stepped foot here before.

'Ted's popped out. He's gone to collect the trestle tables from the village hall.'

Kit nods. She doesn't know why she's here. She doesn't think it was to see Ted, but she's not sure she was intending to see Sibella, either. She should be back at the house, helping everyone prepare for the party. She is all at sea.

'I was going to make some coffee,' says Sibella. 'Would you like a cup?'

Kit nods. She can feel Sibella's careful gaze. 'Yes. Thank you.'

'Take a seat.'

Kit nods again and sits on a creaking wicker chair and then, without warning, something inside of her gives and, before she can stop herself, the tears begin to flow, a torrent of them pouring down her cheeks. She buries her face in her hands. Sibella, abandoning the kettle, joins her for a moment. She passes her a tissue and then presses her warm hand around Kit's cool one, sitting quietly beside her until the tears dry. Eventually, Sibella stands and rummages on a shelf for a cafetière and a tin of coffee. She brings the steaming pot to the table and sits again with Kit. 'You're in shock,' she says.

Kit sighs. 'I know what Lucy wants us to do today, but I don't think I can do it. I can't pretend everything is wonderful.' She pulls at the cuff on her sleeve, drawing it down over her hand. 'Why Lucy? Why now? She's so young. She has so much ahead of her.'

Sibella nods.

'I'm so angry.'

'Yes.'

'How do I stay strong for Lucy? How am I meant to bear this?'

'It's going to be hard.'

Kit sniffs. 'Time doesn't fucking heal. I've been waiting to feel "healed" ever since Ted left, and I still don't. I still feel the loss of him and our relationship. It's an ache that can't be eased.'

Sibella closes her eyes. 'I'm sorry, Kit.'

Kit shrugs. 'It was Ted's choice. He chose you, and perhaps he was right. I hadn't been paying attention to him. We lost our way, a long time ago. But it doesn't make it any easier. I loved him. Still love him, in my own way. But tell me, how do I lose a child and survive that? I don't think I can bear it.' Kit looks up, a twist of anger in her eyes. 'But you wouldn't know how that feels, would you?'

Sibella closes her eyes. 'I lost a husband . . . and a child – a baby, through miscarriage – a long time ago. I know about loss, Kit. I know about holding pain.'

Kit leans back in her chair. The wicker creaks loudly beneath her. She studies Sibella for a long moment then closes her eyes. 'I'm sorry.'

Sibella nods. 'I've never been a mother like you, Kit. You're right. I wouldn't understand how that feels.'

Kit grasps for words. 'I'm – I'm sorry. That day in the market, what I said . . . I didn't know . . . about your baby.'

Sibella shrugs. 'I understood. I *understand*. In an ideal world, I wouldn't have fallen in love with Ted, and he wouldn't have fallen in love with me. In an ideal world I would have found the strength to walk away. I'm not perfect, Kit.'

Kit lets out a hollow laugh. 'Are any of us? I'm sure as hell not. I messed up a relationship with Ted and seem to have failed my girls.' She looks up at Sibella, suddenly distraught. 'You have Ted. Please don't take the girls from me too.'

'I couldn't, Kit. Even if I wanted to. *You're* their mother. They love you.'

Kit's eyes well. She sighs. 'What Lucy is facing, she'll need all the support she can get. It suppose it's up to her, who she turns to, who she leans on. I shouldn't dictate that.'

'She's going to need you, Kit.'

She sighs. 'These lives we live, they are so fragile.'

Sibella nods. 'They are.'

Kit glances around, taking in a little more of her surroundings. There are dried seed heads and thistles bursting out of a jug. A small white skull – animal bones

– placed reverently on a shelf. A pine cone sits on the hearth. Sibella's delicate pieces of porcelain stand in the window, catching the light. In another corner, nestled in a frame, she sees the face of a handsome, dark-haired man gazing back at her. Kit stares at the photo. 'Your late husband?' she asks.

Sibella nods. 'Yes. That's Patrick.'

Kit glances around and feels, momentarily, as if a veil has been lifted from her eyes. They are everywhere: endings. Sibella's entire house seems to be littered with objects of loss, radiating the passing of time, reflecting back the impermanence of life. She turns her head and meets Sibella's gaze directly for the first time since she has arrived at her door.

She wraps her hands around the mug Sibella has pushed towards her. The earthy scent of coffee rises up, familiar and a little comforting. 'How do I accept this? How do I bear the pain? I don't know how to do it.'

Sibella sighs. 'Acceptance is a door you can't even see yet, Kit. It is a long way off. A hard-won process.'

'It feels as if I've had blinkers ripped from my eyes. Death. It's everywhere,' Kit says, looking around again at the kitchen. 'The wind shakes the trees and we fall at random.' Her gaze fixes on the small, white animal skull. 'Is there any point, to any of it?

'I don't know the answer to that. But what I do know is that where there is death and pain, there is life too – and love. It all goes hand in hand.'

Kit looks again. She doesn't know what Sibella is talking about. All she can see is the sheer pointlessness of it all. Why live and love at all, if all that comes from it is pain and devastation? She can't protect Lucy. She can't take the pain for her. She feels her failings as a mother as an acute agony.

'I know you don't want to feel this way, Kit. I know you want to change it. But if you deny the sorrow – the pain – then you deny the joy and love too. You can't have one without the other.'

Kit's gaze fixes on a burst of colour across the room, a small rose bush in a basket on a side table, heavy with yellow buds about to flower. She turns her head and sees a butterfly passing at the window, fluttering up close to the glass until it slides away again on the breeze. Across the room, there is a photo pinned to the fridge, of Ted with his arms thrown around a grinning Chloe and May. As Kit looks more closely, what at first seemed a little macabre – the husks of inanimate, dead creatures and plants – now seem strange, almost beautiful, juxtaposed as they are with the living. One illuminating the other.

'I don't know how to get through today with a smile on my face.'

'Lucy wants to celebrate with you,' says Sibella. 'Today is a day for life. Perhaps,' Sibella suggests gently, 'the day will feel all the sweeter, moving through it in the knowledge that none of us are here for ever. Just a lifetime, however long it turns out to be.'

Kit leans back in her chair. Something in the other woman's words chime. She closes her eyes and lets them settle. When she opens them again, she turns to Sibella. 'It's a shame, isn't it?'

Sibella tilts her head.

'I think we could have been friends.'

Sibella nods. 'Yes,' she says with a small smile. 'I think so too.'

28

Andrew tells her as she is applying make-up in the bath-room mirror. He stands behind her and comes right out with it. 'I know, Eve.'

'You know what?' she asks, her gaze flicking from his eyes back to the black kohl she is tracing across the lash line of her right eyelid.

'I know about the affair.'

Her hand stills, a small smudge of black where her fingers have jerked from their careful path. She places the pencil down on the edge of the porcelain sink and turns to her husband. 'The affair?'

'Yes.'

'Who told you?'

'Does it matter?'

'I suppose not.'

'So you aren't going to deny it?'

Eve drops her head. 'No.'

'Why, Eve? Why him?'

She sighs. When she has considered this moment – this confrontation – the peeling back of the truth of their relationship, it has always played out differently. In her mind, Andrew had always been red-faced and angry, raging at her with fierce indignation. And she would have been righteous and calm, explaining carefully how he had let her down, how she had needed more. But here they are and it's Andrew who is calm, standing there, depleted and sad and all she can think is, 'Yes. Why? Why him?' She doesn't have an answer.

He perches on the side of the bath, his head in his hands. 'I didn't believe her at first. She collared me last night in the pub. I think she's got a soft spot for him. She seemed most put out that he should be carrying on with you.' He gives a hollow laugh. 'She was angry that you should be there in the pub, dining with your husband and kids, while you were messing about with him. She said it was an insult. I thought she was crazy. I insisted she had got it wrong, but she swore blind she had seen you in the pub car park earlier in the week, kissing.'

Eve's stomach sinks. So it had been Stacey. She had been dreading the dinner, worried that she would give herself away in front of everyone, but in the end, it hadn't mattered. The barmaid had done it for her.

'I didn't want to believe her. I was angry at her meddling in our business. But do you know what convinced me?'

She's not sure she wants to know, but she needs to hear him out. It's the least she owes him.

'I replayed the night in my head, and there was one moment that stuck in my mind. As we arrived at the pub, Ryan slid a glass of red wine across the bar towards you. You didn't even have to ask him. Your favourite wine. Such a small gesture, but it spoke volumes. As soon as I remembered, I knew she was telling the truth. Don't you think it was a bit much, us going there for

295

dinner as a family – taking the girls, for God's sake – to the pub your . . . your *lover* manages?' He spits the last words as if they leave a bad taste in his mouth.

'I'm sorry.' Eve hangs her head. 'I know how it looks, but it wasn't my choice. It was Lucy and Tom's. They wanted us to have the dinner there. I had to go along with it.'

'Of course you did,' says Andrew bitterly. He groans. 'And now we have the charade of today to get through.'

Eve nods. This, on top of Lucy's bombshell news is the final straw. She sits beside Andrew on the edge of the bath, feeling utterly defeated. 'I'm sorry. I'm so sorry.' She reaches for his hand but he brushes her off.

'How long?'

'Not long. Weeks. No more.'

'How many times have you slept with him?'

'Once. Twice . . . nearly.' She swallows at the sight of Andrew's anguish. 'Look, I don't expect this to make you feel any better, but I was going to tell him as soon as the wedding was out of the way that it was over, that I didn't want him. I didn't want to lie to you any more.'

Andrew gives a hollow laugh. 'I don't understand, Eve. We had it all. A beautiful home. Two great kids. I *loved* you. I thought you loved me too.'

Eve looks up, into the face of the man she has lived with for the last eleven years. She sees the faded white scar on his cheek from the childhood bike accident he'd told her about on their first date. She sees the amber flecks in his hazel irises that shine in their daughters' eyes, and the small crease between his eyebrows that forms when he frowns, that she knows will forge over time into a deeper cleft mirroring the one on his own father's face. She knows this man and she knows that she loves him and she feels a terrible pain at what she has gambled and lost. He *loved* her. Past tense. She has destroyed something rare, something precious.

Andrew seems to read the sadness on her face, because he reaches out and takes her hand in his. 'It's a big day. I know you're processing what Lucy told you last night. I know we have to get through today as best we can – for Lucy and Tom, for our girls. But we need to talk. We need to . . . decide . . . how we . . . if we want to . . .'

She nods. Part of her wishes he would shout. She wishes he would rage and scream, but instead, he is being so Andrew – so decent. It takes her breath away at how wrong she has got this. Ever since Lucy has shared her devastating news, she has wanted nothing but to draw him close, to feel his arms around her, to rest her head on his shoulder and close her eyes and have him tell her that everything will be OK. Instead, she has pushed him away – hurt him dreadfully – at the time she realises she needs him the most.

He smiles, a small, sad smile. 'You look nice. New dress?'

'No.' She reaches out and straightens the Windsor knot of his tie. 'Crooked. That's better.' She frowns. 'So this was what you wanted to talk to me about last night?'

'No.' Andrew pulls something from his pocket. 'I was going to give you this. I got it for you. Before . . . well,' he shrugs, 'just before.' He hands her a small velvet box. Eve opens it to find a pair of beautiful, art deco diamond earrings. 'I asked Jenny from the office to help me choose them. I wanted to get you something special, as you'd been working so hard to help everyone else these past few weeks but you know how hopeless I am at choosing jewellery. She looks a bit like you so I thought if they looked good on her . . .'

Eve reaches out to touch one of the diamond earrings. Under the bright bathroom lights they glitter like fire.

'I was going to apologise for being so caught up in my work and ignoring you and the kids. I was planning to tell you that I would try harder.' Andrew's face crumples. He buries his head in his hands for a moment, then seems to gather himself.

If Eve had ever tried to picture the moment her marriage collapsed, she would never have imagined it like this, the two of them sitting quietly together in the bathroom, tears in their eyes, a pair of beautiful diamond earrings lying between them.

She touches him on the arm. 'Thank you. Not just for the gift. For today. For being so strong when I know you'd rather . . . you'd rather not go through this.'

He stands. 'I'll go check on the girls. OK to leave in twenty minutes?'

She waits for him to leave the bathroom before she sinks down onto the cool tiled floor, the earring still gripped in her fingers.

29

Ted can't stop moving. There is so much to be done. Shoes to be polished. Shirt to be ironed. Bottles of wine and glasses to be unboxed. A bonfire to be built.

After he'd dropped the trestle tables at the marquee, he'd stood in the lower orchard, surveying the pile of wood gathered for the evening's bonfire. Not big enough, he'd told himself. Not nearly big enough. So he had spent the last forty-minutes dragging wood onto the pile from a huge stash of old storm-blown branches and logs cleared last winter and sitting stacked in a lean-to.

It is hard work. Ted feels perspiration beading on his forehead and splinters stabbing his hands, but he tells himself if he keeps going, if he keeps building the pile, he will somehow remain in control of the situation – the situation he can't bear to think about. One more branch, he tells himself, one more . . . to make everything better.

Sibella had tried to talk to him earlier that morning. They had been lying in bed, listening to the birdsong, when she had gently tested the ground, asking him careful questions about the night before – about Lucy – and about his feelings. But he hadn't been able to talk to her. He hadn't wanted to think about it. He'd told her, too curtly, that there was nothing to discuss. He was going to do what Lucy had asked. He was going to celebrate the day and not dwell on anything sad or anything that he couldn't control. He was going to forget it. That's what he was going to do.

'I don't think that's what she meant,' Sibella had said, gently.

'Don't, Sib. Don't press me.'

Reading his fear and his anger, she had acquiesced with a gentle squeeze of his arm.

He has just thrown a huge sheet of rotten timber onto the pile when he notices Kit walking through the long grass towards the marquee. Even at his distance he can see that she is bowed and pale-faced, dark shadows under her eyes. She carries a tray of glasses, stepping carefully over the uneven ground before disappearing inside the tent.

Sibella had called to tell him about Kit's early morning visit after he had dropped off the tables. 'What did she want?' he'd asked, alarmed at the thought of her there in their home. He hadn't liked to think of the two women together, conversing privately, without him. The thought had made him deeply uncomfortable. Until another realisation had struck him: how terribly alone Kit must have felt, to come knocking at *their* door.

He stands back to assess the huge wooden pile in front of him, then, with a sigh, he throws a last log onto the towering structure, dusts his hands on his shirt and makes for the marquee.

Kit is arranging the glasses on a table in the far corner. She doesn't hear him approach until he is a few feet away. She turns, startled. 'Oh, it's you.'

'How are you?'

Kit shrugs. 'Fine.' She eyes him warily. 'You?'

'Yes. Fine. Keeping busy. There's a lot to do.'

'Yes.'

They stand in silence, the weight of all that is unspoken hanging between them, until Kit can't contain her anguish any longer. She lets out a sob. 'Oh, Ted.'

Seeing her pain, Ted closes the gap and draws her to him. 'I know, Kitty, I know.' At the familiar sensation of her in his arms and the fragrance of her hair, Ted feels a tug of longing – for a time, a place, a woman he once knew.

'It's all wrong.'

'Yes.'

'How did we get it so wrong? How is this the place we find ourselves?'

Ted closes his eyes, surprised to feel the stirrings of a warmth and connection to this woman – this fierce, frustrating, deeply complicated woman. 'I don't know, Kitty. I don't know.'

He guides her to one of the nearby hay bales and they sit quietly as Kit composes herself, Ted brushing at the bark and dust on his shirt sleeves.

'We're going to have to be strong, Kit,' he says, eventually. 'She's going to need us. They're all going to need us.'

'I know.'

Kit pulls at the loose tufts of hay beside her. Looking at her sitting there in her tired, depleted state, he is reminded of a different Kit, a young woman on the brink of exhaustion holding a wailing baby in her arms. Eve, he remembers. It would have been Eve. She had been such an unsettled baby, and Kit had been so miserable, until she had found release through her writing. The memory pierces his heart like an arrow. He feels an unspoken truth rising up and before he can stop himself, the words have left his tongue. 'You were right, you know.'

She looks at him, uncertainly. 'About what?'

'I *was* jealous: of your success, of the ease with which your words seemed to come to you. At the way your career took off. The stronger and the more successful you became, the more I felt empty and useless in contrast.'

'It was never a competition, Ted. I never meant to make you feel that way. I wanted my work to ease your burden, not add to it.'

Ted nods. 'I know.' He gives a dry laugh. 'It doesn't reflect well on me as a man, does it, to be so emasculated by my partner's success?'

Kits smiles. 'Honestly? No. It doesn't.'

Ted laughs again. 'You always were a straight-talker.'

'Not that it's got me far.' She bites her lip. 'I'm so afraid, Ted. It feels as though it's all spiralling away from me. First you. Then Margot. Now Lucy.'

He squeezes her hand, unable to find the reassurances she needs.

Kit sighs. 'You do know, don't you, that I turned a blind eye to Sibella? For nearly four years I let you go to her. No questions asked. No ultimatum. I knew the kind of man you were. I knew the tighter I tried to hold on, the more you would seek release. I knew you needed the attention, the affection. I knew how unfulfilled you were in your work. I thought if I gave you that – if I let you have your freedom – that you would come back to me, eventually.' She sighs and gives him a look of such deep longing that Ted feels something inside of him crack. 'Maybe I should have fought harder?'

Ted swallows. His heart feels so heavy he is not sure he can bear the weight of it pulsing in his chest.

'It will always be one of my deepest regrets that perhaps you never knew how much I loved you.'

'I'm sorry, Kit.'

Kit nods.

'I see now it was cruel. I should never have let it drag on for so long. For what it's worth, Sibella never asked me to choose either. She understood about the girls — that I had responsibilities. But I had to make a choice. It wasn't healthy. For any of us.'

Kit nods. 'You did choose,' she says softly. 'You chose her.'

He hears the pain in her voice and feels a twist of guilt.

'Do you know what makes it even worse?' she asks, after a long moment.

'What?' asks Ted, not sure he wants to know the answer.

'I like her. I bloody like her.'

'I'm sorry, Kit. I'm sorry for all of it.'

She shrugs. 'We are where we are. I suppose we focus on today, as Lucy has asked.'

Ted nods. 'It's as good a place as any to start.'

Kit pats his hand then, with a deep exhalation, pushes herself up from the chair. 'Come on. You're right. There's a lot to do. Not least, you should shower and change out of those dirty clothes. Right now, you're looking a little less like a father of the bride and more Worzel Gummidge.'

30

Margot has dragged the ironing board to the upstairs landing and stands in a square of sunlight in her underwear, pressing a pale blue dress. Lucy eyes her sister's slim frame, her long legs, the startling ink tattoo curling up her left arm. As she lifts her head, Lucy sees the curse of a hangover in her sister's pained expression and her red, bloodshot eyes. She doesn't feel angry. Margot is here, and that is enough, today. 'Will you help me with my hair?' she asks.

'Of course.' Margot switches off the iron, slips into her dress and joins Lucy in her bedroom. She brushes her wild, blonde mane and Lucy closes her eyes, enjoying the sensation of the brush moving over her scalp, Margot's fingers running through her hair. 'So what are we going to do with it?'

Together they fashion a loose up-do before Margot paints Lucy's lips a vivid red, her hand only slightly steadier than Lucy's own. She helps her into the red dress, fastening the zipper running along her spine. 'You look stunning,' says Margot, standing back to appraise her.

'Thanks.'

'Luce,' says Margot, sounding hesitant. 'I'm sorry for last night.'

Lucy nods. 'It's OK. How's your head today? Need a hair of the dog?' she asks, indicating the champagne in the corner of the room.

'No. I'm not drinking today.' Margot's gaze fixes on the suitcase standing in the corner of the room. 'Is that for Monday?' she asks.

Lucy nods. 'Quite the honeymoon, right?'

'You can take one after . . . when you're better.'

'Yes,' she says, squeezing Margot's hand. She doesn't correct her.

'What time are you due at the register office?'

'Twelve.'

'And you're sure you don't want the rest of us to come with you?'

'It's just the legal stuff, isn't it? I think it means more to the parents to witness the formalities. For me, the wedding – the marriage – it starts back here, with all of you.'

'Just think, by the time you return, you'll be an old, married lady.'

'A little less of the old, thanks.'

Kit knocks tentatively on the door before entering. She has changed into a long colourful dress covered in huge flowers and tied her hair up into its usual messy knot. Turquoise earrings glint at her lobes. Margot throws Lucy a surprised look.

'Oh,' says Kit, startling at the sight of Lucy stepping out from behind her sister. 'Oh Lucy,' she breathes, her eyes widening, her lower lip beginning to tremble.

'Don't cry.'

305

'It's OK. I'm wearing waterproof mascara.'

'Do I look all right?' Lucy asks, nervous.

'You look perfect.'

'You look great too, Mum,' Margot says, throwing another surprised glance at Lucy.

'Is it all right?' Kit asks, tugging at the fabric.

'More than.'

'I didn't want to let the side down.'

There is another knock at the door. 'Is everyone decent?'

Margot throws the door open to Jonas. 'As we'll ever be.'

'I wondered if you'd like me to take some photos? A few candid shots, nothing posed. You can all carry on doing what you're doing.'

Lucy smiles. It's obvious from the way Jonas is looking at Margot that he's crazy about her. If she doesn't make the most of this, she's going to have to give her a stern talking to later.

Margot glances at Lucy. 'We don't have to, Luce, it's up to you.'

Lucy flashes her most brilliant smile at Jonas. 'I'd love that. Thank you. What?' she asks, catching Margot and Kit's amused exchange.

'Well, you sure changed your tune,' says Margot.

The sound of a horn blares out on the drive. 'That'll be Tom, back with the car,' says Lucy with a nervous smile. 'Time to go.'

31

With Lucy and Tom out of the house, the place becomes a hive of activity. Furniture is moved. Plates and cutlery are pulled out of hire crates, ice tipped into buckets, bottles arranged. Everyone lends a hand, even Chloe and May who are set to work on folding a stack of napkins and counting cutlery. It seems they all need a job to occupy their hands, to focus their love and attention, and to keep them from their thoughts.

Sibella arrives, looking beautiful in a simple, yellow linen dress. Margot helps her unload jam jars of meadow flowers, cut roses and the arrangements of dried lavender and wheat from the back of her car. Eve and Margot help her dot the flowers about the place – some in the house, some in the marquee – and arrange the lavender and wheat in a stunning display around the entrance to the tent. When they are finished, the air hums with the scent of late summer.

Walking back up from the marquee, they come upon Chloe and May, tumbling down the hillside in a roly-poly race. 'Oh God,' says Eve, spotting the green stains on their once pristine white dresses, the blades of grass caught in their hair. 'The party hasn't even started yet and look at them!'

'Remind you of anything?' asks Margot with a sly smile. 'Lucy always had to win. Didn't she? She'd have a complete tantrum if we didn't let her.' Then seeing Eve's frown. 'Come on. I mean, who cares about a few grass stains? Let them have their fun.' She squeezes her hand. 'There are more important things.'

Eve bites her lip and nods. 'Right. More important things.'

The mood at the house – industrious and focused – shifts as soon as Lucy and Tom arrive back at Windfalls, with both sets of parents in tow. The married couple tumble from Tom's battered jeep, flushed and excited, flashing their rings and their smiles, accepting congratulatory kisses and hugs. Almost simultaneously, a steady stream of vehicles and guests begins to appear down the drive. Champagne corks are popped. Glasses are clinked. Confetti is thrown. Someone, in the excitement, exuberantly throws a bag of rice at the couple, the whole packet clobbering Tom on the side of the head.

Margot hangs back a little, watching. She sees Jonas, dressed now in a slim-fitting dark suit and white shirt, moving through the crowd, unobtrusively snapping the guests unawares. She notes more than a couple of admiring glances cast in his direction and feels an unfamiliar emotion pulling at her. Oh Christ, she thinks. Is she jealous?

She pushes through the lively throng in the garden to find Eve. 'Bloody hell,' she says under her breath. 'There's a lot of them. Do you think we've got enough food?'

Eve nods, her face calm, her eyes scanning the crowd. 'Yes, Margot. We have enough food.'

'Course we do. You're bloody brilliant.'

Eve gives her a small smile. 'Thanks.'

Margot frowns. 'You OK?'

'Not now.' She turns away, but not before Margot has seen the tears brimming in her sister's eyes.

A battered transit van pulls up outside the house, out of which spills a motley crew of Tom's friends, dragging instruments and equipment down to a small, makeshift stage in the orchard. After a brief tuning of guitars and checking of amps, they start up a folksy arrangement of one of Lucy's favourite songs. Margot watches as Lucy shrieks with delight, kicks off her shoes and pulls Tom towards the little stage, for an impromptu first dance. She is a blur of red silk, blonde hair and flashing white teeth dancing barefoot in the grass and Tom, struggling to keep up with her, can't seem to wipe the smile off his face. Margot watches them, feeling a deep ache rise up beside her joy.

The afternoon slides towards evening. The champagne continues to flow. Someone drags a keg of local ale onto a table in the marquee. The lamps hanging in the apple trees are lit. Cushions are requisitioned from the house. With the trickling release of Lucy's news, any caution or careful reserve seems to fade with the growing sense of *carpe diem* that has seized the event. Andrew lights the bonfire and the air is filled with smoke and heat, the crackle of burning wood. It brings a new kind of energy to the proceedings, a certain primal wildness. A DJ takes to the decks in the marquee, the thud of bass changing the tempo of the night.

Margot, standing at a distance, inhales the scent of fire and closes her eyes. Something like fear stirs in her belly. When she opens them again, she sees her mother standing on the other side of the smoke haze, watching her. Their eyes meet over the bonfire and in the glowing light, Kit's eyes reflect the red of the flames. They navigate the space, she thinks, like satellites revolving round the same planet, keeping a careful distance. Margot swallows and turns away. Not today, she tells herself. She will not let the memories claim her today.

Across the marquee, Margot can see Tom, leaning against the bar looking glum. She goes to him and places a glass of champagne in his hand. Their gaze tracks to Lucy, seated on a hay bale laughing and joking with a group of friends.

'She's amazing,' says Margot.

'Yes, she is.'

'She won't pay any attention to me when I suggest she takes it easy today,' he says regretfully. 'But it's impossible to stay annoyed at her. Look.'

Margot smiles, watching Lucy sashay theatrically with a girlfriend across to the dance floor, swishing the long silk skirt of her dress. 'It is impossible,' she agrees. 'Trust me, I've had a lifetime practising.'

They both fall silent and Margot wonders if the word 'lifetime' has jarred for him too. It's not helpful, she knows, but it's hard not to wonder how much time is left. She looks so vibrant, so full of life. Surely, the surgery and the chemo will fix her? It's impossible to imagine a world without the sheer force of Lucy in it.

Jonas appears at her side, his hand at her waist. He removes his camera from where it hangs around his neck and offers it to them both. 'Take a look,' he says. She leans in to the display as Tom scrolls back through the images Jonas has taken. There is one of May, her huge blue eyes looking up over a yellow rose. Lucy looking radiant as she steps from Tom's car, her face creased with laughter. Another of Margot and Eve at the entrance to the tent, heads bent together in quiet discussion, a picture of Sibella looking happy, her head resting on Ted's shoulder. Kit holding court in the kitchen surrounded by a cluster of Lucy's adoring friends. There are shots of the guests laughing and dancing, and one captured through the opening of the marquee, Lucy and Tom in an intimate moment of stillness, foreheads pressed together, eyes closed.

'They're gorgeous,' says Margot, genuinely taken aback.

Jonas nods. 'They're going to be amazing,' he says. 'There is so much love here.' He grabs her hand. 'Margot, you have an amazing family.'

Margot looks over his shoulder and sees Eve over near the band, spinning May around in her arms, her little feet flying out from beneath her. She sees Lucy and Ted, in his crumpled linen suit, dancing in a makeshift circle and Andrew waltzing awkwardly with Kit. She sees them all and smiles. 'Yes, I do.' She turns back to Jonas. 'I'm so glad you're here,' she says, the words out of her mouth before she can stop them.

He smiles down at her, holding her gaze.

Tom clears his throat. 'I think I'll go and dance with my lovely wife,' he says, tactfully.

Jonas leans in towards Margot. 'You look beautiful,' he says.

'Thank you.'

He reels backwards in exaggerated shock. 'I do believe she accepted a compliment.'

She whacks him on the arm. 'Ha ha. Funny guy.'

'Thank you,' he says. 'See, I can take a compliment too.'

Margot narrows her eyes. He lifts his camera as if to take her photo but she bats it away. 'How about you put that down for a moment and kiss me instead?'

When Tom returns, red-faced and puffing from an energetic dance-off, Margot leaves him chatting with Jonas, and heads across to the far side of the marquee, where she can see Eve seated on one of the hay bales in the corner of the tent, her face flashing alternate red, purple, green and blue under the disco strobe light. She is watching Andrew whirl Chloe around the dance floor, his cheeks flushed and his shirt buttons straining against his stomach. Chloe is shrieking with delight, giddy on the lateness of the night and the lemonade she has been sneaking from the bar. Cyndi Lauper is singing about girls just wanting to have fun. Margot protests as Andrew attempts to draw her into their dance party, before plonking herself down next to Eve on the hay bale. They watch the antics out on the dance floor in silence, together in their stillness.

'I think my marriage is over,' Eve says finally, her eyes never leaving the scene in front of them, but leaning in slightly so that Margot can hear the words over the music.

Margot doesn't say anything for a moment. Eve knows about the affair. She doesn't know who told her, but at least she isn't going to have to be the one to do it. This week of surprises just keeps on giving. She turns to Eve. 'You *think* it's over, or you *know*?'

She shrugs.

'What happened?' asks Margot carefully.

'Andrew found out I've been having an affair.'

Margot frowns. 'What?'

'I've been having an affair,' she repeats. 'With Ryan.'

Margot can't keep up. '*You* have? With Ryan? Ryan from the pub?'

'Uh-huh.'

Margot stares, open-mouthed. 'What the fuck, Eve!'

Eve nods. 'I know.'

'I just ... I can't ... *you*? *You* had an affair?'

Eve turns to Margot and narrows her eyes. 'Is it that hard to believe?'

'Sorry, no. It's just you're so ... you're so ...'

'So what?'

'Well ... good. Moral. You always know the right thing to do. You always *do* the right thing. I suppose it's that ... and the fact that Lucy said ... and I thought ...' She catches herself. 'Never mind. It doesn't matter what we thought. Fuck, Eve.'

'Andrew found out last night. He confronted me this morning.'

'How?' But Margot is remembering the night before and a hazy moment in the pub car park, the stolen cigarette, the security light flashing onto a scene, the barmaid from the pub gesticulating angrily, the look on Andrew's ashen-face. The penny drops. The barmaid must have known. She must have been the one to tell him. 'Oh Eve. What are you going to do?'

'I don't know. I'm so ashamed. I had my head turned.

I don't understand it myself. If you'd told me a few months ago that I'd sleep with another man – with Ryan – I would have laughed at you. But I've got to know him a bit over the past few months and I don't know . . . the way he looked at me, the way he spoke to me, made me feel . . . *seen*. He made me feel good. Desired.' Eve looks shamefaced. 'I think I needed someone to see me not just as a wife, or a mother, or a meddling sister,' she adds with a regretful smile, 'but as me, Eve. Ryan made me feel special.'

'You *are* special, Eve.' Margot is still staggered at her sister's revelation. Eve and Ryan. 'How is Andrew taking the news?'

'He's doing that male thing of hiding his emotions. Look at him,' she says.

Margot turns and sees Andrew strutting like Mick Jagger across the dance floor, playing the fool for his daughters. Under his arms, sweat patches are blooming on his shirt and his cheeks are flushed red. When Margot turns back to Eve, she sees that by comparison her sister looks inordinately pale and sad. 'Lucy's news . . . it makes you see the world a little differently, doesn't it?' she says.

Margot nods. 'Yes. It does.'

'We've got it so wrong, Andrew and I. I think, per-haps, we both stopped trying. We lost sight of each other and what's most important. I never thought we'd become *that* couple. The one bickering over school runs and washing-up.'

Margot can't shake the image of Andrew's white face from the night before. 'What did he say? How did he react?'

'He gave me a pair of diamond earrings?'

'He what?'

Eve nods. 'He gave me these.' She gestures to the glittering art deco earrings at her earlobes. Margot's eyes widen even further. 'He's angry,' she continues, 'but mostly sad. I think the earrings were going to be an apology, for being so distracted by his work, for not being there enough. Only it seems that I'm the one who owes *him* the bigger apology.'

Margot reaches out and takes Eve's hand.

'He's a good dad,' Eve adds, watching him with the girls, Chloe's feet now balanced on Andrew's polished shoes as he holds her tight and dances her around the tent in time to the music, the smaller May clinging like a monkey to his back.

'And you're a good mum.' Margot squeezes her sister's fingers. 'You're a good person.'

'I don't feel good. I broke my wedding vows. I've lost Andrew's trust. I've potentially thrown away our entire marriage and all we've built together.'

'If you both want to work this out, you will find a way. And well . . . if not, you'll be OK. You are strong — stronger than you know,' says Margot, fiercely.

'Perhaps we all are, when we have to be?' Eve says, nodding at Lucy, then turning her sliding glance back to Margot. 'Perhaps it's better to have our secrets out in the open. It's painful, but at least we are standing on the same ground now. We can see what is broken. Perhaps you have to do that, before you can even start to think about accepting it, healing it?'

Margot knows Eve is asking something of her. She knows she's asking her to open up. Margot hesitates, wondering if she can find the words, wondering whether she can unburden herself of the darkness she has carried for so long. What was it Jonas had said to her? *Let yourself feel it all. What's the worst that could happen?*

Laughter erupts from the dance floor. They turn to see Lucy, swaying with her girlfriends, arms around shoulders, her face flushed, her hair falling around her face.

'It's hard to believe, isn't it?' says Eve.

'Do you think she's in denial?'

'Wouldn't you be?'

'I keep wanting her to tell us it's a sick joke. Part of her hare-brained scheme to make us celebrate this day, all together.'

'Is she overdoing it, do you think?'

'Probably.'

Margot bites her lip. 'Should we intervene?'

'This is Lucy's night. We've got to let her do it her way.'

Margot glances at Eve in surprise. That *she* should be the one to relinquish control and let Lucy be is unexpected, but Eve nods and with a sigh, leans her head against Margot's shoulder.

Lucy, spying them through the swaying guests, comes and collapses, hot and sweaty, onto the hay next to them. 'Oh my God,' she says, gasping, 'please save me from my brother-in-law's tragic dance moves. I'm dying.'

There is a shocked silence. The three sisters freeze as the truth of Lucy's words registers. Eve looks from Margot to Lucy and then, without warning, all three of them burst out laughing. 'It's not funny,' says Eve.

'It's not,' agrees Margot.

But they can't seem to stop, their laughter mingling with tears, their hands reaching out for each other.

There is a sudden change in the tempo of the music as it shifts from a classic disco number to the gentle acoustic riffs of 'Harvest Moon'. Andrew comes and stands in front of them, a hand held out to Eve. 'It's our song, Eve.'

Eve glances uncertainly at Margot. Margot nods as Lucy pushes her up off the hay bale. 'Go on,' she says. 'For God's sake, go and dance with your husband.'

32

The night stretches – long and rowdy – a carousel of music and dancing and drinking. Andrew gathers up their sleeping girls from sofas in the house and carries them to the car. 'Stay,' he says. 'It's important. You won't have this night again.'

Eve nods. 'Thank you.' She turns away before he can see the tears in her eyes.

In the kitchen, she busies herself with rinsing champagne glasses and scraping discarded plates of food, stacking them by the sink for the morning clean-up. She empties the bin and replaces the rubbish bag. Somewhere out in the orchard, she can hear a guitar playing. There is low laughter and singing. Why is she in here, she wonders? What is she hiding from?

She finds Lucy and Margot stretched out on the grass near the bonfire, propped up on cushions and wrapped in blankets stolen from the house to fend off the cooler night air. The fire has slumped to embers and the mood has settled into something more considered and contemplative as the idea of morning creeps closer. A pale violet hue rises on the horizon, drawing a faint outline over the surrounding hills.

Eve looks at her sisters, Margot with her arms wrapped around her knees, her face lit in the glow of the fire and Lucy lying next to her, looking exhausted, but beatifically happy. She thinks of Andrew and the girls tucked safely in their beds at home. She thinks of the amount of tidying still to do in the morning, when 'tomorrow' has officially arrived. 'Andrew's already taken the girls home, but I should probably go too,' she says.

'Why should you go?' asks Lucy.

Eve shrugs. 'I don't know. Mother guilt. Wife guilt. Guilt guilt.'

'I'm sure Andrew can handle it. Stay. Just a little longer.'

Eve looks at her sisters and realises why she has always felt 'other'. Perhaps it wasn't them. Perhaps it was always her, holding herself at arm's length. She had created the gap, set herself apart, taken responsibilities and duties upon herself that perhaps she hadn't needed to. She nods and sinks down onto the cushion beside Lucy. 'For a little bit.'

'Look what Jonas gave me,' says Margot, producing a spliff from the folds of her dress.

'I don't know where you found him, but I think I might be a little in love your photographer friend,' says Lucy, with a happy sigh. 'He's fit, too,' she adds, nudging Margot in the ribs. 'I hope you're going to let him love you. It's obvious that he does.'

Margot's blushes mirror the warm glow of the fire. Eve frowns at the spliff in her hand. 'Is that a good idea?'

Lucy laughs. 'For fuck's sake, Eve. I've got cancer. I think the least I deserve is a medicinal spliff.'

Margot lights the joint and passes it to Lucy. They sit

in silence for a while, watching the fading bonfire, the way the sparks crackle and fade away into the still-dark sky. Eve accepts the spliff from Lucy and takes a drag. She ignores the amused look shared between her sisters.

'Don't you sometimes wonder what it's all about?' Margot asks, after a long silence. 'If there's any rhyme or reason to it all?'

'All the time,' says Lucy.

'You must think, "why me?"' says Eve, turning to Lucy.

Lucy shrugs. 'Yes. But you know, "why not me?" Life is a lottery. Isn't that what makes it such a wild ride?'

Margot clears her throat. 'Are you scared?'

'I am.' The bonfire shifts, logs collapsing into ash, sparks spiralling up into the sky. 'I'm going to give it my best shot though. I'm young. I'm fit and I've got great doctors. I mean, for fuck's sake, I run a yoga and wellness studio. That's got to be in my favour, right?'

Margot and Eve nod vehemently.

'This diagnosis makes every day even more precious. It makes me want to be more open, to live more boldly and to love more wholeheartedly, in the time that I have. And,' she adds, with a small smile, 'if I can abuse your sympathies,' she turns to Margot, 'and force you to face up to the rifts of the past ... well, then I can die happy and with you lot all thoroughly annoyed with me. Right?'

Lucy is trying to make a joke but Margot has fallen silent, staring into the embers of the bonfire. Her face is ashen and she wears an expression Eve hasn't seen in a long time. Uncertainty, trepidation, as if she is perched on a ledge, wondering whether to jump.

With a sigh, Margot turns to them both. There is a shift in her expression and Eve sees something new in her eyes. Determination. She has made a decision.

'There's something I need to tell you both,' Margot says quietly.

Eve stays silent. She senses Lucy's stillness too, their held breath. They both watch as Margot turns back to the fire. 'It's something I should have told you years ago.'

Eve and Lucy, sensing the precipice Margot hangs on, remain still as their sister begins to speak. They listen as Margot plunges for the first time, with halting words, into her untold truth.

THE PAST

2009–2010

33

At Christmas, Ted invited Eve, Margot and a recently returned Lucy to a Christmas Eve dinner at the pub. It was to be their first proper catch-up since Lucy's globetrotting, and with Ted and Sibella as an official couple. Margot, dreading the idea of an evening of false festivities and close scrutiny, slid reluctantly into the backseat of Ted's car where he sat waiting for her outside Windfalls. Sibella, wearing a red coat and with her hair flowing down her back and Ted – jubilant from a recent return from London where his long-awaited new play, *Attrition*, had opened to critical acclaim – were both in high spirits. Ted seemed intent on grilling Margot on every aspect of her life. Margot slumped down in the back seat and answered their questions with the most perfunctory of replies.

'How are the A levels going?' Ted asked, steering the car round the hairpin bends of the Mortford lanes.

'Fine.'

'You're coping with the workload?'

'Uh-huh.'

'Everything all right with your mum?'

'Yes.'

She saw Ted and Sibella exchange a glance. No doubt they thought her a moody teenager, struggling to accept her father's new partner. Let them think that. It was easier.

Lucy and Eve were waiting inside the pub, perched on bar stools. Lucy, golden brown, her hair knotted in tight plaits and dressed in head-to-toe flowing tie-dye from her stint in India – where three months had turned to six months after a heady but doomed love affair with a fellow yogi – looked impossibly radiant and healthy and Eve, well, Eve looked impossibly tired on a rare night off from looking after baby Chloe.

Ted ordered champagne and regaled them with stories from Theatreland. They pulled Christmas crackers and Margot tried to blend in with them all, tried to look like she was having fun, while saying very little of anything to anyone. When she excused herself, Lucy followed her to the ladies, accosting her at the washbasins. 'Is every-thing all right? You don't seem yourself.'

'Uh-huh.' Margot kept her gaze fixed on her hands, the soap foaming between her fingers, the water scalding hot.

Lucy narrowed her eyes. 'You sure? It's like . . . it's like someone's switched you off. Like a light's gone out.'

Margot met Lucy's gaze in the mirror. 'A light? You've been in India too long.'

'Is it stuff at home? Is it weird being there just you and Mum?'

'She's busy with the final book,' muttered Margot.

Lucy sighed. 'I know it's hard but we've got to give Sibella a chance, for Dad's sake.'

Margot shook her head. 'Sibella's all right.'

Lucy nodded, taking the opening, clearly eager to discuss their father's girlfriend. 'She seems sane, which is a start, right?' She grinned at Margot. 'Wonder what she sees in Dad?'

Margot tried to muster a smile.

'I'm a bit jealous of her hair.'

Margot felt Lucy's close gaze sweeping over her again. She forced herself not to shrink away as Lucy reached out and tugged at the sleeve of her hoodie. 'Isn't this one of Eve's old tops?'

Margot shrugged. 'It's comfy.'

'It's hideous. I need to take you shopping. You're so pretty. You shouldn't hide away.'

Margot remembered the last time she'd felt pretty. The night she had stood on a stage and felt seen and appreciated, an audience applauding her. She remembered Mr Hudson's gaze – the way he had looked at her. The way she had encouraged it. Why would she draw attention to herself? She knows what happens when you do . . . things that hurt . . . things you can't control.

The door to the ladies opened. 'There you are,' said Eve, ducking inside. 'I need in on this. Are we dissecting Dad and Sibella?'

Lucy nodded. 'Quick. Shut the door. What do you make of her?'

'I want to dislike her, but I think Dad's done well. What about you two?'

Lucy shrugged. 'It would help a bit if she wasn't one of those annoying women who looks gorgeous without a scrap of make-up, but yeah, we're in agreement. Though I think we could all do with a little less of his puppy-dog eyes. It's a bit cringe.'

'What do you think she sees in *him*?' Eve asked. 'He's so much older.'

'I asked her that,' said Lucy, matter-of-factly.

Eve gawped at Lucy. 'You what? Oh Lucy. Of course you did.' She shook her head. 'Well, come on then, what did she say?'

'She said he was "sweet and loving" and then said something about him having "a brilliant mind".' Lucy shrugged.

Margot eyed the door. She wanted to be at home, under her duvet, away from the intense family analysis.

'I was just telling Margot she needs to sort out her look,' Lucy said, switching subjects. 'These old hoodies and tracksuit bottoms are doing nothing for her.'

'I like them,' said Margot, jutting her chin. 'Besides, there's more to life than clothes and make-up.'

Eve turned to regard herself in the mirror, tugging at her own loose top, adjusting a breast pad inside her bra. 'God, my boobs are so huge! I thought I would have lost all this baby weight by now. The midwives told me breastfeeding would suck the fat out of me, but they lied. I feel more enormous than ever.'

'Will you two stop already?' Lucy asked. 'You're both gorgeous. If you don't feel good about yourselves, maybe you should try one of my yoga classes.'

Eve and Margot looked at each other and burst out laughing.

'What? It's fun. Yoga is for every body. That's our mantra at the studio. You might enjoy it.'

Eve rolled her eyes. 'Lucy, if I could find an hour to myself without a crying, mewling thing clinging to me demanding milk and nappy changes, do you know what I'd do with it? I'd crawl into bed and sleep.'

Yes, thought Margot silently. Me too.

'It would be good for you,' argued Lucy, unwilling to give up so easily. 'And it might put a spring back in your step too, Margot. You seem so . . . so . . .' Lucy didn't finish her sentence but Margot knew what she wanted to say. She saw them both regarding her in the mirror, her lank, greasy hair, her dull skin, the ugly grey hoodie now a permanent fixture dwarfing her body. She knew what they saw: the disgusting, unlovable truth of her, manifested there for all to see.

Her reflection stared back at her from the graffitied mirror over the sink. It startled her, in many ways, that she was visible in the glass. She felt so hollowed-out and numb. There was something wrong with her, something broken that she wasn't sure could be fixed. She was a husk, emptied out and ready to blow away on the breeze.

Eve yawned. 'We'd best get back out there. They'll know we're talking about them. Besides, the sooner we order dessert, the sooner I can get home to bed. Unless there is a Christmas miracle tonight, Chloe's going to be waking me up at 2 a.m. for another feed.'

Back at the table, Margot slumped into her seat and allowed the conversation and laughter to wash over her. They swapped presents and attempted a little Christmas cheer, toasting with champagne. Ted couldn't take his eyes off Sibella. She sat with her hand on his knee. He acted as if she were a prize, clutching at her like she was some giant teddy bear won at a fairground stall. Eve couldn't stop yawning and checking her watch and Lucy seemed capable of only talking about India and how incredible her trip had been. It was like being behind glass or submerged under water, Margot thought, visible but disconnected from their shiny, happy lives. She was grateful when Ted settled the bill and drove her back to Windfalls.

All winter, Margot held her shameful secret like a hot coal simmering at the very heart of her. She spent hours lying on her bed reading books, listening to music on her headphones or drifting in and out of a strange, numb state: not quite sleep, not quite wakefulness. Occasionally, she'd steal wine from the cupboard in the kitchen, knowing Kit would never notice its absence. She'd drink it up in her room, chasing that buzz, that fuzzy sense of otherness that took her away from herself. Other times she'd buy cigarettes and sit at her bedroom window chain-smoking until she felt lightheaded and sick. She dressed in Eve's baggiest hand-me-downs and let her hair turn into a wild, tangled nest. At school she kept her head down, did the bare minimum to scrape by, and tried to summon the energy to care about it all. She wasn't interested in school plays or exam results. The Bad Thing sapped all her energy. She willed it to be a bad dream, willed it to be gone, but each morning she awoke, knowing that it had happened. It was still there.

On the last day of the Easter term, Margot left the school bus and began her walk home. It had not been a good day. The English teacher had pulled her up in front of everyone for missing yet another end-of-term essay deadline. She had sat in class, head bowed, and let the admonishment wash over her. 'I don't understand it, Margot,' the teacher had berated. 'It's not like you to be so sloppy in your work.' Maybe, Margot thought simmering silently, that's because you don't know me at all. She was tired, irritable and her back had ached no matter how she sat at her desk. It took all of her willpower not to snap back at the teacher and storm out of the classroom. At lunch she had dropped her tray in the canteen and been the cause of much laughter and derision, and she'd spent the rest of the afternoon hiding in the girls' toilets, sitting in a cubicle weeping inexplicably.

A little ahead of her was a group of students, walking down the lane, laughing and joking, Jamie and some others from the *Romeo and Juliet* cast among them. Margot pulled her hood over her head and ducked down onto a nearby pathway leading through the woods towards the river. It was a less direct route, but that way she could take the towpath home to Windfalls and avoid them.

Walking through the woods, Margot felt a little of her irritation lift. The spring sun was gathering strength and the woods were ripe with the scent of wild garlic. Two weeks stretched ahead of her: no school, no bus journeys, nobody to avoid. She knew her mother was in the final, frenzied stages of her novel. 'The last two chapters, darling,' she'd told her with a glazed look on her face that morning over breakfast. Until then, it wouldn't be hard to avoid Kit. Eve was still caught up with the baby and Lucy had hatched a plan to launch her own yoga studio in Bath. She would be able to spend most of the

Easter holidays on her own. Perhaps she'd focus on the late English essay, pull something out of the bag.

Halfway home, among the sun-dappled trees, Margot felt something release inside of her. A physical 'pop', followed by a hot liquid gush flooding down her inner thighs. She stood stock still, shocked at the sensation. It felt as if she'd wet herself. No warning, just a sudden release. Almost as quickly, a sharp band of pressure rose up and gripped her, like a belt pulling tight across her abdomen. Margot reached for the nearest tree trunk, leaning her weight upon it, waiting for the pressure to release. It felt like the worst kind of stomach ache, as if her insides were fighting to leave her body.

As the pain eased, Margot let out a long exhalation and released her hold on the tree. It had passed. She waited for the strength to return to her legs, felt the clammy fabric of her tracksuit bottoms where it clung to her thighs, then began to walk with a little more purpose towards home.

A few steps on and the pain came again, a seizing of muscles so powerful it paralysed her in her tracks. She clutched her stomach, felt the rock hard tautness of it bulging beneath her hands and let out a small whimper. She was afraid. The Bad Thing was coming. It was coming now.

Margot carried on down the path, gripped by pain, staggering between the trees as waves of awful tightening then release came upon her. At one point she bent over and vomited the undigested remains of her school lunch into the undergrowth. She moaned, feeling prickles of sweat breaking out on her neck and forehead. She was so hot. And there it was, another crashing pain rising up within her.

Clutching her belly, she moved with a primal instinct through the trees, away from the path to a denser area of woodland where the Alders grew taller and more closely together. Unable to go any further, she crouched down in the shadows to vomit again onto the leaf-strewn ground, heaving until her stomach was empty and the tears were running down her face. *Help me*, she implored, gazing silently up through the leafy boughs at the faint shard of sky. She didn't know whom she addressed, but she willed for something – anything to take pity on her. *Please help me.*

And then she was sweating and panting and tearing at her clothes, a pressure building in her – a pressure so strong and inevitable that she knew there was nothing she could do to stop it. She dropped to her knees and placed her hands on the muddy ground, bracing herself against the damp earth, moaning and whimpering as the pain took hold of her again, a splitting sensation tearing at her. There was a short release and then it came again and she could do nothing but ride the sensations and let her body purge whatever was coming.

With a loud groan, Margot, still down on all fours, felt something hot and muscular slide from her body. There was a sharp, burning sensation and then she heard something drop with a thud onto the earth. She felt the wetness between her legs, the sweat on her face, heard her breath coming in short pants. She stayed there, her forehead resting on the cool earth, waiting, knowing through some deep internal instinct that it wasn't over. And then, moments later, it came again, another crashing wave of pressure, not as strong as before, but still urgent. There was a second release, another warm and wet thing sliding from her body onto the soil below. She leaned forward again, her face pressed against the ground, and breathed in the mud, the damp leaves and the solid re-assuring scent of the earth holding her up.

She didn't know how long she stayed like that, but when she opened her eyes, it felt as if the world had tilted. The sunlight streaming through the trees a little lower, the air a little cooler on her skin. She could see a misshapen toadstool poking up through the mud, a black earwig scuttling up its grey stem.

She knew there was something she should do, but while her face remained resting on the soil, she could pretend. She could gather herself, come back into herself.

It was only as the air began to cool the slick wetness between her legs, and her sweat-covered skin started to prickle into goosebumps that she moved. Only then did she allow herself to look.

She saw it lying on the ground between her legs. The Bad Thing. A silent, blue baby, slippery with blood, a white-grey cord tangled about its neck, connecting it to a congealed pile of bloody matter lying in the leaves beside it.

Margot studied it for a moment before retching again and again onto the dry earth.

It was almost dark when she eventually shuffled back along the towpath, dirt-stained and weary, following the black slide of the river home. Her hands ached and when she looked down she saw they were black and bleed-ing, her fingernails torn and caked in mud. There was a strange buzzing in her head and though her legs felt as heavy as stone, she stumbled on, a hunched version of herself, autopilot drawing her back to Windfalls. One word echoed over and over in her head. She walked to the beat of it. Gone ... gone ... the Bad Thing was gone.

The jetty below the orchard came into view, jutting out into dark water. Margot hesitated, one hand on her stomach, hearing the echo of long-ago laughter, the sound of bottles clinking. There it was: her mother's studio, looming at her out of the shadows. The place of her undoing. The buzzing in her head grew louder.

So this is where the magic happens?

His voice echoed in her head. She could hear it so clearly she had to wrestle the urge to claw at her ears. Unable to stop herself, she shuffled forward and placed a bloodstained hand on the door handle. Was she in there? Would she help her?

Who did you think about, Margot?

Inside, a familiar smell rose up. It made her want to gag: paper, apples, her mother's perfume. The room was empty but across from the door stood the desk, a perfect pile of stacked A4 pages placed neatly on its surface next to the old black typewriter. She closed her eyes, remembering the sensation of paper pressed against her face, the pressure of his hands on her skin, his thumb pressing into the soft part of her neck, the juddering of the desk beneath her all flooding back in a sickening rush.

You don't know what you do to me.

Feeling the dull, aching emptiness inside of her, Margot let out a howl of rage. She crossed to the desk and in one violent move, swept the stack of paper, the lamp and the typewriter to the floor. The sheets of paper spiralled like a flock of displaced birds. She snatched up the oil lamp hanging on a nail in the wall and threw it to the ground, taking satisfaction in the loud shattering of the glass and the sight of the oil leaking across the floor. She pulled books off the shelves, ripped the gauze curtains from their rails. The pink crystal paperweight flew through the window pane with a crash. This place – the place of her mother's distraction, the cause of their father's departure, the site of her shame – it was to blame for everything.

The box of matches sat on the windowsill. It seemed the most obvious thing in the world to reach for them and strike one against the side of the box. She watched it flare in the gloom, then threw it towards the puddle of oil leaking from the broken lamp, hearing the satisfying *whoomph* as it instantly caught alight.

The flames rose fast. They ran across the floor, dogs licking the legs of the desk, blackening the neatly typed pages of paper lying strewn across the floor, words turning to ash in seconds. Margot, transfixed by the flames, watched for a while, amazed at how quickly they took ownership and lit the whole studio in a bright, smoky haze. She wanted to stay and watch the whole lot burn. She wanted to let it claim her too, but as the fire rose to the roof of the studio and advanced toward her, a deep, primal instinct saw her turn and stagger from the old apple store where she collapsed, choking on the jetty, watching the remains disappear behind a wall of heat and flames.

It could have been minutes, it could have been longer, Margot had no idea how long it took for the figure to emerge from the darkness, running down the path leading from the house. Margot watched with detachment, the woman standing there in her nightdress with her hair hanging loose and wild about her shoulders. 'No!' she screamed, her hands on her head, her face a picture of pure horror as she gazed at the burning building. 'Oh my God. No!'

As Kit turned, Margot saw the jolt of recognition on her mother's face as she caught sight of her crouched on the jetty. Margot, her body numb with exhaustion and shock, watched as Kit's face twisted with sudden understanding and rage. 'What have you done?' her mother cried, pulling at her own hair, fixing her with a furious, burning gaze. 'What have you done? My book! What on earth have you done?'

Margot swallowed, the taste of ash and smoke heavy in her mouth. 'He's gone,' was all she could reply, the words little more than a whisper. 'He's gone.' Overhead the bulbs swayed on their wire, dusty and unlit, while beside her, the dark water flowed endlessly, silently on its course.

34

Lucy lies beside a snoring Tom, blinking in the dim light of her childhood bedroom. She knows she should sleep too, that her body won't thank her for the early start after such a late night, but it's a losing battle. She is still pulsing with adrenaline from the party, and from the horror of Margot's early hours confession. Fragments of their conversation play on repeat in her mind. At the sound of a blackbird calling from the garden, she gives up completely, and slides out from beneath the bed covers.

She pulls on UGG boots and a long woollen cardigan, wrapping it tightly over her pyjamas. There is a familiar, low-lying pain rolling in her stomach, dull enough that she can ignore it, for now.

The house is quiet and still, in complete disarray, like a forest rearranged after a storm. Downstairs in the living room, an unidentifiable wedding guest lies curled beneath a blanket on the velvet sofa, bare feet hanging over one end, soft snores drifting through the open door. The kitchen is a mess. The long oak table is covered in empty wine bottles, dirty glasses and the remains of a cheese platter no one has thought to put away, a wheel of brie oozing into a molten puddle, a bunch of grapes turning brown. An ashtray overflowing with cigarette butts stands next to it. Lucy regards the mess with quiet triumph – all signs of a good party – before letting herself out of the back door and into the morning light. She needs a moment to herself before she can face the clean-up operation ahead.

Outside, the morning air holds the first notes of autumn. The light is bright and clean and beautiful, though lower in the valley, a mist shrouds the river from view. She walks through the orchard, past the ashen remains of the smouldering bonfire, the marquee standing limp with condensation and drooping bunting, a champagne bottle lying discarded in the trampled grass, the scent of fallen apples rising from the earth. The hem of her pyjamas soaks up the morning dew.

A blackbird sings from a branch high above. She wonders if it is the same one that called her from her bed as she wraps the cardigan more tightly around her and heads for the fallen trunk of an old tree resting beside the slow-trickling stream. As she sits, her gaze lands on the carved initials hewn into the trunk of the nearby apple tree: K. T. E. L. M. Five letters marking their place, confirming their family's presence in this landscape, their belonging. She imagines what it would look like without the L. She takes a moment to imagine it being scrubbed from existence and swallows hard.

Her gaze shifts back to the house, standing on top of the hill in the morning light, her family home, a place of dysfunction and chaos, yes, but also love and safety. At least that was how she'd always thought of it. Margot's revelations have shaken her to the core. How had her sister carried such a terrible secret burden for so long? How had none of them seen what she had been through – what she had carried, both physically and emotionally? Why had none of them thought to dig a little deeper? They had all been so quick to interpret her moodiness and destructive act as teenage defiance and anger. And as Margot had built her walls, they had allowed her to slip away. They had turned away. Lucy feels her own sense of shame, for missing the signals – for failing to help.

She remembers the look on Margot's face as she had lain between her and Eve, gazing into the dying flames of the bonfire, and told them about the rape, and of the baby she had secretly carried. She remembers Margot's tears as she had told them about the birth. Stillborn, she'd said – at least, she had thought so. She told them about the silence. The blue baby with the cord wrapped around its neck.

'What did you do?' Lucy had asked, a little afraid of the answer.

Margot had closed her eyes. She hadn't spoken for a long time. 'I didn't want to touch it,' she'd said after a long moment. 'But I couldn't not. I carried him to the river.' *Him*. That one word. It had taken all of Lucy's self-control not to cry, but to stay with Margot, present and silent. 'I wasn't thinking straight.'

'You would have been in terrible shock,' Eve had said gently, reaching out to take her sister's hand. 'Tell us, Margot.'

So she had. She had told them, in faltering words, how

she had decided, at first, to hide the baby in the river. 'I wanted him to disappear. I thought he would float away. Be gone.' But when she had reached the water's edge, she couldn't do it. 'It didn't seem right. The water was so cold and I couldn't let go of him. Not like that.'

Lucy had closed her eyes to hold back her tears as Margot had explained how she had used her bare hands to dig a grave at the river's edge, clawing at the mud with her fingers. 'Underneath the bridge,' she'd told them. 'The river bank was softer, and it was dark and quiet there in the shadows. I thought he would be . . . safe there.' Margot's voice had caught on a sob. 'I know . . . I know it was wrong, but I didn't know what else to do.'

She'd told them both about the terrible walk home and how turning off the towpath, she'd been confronted by the sight of their mother's studio – the place where the attack had happened. She told them how it felt to see it standing there in darkness, goading her from the shadows, and in that moment, Lucy had thought she understood exactly why Margot had done what she had done. She had known that she probably would have done the same.

When Lucy thinks of all her sister has suffered, she feels an overwhelming sadness. Kit would surely understand? Kit would surely forgive the destruction Margot had wreaked, if she could only find a way to tell their mother?

Lucy had heard it over and over last night, as the news had trickled out about her illness: *you are so brave, you are so strong*. Is she brave? She doesn't feel it. She is putting one foot in front of the other and carrying on. What else can she do? It was Margot who had suffered, who had carried so much misplaced shame. It was Margot who was brave, living silently with her secret.

She sees the truth now: they all carry pain. Kit's lost love for Ted, and Eve's crumbling marriage; Lucy's disease and Margot's harrowing past. There is braveness in living, she thinks. There is strength in carrying on. Margot is proof of that and Lucy's hope for her sister, now that she has started to talk about what happened, is that she will find a way to pull down the protective exterior that has kept her from so much and so many. If she can only find the strength to tell Kit what had happened, perhaps there is still a chance the two of them could come back from this.

A figure appears at the top of the garden and walks down through the long grass towards her. 'I don't want to intrude,' Sibella says, drawing a little closer. 'I came to help with the clear-up and I heard you leaving the house.' She holds a blanket out to Lucy. 'I thought you might want this. Don't catch a chill.'

Lucy takes it with a nod. 'Is this how it's going to be from now on: knitted blankets, tea and sympathy?'

Sibella smiles. 'Take it while you can. The alternative is the washing-up.'

'Thank you.'

'I'll leave you to it.'

Sibella is turning away when Lucy speaks. 'I'm afraid,' she says, her voice cracking slightly as the words leave her mouth.

Sibella comes and settles herself on the log and places her hand gently over Lucy's. It feels soft and reassuringly warm. 'I know, love. I know.'

'I was so focused on yesterday's party – the grand

gesture of it. I thought it would bring a sense of accomplishment. Maybe even a sense of peace.' She gives a small laugh. 'And it has, to a degree. Marrying Tom and celebrating with everyone yesterday was exactly what I wanted. Everyone together. I felt so . . . happy and so . . .' she wrestles for the right word, '. . . loved.'

'But today,' she sighs and kicks out at a rock lying on the ground near her feet, sending it skittling away through the grass, 'today I feel pissed off and angry. I can't fix it. I can't fix any of it – my pain, the pain of others.'

Sibella stares off into the middle distance. 'It's not fair,' she agrees. 'What you did yesterday, the way you showed everyone how you want it to be, how you want to *live* right now, it took real courage. It was inspiring.'

Lucy thinks of Margot again and feels a tear trickle down her cheek. It splashes onto her cardigan, forming a dark spot. 'We can hold ourselves so tightly. We build our protective walls and set ourselves apart. But what I see more and more is how much we all need each other.' Lucy swallows back a sob, thinking again of Margot alone in the woods, cradling her stillborn baby. What she had gone through, birthing him all on her own before taking the poor infant and burying his body in the mud beneath the stone bridge with her bare hands, a last act of desperation, only the river to bear witness.

Sibella, unaware of Lucy's thoughts, squeezes her hand tightly. 'You can't fix everyone else's problems, Lucy. You aren't responsible. Forgive me if this sounds like meddling, but I wonder if it isn't time for you to think about what you need, right now, to keep yourself strong?'

'Isn't that selfish?' Lucy manages a weak smile. 'I think there are a few people who already think I'm selfish for forcing everyone back together yesterday.'

'I don't think anyone could call you selfish, Lucy. Yesterday was wonderful. You showed incredible strength of heart. It was a day filled with memories that your family will cherish in the days to come, whatever they bring. But your wedding to Tom isn't the end. It's not the end of your story, is it? You're still here. Alive. So live, Lucy. Live to the best of your ability.'

Lucy gives a small smile. 'Not dead yet, right?'

'Exactly. Each day is a gift.'

Sibella leaves her sitting on the old tree trunk. Lucy watches her go, not quite ready to move. Gradually, in her stillness, other, happier memories from the previous night return to her: twirling with her friends under flashing lights; Chloe and May laughing with their dad; Eve sitting on a hay bale, resting her head on Margot's shoulder; Tom drawing her close and whispering how proud he was to be her husband; Andrew holding out his hand to Eve and inviting her to dance; Ted and Kit sitting on deck chairs beneath the stars, quietly conversing.

Gazing around the orchard, her eyes land again on the five initials carved into the old apple tree. This time, the sight of them brings comfort. The love will remain, she realises. The love they hold for each other will still be here, even when she no longer is.

A breeze shifts the tree branches overhead, sending a small flurry of copper leaves spiralling to the earth. Lucy turns her face to find the sun, allowing it to warm her cheek. She knows the day heralds the equinox, when the northern hemisphere will begin to lean away from the sun. Today, the earth is in balance, but soon the nights will be longer than the days. Summer is giving way to autumn. Lucy watches as one brown leaf lands on the stream and floats away on the current towards the river, part of the endless flow. The light, settling on the mist in the valley, is almost too beautiful. She feels herself surrender – to the beauty, the love, the pain, the sadness, the joy of living.

What does she need right now? She needs to return to her family. She needs to hug her husband and thank her family for a wonderful day. But first, she thinks, gazing down into the valley, there is something else.

The white mist gathers round her in a fine veil as she wanders down through the orchard and beyond the wooden gate to meet the riverside. Everything is muffled, shrouded in strange silence. It is a feeling of separation, a peculiar sensation, as if she steps into another world. At the bottom of the valley, the river stretches out pale grey and flat, merging on the horizon with the mist to create a seamless blank canvas, eerily pretty and still. She walks onto the jetty and shrugs off her clothes. The cooler air brings goosebumps prickling on her skin. Standing at the edge of the wooden platform, she looks down into the smooth water, as pale as milk. It stretches out, a sheet of glass, to meet the white horizon – blank and formless in the mist. The overhanging trees are faded and smudged, as if an artist has taken an eraser and blurred their edges, blending them to white. The silent river waits to embrace her.

With a deep breath, she dives out towards its centre.

The cold water claims her. The shock is electric. It

envelops her traitorous body. As she pushes for the surface, she feels her wild, beating heart, her breath rising hot and urgent in her throat, her undeniable, incredible aliveness. She floats on the surface of the river and experiences a certain peace. She feels herself connected to the flow of life all around. Here I am, she thinks. Here I am.

35

Margot sits on the window seat, gazing out at the black silhouettes of the trees bristling on the surrounding hillside, birds' nests caught like knotted tangles in their leafless branches. Lucy lies nearby in her old bed, her eyes closed. Tom sits slumped in a chair at her side. None of them have moved for a while, though every so often Tom reaches out to stroke Lucy's hand, to twist the loose gold band on her ring finger.

The hospice nurse, a middle-aged woman called Pam, comes in to check on Lucy. She adjusts the drip standing sentry at the bedside before turning to Margot and Tom. 'Long night,' she says. 'How are you holding up?'

Margot nods. She doesn't have the words.

Lucy opens her eyes. 'The window,' she gestures.

Margot looks out at the winter landscape, everything brown and grey in the early morning light, a world devoid of colour. 'I don't know, Luce. It's cold out.'

'Worried I'll catch my death?' Lucy asks, her voice a dry rasp. Tom buries his head in his hands. Lucy reaches

344

out and caresses his arm with a finger. 'I need to feel the air on my face.'

Margot looks at Lucy, at her frail limbs, her thin face, grey and collapsed in on itself, at the dark shadows under her eyes. Who is she to deny her sister this?

She turns and wrestles with the catch on the window, opens it with a thump, feels a rush of cool air slide into the room. She lays another blanket over her sister's narrow frame before pulling her own cardigan more tightly around her body. It *is* cold, but it feels good to let a little of the outside in. A reminder of the world beyond this strange, stilted bedside existence where each breath feels painful and hard won.

Through the open window the first bird lifts its voice in morning song. Lucy closes her eyes. 'That's better,' she says. 'I can breathe now.'

It was Lucy who had wanted to return to Windfalls. 'Take me home,' she'd told Tom. 'Please.' It was, she'd said, the only place she wanted to be.

Margot had taken the phone call from Ted and caught the first train south from Edinburgh. As the carriage had juddered and swayed its way to London, she'd remembered travelling the same tracks the previous September, that day a different sort of trepidation flowing through her veins.

The journey was more familiar now. She had been back and forth since the wedding, accompanying Lucy to her medical appointments, sitting with her through those interminable hours of treatment when she'd been hooked up to the IV and given the chemo drugs designed to slow the advance of the tumours. Sometimes they'd chatted.

Sometimes they'd watched reruns of favourite shows or played podcasts on an iPad, splitting the headphones so they could listen together. Sometimes Lucy slept and Margot had sat reading next to her. Sometimes she had left her and wandered out to the small patio area where she would chat to others who were accompanying friends and family in treatment, or sit quietly and simply stare at the sky and breathe, thinking about how extraordinary her sister was and the sheer impossibility of her not being in the world.

After those gruelling visits to the clinic, Margot sometimes slept on Lucy and Tom's sofa, or dropped by to see Eve and the girls, but mostly she returned to Windfalls. In the face of Lucy's illness, she and Kit had reached an uneasy truce. 'Tell her,' Lucy urged her, more than once. 'Tell her what happened.' And Margot would nod and reassure her sister that she would – in time. But not now, when Lucy was feeling better. And Lucy had shaken her head – her hair shaved and her scalp wrapped in one of her Indian silk headscarves – and told Margot how annoyingly stubborn she was.

They had talked about Mr Hudson. On one of those long, protracted afternoons at the clinic, Margot had told her sister how she had found the courage to look for him online. He hadn't been hard to find. His name had appeared almost immediately in the search engine results, linked to a string of news articles about a teacher in Manchester who had been prosecuted for indecent assault and was currently serving time in prison. Several of the articles had been accompanied by photos of the offender being ushered from a police car into the courthouse. The sight of him had made her breath falter. Time had not been kind. He'd looked harassed and bloated, a softer, older version of the man she remembered. She had stared at the photos for a long time, feeling her anger rise at what he had put her through – what he had taken from her. Worse still, she was not the only one. If she had found the courage to speak up, would she have saved someone else from the same ordeal?

'You were terrified, ashamed. What you went through . . . it's understandable that you felt you couldn't tell anyone,' Lucy had said, gripping her hand. 'But it's not too late. You can still tell the police.'

'Why would they believe me, after all this time?'

Lucy had looked her in the eye. 'There's evidence, Margot. You buried it, but it's there. Your baby.'

Margot had dropped her head and wrapped her arms around herself, her fingers unconsciously caressing the small dark heart in the crook of her elbow. She'd nodded. 'I've tried so hard not to think about him, but ever since I told you and Eve, I keep thinking . . . I can't leave him there. It's wrong.'

Lucy nods. 'I know. Perhaps there is a way. Perhaps . . . a proper burial?' she had suggested tentatively. 'It might help?'

Margot had nodded, unable to look at Lucy, letting the tears fall into her lap.

Lucy had squeezed her hand. 'When you're ready.'

Margot had been at Windfalls the afternoon that Lucy had told them all she wanted to stop – that the treatment was no longer having any effect. Lucy and Tom had spoken with the doctors and she had taken the decision that it would be better to focus on the time she had left, with the support of the palliative care team, rather than enduring more punishing cycles of chemo.

Margot hadn't wanted to accept Lucy's decision, but she had known she had no right to challenge her, not when she had seen first hand the toll of the treatment. The last few months had been a terrible endurance and Lucy had borne the drugs with a stoic courage. But watching her suffering had been painful for them all. Lucy had been so strong that Margot had convinced herself of a miracle. She doesn't know if she can bear what is to come.

It's Margot who tells them. She leaves Tom in the bedroom and goes downstairs to where Eve, Kit and Ted sit silently in the kitchen, empty mugs and a cooling teapot in front of them. She stands in the doorway and, at the sight of her, they understand. Ted releases a soft sigh.

She nods. 'Pam says you should come now.'

Kit turns her face. 'I can't.'

'Come on, Mum,' says Margot. 'For Lucy.'

Eve touches Kit's arm. 'We have to.'

It is Ted who helps Kit from the chair and supports her up the stairs to Lucy's room. Pam adjusts the drip at the bedside then steps back to allow the family around the bed. Eve puts her arm around Tom. Margot stands alone by the window seat. The ache in her chest threatens to cleave her in two.

'I've increased the medication,' says Pam. 'She was in a lot of pain.'

Kit goes to Lucy and strokes her cheek. She brushes her daughter's forehead and bends to kiss her. Lucy's breath is a slow, irregular rasp.

Margot watches Eve kiss her sister. She sees Tom reach for Lucy's hand and press it to his lips. 'I love you, Luce,' he says. 'I'll always love you.'

Kit lets out a strangled sob and Ted reaches for her, supporting her at the end of the bed. Margot thinks her heart will burst. She turns and faces the window, counting the slowing of Lucy's rattled breathing. A pale sun is rising over the hills, emerging between the clouds and momentarily shining silver on the twist of river in the valley below, visible between the leafless trees. She remembers the morning after the wedding. She remembers walking out into the garden, following her sister's footprints in the dew-soaked grass until she had come upon her floating on the surface of the misty river, arms outstretched, eyes closed and a beatific smile spread across her face. She remembers how she had watched her from the cover of the trees, marvelling at the strange peace of the scene, and at her sister's spirit, thinking back on all the other times she had watched Lucy swim and play in the river as a younger girl, wild and carefree.

Margot thinks of her sister in her place of joy and it's only as her attention returns to the room, that she realises the bird has stopped singing. Outside the window, a thin veil of rain begins to fall.

It is Pam's suggestion. The nurse mentions her idea to Margot, explaining that she has found it sometimes helps some family members to say goodbye. As soon as the thought is in her head, Margot knows it is something she would like to do. While Ted phones the undertaker, Margot goes outside to find Sibella. 'Would you help with something? Mum can't face it and Eve needs to gather herself before she goes home to tell the girls.'

'Of course,' Sibella agrees. 'Whatever you need.'

The rain has stopped as quickly as it began. The winter sun filters across the wet trees, turning the bare landscape into a dazzling mass of light. The drops cascading off the branches form a shifting silver waterfall that takes her breath away. She can't look away, the beauty somehow intensified by her pain.

The emotion swells and mingles with the ache of loss – her feelings amplified – until tears burn in her eyes and the shimmering landscape blurs. She turns her face to the sky and whispers words of gratitude and love.

Bowing at the river's edge, Margot fills a small flask and carries it reverently back to Lucy's room, where she finds Sibella waiting for her with clean cloths and towels, as well as a basin of warm water. Sibella watches silently as Margot adds the river water to the basin. She isn't quite sure why it has felt so important to carry the river home to Lucy, but something about the gesture feels right. As if the water she loved might somehow help bear her onwards, to her final resting place. 'A last swim,' she says, turning to Sibella, attempting to explain, her throat aching with love and sorrow.

Sibella nods and passes Margot a cloth.

As they wash Lucy's body, Margot is struck by the fact that it is Lucy, and yet it is not. The more she tends to her sister's body, the more clearly she understands that Lucy is no longer with them. Whatever made Lucy so inimitably Lucy is no longer there. It is eerie and strange, yet Margot finds it comforting to touch her, to care for her sister in this final act of love. She can't help glancing once or twice at the open window. Where are you, she wonders? Where have you gone? Her stillness, her coldness, is baffling.

They carefully remove the wedding ring from her finger. Margot steps back and feels a hot rush of anger at the sight of Lucy's sunken face. She should have had more time, time for pregnancy and stretch marks, wrinkles and liver spots and wispy white hairs on her old lady chin. It's so desperately unfair. She tries to remember the beauty of her sister. She tries to lock away for posterity the memory of Lucy at her most radiant. Not this ravaged version, her body devastated by illness. One day, Margot will be an old lady, yet Lucy never a day older. It's hard not to feel robbed. She sighs. 'She looks at peace, doesn't she?'

Sibella nods. 'She does.'

Margot uncurls Lucy's hand and tucks a smooth river stone into Lucy's fingers before pressing them back into a tight fist. Satisfied that they have done their best, they leave the room.

She finds Tom and Eve outside on the patio. They sit shivering in the cool morning light, their breath ghosting in the air, driven as if by some unspoken agreement to escape the compressed atmosphere of the house. *Open the window*. She remembers Lucy's final request and looks to the blank sky, blinking back the tears. Already it feels wrong: three of them sitting at a table where there should be four. She reaches out and squeezes Tom's shoulder as she passes. He is rigid beneath her touch and Margot senses what an effort it is for him to hold himself together. She takes the seat beside him.

'I thought you'd left,' says Margot, turning to Eve.

'Just summoning the courage.' She bites her lip. 'I can't bear to tell the girls.'

'Will Andrew be there?'

'Yes.' Eve lifts her head to meet Margot's gaze. 'He moved back in last weekend.'

Margot eyes her. 'That's good. Are things... OK?'

'He's been brilliant these past few weeks. Solid. We've talked. We both want to make it work, and not just for the girls' sake. I think we've both come to realise... what's important. Lucy's illness has shone a light on what really matters. The rest...' she shrugs.

Tom clears his throat. 'That would've made Lucy very happy.'

Eve nods. 'I told her yesterday.' Margot watches Eve and Tom share a look of understanding. Yesterday. The word seems to catch in the air, reminding them all how 'yesterday' will always be a memory now, how different all their days will be from this point on.

Eve lets out a long sigh. 'We'll have to start thinking about the funeral.'

'Lucy left a list. She had some firm ideas of what she wants.' Tom's blue eyes swim, but he manages a wry smile. 'And what she definitely *doesn't* want.'

Margot remembers the rows and tensions surrounding the wedding. 'Of course she did.' A robin hops in a hedgerow, rustling the foliage. Margot turns and notices the flash of its red breast. The colour reminds her of Lucy's wedding dress – how beautiful she had looked – and the thought makes the ache in her chest throb.

Tom rests his head in his hands. He sits silently for a moment, then seems to pull himself up, rubbing his hands over his face. 'I'm so tired. I almost forgot. Lucy wrote letters to you both,' he says. 'She asked me to give them to you . . . after.' His voice cracks. He reaches into his jacket and pulls out an envelope. 'Margot' is written on the front in Lucy's looping handwriting. There is another for Eve. Margot takes up the envelope with her name on and grips it tightly as Tom heads back inside the house.

Through the window, she watches Tom enter the kitchen, where Kit, Ted and Sibella sit at the table. Ted stands to greet him. He shakes Tom's hand, then pulls him closer, drawing him into a half-pat, half-hug embrace, the type certain men perform in times of high emotion. Tom moves as if to pull back, then collapses, leaning into his father-in-law, his shoulders heaving. Ted, after only a second's hesitation, holds him more tightly, and after a while, Margot realises she is no longer sure which of the men is holding the other up.

Her eyes welling with tears, she turns her gaze to where Kit sits nearby, her mother's head bowed low. Though perhaps as if sensing the weight of Margot's attention, Kit shifts in her chair and raises her face to the window. Margot sees her mother's small nod of acknowledgement and the saddest of smiles breaking on her lips. Margot returns the nod. Lucy had told them that she wanted her wedding to bring them all back to each other. If the wedding hasn't, perhaps her death will, for here they all are at Windfalls again, connected in their love and their grief.

'I'm not sure I can read it yet,' says Eve, taking her envelope from the table and stowing it carefully in her coat pocket. 'I think I might save it for another time.

When she feels too . . . far away.' She shivers. 'I'm going in. Are you coming?'

The robin hops between the hedgerow branches, rustling the leaves, before taking off with a sudden flutter of wings into the valley below. Margot glances at the envelope. 'Not yet,' she says, turning to look beyond the orchard, to where the water glints through the trees.

36

All is still beside the river. Silence hangs in the air. Margot folds the letter carefully into its envelope and sits on the jetty, looking out over the mirrored water.

To read Lucy's letter, to hear her voice, brings an ache of longing. Grief grips her heart like a fist. Already, she feels the absoluteness of her sister's absence. Where once there were shared jokes, stories and experiences, only she holds them now. The sisterly language that belonged to them both is hers alone. No more, *do you remember the time . . . ?* The thought brings intense pain.

Tomorrow will be the first full day that she will live without Lucy. Tomorrow, she will wake and after a split second of peace – that moment between sleep and consciousness – she will have to remember that Lucy is no longer in the world. How many mornings will it take for her to accept the impossible truth? How long before Lucy's death has become a part of her, a sad fact in the string of moments making up her life?

She grips her sister's letter in her hand and looks down into the slow-moving water. *It takes courage to love*, she had written. *But where there is love – and I know there is love here — there is also hope. Don't give up. Talk to Mum.*

Margot closes her eyes. Sitting there on the jetty a carousel of memories revolve. Behind her closed lids, a wire of bobbing light bulbs glints and sways. Her tongue tingles with the remembered fizz of cider. She hears the echoes of laughter, remembers the grip of fingers pressing into her neck. She opens her eyes and refocuses on the deep green of the water. She lets out a breath. She will tell Kit. She will honour her sister's last request. She will find the strength to sit down with her mother and explain what happened that summer, and in the months that followed. She doesn't know how Kit will respond, but she will give her the opportunity to hear her, if nothing else. Maybe, just maybe, Lucy was right. Maybe the truth will be the bridge they can finally meet upon.

She looks around at the river, the jetty and the charred remains of her mother's old studio hidden in the shadows of the tangled undergrowth. This place has haunted her for so long. It has born her deepest shame and held her darkest secrets. It has reared up in her nightmares and held her caught in a past she hasn't yet outrun. Yet looking again, she sees the old rowboat where Eve would sit and read her books. She sees the rocks where they scrambled up to leap out into the water. She sees the smooth surface of the river where Lucy would float, face turned to the sky. She sees all her family memories nestled in this one place.

Something Lucy had said to her chimes: where there is love.

For too many years, this river has been a place of pain. Yet is also a place of joy. Perhaps, this place — this silent

356

river — is all of these things. Or perhaps it is none. Perhaps it just *is*. Margot understands now that what she has been frightened of facing is not her mother's studio, nor the river, nor Windfalls but the hurt place inside of her — the dark wound she has carried for so long. This is what Lucy has been asking her to confront.

Joy. Pain. Life. Death. Each casts the other in sharp relief. Sitting on the jetty, thinking about Lucy's life — and death — it's as if Margot can feel her heart beating a little more fiercely, her breath coming a little more forcefully. *It takes courage to love.*

Feeling the chill of the March morning seeping into her bones, Margot stands and makes for the gate leading up through the orchard. With her hand on the metal latch, she hesitates. She turns and eyes the timbers of the old studio lying slumped in the shadows. The clouds shift overhead, sending a shaft of sunlight strobing across the valley. Margot's gaze is caught by something pale, glinting in the long grass near one of the collapsed beams. She moves closer and bends down, her hand closing around a egg-shaped object. She knows what it is before she has even brushed the layer of dirt from its surface. She remembers the rose-pink crystal, the treasured piece of quartz that had sat on her mother's desk for all those years. Weighing it in her hand, she recalls the night of the fire and the sound of smashing glass as she had thrown it through the studio window. Has it been lying here forgotten all this time? Turning the stone, it glitters pale pink in the morning light, refracting the sun like ice. She holds it in the palm of her hand. Something important — something to be returned.

*

The trees in the orchard stand like old friends marking her path back to the house. She enters through the back door. Upstairs, Jonas waits for her. In a moment, she will follow the steps to her bedroom. She will lift his arm and nestle in beside him, pressing her body against his, holding his warm hand against her heart. His other arm will wrap around her, his fingers unconsciously tracing the ink on her upper arm in what is now a familiar gesture, mapping the vines and the small dark heart in the crook of her arm. He will murmur soft words into her hair and Margot will close her eyes.

She hesitates at the bottom of the staircase, one foot on the lowest step. The rose quartz crystal is a warm weight in her hand. Slowly, she turns to the open doorway of the kitchen, to where Kit now sits alone, staring out of the window. Margot hesitates. She hears her mother's soft sigh. She lifts her foot from the step. 'Mum,' she says, going to the open door, squeezing the quartz in her hand. 'Mum, can I talk to you?'

Kit looks up. She gives a slow nod and pats the empty chair beside her. 'Come,' she says.

Margot takes a breath and enters the room.

ACKNOWLEDGEMENTS

Thank you to my agent, Sarah Lutyens, and all at Lutyens and Rubinstein for their continual support. Thank you to the publishing teams at Orion in the UK, Hachette Australia and HarperCollins in the US, with special thanks to Clare Hey, Vanessa Radnidge and Emily Griffin for their clear editorial vision and care.

Huge thanks to all the booksellers and librarians shepherding books to readers and keeping the love of the written word alive and thriving.

Lastly, but most importantly, thank you to my family and friends, for their love and support, especially my parents, John and Gill, my sister (and first reader) Jess, my brother Will, and, of course, my very best creations, Jude and Gracie, for putting up with me and making me smile through it all.

This book is dedicated to my brother, Will – one of the kindest, most generous-hearted men you could hope to meet.

CREDITS

Hannah Richell and Orion Fiction would like to thank everyone at Orion who worked on the publication of *The River Home* in the UK.

Editorial
Clare Hey
Victoria Oundjian
Olivia Barber

Copy editor
Justine Taylor

Proof reader
Kati Nicholl

Audio
Paul Stark
Amber Bates

Contracts
Anne Goddard
Paul Bulos
Jake Alderson

Design
Debbie Holmes

Joanna Ridley
Nick May

Editorial Management
Charlie Panayiotou
Jane Hughes
Alice Davis

Finance
Jasdip Nandra
Afeera Ahmed
Elizabeth Beaumont
Sue Baker

Production
Ruth Sharvell

Marketing
Amy Davies

Publicity
Alainna Hadjigeorgiou

Sales
Jen Wilson
Esther Waters
Victoria Laws
Rachael Hum
Ellie Kyrke-Smith
Frances Doyle

Georgina Cutler

Operations
Jo Jacobs
Sharon Willis
Lisa Pryde
Lucy Brem